'*The Liars* is a propulsive thriller that covers some serious subject matter. Switching perspectives between a number of characters—including a killer—it keeps the reader guessing about motives, secrets and how it will all end.'

—*Weekend Australian*

'A timely psychological thriller that will open your eyes.'

—*Who Magazine*

'A textured psychological thriller that encompasses voices of truth, lies, deceit, deception and benevolence, *The Liars* is a first rate read that I mightily recommend.'

—*Mrs B's Book Reviews*

'A heart-stopping tale told across different generations.'

—*Canberra Times*

'Petronella McGovern has woven a story of unfathomably good twists, turns and unforeseen outcomes. Her intelligence, wisdom, insight and understanding shine through on every page. Yet again the bar has been raised in terms of writing excellence by an Australian writer. I loved this book, and shall be on the lookout for her future books.'

—*She Society*

'A psychological thriller that is about much more than crime.'

—*New Zealand Women's Weekly*

Praise for
THE GOOD TEACHER

'An emotionally charged and intriguing novel that goes down some unexpected paths. Jolting surprises and a strong cast of characters will keep you reading well into the night.'
—*Canberra Weekly*

'A fast-paced, heart-stopping thriller full of gripping tension, twists and turns from bestselling author Petronella McGovern.'
—*Who Magazine*

'Intriguing . . . a lively, well-plotted tale about generosity and betrayal.'
—*Sydney Morning Herald*

'I loved this book . . . absolutely engaging from start to finish, and kept me reading into the wee small hours.'
—*Living Arts Canberra*

'Taut, tight and terrific, an addictive read.'
—*Blue Wolf Reviews*

'McGovern has created a compelling and well-plotted second novel . . . deserves a place at the top of your must-read list.'
—*Pittwater Life*

'McGovern's books take us to people and places we know, the characters ringing so true. And the books are addictive, leaving you guessing to the very end and wanting more.'
—*Canberra Times*

Petronella McGovern is the bestselling author of *Six Minutes*, *The Good Teacher* and *The Liars*. Her books have been nominated in the Ned Kelly Awards, the Davitt Awards and the Australian Independent Bookseller Awards. *The Liars* was selected in the Top 100 Big W/Better Reading list for 2023. Petronella has a Master of Arts in Creative Writing and tutors in creative writing. She grew up on a farm in central west New South Wales and now lives with her family in Sydney, on Gadigal Country. Her new novel is *The Last Trace*.

www.petronellamcgovern.com.au

This book was written on Gadigal Country, where I am constantly inspired by the sandstone caves and rocks, the bush and the sea. I acknowledge the Gadigal people of the Eora Nation as the Traditional Custodians of this land and coastline, and I recognise their continuing connection with this beautiful place.

THE
LIARS

PETRONELLA
McGOVERN

ALLEN&UNWIN
SYDNEY · MELBOURNE · AUCKLAND · LONDON

This edition published in 2024
First published in 2022

Allen & Unwin
Cammeraygal Country
83 Alexander Street
Crows Nest NSW 2065
Australia
Phone: (61 2) 8425 0100
Email: info@allenandunwin.com
Web: www.allenandunwin.com

Allen & Unwin acknowledges the Traditional Owners of the Country on which we live and work. We pay our respects to all Aboriginal and Torres Strait Islander Elders, past and present.

 A catalogue record for this book is available from the National Library of Australia

ISBN 978 1 76147 060 8

Set in Adobe Jenson Pro by Bookhouse, Sydney
Printed and bound in Australia by the Opus Group

10 9 8 7 6 5 4 3 2 1

 The paper in this book is FSC® certified. FSC® promotes environmentally responsible, socially beneficial and economically viable management of the world's forests.

To the power of female friendship.

*I feel very lucky to have so many incredible women in my life,
I appreciate you all.*

*Especially the keepers of my own teenage secrets—
thank you for our lifelong friendship:
Christina, Tash, George, Lucy, Nicky and Katie.*

PART ONE

BIRTHING SEASON

Female humpback whales go to extreme lengths to keep their babies safe. When a mother senses danger, she flips over and pulls her calf onto her belly, lifting it out of the water away from the predators. But killer whales are relentless in their attack. They separate the calf and drag it away. The mother fights back.

It can be a fight to the death.

1

MERI

THE LOCATION APP ON MERI'S PHONE PINGED AS SHE WAS SHIFTING THE last cardboard box. She knew what the notification would say: *Taj has 0% battery. Ask him to recharge.* Her son was always forgetting to plug in his mobile, unlike his twin sister.

'What's in the box?' her husband asked from the other side of the garage.

'Mum's old *National Geographics*, I think.' Meri hadn't been able to throw them away in previous clean-ups.

After brushing off the dust, she slid a knife through the crusty tape. But instead of a magazine cover with the distinctive yellow border, she found a pile of exercise books. The top one had a heart-shaped label: *Meredith Carmody, Year 9 English, Kinton Bay High School, 1998.*

Year 9. The same as her twins now.

Turning her back to Rollo, she shielded the book with her body and flipped it open to a story in her neat teenage handwriting.

THE KILLING CAVE

A furious wind shrieks through the Killing Cave, echoing off the dark sandstone walls. It's an angry clamour of ghosts— the ghosts of tough men, convicts and soldiers who perished in their search for new lands.

As she read, a shiver ran through her. What the hell were these school books still doing in the garage? She'd meant to throw them out years ago.

A memory came to her—searching through the big thesaurus in the school library to find the perfect adjectives for this story. God, such horrendously melodramatic writing. Not that Meri would be showing anyone, especially not Rollo. They never talked about the cave in Wreck Point National Park. No-one did. Hopefully the whole area was inaccessible now.

Rollo was stacking crates of snorkelling equipment on the metal shelves. If she did show him the story, would he brush it off with some patter about the past being past? Although the past was with them every day: they lived in her childhood home and the twins went to their old high school. Her husband even sported the same blond shaggy haircut as back then; Rollo couldn't be bothered trying a new style. That was his attitude: *If it ain't broke, don't fix it.*

'Do I need to put that box of magazines back on the shelf?' he called out to her.

She could hear the relief in his voice to be doing this job again—moving the summer gear off the boat to make room for a full load of whale-watching passengers. Forty *paying* customers. Maybe they could afford to get the leaks in the roof fixed at last.

'No, it's not the *National Geographics*—just some of Mum's old papers.' After years of avoiding the topic of the Killing Cave, the lie came easily. 'I'll put them in the recycling.'

Meri lugged the box to the bins beside the garage. Out of Rollo's sight, she opened the exercise book again.

*Underneath the howl of the ghostly wind is another sound—
the deep drumbeat of a relentless sea smashing against the
rocks thirty metres below. The mouth of the cavern opens onto
the tall, majestic trees of the forest, but there must be a secret
crevasse leading to a hidden pathway between the rock platform and the ocean.*

The description went on for three full pages. At the end, in red pen, were Miss Wilcox's comments: *An intense, atmospheric piece, Meri. Well done on conveying the sensory details but I want you to dig deeper into this story. Tell us exactly who are the ghosts? How did they die? Why are they angry? Keep going and show me next week. Excellent work! 19/20.*

Miss Wilcox. Their enthusiastic young English teacher. Meri must have written the story in first term; later, they'd stopped talking about the cave, and their teacher had gone.

Meri ripped the exercise book in half, tugging at the old staples. Pages scattered onto the ground. Gathering them up, she scrunched them into a big ball and threw it in the bin. Then she dumped the rest of the exercise books on top.

Somewhere in those pages, adorned with pictures of Big Ben and the Union Jack, was a plan for her future career—working as a journalist on BBC television. A teenage dream, inspired by her father. Before he'd abandoned them.

Above the back fence glowed the same old view of the same old sky. A view she'd had forever. Tonight, it resembled an oil painting, feathery wisps of pink and gold clouds luminescent on a violet backdrop. Ha, she still liked descriptive words after all.

Twenty years since school and she'd never experienced a northern hemisphere sunset, never been to the BBC news studio. At least she'd made part of her dream happen: working as a reporter on the *Coastal Chronicle*. Not quite the hard-hitting journalism she'd imagined.

Staring at the clouds, Meri sighed and tried to follow Rollo's optimistic approach. *How good is life?* he'd say. She began counting out five things for which to be grateful.

1. *This beautiful sunset.*
2. *Another week of July school holidays, which means more whale-watching bookings.*
3. *Taj and Siena are happy, doing well at school, and hanging out with nice friends. Taj's strange pains from last term have disappeared.*
4. *Tonight, we'll eat the chicken casserole Rollo has cooked and watch a movie on Netflix. Ah, the excitement of a Saturday night in Kinton Bay. Oops, that isn't quite gratitude.*

She was trying to think of a fifth thing when Rollo appeared from the garage, wiping his dusty hands down his boardies. Most of the men in Kinton Bay wore shorts all winter, as if to say, *We live in a seaside town, it can't possibly get cold here.* Of course, it did. Right now, the temperature was dropping with the sun. Meri zipped her hoodie to halfway.

'I'm all done.' Rollo grinned. 'You ready for a drink?'

'Sounds good.'

Before going inside, Meri checked the location app. It listed Taj *At Home* because his phone had died—really, he was working at the fish and chip shop on Dolphin Street. With tourists returning at last, he had more evening and weekend shifts. Siena's location showed an address in Harbours End—Jasminda's house, where she was having a sleepover.

Best friends' sleepovers: they had been Meri's alibi for parties when she was a teenager. For a few seconds, Meri could smell the earthy dankness of the Killing Cave. Taste the sweetness of a Bacardi Breezer. Feel the hard rock jutting into her back, rough hands fumbling under her shirt. Fear and bewilderment paralysing her. Those first parties at the cool teenage hangout—Meri and her friends had been so excited. So naïve.

Swallowing hard, she focused on the sunset again. As much as she'd tried to block out that year, the fear remained. The danger of being fifteen—the age when everything had changed.

That was why Meri insisted on the location app now. So she knew her teenagers were exactly where they should be.

Safe.

2

SIENA

THE UTE HIT A DIP IN THE DIRT TRACK, BOUNCING THE PARTY OF teenagers in the tray. While the others hooted, Siena gripped the cold metal edge with one hand and clutched the mobile with the other. She had to take extra care 'cos it wasn't her phone—she'd swapped with Jasminda. Mum would freak if she turned off the location app, so she'd left it at her best friend's house in Harbours End.

The darkness made it hard to see how far they'd driven into Wreck Point National Park. They'd entered through the main gate about five minutes ago. Siena had been wondering how the party gang broke in each time, but they just opened it with a key. From Hayley's dad.

Mottled trunks shimmered in the headlights, ghostly sentries lining the track. Forest red gums. *Eucalyptus tereticornis*. She'd had to practise saying the Latin name for her YouTube video on the last project: protecting koala habitat. Forest red gum leaves were their main food source. At school, almost twenty kids had joined her new koala club. No-one from this gang though; if they knew about it, the teasing would be brutal.

The guy on her right, Axel, had a guitar nestled between his legs, and his thigh pressed against hers. Every time they went over a bump, he slid closer. Siena inched away from his touch again. But it was impossible to maintain a gap with so many bodies crammed into the back of the ute. Twelve? Thirteen people? Arms and legs entwined.

At school last term, Hayley and her friends had been talking about Axel—an older guy who kept turning up to the summer parties. He had some kind of connection: Was he Jackson's cousin?

'Have you been out here much?' she asked him.

'Heaps.' Axel took a swig from his VB can. Gulped then grinned. His eyes raked across her chest. 'You'll enjoy your first time.'

Siena let go of the ute's side and crossed her arms over her baggy black jumper. With her dark hair in two long plaits, she knew she looked even younger than fifteen. How old was he? Hard jaw, rough stubble, brown wavy hair nearly to his shoulders—at least twenty. Sleazy with a capital S. Any other time, she would've told him straight: *You're too old to be hanging with schoolgirls.*

Not tonight. Tonight, he was her ticket to the cave—a secret party in a secret location.

Although Siena had no intention of partying with this gang.

With Axel eyeing her up like another cold beer to drink, Siena realised, too late, that she shouldn't have come alone. But Jasminda had reckoned it would be easier to cover for Siena if she stayed at home. 'And that group won't let me hang out with them anyway,' her best friend had said. 'I'll ruin your chances.'

Jasminda was probably right: she'd only arrived in KB four years ago and her parents were both tech specialists who worked at the council. Unlike Siena's dad, who was considered cool, and had grown up with Hayley's father, Owen.

When the school holidays started last week, Siena had tried to find the cave with her mate, Kyle. Twice, he'd borrowed his sister's car and driven them out here on his P plates; Mum would die if she knew. Kyle understood the history of this place. He'd spent heaps of time in this national park; this was his Country. But they still hadn't been able to find the cave. Each path they followed brought them down onto the small half-moon of Wreck Beach, or back into the dense bush.

Her parents thought the trips to the national park were with Jasminda for a geography assignment. If they knew the real reason, Dad would say: *Why do you wanna dredge up the past?* And Mum would insist Siena go old school—use her newspaper records and the Kinton Bay Historical Society.

But Siena wanted to tell the real story, not repeat the same old lies. Even if only her teacher and history class heard her presentation, it might start waking up this closed-minded town.

The big bonus of this project was hanging out with Kyle. But when they hadn't been able to find the cave together, she'd come up with this plan.

The party gang always boasted about their wild nights in the cave. At six o'clock this evening, she'd tracked them down near Main Beach. The girls were from Year 9, the boys older. This was a normal Saturday night for them—quick feed from the fish and chip shop before driving into the national park for a drinking party.

Hayley had introduced her to Axel. 'This is Siena. She's a nerd. The smartest in our year.'

Her brother would have disagreed: *You're not top in maths, I am.*

Siena watched Axel strumming his guitar, his voice deep but off-key. He had all the moves: flicking his hair; tapping his foot to the beat; the slow, sexy grin. A bad boy. That was why the girls were fighting over him.

'Let me come to the cave,' she'd said. 'I'll film you singing and put it online. I've got a YouTube channel.'

Hayley had made a face and whispered to her friends, but Axel was keen. 'Cool. The acoustics are epic out there.'

At the end of the fire trail, the ute rolled to a standstill. Red gums rose around them, branches stretching high above their heads, blocking the faint moonlight. With the engine switched off, Siena could hear the forest alive in the darkness.

A harsh rasping call. The masked owl.

A warning to stay away.

And then movement and laughter as the group scrambled out—some jumping over the side, others climbing down the tailgate. Siena moved fast to get away from Axel, onto solid ground. In the mass of bodies, Hayley tripped on the rubber mat and lurched off the ute. Siena was in exactly the right spot to catch her.

'Huh, Siena the virgin,' Hayley slurred. 'You're gonna have a good time tonight and get luck-luck-lucky! But keep your hands off Axel—he's mine.'

As if Siena wanted a good time with any of this gang.

Around them, the guys heaved cases of beer onto their shoulders. Bottles clinked in backpacks.

'Let's get this party started!' Hayley shouted.

The others whooped and shone their torches crazily into the treetops. Jerks, they'd disturb the koalas in their night-time feeding.

From the fire trail, there was no sign of a path. But the gang set off between the low bushes, their torch beams creating circles of light among the ferns. Siena tried to memorise the entry point.

In the black of night, the ocean sounded close, waves crashing against rocks.

Wreck Point. Where it had all started.

'Come on, babe!' Axel grabbed her hand and pulled her along the track. Siena tried to extract her fingers, but instead of letting go, he caressed her palm with his thumb.

'Wait a minute,' she said, stalling. 'I have to do up my shoe.'

She crouched down, pretending her lace had come undone. Ahead, sneakers pounded the earth, and the smell of weed drifted in the air. Figures faded into darkness. From what she'd heard, the gang would traipse through the scrub to the cave. They'd light a campfire, drink, smoke and party. They'd frighten the nocturnal creatures. Crush plants and insects underfoot. Disrespect the animals. The land. The history.

Siena shivered.

'You cold, babe?' As she stood up, Axel draped a heavy arm over her shoulders.

Her assignment would be worth it, as long as she didn't have to put up with much more of Axel's sleazy crap. They'd lead her to the cave and she'd come back next week with Kyle. Then she would vlog it on her YouTube channel as an introduction to her history assignment.

'Let's go!' Axel nudged her and his guitar banged against her hip. Pushing it away, she noticed the skull-and-crossbones strap for the first time.

Somewhere in front of them, one of the guys let out a howl, long and low. The eerie noise curled upwards and hung in the treetops. Axel's arm had crept around her lower back. Freaking hell, she needed to get away from him.

'You know what they call this place?' he whispered, his breath hot and beery against her cheek.

Of course she knew. That was why she'd come.

'You are now walking towards'—he paused for effect, like a bad actor in an American teen slasher movie—'the Killing Cave.'

Axel slapped her bum. To give her a fright. To get a quick feel.

Despite his corny performance, Siena jumped. This scumbag had no idea of the bloodshed that had happened here.

The sheer terror of the girl and her family.

A girl my age.

With legs trembling, Siena stepped forwards into the black night.

3

MERI

MERI WAS DRIVING PAST ST PAUL'S, ON HER WAY TO THE HOSPITAL, WHEN her phone beeped. The Sunday morning service had finished so she could park in front of the sandstone church to check the text message.

Jasminda's mum will drop me off after lunch.

On the location app, the small circle of Siena's face was still at Melaleuca Drive in Harbours End. Meri had checked it four times last night and as soon as she'd woken up this morning. Finding that old exercise book had made her even more vigilant than usual. According to the app, Siena hadn't left the house at all. Good. No spontaneous parties on the beach. Her daughter didn't have a boyfriend yet; that would be an extra level of worry.

Rollo refused to download the location app. 'We don't need helicopter parenting in Kinton Bay, hon. We know almost everyone in town.' But sometimes she'd whisper the name of his old school friend and he'd stop arguing about it.

At least her husband agreed that Siena's passionate nature made her more vulnerable. Since primary school, she'd been on one mission after another. First, saving the loggerhead turtle, then the sea lion, then the southern corroboree frog. In their small high school, she'd been campaigning for LGBTQIA+ awareness, ending violence against women, and more support for mental health. Her latest crusade was back to nature again— protecting the local koala habitat. She threw herself into every cause with such intensity.

Meri was proud of her daughter, sure that some of Siena's activism had been inherited from her. At uni, Meri had marched against the war in Iraq and protested about refugees in detention. She'd written articles for the student paper on the gender pay gap and abortion laws.

News and newspapers, issues and investigations were in their blood. Meri's dad used to discuss politics at meals, condemning the greed of Wall Street and cheering on the trade unions. He'd grown up in London's East End, his own father a printer and union rep at *The Guardian*. The stories had fuelled Meri's ambition to live in England and report for the BBC.

Taj cared about causes too, but he didn't seem to feel things as deeply as his sister; it meant Meri watched Siena more closely.

'I'm responsible,' Siena complained. 'I don't need this stupid location app.'

'I have to keep you safe. It's my job as a parent.'

'But I'm almost an adult!' Siena would yell. 'Back in your day, fifteen-year-olds were working down the mines.'

'Ha ha. Smart arse.'

'Seriously, Mum. In your day, there were no phones. You had a free-range childhood.'

And look what happened to us.

*

From up here by the church, Meri could see the township of Kinton Bay nestled in a horseshoe shape around the harbour. St Paul's had been built in 1864, the sandstone blocks carted to this spot on the hill. The town founder, Geoffrey Kinton, had envisioned equality for all men and a settlement without a church—a world away from the class structures of the old country. But as the town grew, so too had the number of births, deaths and marriages. Another founding family, the Redpaths, lobbied for a church and won. Meri had been at St Paul's for all the significant moments in her life—she couldn't imagine Kinton Bay without it.

The bay sparkled, the sunshine a silver shimmer across its middle. A few yachts and cruisers dotted the water, a jet ski zigzagged around Grotto Rocks. Rollo's catamaran was powering up the bay, about to pass through the heads and out to sea. A full boat of paying passengers. Meri sent a quick prayer towards St Paul's: *Please let them see lots of whales and tell their friends to book a cruise.*

Visitors liked the small-town feel of Kinton Bay. Five thousand permanent residents plus holidaymakers in summer: families from inland farms on their once-a-year beach holiday; backpackers who felt they'd discovered a hidden treasure; and grey nomads enjoying the slower pace of life. Some had fondly labelled it 'the seaside town stuck in the nineteen-seventies'.

But the town—and Rollo's whale-watching business—needed the tourist dollar. At the marina, two of the five restaurants were closed for winter. Meri suspected one had gone bust. She should look into it, write a story for the *Chronicle*. But there was no point: Neville didn't like to report 'bad news'. He'd prefer to promote the new wine bar opening in Spring.

The town's development committee said the trouble with Kinton Bay was its location: a bit too far from Sydney for a day trip, and too small to compete with the nearby tourist hubs of Port Stephens and Port Macquarie. What would Geoffrey Kinton think of the town he'd founded? Scrambling to make a profit in summer, struggling for cash and visitors in the off-season.

A tall wire fence encircled the block of land next to St Paul's. The sign read: BLUE WATERS PANORAMA RESIDENCES, but it was a patch of dirt, the only building so far a small portable shed. Would Geoffrey Kinton have welcomed the developer pushing for multistorey apartments here? Better than a church, he'd probably say, but Meri foresaw a white elephant, vacant for nine months every year. Great views for the guests, though. Down below, in the green stretch of park along Main Beach, the bronze statue of Geoffrey Kinton glinted in the sun. Across the road stood the cafes, surf shop, and Mick's fish and chips, where Taj worked. The street behind had the supermarket, two clothes stores and a chemist. The *Coastal Chronicle* office was the next block back, along with the Red Cross shop and the Historical Society. Halfway up the other hill, on the road leading out of town, squatted two low, flat buildings surrounded by trees—the bowling club, and Meri's destination this morning, the hospital.

Behind her, obscured by undulating slopes and pockets of bush, sat her own house.

Sunlight reflected off the brass bell atop St Paul's. The UV index must be high today. She tapped out a quick text to Siena: *Put on sunscreen.* While the twins didn't remember attending the funeral here, they knew the sparkling sun had killed their grandmother. At forty-seven. Way too young.

But the sunshine wasn't going to last. The weather bureau had forecast one of the biggest storms this decade, starting tonight. Oh god, the leaks in the roof . . .

⌒

Inside Kinton Bay Community Hospital, Meri located Glenda O'Riordan in the Seahorse Ward. The older woman was sitting up in bed, flicking through *Woman's Day*. A section of her pinky-purple hair had been shaved and her scalp sported a large gauze bandage.

Glenda also had twins—Blake and Derek. They were two years older than Meri but neither would be visiting their mum today. From a young age, they'd been notorious around town. Meri's father had given them a weekend job at the bowling club 'to keep them out of trouble' but it hadn't lasted long. Funny how things turned out. Back in high school, Meri never could have imagined her own father leaving town and the O'Riordan twins' mother virtually becoming part of her family. And not in a million years did she envisage marrying their friend, the scruffy stoner Rollo. What had they called their gang? The Wrecking Crew. God, that school book was bringing it all back.

'How are you feeling?' Meri patted Glenda's hand and placed packets of chocolates and nuts on the tray table.

'Bit fuzzy from the drugs.'

Bruising spread across Glenda's face from her nose to her right ear. Bloody hell, she looked like she'd been in a brawl at the Time'n'Tide.

'You're looking good.' Meri offered up a comforting lie.

'Thought it'd be the fags or the booze that got me. Not this.'

Two days earlier, Glenda had tripped down her back steps with a basket of wet washing in her arms. She'd landed head-first on the concrete path. Luckily Ninetta Nelson had dropped in ten minutes later and found her dazed and bleeding among the scattered shirts and undies. Weird, though. Meri thought Ninetta and her son Lance didn't usually socialise with Glenda now that their construction company was attracting big investors.

'You'll be fine,' Meri insisted. 'Think of this as a nice rest from work.'

Glenda had spent decades looking after others, cooking and cleaning. When Meri's father was managing the bowling club, Glenda had worked there. Later, during Mum's treatments, Glenda was the glue that held them all together: babysitting the twins while Meri drove Mum to specialists in Newcastle; preparing lunches and dinners; always chatty as she kept the wheels turning. Mum had appreciated Glenda's easy way; the twins loved her songs and stories. Rollo joked that she'd saved their marriage. Her help had given Meri precious time with Mum at the end; she would always be grateful to Glenda for that.

'I'm not used to people waiting on me.' Glenda shook her head. 'I reckon the kitchen here could do with my two cents' worth. Overcooked chicken and undercooked veg.'

'Let them look after you, even if it's not the best food.' Meri opened a bag of mixed nuts for her. 'Siena will come in this afternoon.'

Glenda picked out the cashews from the packet. 'You're blessed to have a daughter. Girls look after their mothers.'

Her own twins were nothing like the O'Riordan boys; Meri was raising her son to be just as caring as her daughter.

'Taj is doing an assignment today. Whales again for every subject.' Meri laughed. 'He thinks the teachers haven't twigged. He could bring you fish and chips after work tonight if you're still hungry.'

For almost two weeks last term, Taj had been home sick with stomach pains. Unusual for him. All the medical tests had come back normal. Just as Meri had begun to worry about anxiety and bullying, the pains stopped. Now, he was catching up on his schoolwork over the holidays.

'I keep falling asleep early,' Glenda said. 'What about lunch tomorrow?'

'Absolutely. Taj will deliver Kinton Bay's finest fish and chips to your bedside.'

'With seafood sauce, please.' Glenda grinned. 'Did I tell you they've approved Derek's parole?'

Meri managed to smile. 'Great. When?'

'Tenth of November. Only five months away. He'll be home for Christmas!'

'Wow. Christmas,' Meri repeated. The worst kind of Christmas present for Kinton Bay. Rollo and Owen would start planning how to avoid their old mate. Not easy in a small town with one pub.

Meri glanced up and found a distraction: a large bouquet of flowers above Glenda's bed, almost too big for the vase and the shelf. 'Impressive bunch! Who sent those?'

Glenda's grin drooped. 'Lance and Ninetta dropped by earlier with them.'

Trust Lance to splash cash on the biggest bouquet. But why was he visiting Glenda?

'That was nice of them,' Meri said, hoping Glenda would explain. 'And lucky that Ninetta—'

Glenda groaned. In the hospital gown, without her usual bright blouse and gold necklace, she seemed shrunken and scared.

'Are you okay? Did Lance upset you? Or does your head hurt?'

The older woman didn't answer, but stared at the blank wall opposite her bed. 'I want purples and pinks at my funeral,' she finally whispered. 'Same colour as my hair. Purply-pink balloons. Flowers. Everything.'

'Fuchsia,' Meri said automatically. Her mind was elsewhere: Mum's funeral at St Paul's twelve years ago, the twins asleep in a huge double stroller which took up most of the aisle. It was because of Mum's illness that Meri had gone ahead with the unexpected pregnancy—she'd assumed Mum would have more days to spend with her grandkids.

'What's fuchsia?' Glenda asked.

'Purply-pink. Like the flower. Sorry, you know I work with words.' Meri's cheeks were burning in a similar colour. Oh god, did Glenda have some bad test results? 'You gave me a shock talking about funerals. But don't be silly, Glenda. You're not going to die.'

'I dunno, I just feel . . .' Glenda reached for Meri's hand. 'Promise me something.'

'Of course. Anything. You've been our guardian angel.'

Meri expected a simple request, like organising a substitute cleaner for her clients.

'Use your newspaper. Use your police contacts.' She pinned Meri with her blue eyes and tightened her grip. 'Do everything you can to find Blake for me. I want to know what happened to my son.'

Forcing herself not to pull her hand away, Meri nodded.

But she couldn't follow through on the promise. She just couldn't start an investigation into what happened the year she turned fifteen.

4

Student: Taj Britton
Year 9 Science / Biology, Mrs Dalla Costa
Assignment: Reproduction cycle of humpback whales

Mother love—birthing and protecting their calves
Humpback whales migrate from Antarctica in May each year
to give birth in the warm, subtropical waters off Queensland.
They swim south again with their new calves in October. It's the
longest mammal migration in the world—over 5000 kilometres.

The mothers are pregnant for a whole year, and the calves
are born tail first. The calves survive on their mother's milk, just
like humans. A mother whale can produce 600 litres of milk a
day. Their milk has a lot more fat than ours, and is as thick as
toothpaste. All that fat helps the calf develop blubber to keep
it warm during the big swim back to Antarctica.

On the long migration south, predators try to attack the
calves. The mum has a special way of communicating with her
baby so she can keep it close; these whispering sounds are so

23

soft that they go undetected by killer whales. Scientists only discovered this survival technique a few years ago.

Even though a male whale escorts the mother and new calf, pods of killer whales can surround them. When the mother senses danger, she flips over and pulls her calf onto her belly, lifting it out of the water away from the predators.

Whales sometimes protect other species, like seals, in exactly the same way. This is an example of altruistic animal behaviour.

5

MERI

THE SMELL OF ROAST CHICKEN FILLED THE KITCHEN. MERI COOKED A roast most Sunday nights in winter, just like Mum always had. Thankfully, the twins were no longer in their vegetarian phase— that had made family meals more difficult. Siena still didn't eat 'baby animals'. Fine by Meri, lamb and veal were too expensive anyway.

Siena was setting the table in the corner while Taj fed carrots to the dog.

'Can you take some fish and chips to Glenda for lunch tomorrow?' Meri asked her son.

'Yeah. As long as I can sleep in.' Taj yawned. 'I still have to finish my assignment. Dad, can I ask you some whale questions after dinner?'

'Sure,' said Rollo. 'Do you want a wine, Meri?'

Nodding, Meri waited until they'd all moved out of the way to open the oven again. She didn't remember the kitchen being so crowded when she was growing up, but then her dad wasn't often home for dinner.

'Glenda was really chatty when I visited,' Siena said. 'She was telling stories about Blake. Asked if we had any photos of him. Do we?'

Dishing out the crispy potatoes, Meri pictured Blake—black greasy hair, cap on backwards, flannelette shirt, ripped jeans. Smirking.

'No, he and Dad were two years above me. I wouldn't have any.'

'What about you, Dad?'

Sitting at the table, Rollo shrugged. His long hair flopped over his eyes. 'We didn't take many pictures. Not like you guys with your phones.'

'Can I look through the old photos anyway?' Siena asked.

'After dinner.' Meri put the heaped plates onto each placemat. She hoped Glenda's mood had improved with Siena's visit. 'Did you entertain Glenda with some of your stories?'

'I told her I'm going to be a journalist.'

'Following in your mum's footsteps.' Rollo smiled at Meri.

'No. Nothing like Mum. Newspapers are dead. I'll be online. Global.'

'It doesn't matter how it's delivered. You still have to find and report the news.' Teenagers—they always thought they knew better than their parents.

'No offence, Mum, but online is the future. And no-one reads the *Coastal Chronicle*.'

'Old people do,' Taj interjected. 'I bet Glenda reads it.'

'But there's no actual news in there, it's just . . .' Siena screwed up her face in the ultimate expression of teenage contempt. 'It's just . . . advertising.'

Rollo patted Meri's forearm, a warning for her to stay calm.

'It's not *just* advertising. And it's online too.' Meri spoke through gritted teeth. 'It's community news. Important to the people who live here.'

'It's not the real news, though, is it? You've said so yourself, Mum. What did you call it? A business-friendly version of the news. The positive spin.'

Meri stabbed at her roast pumpkin, sending a row of peas off her plate onto the floor. Before she could retrieve them, the dog had gobbled them down. How was it that her daughter could pinpoint her weak spot so easily? All those times Meri had complained to Rollo about her editor, the advertisers, the commercial pressure on a story—Siena had been listening.

'Global online news sounds great.' Meri went for her own positive spin. 'You'll be a good journalist because you care about the world.'

'That's exactly what Mr Durham said in our careers chat!' Siena sat up taller. 'He told me I'm the sort of person who can make a difference in the world.'

Two decades ago, a much younger Mr Durham had encouraged Meri in a similar vein. Back then, she'd believed him.

'I had dreams too, you know,' Meri began. 'I planned to work in London. On the BBC as a—'

'Meri, you're doing an amazing job at the paper.' Rollo lifted his beer in a toast to her. 'Kinton Bay is so lucky to have kept you.'

Kept me. Ensnared me. Trapped me.

Rollo had never planned to leave—he was always content.

'Hey, Dad.' Siena turned her attention away from Meri. 'I think we should change the name of the boat.'

'Why?'

Rollo had worked on the *Sirius* since he was twenty, then bought it a decade ago when the owner retired.

'*Sirius* was the main ship in the First Fleet.' Siena gave a snort of disgust.

'So what?'

'But the *First Fleet*, Dad.' Siena shook her head at him. 'The Invasion.'

'That was a long time ago. Anyway, she was named after a star.'

'You should call it *Migaloo*,' Taj said. 'Did you see him today?'

'If Dad had seen Migaloo, we'd all know about it.'

That would certainly make it into the *Chronicle*—a rare sighting of the famous white whale, one of a few albino humpbacks in the world. The crew was always on the lookout but mostly Migaloo seemed to swim past Kinton Bay in the dead of night and appear further north at Byron Bay the next day. In twenty years of whale watching, Rollo had seen him just once.

'MV *Migaloo*.' Siena sounded it out slowly, then grinned. 'That's perfect, Dad. Let's do it. We can have a renaming ceremony at the marina. I could report on it.'

Meri rushed in before Rollo could answer. 'I'm sure there are already boats with that name. Siena, why don't you do some research first?'

Her husband liked to keep everyone happy—he'd probably just say, 'Too easy, mate,' and ask Meri to sort it out. But it wouldn't be easy. Nor cheap. Changing the name of the boat would mean updating the registration, the paperwork and the website. They were still paying off the loan, along with the yearly costs of repairs and new safety equipment, registrations and licences. The lack of tourists during the lockdowns had set them back. As much as Rollo loved the business, without Meri's stable income they wouldn't have been able to keep Seabreeze Cruises afloat.

⌒

When the twins had disappeared to their bedrooms, Meri passed her husband another beer and told him about Derek's release date.

'Ah, fuck. I wonder how long he'll be out this time.'

'He'll want a reunion with you and Owen. And with Lance.'

Rollo sighed. 'No-one else wants that. 'Specially not Lance.'

The Wrecking Crew: Derek and Blake. Lance, Rollo and Owen. Her editor's son, Scott. A few other boys on and off. Most of them still lived in the area. Not like the girls from high school. All her friends had gone.

'Another thing . . .' How would Rollo react to this? 'Glenda begged me to find Blake.'

Her husband took a swig of beer, then bent down to rub the dog's belly. When he finally spoke, he kept his eyes on Pirate.

'It's up to the police,' he grunted. 'Anyway, you already tried.'

Not very hard. Meri could've done more. Asked her editor to run a campaign. Written articles about Blake's disappearance to jog memories. Gathered information. Urged police to interview the Wrecking Crew and the girls from school about their last encounters with Blake.

Meri could have—should have—told the truth.

6

SIENA

AFTER DINNER, SIENA PULLED OUT THE SHOEBOXES FROM THE BIG cupboard in the study, looking for photos of Blake. Sitting cross-legged on the floor, she opened the first box. Pictures of two chubby, dark-haired toddlers stared up at her.

'Oh my god, Taj, we were soooo cute!' Siena yelled. 'Come and look!'

'In a minute.'

That was Taj's answer to everything. *In a minute.* He was always in his room, on his computer. She'd asked him to subscribe to her YouTube channel; now she had a grand total of forty-six subscribers. Mostly kids from school. Siena hadn't mentioned it to her parents—Mum would freak out about privacy and online grooming. As if a paedo would be interested in her videos on koala habitat.

Instead of her brother, Mum appeared in the doorway. Siena showed her the photo.

'You two were divine,' Mum said. 'Those big brown eyes. You cuties got away with so much.'

Siena picked up another picture: her parents standing on Main Beach at sunset, both of them so young with nervous smiles. It looked like Mum had stuffed a basketball up her jumper.

'Wow, you were huge! And your hair's so short.'

'I cut it off just before you two were born. I thought I wouldn't have time to manage my curls. But it went so frizzy. I never made that mistake again.'

For as long as Siena could remember, Mum's haircut had stayed the same—dark brown curls that sat on her shoulders. When Siena was little, she'd wished for curls too, but now she liked her straight hair. Most days, she plaited it to stop the knots. Today she wore it out to hide the bruises on her neck.

The bruises hurt. And they definitely looked like fingerprints. Siena kept touching them, as a reminder that she'd made it out alive. That bastard. How dare he!

Mum pointed to a photo of Siena and Taj in highchairs, with Glenda standing between them, a spoon in each hand. 'She was magic with you guys,' Mum said. 'I felt so bad that I couldn't look after you all the time, but Granny needed me.'

Did Mum have tears in her eyes? Mother guilt. God, if she knew what had happened last night, her tears would flood the room.

Taj slouched through the doorway and Siena passed him the photos.

'Nice hair!' Taj laughed. 'You look like a boy.'

'Ha ha.' Siena jabbed a finger into his thigh. 'Well, your hair's exactly the same as when you were two.'

'Look at Glenda feeding us.' He studied the picture. 'She's so young. I'll take this to show her tomorrow.'

'Mum, is Derek allowed to visit the hospital?' Siena could only imagine how sad Glenda must be without either of her sons. 'When's he coming out? Is it this year?'

'I'm sure they've been talking on the phone.' Mum changed the subject. 'Whose turn is it to take out the bins?'

'Not mine,' Taj said quickly, then mouthed at Siena: 'Loser.'

Mum didn't see him, of course. 'Okay, Siena. Can you do it now so you don't forget? And there's a pile of papers in the kitchen for recycling.'

Jeez, Mum treated her like a child. Siena *always* remembered bin night. Sometimes Taj forgot when it was his turn, and Mum had to leap out of bed at dawn, in her PJs. That was never a good start to the week.

Pirate threaded around Siena's legs as she carried the rubbish and the recycling outside. The black labrador would make a good spy, blending into the shadows so much that Siena almost tripped over him. The darkness felt thick and heavy—clouds blanketed the night sky and thunder grumbled softly. So annoying; they'd only had one week of school holidays and now it was going to rain for the rest of it. Half the hols ruined. After dumping the rubbish in the red bin, Siena discovered the cardboard recycling already full to the brim, with school books on top. The labels all read: Meredith Carmody, Year 9.

Why had Mum tossed these without showing her and Taj? Siena sifted through them: science, maths, French. An exercise book torn in half—English, Miss Wilcox. Had Mum ripped it up recently? Further down, sandwiched between religious education and geography, Siena found a red notebook.

The Diary of Meredith Carmody, 1998
THIS IS PRIVATE!!!
NATHAN—that means you. DO NOT READ!

As far as Siena knew, Uncle Nathan didn't read anything. It was the big joke every Christmas—a sister who loved to write and a brother who hated to read.

Wow, Mum's diary. What a find! Flipping it open at random, Siena studied the careful teenage lettering.

9th March 1998
Kristie got us invited to a beach party with the senior years. It's this Friday night, Friday the 13th, and I can't wait! Kristie keeps making dramatic announcements. 'This is it! Everyone says Year 9 is the party year. Bring it on—our future is here and it's going to be ACE!'

Our future: we've made a pact to go to New York after the HSC. No Gold Coast schoolies trip for us. (Loretta will have to convince her parents to let her go.) Kristie keeps saying, 'Kinton Bay is too small for us. We're outta here as soon as we finish school.'

Dad has promised Nathan $500 if he studies hard in Year 11 and 12. It's supposed to be for an overseas trip but Nathan is so boring—he wants to get a car. He'll never leave Australia. Dad's stories of backpacking around Europe are The Best. That's where life is really happening. I can't wait to get over there!

How bizarre to read Mum's thoughts from Year 9—nothing like today's helicopter parent, stickler for homework, destroyer of fun. Who were Kristie and Loretta? Had they both left Kinton Bay without Mum? Gone to New York together and never returned?

And the diary mentioned 'Dad', the grandfather she'd never met. Mum didn't seem to hate him at this point. Siena skimmed through a few more pages. Oh god, Mum would be so embarrassed by these teenage ramblings; she hardly sounded like a future journalist.

The party is at the Killing Cave!! So rad! I'm wearing my new denim overalls.

The Killing Cave.

A chill ran down her back. Mum had been to parties out there too.

Pirate whined as thunder boomed closer and a flash of lightning split the darkness. Siena shoved the diary into the waistband of her jeans and pulled her jumper over the top. Dragging the bins out to the street, she wondered about the parties back then—were any of those guys the same as Axel?

She'd videoed him in the cave, focused on him strumming his guitar—her cover for being there. Between songs, Axel had turned to her and started narrating.

'I'm gonna tell you a ghost story, Siena. It's the story of the Killing Cave. Back in the nineteen-nineties, a gang camped out here. They were called the Wrecking Crew. To join the gang, each man had to have sex with a virgin here in the cave. Pop her cherry. As the gang grew bigger, the girls got younger.'

Around the campfire, the other boys had guffawed; the girls ignored them.

Axel whispered into her ear, too low to be caught on camera, 'How old are you, Siena?' He taunted her: 'Are you a virgin?'

That fucking bastard.

Another crack of lightning lit up the empty street for a second, illuminating a line of wheelie bins along the kerb. The rain came in one great torrent and Siena bolted for the front door.

Before going inside, she rearranged her damp hair to cover the bruises on her neck, wincing as she touched them. This morning, they'd been dark purple circles, the shape of his fingers and two thumbprints.

She hoped his injury hurt as much as hers.

7

A week of non-stop rain. Gusts of wind. Trees toppling. Waves battering the beaches.

All of the mid-north coast is affected but it's Kinton Bay they show on the news. Water swamping the marina, flooding into the mangroves, gushing down the streets.

I recognise the aerial shot of Wreck Beach, whitewash swirling in the small bay, huge seas smashing the point. As the camera pans out, I spot a bare sandstone platform among the trees—it must be the roof of the Killing Cave.

Is it protected or will the water be rushing into the cavern and its crevasses?

8

SIENA

EVERY DAY THIS WEEK, SIENA HAD WONDERED IF SHE COULD GET OUT to Wreck Point but the storm hadn't stopped. Lightning, thunder, wind and constant rain. The town was drowning. And the animals too: exhausted turtles washed up on the beach; seabirds blown off course; wombats and echidnas trapped, dead in their flooded burrows. Hopefully the koalas had stayed safe in their trees. Siena helped at the vet clinic with a joey whose mother had died; she couldn't bring the tiny thing home because of Pirate. Her other job was emptying the buckets in the laundry, the hallway and her parents' bedroom; the roof leaked constantly.

It was five days since she'd followed Axel and the party gang to the Killing Cave. Would she be able to find the track again after all this rain? The *Chronicle* said it had broken seventy-year records.

Friday morning and the skies were finally clearing. Kyle had borrowed his sister's car and, after dropping Brooke at work, he pulled up outside Siena's house. No-one else was home. Mum and Dad didn't know about Kyle; they wouldn't approve of a friend who was two years older with a driver's licence.

She'd met Kyle organising a small group for the school climate rally in Newcastle. Siena had felt an instant connection to him: his love for Country, the animals, history, culture—his passions reflected her own. He'd already done work experience with the ranger in the local national park, and for the September holidays he'd lined up more a few hours south. The park there was run by the traditional owners, and Kyle couldn't wait to learn about the land from them. While his sister worked at Bay Beauty, the only beautician in town, Kyle was more into natural beauty. And Siena knew he'd achieve his dream: to become the first Aboriginal ranger at Wreck Point National Park.

'I still can't believe you did it,' Kyle said, grinning, as she got into the passenger seat. 'You found the cave. Without me!'

For a few seconds, Siena thought he was leaning in for a hug; that was how she greeted most of her friends, but not Kyle—this guy who was more than a friend but not yet a boyfriend. She waited and his hand came up for the usual fist bump, then his fingers moved to her hair.

'You hardly ever wear it out,' he said.

She hoped her cheeks weren't going bright red. Did Kyle think she was trying to look pretty for him? The bruises on her neck were evolving, yellow now rather than purple. She'd managed to hide them from everyone in the house all week.

On Tuesday, Hayley had sent her a WhatsApp message. Hayley Shuttlewood, who never contacted her. *Where's Axel? What did you do? No-one's seen him since Saturday night.*

Siena had replied as politely as she could: *Sorry. I don't know.*

Hayley's last three Insta posts featured pics of her kissing Axel, with the tagline in capitals: *MY BOYFRIEND'S MISSING! HAVE YOU SEEN HIM?*

'Your hair's so long.' Kyle's voice was deeper than usual as he touched the ends. Siena stared into his brown eyes framed by long lashes. Sexy and smart. Oh god, was this it? Her first kiss? She'd brushed her teeth just before—would she still have the taste of toothpaste in her mouth? Her stomach did a slow flip-flop. This was definitely the moment.

Her phone beeped.

'Is that your mum checking up on you?' Kyle grinned even wider than before.

She smiled back, face aflame now.

'Of course.' Helicopter mum spoiling the moment. She read the text aloud. *'Be careful in the bush. Has Jasminda's mum checked if the trails are open?'*

'Tell her I'll be careful.'

Siena burst out laughing. Mum had already been worrying about Jasminda's mother, an experienced driver. She'd freak if she knew that Siena was going into Wreck Point National Park with a P-plater.

The fire trail was the consistency of a Maccas thickshake, every groove and pothole filled with mud. The car inched its way along the track, slipping and sliding. Nothing like the ute roaring through on Saturday night, with the party gang bouncing around in the back, howling like wild animals.

'It's the wrong season for all this rain.' Kyle squinted through the foggy windscreen. 'Did you know that the Wiradjuri people have made an amazing calendar of their six seasons? It's all about using the land sustainably. Like, you don't eat certain fish in the season they're spawning, so there's enough fish later. We need to do one for our Country.'

'That makes much more sense than English seasons.' Siena was embarrassed she'd never thought about it before. 'Australia is sooooo dumb. We have all this traditional knowledge and we just ignore it.'

When they reached the end of the trail, Kyle stopped the car and breathed out a long sigh.

'That was intense, man. Now, let's find this cave.'

Siena pulled on her backpack and studied the scrub around them. The storm had torn through here: bushes tilted in the soggy ground and the air smelt like a musty soup of soil and mould and eucalyptus. Leaves hung heavy with water droplets. The kookaburras and currawongs were silent, still spooked by the crazy weather. Siena scanned the undergrowth for the path. After a few false starts, she noticed a beer can in the mud.

'This is it,' she said, and raced ahead of Kyle, keen to show him the cave.

After ten minutes of traipsing through mud and puddles, the ground became rougher and she led him up a causeway of rocks. They were right behind the headland now. The wind whispered around them.

The path seemed different than she remembered; had she taken a wrong turn? A huge boulder towered over them.

And then she saw the gap with sheer stone on either side. A gap only big enough for one person, but Axel had squeezed in behind her that night. Touched the back of her thigh. She'd stumbled over the rocks, trying to get away from him prodding her bum. Like a cow on Uncle Nathan's farm being pushed up the ramp onto a truck, to be carted off to the slaughterhouse.

'We're almost there,' she called over her shoulder to Kyle.

They were through the gap, and up onto the rock platform.

'Siena, you found it!'

She turned towards him and he gave her a double fist bump. His hands dropped down to her waist and suddenly he was picking her up and swinging her around. 'You were so brave coming up here alone with those jerks.'

When Kyle stopped spinning, Siena still felt dizzy. His arms remained around her, his body so close to hers. He leaned down and brushed his lips against hers. Their noses bumped. *Oh Kyle, my first-ever kiss. Am I doing it right? Wait till I tell Jasminda!* Looking at him felt too intense so Siena closed her eyes. His fingers were now cradling her chin, lighting a line of fire along her jaw. He tasted of orange juice and smelt like deodorant, strong and musky. She reached into his hair, felt the thick, closely cropped locks.

This kiss, this moment, could last forever.

Except she'd forgotten how to breathe. She pulled away and gulped mouthfuls of air. Would he have this effect on her every time?

'Wow.' Kyle sighed out the word slowly. He took her hand. 'That was . . . just wow . . . Well, let's have a look around.'

But as Kyle entered the mouth of the cave, she watched his face drop. She'd given him an edited version of last Saturday night, avoided showing him the video—she knew it would upset him.

At night, with the campfire casting strange shadows, she'd felt the terror of the place. Now, she could see the damage and litter left by those wild parties—crushed beer cans, plastic bags and broken glass. Obscenities scrawled onto the walls. A penis drawn in black texta with words underneath: *Jackson has the biggest cock*. Lines of white paint for a game of noughts and crosses. *Hayley loves Axel* written in silver pen inside a heart. And some fainter words. *Kristie gives great head*. A star shape. *Fuck off Derek*.

Kyle kicked at a beer can. It clunked loudly and the sound echoed through the cave.

'Dirty bastards,' he muttered. 'Are you going to film it?'

While Kyle rubbed his hand over the rock, Siena went back to the entrance, pulling out her GoPro. First, she captured the view of the green-grey forest in front of her, and then she swivelled around to show the mouth of the Killing Cave. The semicircle of rock rose in a smooth curve. Despite the cloudy sky, the ceiling of the cave glowed golden. It must be magnificent in the sunshine. Thousands of years of erosion had created this wonder of natural architecture. If she hadn't known its human history, Siena could have believed the cave was welcoming, a golden canopy protecting her from the elements. Almost like a womb, the Earth's womb.

But it had been defiled.

The whine of the wind around the cave's entrance forced her to speak up for the voice-over.

'In 1847, the *Lady Emmeline* was sailing from Sydney to the settlement of Port Macquarie when it got caught in a storm. A bit like the one we had this week. The captain decided to shelter in the bay here, but he misjudged the heads and slammed into what's now called Wreck Point. The ship broke apart and the captain and many of his passengers went down with it.

Others dragged themselves out of the water and up onto the beach. They sought shelter from the storm here, in this cave.'

Kyle had disappeared into the gloom. As far as they knew, the cave had never been properly mapped. Imagine if they found a digging tool or a stone axehead—everyone would have to acknowledge the significance of this place then.

'The local people spotted the shipwreck,' Siena continued. 'They pulled the dead bodies from the water. Then they found the survivors hiding in their cave. They brought them food and fresh water. They saved their lives.'

A crack of thunder made Siena jump. What the hell? The storms were supposed to have finished.

'Shit, we'd better get out of here.' Kyle emerged from the shadows. 'I can't drive that track in the rain.'

'But I haven't finished,' said Siena. 'And I was going to clean up the rubbish.'

'We'll come back next week.'

Surely it wouldn't start raining again? But Kyle was already climbing down the rocks. Shoving her camera into her backpack, she ran after him. Another thunderclap filled the air and Kyle moved even faster.

Rushing to catch up with him, her eyes on the ground to avoid the puddles, at first Siena didn't realise they'd come down a different way. This path was steeper, littered with twigs and wet leaves. On each side rose large boulders. Water must have poured off the rocks higher up, creating a river along this track.

'It's the wrong path, Kyle,' she called. 'We must be on the ocean side.'

He glanced around. 'You're right, the waves sound really close. I'll climb up and have a look.'

His long legs made it easy for him to scale the boulders. She could see the bottom of his mud-spattered jeans and hear his sneakers squelching with each step. Then he was out of sight, on top of the rocks.

'Can you work out where we are?' she shouted.

Waiting for Kyle to reply, she reached into her backpack for the GoPro. Maybe she could finish filming.

'It looks like the place Gran talked about.' Kyle's words drifted down, his voice shaky. 'I don't think we should be here.'

But Siena wanted to see. Clambering up, she put her foot on a pile of debris. It started to give way and she scuttled sideways. A mess of mud and sticks cascaded to the ground through a hole in the boulder. A few steps later, with both feet on solid rock, she rested a moment, listening to the waves pounding into Wreck Point. This must be the path linking the headland to the cave; the same path the survivors had taken after the shipwreck.

Standing on top of the boulders, Siena spun her GoPro in a circle. The storm had blown down bushes and trees, leaving a moonscape of ancient rocks. Rocks that had witnessed the passing of thousands of years. A mossy ledge sloped upwards on one side. They were right underneath the cave.

'We shouldn't be here,' Kyle repeated. 'Why'd you come up?'

'Sorry, I wanted to see it. I'll be quick.'

He scooted past her and disappeared into the bush below.

Siena switched on the camera and continued the story from where she'd left off.

'And then on the third day, Geoffrey Kinton, a former convict, decided he wanted more than food. He cornered a local girl in the cave, and decided to take her—just like the colonials had taken this whole land.'

Kinton would've had the same look in his eyes as Axel on Saturday night. *You're mine.*

As Siena told the story, a shudder snaked from her bruised neck to her cold, wet feet. She was standing where the first people had once stood, staring at the same rocks, the same landforms. Where those families had been massacred. She imagined their confusion in those last moments. They'd tried to help the strangers who'd appeared on their land like aliens from another planet, and they'd been killed for it.

A shout broke into her audio. Damn Kyle! Now she'd have to edit it.

'Fucking hell, Siena. I've found a skull.'

9

POOLE

DETECTIVE CHIEF INSPECTOR DOUGLAS POOLE BROUGHT UP THE LIST on his laptop, readying himself for a conversation with the mayor. The storms had caused a huge amount of damage in Kinton Bay and the surrounding areas. Over a hundred call-outs for the SES. A collapsed wall at the bowling club. Elderly residents evacuated from Banksia Gardens. Power lines down at Harbours End. Several boats battered against pylons at the marina, three irreparable. Muddy water had poured into the ground floor of the new council building—that was part of the reason for his phone call to Mayor Redpath.

The old-timers said they hadn't seen it this bad since 1950.

Surprisingly, no reports of serious injury. For once, everyone had heeded the warnings.

Poole's rented home, a fairly new brick house, had survived the deluge, although Caroline was still worried about the big gum tree in the backyard. But it hadn't moved. Nor had Caroline. He'd convinced her to use Zoom and deliver her lectures from her study, rather than attempt a slippery four-hour drive south to Sydney.

Poole picked up his phone. 'Mayor Redpath, how are things with you?'

'Very difficult,' she moaned. 'We've got the truck coming at three o'clock to pump out the basement of the council building. Can you send some officers to help with traffic diversion? Our workers are frantic.'

'Of course.'

His own teams were frantic, the whole town was frantic, but the mayor had a knack of always asking for more. To give her some perspective, Poole read out the list of damage.

'Oh my gosh,' she squeaked. 'I don't know how we're going to manage the clean-up. The tourists were finally returning, and now . . .'

'Kinton Bay will bounce back,' Poole reassured her.

That seemed to give Emmeline Redpath a lift, and she hung up with an almost cheery, 'Thank you, Doug.'

Pleased with his diplomatic skills, Poole made a note to allocate two officers to traffic control outside the council building this afternoon. Two years in charge of KB station and Poole had finally figured out the small-town politics of this community. And now, he was also proficient in the management side of things—supervising staff and processes, the never-ending paperwork and the tight budget.

A text from Caroline flashed up on his mobile. *Getting my workout this morning!* She'd attached two photos: a group of volunteers sandbagging near the mangrove swamps, and a close-up of her bicep. Laughing, Poole typed a quick reply: *You're an Amazon warrior.*

His wife was almost the polar opposite of Mayor Redpath— independent, self-assured, strong in every sense of the word.

Tomorrow night they'd celebrate their eighteenth anniversary with dinner at the marina. All those years ago, he'd been working with the Sex Crimes Investigation Team when Caroline contacted him for her research. At the end of the interview, she declared: 'I've never met a man more dedicated to the protection of women.'

While Caroline hadn't been keen on a sea change from their lives in Sydney, she'd agreed to give it three years. The promotion was a reward of sorts for his role in identifying a corrupt detective. Poole suspected that certain people were also keen to move him away; despite the accolades, no-one liked a dobber. But bent coppers made his blood boil. While everyone else was slogging away to nail an offender, those bastards were on the inside fucking it all up.

If it were solely Poole's decision, he'd stay in Kinton Bay as long as he could. He knew that his approach to community policing was making a difference, even though he'd always be an outsider. Kinton Bay had five founding families—the Kintons, Evanses, Hoxtons, Redpaths and McCormacks; a close-knit town where everyone knew everyone, and half were related.

When Caroline was younger, she'd come to Kinton Bay on holidays. Poole thought she might remember some locals and re-connect but it had been too long ago. She'd made a few friends through her running group and on the development committee. It was difficult though, because she was travelling back to Sydney Uni for work three days a week. And, of course, because they didn't have children. That was how others made friends—through their kids' school and sports.

He guessed that some people deliberately avoided Caroline. An associate professor in criminology married to the chief inspector was an intimidating combination. Their loss—they'd never know that this tall woman with spiky platinum-blonde hair was not only clever but had a devilish sense of humour and a gung-ho attitude to life. She needed it as an antidote to her work.

Another text popped up. *Sandbagging finished. Houses protected. Amazon warrior off for coffee.* She'd sent a new photo, he recognised Glenda O'Riordan's house in the background.

In Poole's first week on the job, Glenda had bailed him up outside the supermarket, begging him to find her son. He'd read the old file—the investigating officer had concluded that Blake had run away to Sydney; this was supported by an anonymous sighting of the boy in Kings Cross. Poole had re-interviewed Glenda, checked the databases, contacted Kings Cross station and the Missing Persons Registry. He'd taken new DNA samples from Glenda and sent them for analysis against unidentified bones held in the Bone Room in Glebe morgue. No success with any of it.

Glenda would be aware of National Missing Persons Week coming up; he'd pay her a visit before then. The media release was still awaiting his approval—he could probably do that now before the next call about storm damage. Poole opened the document on his computer.

MISSING BUT NOT FORGOTTEN: CAN YOU HELP FIND THEM?

In National Missing Persons Week, we ask for your help in finding Kinton Bay's five long-term missing individuals. These people are not simply photos on a website—they are parents and children, family and friends. The police have never given up searching for them, and your information might assist in providing answers.

Regina Neary: The three-year-old girl went missing early on New Year's Day at Harbours End caravan park in 1971. A witness saw Regina being strapped into the back seat of a green Ford Falcon and driven away at speed. Neither the car nor the driver has ever been located.

Blake O'Riordan: The seventeen-year-old high school student was last seen leaving Kinton Bay High School on the afternoon of Friday 14 August 1998. There is a possibility that he travelled to Kings Cross in Sydney.

Greyson Creighton: The twenty-three-year-old nurse from Brisbane was on a work placement at the Community Hospital. He finished his night shift at 5 am on 10 December 1998. He may have gone for an early surf as his broken surfboard washed up at South Cove later that day.

Stefan Schwarzenbeck: The twenty-one-year-old Swiss backpacker left the Time'n'Tide Hotel around 11 pm on 20 November 1999. A witness reported seeing him swimming at Grotto Rocks at midnight.

Fabian Lavigne: The sixty-three-year-old businessman went missing on 30 October last year. He was last seen at 10:45 pm walking down Dolphin Street towards Main Beach. Fabian had received threats following a COVID outbreak in his resort.

Anyone who has information on any of these cases is urged to come forward. A single piece of information—no matter how small—may help us determine what happened to somebody's loved one.

When Poole had first arrived in Kinton Bay, he'd reviewed each of these cases. The coronial inquest into Regina's disappearance found a high likelihood that she'd been kidnapped and was now deceased. Her case had been referred to the Unsolved

Homicides Unit. Both Greyson's and Stefan's disappearances were attributed to probable misadventure. Stefan's parents had pushed for maximum publicity to get answers about their son but, despite a reward of five hundred thousand dollars, no leads had come through. Blake's file was the thinnest and his case had never gone to the coroner. Of them all, he seemed the most likely to be alive today.

On Monday, Poole would send the release to local media, along with a special note to Meri Britton. Over the past year, the *Chronicle* journalist had asked numerous questions about the investigation into Fabian Lavigne.

Fabian was the only one to have gone missing under Poole's command. Just before the pandemic, Fabian and his wife, Yuki, had invested millions building a new eco-resort twenty kilometres out of town. Luxury accommodation aimed at overseas tourists. But their first—and only—foreign guests left behind a deadly trail. Fabian caught the virus and passed it on. Three locals died, another five suffered ongoing effects. The town turned on him with angry phone calls and anonymous death threats.

Trying to make amends, Fabian had offered cash payments to those who'd been affected. But he was already deep in debt. Yuki juggled loans and deferments and bills for six months while Fabian hit the whiskey bottle. And then one Friday, he didn't return from a late-night drinking session at the Time'n'Tide. With the anonymous threats earlier in the year, Yuki was convinced her husband had been murdered. Poole investigated the vindictive emails and letters but found no evidence that any of the people behind them had followed through. The most plausible explanation was suicide.

In the nine months since the disappearance, Yuki had promoted the eco-resort to wealthy Sydneysiders who couldn't travel overseas. Her adult children had stepped in to help. They'd rebranded it Shearwater Resort, named for the migratory seabirds. The place had become a success. If Fabian knew, he'd be kicking himself.

Poole emailed his approval for the media release, yawned and stood up from his desk. He needed a coffee. His whole team was exhausted from long days dealing with the storm. It finally seemed to have passed, although the sudden thunder at lunchtime had put the station back on high alert.

Before Poole could leave his office, Constable Wes Terry appeared at the door. The young local had come through the Indigenous recruitment program. Smart and enthusiastic. Poole liked his positive attitude, a counterbalance to the cynicism of the older blokes at the station. And sometimes his own.

'Sir, we've had a call from a couple of teenagers in Wreck Point National Park,' the constable said. 'They've found a human skull.'

'A skull?'

Kids could mistake an animal tibia or femur for human bones, but there was no mistaking the shape of a human skull. Poole's mind automatically ran through the missing persons list. Had Fabian Lavigne walked into the dense bush of the national park last year and shot himself?

'Yep, a skull,' Constable Terry repeated. 'Between Wreck Beach and the big cave.'

'Right, let's get a team out there.'

Wet, muddy and remote—not an easy task for a search team. After all the rain, the site would be difficult to access and any forensic evidence likely to have washed away.

'Sorry, sir, one more thing,' Constable Terry said. 'The teenagers reckon it's historical. They found the skull in the same location as a massacre of our people in 1847.'

Poole hadn't heard of an Aboriginal massacre around here but more sites were being catalogued each year. The huge storm could have unearthed fossilised bones from colonial times. If that were the case, he'd have to call the Aboriginal Liaison Officer and a raft of specialists from the Office of Environment and Heritage to an Aboriginal Cultural Heritage Adviser and archaeologists.

Constable Terry shifted his weight from one foot to the other.

'Okay.' Poole nodded. 'We'll call the ALO on the way and you can fill me in on the history. Is there something else?'

'The boy who found the skull. Kyle. He's my cousin.'

Of course. Everyone was related in Kinton Bay.

'Thanks for letting me know.'

Poole collected his radio and phone from the desk; he'd grab a coffee to take in the car with him. But still the constable didn't move. When the young man finally spoke, it came out in a rush.

'The other teenager is Siena Britton, the journalist's daughter. Kyle said that as soon as they found the skull, she uploaded a video to YouTube. And she's sent it to all the media in Sydney.'

Shit. Poole would have preferred some time to start an investigation before the media merry-go-round began spinning.

10

MERI

MERI HOPED FRIDAY MORNING'S EDITORIAL MEETING WOULD BE QUICK.
She needed to finish the story on the damage to the marina,
track down an evacuated resident from the nursing home, and
be at the flooded council building by three o'clock. And she
wanted to ask her editor about Glenda's request. As a courtesy.
Neville hadn't been interested in reporting on Blake O'Riordan's
disappearance for the past two decades and he was unlikely to
change now. That suited Meri just fine.

The three journalists, advertising manager and editorial
assistant had gathered in the meeting room.

'What goes up when the rain comes down?' Neville loved to
start every editorial meeting with a joke.

'What?' The editorial assistant played along.

'An umbrella!'

It wasn't as bad as some of his other offerings. The team
obliged him with a brief chuckle.

'Thank god the rain has actually stopped,' Meri said.

The three journalists—Meri, Josephine and Hugh—had
been out in the worst of it every day, finding stories and taking

photos. Neville, meanwhile, had only left the office once or twice all week. His bright yellow polo shirt matched his sunny mood today. He had a whole wardrobe of shirts from local businesses—this yellow one sported the logo of Lance's Construction & Development. Apparently, Lance had been helping out with sandbagging down by the mangroves, near Glenda's house. Thankfully her house hadn't flooded.

When they were growing up, that area had been nicknamed Stinking Bay. It was boggy and smelly at the best of times. Lance couldn't possibly be interested in developing it, but why else would he be so keen to assist Glenda all of a sudden? He'd done exactly the same thing to Meri after Mum had died—turned up on the doorstep, ostensibly to help Rollo with any maintenance, while assessing the potential of the house and its large block. For a few months, Lance campaigned so subtly that Meri, in her grief, hadn't realised his motives. Until they were almost signing the paperwork on a small house in one of his new developments. That was Lance's special skill—taking advantage of vulnerable people.

After Neville had decided on the front page for tomorrow's print edition, he turned to Meri. 'So, Proclamation Day in eight weeks. How are your stories coming on?'

She refrained from rolling her eyes. Every year, they ran the same articles to commemorate the proclamation of Kinton Bay as a town. And every year, Neville Kinton treated Proclamation Day like a family anniversary party. His great-great-great-grandfather Augustus Kinton had grazed sheep and grown potatoes on the hill where St Paul's now stood.

'All underway.' Meri counted off the stories. 'An interview with Olive and a piece from the historical society. Photo shoot of

Geoffrey Kinton's descendants beside his statue.' Neville would be front and centre, beaming from ear to ear. 'Column from the mayor. Announcement of this year's Living Legends awards.'

'Excellent.' Neville nodded. 'And what about the development committee?'

'I'll get a few paragraphs from them on upcoming projects.'

Both of their spouses were on the development committee. Rollo's big moment had been creating The Whopping Whale Festival six years ago. The annual festival had gradually attracted more and more visitors and media, but then the pandemic had hit. Last month, they'd held a mini version: an exhibition of photos at the council chambers, some online whale videos, and live music at the pub. A fun night, but the locals saw whales from their own fishing boats—none of them would spend their hard-earned cash on a cruise ticket. By the time Rollo got home from the pub, Taj had branded it *The Not-So-Whopping Whale Festival*.

'It'd be good to have a female voice from the development committee,' Neville said. 'Can you interview Caroline Poole? Ask her about the plans for those apartments near the church.'

'I've already done two stories on the Blue Waters Panorama Residences,' said Josephine, the youngest journalist.

Neville and his wife owned a small block of flats near Main Beach which they leased out for short stays. Was he worried about the new development affecting his rental income? Like most people in town, Neville's family relied on the tourist dollar.

'Okay, let's have a piece on the new bar at the marina then,' Neville directed. 'Phil has already locked in some advertising from them. A good news story!'

Good news. Neville should've had the phrase tattooed on his forehead. Just as Siena had pointed out at dinner last Sunday, Neville liked upbeat stories. Even more so if they brought in advertising for the paper and tourists to Kinton Bay.

In her early days at the *Chronicle*, Meri's draft copy had come back covered with red scrawls. *More positive. What's the upside?* Now, the small team of journalists looked for a positive angle automatically. Sometimes, during the bushfires and the worst COVID-19 outbreak, it was almost impossible to find, but they'd persisted. When their parent company closed some of its other regional papers last year, the *Chronicle* survived and was sold to a new group, Regional Express Media. Neville claimed the credit: *It's down to my success in maintaining a fine balance of news and advertising and business development.* But his approach was like doing a deal with the devil—they couldn't report properly on any local business issue.

'I can write the piece on the bar,' Hugh offered. Meri smiled at him gratefully.

'Good.' Neville ran his hands through his hair—still long on the sides but receding on top. 'Okay, that's it. We've covered everything.'

When the rest of the team filed out, Meri stayed behind.

'Can I have a quick word, Neville? I was wondering if we could run a campaign about Blake O'Riordan's disappearance. His mother has been in hospital and she asked me . . .'

Meri was sure he'd brush her off straight away. And it was for the best. Glenda wouldn't want to hear what came out once they started investigating.

'Blake O'Riordan.' Neville grimaced, then cracked his neck from side to side. His neck-cracking generally meant *no*.

'Who wants to read about a teenage runaway from years ago? Blake buggered off to Kings Cross. He wanted to leave.'

That had been the police theory at the time, now cemented by each retelling.

'Why do you think he never contacted his mother or brother?'

'I bet he died. Those runaways always do. Heroin overdose. Turf war. Bikie shootout.' Neville shrugged his shoulders to finish his neck exercise. 'Either his body wasn't found or the police never connected the dots. It was the early days of DNA testing.'

Over the years, Meri had considered various theories about Blake. He was in Sydney, having a great time, drinking, smoking, being a bastard. He was dead, killed in a fight. He was alive, hiding out from the police after his latest crime spree. Or he'd turned police informant and gone into witness protection—that would explain why he couldn't contact his mum.

Blake's disappearance had never received much media atten-tion, especially compared to the missing backpacker from Switzerland who became international news the following year. Meri understood why: Blake came from Stinking Bay; he wasn't photogenic; he wasn't smart; he wasn't funny; and he wasn't nice. But along with her editor, Meri knew she'd been complicit in under-reporting.

Each year, before the anniversary of his disappearance, Glenda would ask if the *Chronicle* could run a special feature on Blake. Neville always convinced her to buy a 'discounted' ad in the memorial column instead.

'Missing Persons Week is coming up next month,' Meri said.

'Uh-huh.'

Was Neville actually considering it? Oh no. She'd only asked so she could answer Glenda truthfully.

'But if it's the wrong month . . . after the storm . . .' Meri tried to backtrack, hating herself for it. Maybe it *was* time to get the truth out. If she had to write the story, could she deliver her own information, anonymously?

'Mmm . . .' Her editor tapped his fingers on the table, a habit that irritated the whole team. 'This storm has been hard enough for the town. We don't need to go digging up old issues. People need a bit of good news right now.'

For once Meri agreed. Now she could tell Glenda she'd tried. Despite her relief, that last cup of coffee gurgled inside her. Not such good news . . . she was turning into a younger version of her editor.

After lunch, Meri was summoned to his office. Neville told her to shut the door.

'Someone called with a tip.' Neville had friends phoning him constantly. 'They've found a skull at Wreck Point. Fabian, I'm guessing. Can you drive out and get some details?'

A skull. Meri took a deep breath, closed her eyes for a moment and pictured Fabian. The French man. Always smartly dressed, wearing expensive shoes and a constant frown in those last months; his wry take on the world had been extinguished by the pandemic. But he didn't seem the type to walk into the forest—Meri had imagined him sailing away in the yacht he used to own, and ending it out in the deep blue sea. His poor wife. Yuki had shown her the threatening emails but, of course, Neville refused to look into the story. Without telling him, Meri had conducted her own investigation, looking at the possible suspects. She'd interviewed Lance and the other guys on the development committee. But like the police, she'd found nothing. Every second Friday, Yuki still turned up to the office with coffee and cake, and asked her to keep investigating.

Maybe they'd just found the answer.

⌒

Turning into the entrance of the national park, the car slid in the mud. Meri yanked on the steering wheel and slowed to a crawl. She'd been right to tell Siena it was too muddy to come out here today. The location app showed her daughter was still in the park. Before leaving the office, Meri had called and texted but got no response. Perhaps the girls were in a black spot with no signal. If Siena had seen the police in the forest, she would've rung straight away, alerted her to a possible news story. Meri would feel better, though, if her daughter called back; if she knew for sure that Siena was nowhere near the discovery of a skull.

The skull. A frisson of anticipation tingled through her—a proper news story at last. Sad and tragic but nothing like reporting on the new roundabout in Dolphin Street or the school fete. If it was Fabian, she could help provide answers for Yuki and solve the mystery for the community. And if it was someone else, then that would be an unexpected story with Meri first on the scene.

Ten metres along the fire trail, a police officer stood guard, his vehicle parked at an angle to block the route. Young Wes Terry. When Meri interviewed him last year about starting the role, he'd been so enthusiastic. How was he finding it now, arresting old classmates from school and teammates from rugby league? Attending a car accident and recognising a friend behind the wheel? It must be easier to work anywhere other than your own home town.

'Sorry, Mrs Britton, there's no entry in here,' Constable Terry said after she'd wound down her window. 'You'll have to turn around.'

Meri inched her car back and forth in the mud while the constable guided her with hand signals. Soon she was facing the main road.

'Do you know when the chief inspector will be able to speak to me?'

'I don't think there's much to say at this stage.' He shrugged. 'Forensics will arrive tomorrow.'

'Can you tell me where the skull was found?'

'Quite far into the bush, in a really rocky spot. It'll be tricky to get equipment in.'

'Do the police have any leads?' Meri asked, desperate for a hint. 'Do they think it's Fabian?'

'Sorry, Mrs Britton. You'll have to wait to hear from the chief inspector.'

'I understand.' She smiled her acceptance, before asking one last question. 'My daughter is somewhere in the national park with her friend. You've closed the track but they'll be able to get out, won't they?'

Constable Terry took off his cap and circled it through his hands.

'I thought that's why you got here so fast.' He leaned into the open window. 'You know who found it, don't you? Haven't you seen the YouTube video?'

11

SIENA

YouTube
Siena's Stories | #TheKillingCave
13 views

My name is Siena Britton and I'm reporting from Wreck Point National Park. My town, Kinton Bay, calls itself the perfect summer holiday spot. You can swim, go fishing and snorkelling, ride a quad bike in the sand dunes, all that kind of stuff.

But beneath the sunshine and the fun, Kinton Bay is hiding a dark secret.

Right here is the tragic resting place of three Aboriginal families. Men, women and children. These generous people were feeding shipwrecked survivors who'd taken shelter in a cave just over there. And then on the third day, Geoffrey Kinton, a former convict, decided he wanted more than food. He cornered a local girl in the cave, and decided to take her—just like the colonials had taken this whole land.

Her family tried to save her, and they were shot dead. Their lives cut short, their bodies thrown down from the cave to these rocks below my feet.

My school assignment talks about how history is told from the point of view of the victors. Well, Kinton Bay is a perfect example. The white men were never held accountable. Instead, they took this land and built a village here in 1847. Our town is even named after Geoffrey Kinton, the rapist and murderer.

Today, local teenagers come to the cave, known as the Killing Cave because of its dark history. They party, they drink, they graffiti the walls. They continue the desecration that began almost a hundred and eighty years ago.

I'm calling for two things: a memorial to the victims of this massacre and for our town to be renamed to honour the traditional owners. We need to right the wrongs of our whitewashed history and acknowledge these horrific killings. This is not just a tourist town for—

Fucking hell, Siena. I've found a skull.

Oh my god! Oh my god! That's Kyle. Sorry about the swearing.

All that rain from the storm must've uncovered their bones. The past is talking to us and we have to listen. This is such a significant moment. Oh my god! I'm shaking. Sorry if the picture is shaking too. I can't believe this.

But I'm going to post this right now, from here—unedited. And I'm sending it to all the media across Australia. We need to make a change.

Kinton Bay has to listen now.

12

MERI

GOOD GOD, SIENA HAD FOUND THE SKULL. THE THOUGHT HAD NIGGLED at Meri earlier and she'd ignored it. But who else would've been out in the waterlogged national park today.

'You need to let me through.' Meri pointed at the barricade. Her voice went high. Panicky. 'She's a minor!'

The constable leant inside his car and radioed Detective Chief Inspector Poole. She strained to hear the conversation, without success.

'The boss says it's all good,' Constable Terry reported back. 'Siena's fine. He'll bring her home a bit later.'

'But I should be there,' Meri insisted. Her poor sensitive girl. She'd be so shaken at unearthing a skull. 'Siena needs me.'

'She's okay, seriously,' the constable repeated. 'You can see on the video.'

'What is the video you're talking about?'

Meri didn't understand why she couldn't see her daughter, and why there was a video already? Aside from the worry of Siena's involvement, this was Meri's breaking news.

Constable Terry took her mobile and brought up a YouTube channel. Bloody hell, Siena had a YouTube channel! The video ended with Siena standing on a rock while a boy yelled off-screen about finding a skull. Kyle, not Jasminda. Must be Kyle Cooper in Year 11 who led the NAIDOC assembly last term.

Why don't I know about the YouTube channel? Why didn't she ring me immediately? Obviously, these were questions that Constable Terry couldn't answer. Meri planned to stay right here until a police car came out carrying her daughter.

As she was watching the video for a second time, her phone rang.

'What's happening?' Neville asked. 'Is it Fabian?'

Without mentioning Siena, Meri explained that access was blocked.

'Right, well, if you can't get closer, take a shot of the national park sign and come back to the office,' Neville said. 'You need to finish the marina story and be at the council building at three.'

'I'll stay here a bit longer,' Meri replied.

Neville said 'No' as Constable Terry shook his head. For god's sake, she should be allowed to see her own daughter. Meri rang Siena again; no answer. She didn't have Poole's mobile number, she always had to contact him through the station.

'You'll need to move your car, Mrs Britton,' the constable said. 'The ALO has to get through.'

Meri turned to see a blue four-wheel drive chugging along the muddy track. ALO: Aboriginal Liaison Officer. The video had talked about a massacre. Could she catch a ride further into the forest with him? Or should she leave, as they were all requesting her to? Chief Inspector Poole was a good man—she knew he'd look after Siena. But still . . .

'Mrs Britton, please,' the constable begged. 'Your car is in the way. It's important.'

'Okay, okay,' Meri snapped. 'But ask the chief inspector to ring me. Urgently.'

'Of course. He's just pretty busy right now.'

Driving back to the office, Meri mulled over the words in the video. *Our town is named after Geoffrey Kinton, the rapist and murderer.* In primary school, Meri had done a project on their town founder. Kinton, a bricklayer from Birmingham, had been arrested in a riot demanding the right for working-class men to vote. He was transported to Australia for the crime of sedition. After seven years in Sydney, Governor FitzRoy sent him on an expedition to explore the bays north of Newcastle. This was to keep Kinton's progressive views about democracy away from the capital. In a storm, the ship smashed into the rocks and the heroic Kinton rescued most of the passengers. He chose a sheltered spot to set up camp, and that camp became the township of Kinton Bay. In line with his democratic beliefs, the first public building Geoffrey Kinton erected was a town hall. The part that made Meri and her classmates smirk was that Kinton had fathered sixteen children. He'd practically populated the new town by himself.

The information given by Meri's teacher had not mentioned the traditional owners and the murder of three local families. She'd only heard that story a few years ago. One of the Aboriginal Elders, Aunty Bim, had asked why she should accept a Living Legends award when Proclamation Day caused them so much heartache. Bim Cooper, Kyle's grandmother.

These days, they taught some Aboriginal history and culture at Kinton Bay High School, more than Meri had ever learned there. Not the massacre, though. It was rumoured that the Killing Cave got its name from the actions of a shipwrecked soldier: exhausted and dehydrated, his mind ravaged by syphilis, he'd stabbed two men to death for a cup of water, then walked into the ocean, looking for the boat. A sexual disease, madness, thirst, drowning: it had all the elements to create horrified fascination in school kids. The stuff of urban legend. Had Geoffrey Kinton made it up to cover his own crime?

⁓

Staring at the blank document on her computer, Meri wondered how to frame the story. Mentioning the historical aspect would put Yuki's mind at ease but could police forensics determine the age of the skull straight away? She was still waiting for Chief Inspector Poole to call. In the meantime, Aunty Bim might provide background on the massacre; Meri found her contact details, but the call rang out.

Google alone was answering her questions: *In a century's time, only your teeth will remain. Your bones will literally have turned to dust.* Flicking to another webpage, she read that the acids in fertile soils could dissolve bones in thirty years. Well, that ruled out any historical link. Or did it? The soil at Wreck Point wasn't exactly fertile. *Skeletons can fossilise in salty ground.* If the skull had been inside the cave, that added another layer of possibility. The bones of an extinct marsupial lion had been protected inside a cave system under the Nullarbor Plain for hundreds of thousands of years.

When Neville walked past her desk, she asked his advice. 'Should I wait until I can speak to Chief Inspector Poole to write this piece?'

'Yes.' Neville balanced his empty coffee mug on top of the partition. His answer was hardly surprising—her editor would rather not run any story about death.

'Gossip will spread around town,' she said. 'We have to report something.'

'That video . . . I saw it.' He drummed his fingers on the cup, making a tinny sound. 'Why did your daughter email it out to the media? Did she send it to us? Have you spoken to her?'

'I . . . um . . . haven't been able to speak to her. She's still with the police.'

'Well, that's ridiculous. She's your eyewitness.'

Heat spread from Meri's throat and blossomed across her face. Her daughter was embarrassing her professionally, *and* she'd lied about her trips to the national park. This would never happen to Kimberley. Her uni friend had made it to the BBC in London, with no children to impede her ability to do her job fearlessly. Kimberley had just won an award for an investigative report that led to the arrest of human traffickers. Her stories had impact. She wasn't constrained by kids and a dogma of good news.

'I'll try again,' Meri said to Neville. She watched him walk into the office kitchen before calling Rollo.

'Is Siena home yet?'

'Nope. Did you see her on the TV news?' Rollo spoke slowly. Had he been drinking?

'The regional news?'

'No, Channel Ten. They played some of her video on the five o'clock news.'

'Are you kidding me?'

Her own daughter hadn't called her first; instead she'd sent the video to the whole nation. The TV channels had got the scoop, not Meri.

And then Neville was back by her desk, fresh cup of coffee in hand.

'Have you spoken to your eyewitness?' he asked.

'Not but it's on the TV news.' She tried to bury the anger, keep her tone neutral. 'So we'll need to put a story online.'

'This is going to be bad for tourism.'

You're a journalist, Neville. Don't you want to find out who it is? What happened in the forest?

Biting her tongue, Meri shook her head. 'It's going to be bad for the dead person's family.'

13

The story is on every news channel. Five o'clock, six o'clock, seven o'clock.

The first time I see it, I'm holding a glass of water. It falls from my hand. The liquid runs out in a long dark stain across the floor. Thinner than blood.

Blood would ooze.

'Human remains have been found by teenagers in dense bushland near Kinton Bay on the mid-north coast. Police have cordoned off the site. Forensics are working to identify the remains and the circumstances of the death.'

On the seven o'clock news, the presenter is a young Eurasian woman, bright red lips, wide brown eyes, almost sexy in her tight yellow dress. Too colourful, too attractive to be talking about death.

'We have footage from one of the teenagers who made the discovery. Local high school student Siena Britton was in the national park doing a history assignment.'

Siena.

She's talking about Geoffrey Kinton and an Aboriginal massacre in 1847.

So serious.

So wrong.

Forensics will take one look and know the skull isn't that old.

Swallowing down the bile, I put my head in my hands, wrap my hands around my own skull.

The watermark on the floor is in the shape of a footprint. But I've left no footprints in the forest. No evidence.

When I take my hands away from my head, my fingers are shaking.

I've imagined this moment. Over and over. But still I haven't figured out my response.

My thoughts jump and tumble, old memories, nights of darkness. Through it all shines one image.

Siena's face.

She has no idea of what she's just unleashed.

PART TWO

BOILING SEASON

The excitement of a whale hunt attracted a particular type of man. A live whale had the strength to drag a ship underwater. A dead whale was almost as lethal. The crew had to move carefully in the rivers of blood and oil that flowed as they cut up the carcass. Long strips of blubber were carved off and boiled in metal pots. The dead whales were decapitated and peeled like oranges.

14

ROLLO

ROLLO SLUMPED IN THE LOUNGE CHAIR, STARING AT THE BLANK TELE-vision. He'd finally switched it off. Every news bulletin had prompted a stream of phone calls and texts, all along the same lines.

What the hell is Siena doing, mate?

Tell your girl to pull her head in.

After all this town has been through, we don't need this shit now.

This will kill the spring holiday trade.

None of them seemed to care about the human remains.

Except Owen.

His text was different from the rest.

Is it Blake?

Rollo's fingers hovered over the keypad, typed a few words. *No way, mate.* Then deleted them. A second attempt: *I hope not.* Backspaced again. He really wanted to say: *What makes you think I'd know?* Out on the boat, they didn't speak about Blake. Or Derek. Or Lance.

How did Siena find the Killing Cave anyway? No-one had talked about it for years. An image came to him of the cave, a dark, gaping mouth ready to swallow them into the depths of the earth. Girls dancing in the firelight, their shadows long and skinny, leaping along the walls, as if they were monsters escaping from inside the sandstone. Rollo's gut contracted. Doubling over on the couch, he rubbed his stomach, then ran his hand down to the back of his leg, touching the lumpy, scarred skin. His surfboard tattoo hid the worst of it. The scar was aching too. One of those phantom pains, maybe. From what had been lost.

⌒

By the time Siena bounced in the back door, Rollo had knocked back four beers and replied to Owen. He didn't mention Blake's name.

Meri said ID will take weeks. She reckons it's Fabian.

Weeks . . . They'd all be on edge until the remains were identified.

He went into the hallway to greet Siena.

'Dad, did you see the news? Sorry I couldn't ring you—the police took our phones. I had forty missed calls! I bet Mum's desperate to talk to me.' She paused for breath, only for a second. 'I can't believe it. They showed my video on TV. It's incredible. I sent it out but I didn't think anyone would actually *use* it. It was so sad finding the skull. I was shaking. Literally shaking. But it means we can start making things right. Get justice for what Geoffrey Kinton did.'

While dealing with the phone calls and texts, Rollo had tried to work out the best approach to take with his daughter. He'd asked himself over and over: why did Siena have to be the one who found it?

'Are you okay, honey?' He wrapped her in a hug. 'Must've been a shock.'

'Yeah, it was.'

'Do the police have any ideas about who . . .' He stepped back, watching her face.

'Well, they listened to what we said about the massacre. They have to do forensic testing to find out how old the skull is.'

Rollo's phone was ringing again. He'd left it on the coffee table in the lounge room. Another fuming business owner, no doubt. When would Lance Nelson call?

He had to warn Siena, but gently. When she got riled up, she became louder and louder.

'Listen, honey, we have to tread carefully with all this . . . stuff. Some people might get upset.' He shrugged, as if to dismiss their views. 'We've been through the bushfires and then we had the lockdowns. And now this flood. People are worried the tourists won't come back.'

'What are you saying?' She glared at him. 'We shouldn't talk about Geoffrey Kinton murdering three families because it will scare off the tourists?'

'I'm not saying that. But others . . . they're trying to fill their holiday houses and their cafes. They might say we should let history be history.'

'This town is so racist.' The bounciness had gone; her body was rigid with outrage. 'It's not *history*, Dad. It's still affecting everything now. There's intergenerational trauma. Kyle explains it better than me.'

Rollo tried to remember which of her friends was Kyle. 'Did he put you up to this?'

'No! I'm doing a school assignment. I'm studying how we're whitewashing history. Aunty Bim told me all about the massacre.'

Aunty Bim Cooper, the Aboriginal Elder on the development committee. When Rollo had joined, she'd invited him to use the title, Aunty—it meant she was a custodian of knowledge and lore.

'But what if they're not Aboriginal bones and all this trouble has been stirred up? Aunty Bim won't be happy.'

'That's what I mean about whitewashing—you just did it then.' Siena stuck out her bottom lip. 'We need to address our hidden history.'

Address our hidden history. She sounded like she was still doing a speech on the telly.

'Why don't you let Aunty Bim deal with it? You don't need to get involved, honey.'

Siena turned her death stare on him. 'Seriously, we're all involved, whether you like it or not. Aren't you proud of me?' she asked. 'Mum'll be proud.'

"Course I am.' Meri though . . . On the phone, she'd been as mad as a cut snake.

'Thanks, Dad.'

'You're a clever girl,' he added. 'Much braver than I was at fifteen.'

Rollo didn't know which option was worse: the evidence of an Aboriginal massacre driving away Kinton Bay's tourists or proof of Fabian's death by suicide—another casualty of the pandemic.

But what if it was neither?

15

SIENA

WITH A PILLOW PROPPED UNDER HER CHEST, SIENA LAY ON THE BED staring at her YouTube channel. She still couldn't believe she'd been on the TV news. And her video had been viewed nearly a thousand times!

Should she upload the footage of the party next? She'd forgotten to mention it when Detective Chief Inspector Poole had interviewed them; his questions were all about the skull.

Kyle had found it at the base of the rock. She must've dislodged it when she climbed up. While he stood staring at it, Siena had crouched down and brushed off the twigs and leaves before picking it up. It was coated in black mud but recognisable as a human skull. A life.

She'd held someone's head in her palms.

'You shouldn't be touching it!' Kyle had shouted at her. 'That's so disrespectful. Shit, we have to get out of this place.'

The shock of his shout and the sliminess of the mud made her drop it. The skull thudded back into the sludge, rolling slightly to one side. She was surprised it didn't break; the bone had felt thin and fragile.

'Sorry, I wanted to make sure it was real . . .' The mud wouldn't come off her fingers. Without thinking, Siena had rubbed her palms down her jeans.

'Gran says we're related to the people who died here,' Kyle whispered. 'My ancestors. Imagine all the family I would've had.'

For her history assignment, Siena had written the story as Kyle's grandmother had told it to her.

When the white man put his hands on the girl, she kicked and screamed. The others came running into the cave to free her. Everyone shouting. That Kinton, he had a gun. How could our people defend themselves against his bullets? Then Kinton set up camp in the bay and our other families stayed away. Scared he'd shoot them too. They say he kept the girl for a while. Used her knowledge for fresh water, fishing and cooking. Used her knowledge to survive.

Siena wondered about the teenage girl. Her family massacred before her eyes. Because of what a man wanted from her. And then she'd been put into slavery, serving him, while grieving her mum and dad, her brothers, sisters and cousins. He'd named her Rose.

'Your gran talked about the Great Forgetting,' Siena had said, standing guard by the skull. 'Well, the answer is to tell everyone. That's why I'm sending the video to the news channels.'

'You should check with Gran first.' Kyle phoned her but the call went to voicemail.

Siena didn't want to wait; she had to get the news out before anyone had a chance to suppress it.

From Kyle's latest text, it didn't sound like Aunty Bim was angry.

Wow, it was on the news! Gran wants to tell her own story. Can you get her an interview?

Aunty Bim said she'd told everyone about the Killing Cave in the nineteen-seventies. No-one had listened. She'd tried again in the late nineties, after the government brought in National Sorry Day. No-one had listened. She'd kept trying over the years. The town just didn't want to know. If Siena could get the TV news to interview her now, would people finally start to take notice?

Comments were popping up under Siena's video. She recognised a few names. The first message was from her history teacher.

Mrs Genares: *This is an important discussion, Siena. It shows the very act of correcting history.*

Alexandra Kinton: *Geoffrey Kinton was not a murderer. This is a false allegation about the wonderful founder of our wonderful town.*

ST: *There was no massacre. Where are your facts?*

Layla: *Do we have Koala Club next week or will you be too busy, Siena?*

Raine: *Thank you for your truth-telling. Change the name of Kinton Bay!*

Wallingo: *Fuck off with your lies and your ugly mug.*

Her first ever troll. Siena giggled. Excellent—that meant she was making a difference. Just like her careers adviser, Mr Durham, had said she would.

The phone buzzed and Glenda's name came up.

'I saw you on telly, love.' She sniffed. 'Did the police say . . . do you think it's Blake?'

'Blake? No, it's in the spot where there was a massacre almost two hundred years ago.'

'Are you sure, love?' Glenda sounded so sad.

Her missing son went to Kings Cross for drugs and girls—that was the story Siena had heard. He couldn't be dead in Wreck Point National Park. Someone would've known.

The back door opened and banged shut. Before Siena could move off the bed, Mum was striding into her room. Rushing out a quick goodbye to Glenda, she sat up, ready for her mother's praise; Mum would be so proud of her journalistic initiative.

'Why didn't you ring me first?' Mum stood over her, hands on hips. 'Why didn't you send the video to me?'

Shifting backwards on the bed, away from her mother's anger, Siena hugged her arms around herself, curling into a tight ball. 'The police took my phone.'

'They shouldn't have interviewed you without a parent present.' Mum didn't shout but Siena felt the controlled fury in her words. 'Why didn't they call me?'

'I don't know. They just asked us how we found the skull. They weren't accusing us of anything.'

'You had the right not to speak to them. You're a child.'

'I'm *not* a child.' *Here we go again, Mum treating me like a baby.* That was precisely why Siena hadn't sent the video to her—she wanted to prove herself. And because Mum's paper only printed the good news but she wouldn't mention that right now; Mum would get even crankier. 'I'm almost an adult and I didn't have anything to hide from the police.'

'Well, you've certainly been hiding things from us.' As Mum leaned closer again, she could smell the coffee on her breath.

'You set up a YouTube channel without discussing it with me. And you told me you were bushwalking with Jasminda.'

'I didn't want you telling me what to write for the assignment. Kyle was helping me and I interviewed his grandmother. The story has been passed down the generations.' She hoped her explanation would appease her mother. It didn't.

'You lied to me!'

'It's not like I'm doing drugs,' Siena yelled. 'It's a school assignment.'

'You lied. And you've embarrassed me professionally.'

I hate her. I hate her. I hate her. Squeezing her eyes shut, Siena felt tears leaking out. She dropped her head onto her knees and dragged a thumb across her eyelids; she didn't want to give Mum the satisfaction of seeing her cry.

'I didn't mean to embarrass you.' It was the closest she could come to an apology. 'I thought you'd be proud of me.'

This time, her mother seemed to listen. Sighing, she plonked herself down on Siena's bed and patted her shoulder. 'Are you upset about seeing the skull?'

'A bit freaked out. I touched it. I didn't mean to. Kyle was really mad at me.'

'Why do you think it's from the massacre?'

'It was in exactly the spot where Aunty Bim said—right underneath the cave.'

'Unless the skull was protected in the cave, it's unlikely to be that old.' Mum rubbed her temples with her fingertips. 'Bones turn to dust after about twenty-five years.'

'Really?' Siena hoped Mum was wrong. She had to be—this was the evidence that Aunty Bim needed to make everyone listen.

But what if Mum was right? What if she'd held Blake's head in her hands? That would be totally creepy.

'Did you go out to the cave when you were a teenager, Mum?'

Mum shook her head, got up and left the room without saying another word.

Siena lay back on her bed, staring at the ceiling, unable to believe that her school assignment had become national news.

And that her mother had just lied to her, outright. Hypocrite.

Yesterday, when Siena had been searching through Mum's diary for any references to the Killing Cave, she'd recognised another name, one that Axel had mentioned.

The Wrecking Crew.

10th March 1998

Kristie heard they've given themselves a gang name, the Wrecking Crew. From what we can tell, the gang is made up of Derek, Blake, Lance, Scott, Rollo and Owen. Kristie's brother said they've got a list of virgins and our names are on it. Is he telling the truth? Or is he just trying to stop us from going to the parties so we don't see what he gets up to with his girlfriend? I don't know if the others feel the same—I can't wait to lose my virginity!

Eww. Was Siena going to read about her mum's first sexual encounter in this diary? No wonder Mum had thrown it in the bin. But surely Dad wouldn't have been in a gang that listed virgins to pop. He wasn't a chauvinist pig; he treated Mum so well and cooked dinner most nights. And he never made sexist jokes like Owen did. Her father couldn't have been one of the Wrecking Crew.

But Mum had lied to her just now—she'd definitely gone to parties there. Siena pulled the diary out from underneath her bed and started reading a new page.

13th March 1998

I can't believe we're going to a cool party, a party with bonfires and beers and boys!!! Mum and Dad think I'm having a normal sleepover at Kristie's, but there's nothing normal about Friday the Thirteenth!

We squash into the back of Kristie's brother's car. Loretta's body spray makes me sneeze. It's a new Impulse flavour— Melon Madness.

When we get to Wreck Point, the bonfire on the beach glows in the darkness, sparks flicker between ribbons of white smoke. Pearl Jam is blaring from the boombox and a few couples are dancing. Just like the parties on Beverly Hills, 90210!

'This is freaking ACE!!!'

Loretta tells me to take a chill pill and keep my voice down.

Kristie is already looking for her crush—a guy in Year 12. We spot him, along with all the other cool seniors. They're in the same year as Nathan but he's way too daggy to be invited.

In their new boob tubes and choker chains, Kristie and Loretta could pass for seventeen. I look like a six-year-old in my denim overalls, even though I left one strap undone, like they showed in Dolly. *The girls by the fire are in tiny singlets and denim shorts.*

'Here, have a beer.' Kristie's brother is passing them around.

I tip up the can so fast that the beer froths inside my mouth. Not the greatest taste. Maybe we could get some Bacardi Breezers next time—they're yummy.

We sit on the logs by the fire and a group of Year 11 boys come over. It's the Wrecking Crew. Derek and Lance offer us rum and Coke from a big plastic bottle. They lie on the sand next to us, their faces shining in the light of the flames.

The alcohol makes me bold. I turn to Lance. If I squint hard enough, he looks like Dylan from 90210. He's definitely a bad boy.

'Do you have a list of virgins?' I can't help giggling. 'Are we on it?'

Siena slammed the diary shut. Sheesh, Mum was fifteen—what was she doing? Did she lose her virginity that night? *Tell me it wasn't with Lance the construction guy!* That slimeball. At every event, he flirted with Owen's wife and the waitress from the pub, as well as any attractive tourists.

And Mum was accusing *her* of behaving badly. Seriously. For going into the national park to do a school assignment. Not to drink or to party or to have sex.

Stuff Mum. Stuff them all. She'd give them something else to talk about.

Opening the YouTube app on her phone, Siena uploaded the video of last Saturday's party.

16

POOLE

DETECTIVE CHIEF INSPECTOR POOLE HELD THE MEDIA CONFERENCE outside the police station on Saturday morning. He surveyed the journalists in front of him—two from radio, one from regional TV, one from the Newcastle paper, and Meri Britton from the *Coastal Chronicle*. Over the past two years he'd built relationships with these people. There was one reporter he didn't recognise—no doubt attracted by Siena's footage. He nodded at Meri and took a deep breath: of all the people to find the skull, it had to be a journalist's daughter. He hadn't called Meri yesterday afternoon, assuming he'd speak with her when he dropped Siena home. But the girl had said not to come in, that her mother wasn't there. She was certainly strong-minded—he'd have to keep an eye on her, the amateur YouTube journalist.

Back in Sydney, Poole had seen the media as a necessary evil—a channel for speaking to the public but also one that could jeopardise a trial after months of police work. In Kinton Bay, he'd aimed to become a friendly public face, holding regular press conferences and publishing casual videos on Facebook. Much of the liaison work involved chatting informally to journalists about marine safety, road rules and domestic violence. Here, Poole felt they were working together to prevent crime. Community engagement and community-based policing in action.

He would definitely need the community's help to solve this case.

'Thanks for coming out on a Saturday morning,' Poole began. 'Skeletal remains were discovered in dense bushland in Wreck Point National Park yesterday afternoon. We've established a crime scene, and a forensic team is examining the area right now. As you can appreciate, after the storm we've had, it may take some time to locate any related evidence. The dog squad is assisting with a search of the area.'

'Is it a suspicious death, Chief Inspector?' asked the radio journalist.

'We can't say at this stage. Forensics will be working to understand how the person died.'

'Do you know who it is? Any obvious identifying factors?'

'Not at this stage, as I said.' Poole shook his head. 'We're keeping an open mind.'

The female TV reporter stepped forwards with a microphone. Her cameraman was filming every word. 'The teenagers who found the skull believe it's from a massacre of Indigenous people nearly two hundred years ago,' she said. 'Do the police agree this could be the case?'

'I can't comment at this stage.' Poole knew he was repeating himself but the phrase, *at this stage*, was the best way to convey their meticulous processes. 'We need to let forensics do their job.'

'Surely you can tell the difference between two-hundred-year-old bones and recent remains?' The reporter pursed her lips at the apparent stupidity of the police.

'It depends on environmental factors.' Poole didn't want to discuss the decomposition of a corpse, especially not if the deceased person's family was listening. He drew himself up to his full six feet and five inches. 'We will allow the forensics team to do their examinations and then we'll have some concrete information to assist in the identification process.'

'Excuse me, Chief Inspector. Can you confirm that the teenagers who found the remains were interviewed without a supervising adult present?'

Ah shit. Meri Britton was arcing up over her daughter's involvement. Poole didn't need that on the television news.

'Mrs Britton. Thank you for your question. I'll discuss that with you afterwards.'

Meri scowled and the other journalists pressed closer, as if they'd sniffed the foul stench of police misconduct.

'Is there a reason you can't tell me in front of everyone?' she asked.

This wasn't how his media conferences usually played out. He didn't want to make an enemy of Meri Britton. Damn. He should've found the time to speak with her yesterday, even though he'd been so busy.

'Have you asked your daughter about this?' Poole raised his eyebrows, a warning signal. 'I'm happy to talk to you privately after we've finished up here.'

'She said there was no supervising adult.' Meri obviously hadn't understood his look. 'You took her phone and went through it. Without adult permission. She's only fifteen.'

'The teenagers were merely witnesses.' He spoke gently. 'She showed us the video she'd made.'

'But why didn't you let me into the forest?' Meri's voice rose in pitch. 'Is it because I'm a journalist?'

Poole felt sorry for her; although he didn't have kids, he imagined this would be pretty hurtful. 'Mrs Britton, as I said, I'd rather have this chat in private, but as you're insisting on discussing it right now, I'll explain. We told the teenagers we were going to call their parents. The individual in question begged us not to call her mother or father. The teenagers wanted to speak with us freely and were happy to show us their mobiles. There was no wrongdoing and no attempt to hide any information from you.'

'Oh, for god's sake,' Meri muttered before picking up her satchel and rummaging around in it. The other journalists watched her, then turned their gazes back to Poole. Accusing gazes this time; he'd embarrassed one of their own.

⌒

After hosing the layers of mud off his gumboots, Poole left them in a corner of the garage to dry. At least the mud from the national park didn't stink like the foul thick stuff down in the mangroves. Still, he'd need a shower before dinner. A late dinner. They were supposed to be celebrating their anniversary at the seafood restaurant overlooking the bay, but Poole had texted Caroline to cancel. The afternoon and early evening had disappeared as he traipsed through the forest and trawled through the old missing persons reports.

When he entered the house, Caroline was stirring something in the wok, a gin and tonic in her other hand. She wore a bright blue skirt with a geometric pattern, her platinum hair gelled up. She must've been dressed already when he sent the message.

'Sorry about the restaurant,' he said. 'Maybe next weekend?'

As usual, it was a promise he didn't know if he could keep.

'Don't worry.' She smiled. 'I've whipped up a green chicken curry. With extra chillies for you.'

'Sounds good.' He leaned forwards to kiss her. 'You look lovely. As beautiful as the day I married you.'

'Well, you look muddy, darling,' Caroline shot back. 'Do you want a beer now or after your shower?'

'No beer tonight. I've got a special bottle in the back fridge.' Piper-Heidsieck—Caroline's favourite. It had been their wedding day champagne and he'd bought it for every anniversary since. More expensive than what he used to drink, but Caroline had introduced him to the finer things in life.

As Poole soaped away the dirt from his afternoon in the national park, he recalled the morning of his wedding. His best man had slipped him a medicinal brandy: *You're ten years older than her. You're supposed to be the cool, calm, collected one.* But Poole couldn't believe his luck—that the smart, funny, sexy young Caroline had agreed to spend the rest of her life with *him*, Douglas F. Poole. F for Frederick, after his father and grandfather. A name handed down to each new generation.

Except the next one. Caroline didn't want kids.

'She's young, she'll change her mind,' his mum had said. His dad had wondered aloud: 'Will there be another Frederick Poole?'

But any future Fredericks were nebulous, unknown things, while each night, Caroline lay with him, electrifying every nerve ending in his body, including his mind. Life was a compromise, his parents should've known that at their age. He'd been with his previous girlfriend for eight years; they'd talked babies and houses. Made plans. But when he finally popped the question, she turned him down: 'I can't do it. You're already married to your job.' Thirty-five years old, on the cusp of it all, and suddenly single. He lost his belief in romance, hadn't expected to fall in love ever again. Meeting Caroline was a complete surprise.

Not long after their wedding, his sister had her first child, Freda. A female Freddie. It wasn't quite the right tradition but his parents seemed happy enough. Occasionally, Poole had played with his niece and imagined her as his own. But then work became so busy for both him and Caroline that children seemed an impossibility anyway.

While eating the curry, they managed not to talk shop. Caroline twirled her new silver bangle so it glinted in the candlelight.

'Thank you for my anniversary present. It's beautiful.'

And then, as she sliced up the lemon tart for dessert, all her questions came at once.

'Did you find anything else near the skull? Do they really think it's historical? When will an identification be made?'

He laughed. 'You've been waiting all dinner to ask me, haven't you?'

'It didn't seem a very romantic conversation for our anniversary.'

'The ID could take weeks—months if we don't have matching DNA on file.'

'Do you think it's Fabian?'

He'd rung Yuki and told her about the skull but warned that it was difficult to gauge the date of the remains until they had forensic results.

'I don't know. I was reading up on the Swiss backpacker who disappeared in 1999.' The file held photos of a tall young man with blond hair and expensive sunglasses. In one picture, Stefan Schwarzenbeck posed on a boat in Sydney Harbour, the iconic bridge behind him. 'Imagine losing your son on his travels, half a world away.'

'Terrible.' Caroline dolloped a small spoonful of cream onto both of their dessert plates. 'Although I imagine Yuki would say it's just as bad to lose your husband at home.'

'Or eight hours from home, like Greyson Creighton.' The nurse from Brisbane had gone missing a year before the backpacker. Who knew what Greyson's future might have held? He could've saved lives, made a difference during the pandemic.

All these families, waiting, wondering what had happened to their men.

Poole hadn't mentioned a fourth name: Blake O'Riordan. There had only been a cursory investigation under Inspector Nelson's command. Was the man inept or lazy? Or both? Poole hadn't found anyone to ask—surprisingly, all of the officers from back then had left Kinton Bay.

What would Glenda do if the skull was Blake's?

17

MERI

MERI LEFT THE MEDIA CONFERENCE WITHOUT SAYING A WORD TO THE other journos; their sympathetic grimaces made her want to fling herself off Grotto Rocks. The story would spread around the newsrooms: *Meri Britton could've had the scoop but her daughter didn't want her involved.*

After all these years, the one time her daughter might have actually helped her career . . .

On the day Meri's friends graduated from university, flapping around in their old-fashioned academic gowns, she'd been waiting for her mother to come out of surgery. Kimberley had invited her to Sydney. 'Celebrate with us! We'll go drinking with the whole gang,' her friend said over the phone.

But Mum needed her. And some of the gang had already jetted off overseas. Dave had even asked her along on his trip: China first, then the Trans-Siberian Railway. He'd ended up in Tajikistan. Adam went backpacking around Greece and Italy. They all sent postcards. She sat by Mum's bed imagining herself inside those pictures—the piazza in the medieval city of Siena, the mountains and lakes of Tajikistan, the Forbidden Palace in Beijing, the Red Square in Moscow. When her accidental twins arrived just three years later, she named them for those exotic places: Siena and Taj. A permanent reminder of her goal to travel. Some time in the future, she would drink an espresso standing at a cafe in Siena and scoop ice-cold water from a glacial lake in Tajikistan.

When Meri dropped out in second year, her friends had all asked the same question: 'Why can't your dad look after your mum?'

Her answer was brief. 'He lives in Perth.'

Her father had left the family home in August 1998—a week after Blake disappeared. In the months before, Meri had tried talking to Dad about the parties in the Killing Cave, but he was always at work. Most nights he didn't get home until after she was in bed, and a tense silence often accompanied them at the breakfast table. Her parents didn't scream and shout; they just stopped speaking to each other. Turned out he was more interested in Bonnie, the events manager at the bowling club, than his own family.

His leaving tore them apart. Mum started working full-time at the childcare centre. In the evenings, she was always off volunteering somewhere—helping with card games at the nursing home, adult literacy classes at the church, knitting for newborns in the hospital. It was like she had to fill every spare minute. And then when Nathan finished school, he got a job as a jackeroo and went to Queensland for eight months.

Dad was the glue that had held them together.

Meri missed everything about him. His deep laughter, his spaghetti bolognaise (the only meal he could cook), his enthusiasm about her creative writing, his Monday night treat of takeaway hamburgers (the only night he didn't have to work at the bowling club), his discussions about current affairs, his tight hugs. His ability to make her feel that everything would turn out okay.

Dad was supposed to be the one who fixed everything. But he deserted Meri when she'd needed him most.

Whenever Dad had called from Perth, Meri was sure he'd say, *I made a mistake. I'll be home soon.* He never did. Instead, he flew back for occasional visits which became more and more awkward; he'd lost track of the rhythm of their lives, and they'd lost track of him.

Three years later, as she was studying for her HSC exams, Dad rang. Relief flooded through her—despite everything, he'd remembered his promise of five hundred dollars for a trip after she finished school. Not enough for New York but maybe Melbourne. Kristie had moved there with her family—it would be great to visit her. Meri was working at the gift shop on Saturdays, saving up, but it wasn't enough.

'I've got some exciting news for you.' Meri could hear him smiling down the phone; he knew how much the trip would mean to her. 'Bonnie and I are having a baby. A little girl.'

The final betrayal. Her father had forgotten about her future and now she was being replaced. By an innocent, unblemished baby daughter. Meri was done. She cut all contact.

When she had to quit uni to look after Mum, she blamed Dad. If he hadn't left the marriage, she would have finished her degree. At least Neville Kinton had taken her on part-time, as a low-paid cadet.

Now, every time Meri tuned into the news, she was reminded of her failure. On ABC TV, Adam reported from Europe.

In *The Sydney Morning Herald*, Prisha broke the latest scandals from Parliament House. Cameron's impassioned words explained climate issues in *The Guardian*. Fatima worked for CNN in India; Dave on an American radio station; Nicci in film production in Hollywood; and Kimberley, of course, for the BBC in London.

In first year uni, she'd promised Kimberley that they would meet on the steps of Nelson's Column in Trafalgar Square. But she never made it.

⌒

Meri stomped in the back door, slamming it shut behind her. Pirate came rushing down the corridor to greet her. The only loyal member of this bloody household.

'Siena, are you home?' she shouted.

'Hello to you too,' Rollo called from the kitchen. 'Kids are out. Do you want coffee? I've just made a pot.'

Why was he so fucking jovial all the time? Dumping her bag on the kitchen table, she noticed that Rollo had already taken out a mug for her.

'Siena has embarrassed me,' she said. 'Both of us. She told the police not to call us when they were interviewing her.'

'Oh well, you know what she's like.' Rollo shrugged. 'Thinks she's grown up already and doesn't need us.'

'But she shamed me. In front of the police and the other journos.'

'They all know how teenagers are.' He pushed down the plunger in the coffee pot. 'Don't take it personally, hon.'

'But it *is* personal. She didn't want *me* there, her own mother. Why do you always excuse her behaviour?'

'Come on, Meri, why are you so hard on her? She's a good kid. They both are. We're lucky they're not like me at that age.'

He'd been a teenage druggie, nicknamed for his skill in rolling tobacco papers. But when she moved back to Kinton Bay to care for Mum, Rollo had become a completely different person. He'd never touched marijuana again.

'Yep, we're lucky,' she said, taking the mug of coffee from him. 'That they didn't turn out like you. Or Derek.'

She could hear the meanness in her voice. Rollo ignored it and changed the subject.

'Have the coppers got an ID on the skull?'

'Not yet. Poole was unusually tight-lipped.'

'The opposite of Caroline on the phone today then. She was chatty as usual.'

Rollo often came home from development committee meetings repeating Caroline's thoughts on an issue. Meri had done a few interviews with her—a smart, super-fit woman who was definitely achieving her dreams. Up and down to Sydney all the time, travelling for a half-marathon in Coffs Harbour or Brisbane, off to a conference in Melbourne. No children to clip her wings.

'So she rang you about Siena's video?' Meri asked.

'Yep. But she wasn't ranting like everyone else. She said we should listen to Siena.' Rollo took a sip of his coffee. 'I reckon it's a storm in a teacup. It'll all blow over.'

'Maybe. What about Lance? Did he call?'

Lance would have plenty to say about Siena's video plastered across national TV. And none of it good. When Fabian's guests brought in the virus, Lance accused him of destroying the town single-handedly. As if Fabian could be held responsible for a worldwide pandemic. *That fucking French wanker thinks he's so cool in his Gucci loafers.* Lance owned a pair of Gucci sunglasses himself. *Fabian should be selling the clothes off his back to pay for what he's cost this town.*

'Nah, he didn't ring.'

Strange. Did this mean Lance was saving up his vitriol? Hopefully he wouldn't take it out on Aunty Bim at the next committee meeting. They'd had a few arguments before—Lance thought he could just build over protected Aboriginal rock carvings and middens.

'Had you heard of the massacre?' Meri asked.

'Aunty Bim told me. But there's always been stories about the cave.' Dangerous territory, discussing the cave. 'Like the one about the surfer being taken by a shark on Wreck Beach and his ghost coming back to haunt the cave. And the syphilis story, of course.'

The telling and retelling of ghost stories and urban myths. But none of their parents had talked about a massacre.

By the time she hooked up with Rollo, five years had passed since those parties at the cave, and he had broken away from Derek and Lance. He'd fallen into his dream job—working on the whale-watching boat—and exuded a relaxed satisfaction with the world. She'd envied his transformation, wished she could achieve the same. Those early secret nights with him had been a perfect release from days looking after Mum. They hadn't wanted to spoil it by reliving their tricky school years.

Her phone buzzed, an unknown number.

'Hello, Mrs Britton. This is Stu, Yuki Lavigne's son. We're wondering if you know anything more about the . . . findings . . . in the national park?'

'I'm sorry, Stu, only what the police have said already. We have to wait for the forensic report.'

Meri had first met Stu at the re-opening of the resort—he'd left a high-powered job at an investment bank in Melbourne to come up here and help his mother.

'But your daughter found it.' Stu cleared his throat. Polite but insistent. 'You must know something. Were there any clothes or other items linking the remains to my father?'

'No, I don't believe so.' Bloody Siena—placing her in this impossible position. 'Listen, they'll have the results pretty quickly if it's Fabian. His DNA is on record.'

'And maybe it will stop Mum going on about him being murdered.' He sighed. 'She can't face the other option. It'd be a relief to find him and understand what happened.'

'Of course. I'll call you if I hear anything.'

As she finished the call, Rollo put the mugs in the dishwasher and took his wind jacket from the back of his chair. 'I'm going down to the marina,' he said. 'Helping with the clean-up. Frank's catamaran smashed against a pylon.'

Meri closed her eyes for a moment, feeling grateful:

1. *Thank god, our own boat hasn't been damaged in the storm.*
2. *Thank god, Stu's call prevented further discussion of the cave.*

What would Rollo say about her focusing on these two things for gratitude? In his world, everything was good. Even with the storm damage, the leaking roof, the erratic cruise bookings, and now their daughter uncovering a skull in the national park.

As he kissed her goodbye, she asked about the kids.

'Taj finishes work at five. Siena has gone to clean Glenda's house. She asked if you could pick her up and bring something for Glenda's dinner.'

'Fine.' A cook and a taxi driver to do her child's bidding.

'Don't be like that.' Rollo pulled her against him. 'She just found a dead body.'

'A skull, not a dead body. But then I wouldn't know, because she won't talk to me about it.'

Meri knew she was being petulant, acting like a child herself. But none of them had ever supported her work—the children demanded her attention and Rollo's cruises took precedence over everything else. She was always the one juggling and compromising, putting her own ambitions aside. And now, in this one moment when her daughter could've helped her career, Siena had done the opposite.

After Rollo left, she pulled out her mobile and checked the location app. Yes, Siena's face came up on Glenda's street. As usual, Taj's phone had run out of battery. She googled Siena's YouTube channel and glanced at the number of subscribers. Five hundred and sixty-three. Where had they all come from? The general public? She'd better check that Siena had the comment option switched off.

A new video had been posted. Shot at night. Teenagers around a campfire. Someone was playing a guitar. Firelight danced on the ceiling above them. A rounded, golden ceiling. Wait—where was this? Oh no, Siena had been to a party in the Killing Cave.

The first comment below the video was typed in capital letters. *TAKE THIS DOWN, YOU STUPID BITCH. WHERE IS AXEL?*

18

SIENA

SIENA WOKE WITH A START. LISTENING TO THE DARK, SILENT HOUSE, she could feel the *thud-thud-thud* of her panicked heart. The images in the dream came back to her. A muddy skull. Axel lobbing it like a rugby ball across the cave to Jackson. The pair tossing it back and forth, faster and faster. Then slamming it into the campfire. The skull exploding as it hit the flames. Black blood spurting out, drenching her face, splattering the walls of the cave.

Calm down. Just a dream.

The numbers glowed on her iPhone. 5:23. Way too early, too dark to get out of bed.

Bringing up her YouTube channel, Siena read the latest messages under the party video. Mum had told her to turn off the comments, but Siena wanted everyone to debate the story online. And they were. The latest agreed with her: *It's a disgrace! These vandals should be arrested for defacing public property, trespassing and wanton destruction.* But the previous comment must've been written by someone in the party gang:

You fucking nerd. We felt sorry for you and you fucked us over. Don't forget: we know where you live.

The video she'd posted began with Axel in the cave, his body swaying as he strummed his guitar. His first song was a ballad, but then he switched to rock, his voice screeching out the lyrics.

Next, Siena panned to a small group shotgunning beers. One boy choked and the beer spurted out of his mouth, down the front of his shirt. A couple nuzzled on the ground, kissing, breaking apart only to take a drag on the joint going around.

From this point, she'd edited out the worst bits. The video showed clips of the girls scrawling graffiti on the wall of the cave. Hayley spelt out *I LOVE VODKA* in wonky drunken letters. Jackson could be heard calling out: 'Write *JACKSON IS HOT!*'

Siena had cut to pictures of discarded beer cans, cigarette butts and chip packets. Apart from Axel singing to the camera, none of the faces could be identified in the dim light. Partly, she was worried about being arrested. Every year at school, they were given the 'staying safe online' talk; the teachers stressed that it was illegal to publish naked photos without consent. And Siena didn't want the girls being seen like that anyway.

So the video didn't show what had happened next.

Despite the winter chill, Jackson and another guy stripped. They ran naked around the cave, yelling and whooping.

'Get your gear off, girls,' they shouted. 'Show us yer tits!'

'Fuck off,' the girls replied, laughing. But Hayley stood up, stumbling slightly, and started to unzip her jumper.

'Hayley! Strip! Hayley! Strip! Hayley! Strip!'

The chant echoed around the cave. Someone began a slow clap, each loud noise like a gunshot, and the others joined in.

Oh no, what had Siena got herself into? Would they be chanting for her to undress next?

Hayley shimmied her skirt down her legs, and the chanting and clapping sped up.

'All the way, Hales! All the way! Take it off! Take it off!'

She pulled her t-shirt over her head and snapped the clasp on her bra.

'Ta-da!' Hayley yelled, her arms out wide. In the golden glow of the fire, she appeared like Venus in the Botticelli painting—red hair streaming around her shoulders, breasts white, the only covering the black triangle of a G-string.

'All hail Hayley,' she slurred, twirling in a circle as if she was on stage.

'Hot as hell, Hales!' the boys yelled.

'You're beautiful,' came the cheer from the girls.

She twirled again, her bare bum at Siena's eye level. A line of freckles dotted the middle of her left cheek. Did Hayley know those freckles existed?

'Come to me, baby,' Axel demanded.

Hayley danced over to him, her movements disjointed, feet clumsy. He held out his arms and she fell into him. Axel groaned. 'You're fucking heavier than you look.'

She put an arm around his neck to steady herself. Licking up her neck, Axel crooned, 'You want it tonight, don't you, baby?'

'They all want it tonight,' jeered the naked Jackson.

Siena tried not to look at Jackson's penis but her gaze went straight there. It seemed to be getting longer and straighter. Ugh. Disgusting. Could she creep out of the cave unseen and find her way back in the dark by herself? Beg Kyle to pick her up from somewhere in the forest?

A hand touched her back and she flinched.

'Ohhh, we've got a nervous chick here.' Jackson tugged on one of her plaits and sniggered.

Shuffling sideways to get away from Jackson meant moving closer to Axel and Hayley. She whipped her gaze between them, unable to take her eyes off the bare bodies. Axel stroked his hand over the black triangle of Hayley's underwear.

'Axel, I'm feeling a bit . . .' Hayley broke off with a retching noise. He scrambled backwards as vomit erupted from her mouth and splattered across the rock.

'Fucking hell!'

Hayley retched a second time as everyone was jumping away from her.

'That stinks,' said Zoe.

None of them moved to help. Siena gathered Hayley's discarded clothes and was about to pass them to her when Jackson stopped her.

'Let me rinse her off first.'

Standing above her, he poured his can of beer onto her face and hands.

Hayley yelped. 'Jackson, you jerk. Now I'm freezing.' She rubbed at the liquid. 'And I stink of beer.'

'Better than vom.'

Hayley took her skirt from Siena and wiped it across her chest, soaking up the beer. Once she was fully dressed, she crouched by the fire.

'Do you want another vodka?' Axel asked.

'Leave her alone.' Zoe walked over to her friend and squatted next to her. 'You all right?'

'Yeah . . . I could have another vodka.'

Siena closed her eyes at the stupidity. Drink until you vomit, then drink again.

'Why don't you have one, too, Siena?' Axel was suddenly by her side, holding out a bottle. 'You haven't had much tonight, babe.'

She hadn't had *any* vodka. Pretending to take sips while pouring it out behind her.

'You can chug it.' Axel pressed a bottle into her hand. 'Catch up with the rest of us.'

Although Axel didn't seem drunk himself.

'I don't really drink vodka,' she said.

'Well, how about a cap then?' He put his hand into his pocket and produced a small plastic bag of white pills.

'Ah, no, that's okay.'

'You're missing all the fun.' Axel put a pill on his tongue and swallowed it down with a slug of beer. 'But maybe we can have a more natural type of fun?'

He ran his thumb down the side of her jeans, then back up to her hip.

'I've got a boyfriend,' she lied and made herself smile while she removed his hand. It came straight back to her thigh. 'And you've got Hayley.'

'You'd be so sexy if you let your hair out. A stunner.'

He leaned in and pressed wet lips against her neck, her ear, her cheek. The others hadn't noticed; Hayley and Zoe were sitting by the fire, facing the other way.

'No means no, Axel.' She said it with confidence, just as they'd been taught at school. Just like her mum had trained her—you're in control of your body, not anyone else.

'Aw, babe, don't be like that. I'm the one who let you come.'

'Thanks, Axel. I'll send you the video tomorrow.'

'How about a little gratitude, Siena.'

His hand had been caressing her cheek; now the fingers jammed into the soft tissue of her neck. She scuttled backwards and felt rough rock; she was trapped against the wall of the cave. Ducking, she tried to break free from his grasp, but Axel lurched forwards, pushing her down, his full weight on top of her.

'Please get off me,' she wheezed. 'I can't breathe.'

Oh god, he was suffocating her. His hands were around her throat, stones dug into her back. No escape. His tight fingers against her windpipe made her panicky. Her breath became even more ragged. With her left hand, she scrabbled around for any object in reach: a can of beer, a backpack, a stick. Nothing. And then her fingers hooked on something hard. A rock. Small enough for her to lift, heavy enough to do damage.

'Come on, babe. Let's have some fun.'

'I said NO!'

Siena grasped the rock in her palm and swung it as hard as she could, smashing up into Axel's temple. He fell off her and lay motionless on the ground. She bolted over to the campfire and positioned herself close to Hayley and Zoe, hoping for some kind of safety with the girls. Taking deep shaky breaths, she checked the reaction of the group—none of them had noticed what had happened.

Axel groaned and sat up.

'Can't hold your liquor, mate?' Jackson teased. 'Just don't go spewing like Hayley.'

'Shut up,' Hayley shouted.

'It's not . . .' Axel started. Was he embarrassed that a girl had got the better of him?

She stayed away from him for the rest of the night, sick with fear about what he might do next. But he blanked her completely and said nothing to his mates. When they drove back to town, Siena asked to sit in the cabin. The ute pulled up behind the bowling club. Jumping out, she hurried to escape them. She thought she'd succeeded until she heard footsteps.

'You crazy bitch.' Axel's fingers dug into her arm and he pulled her around to face him. 'You don't do that sort of shit to me and get away with it.'

Siena glanced up and down the empty street. No people and no cars at this time of night. The pub was already closed. They were outside the surf shop, away from any houses where people might still be awake. In the green light from the store windows, Axel resembled a savage Rottweiler, snarling and grimacing. Cold dread made her legs heavy, cemented her to the pavement. Why did she go to the cave alone with these jerks? Stupid. Reckless. She touched her mobile in her back pocket—could she somehow text Kyle?

She heard the car before she saw it, a low thrum coming from the marina carpark. When the headlights appeared on Dolphin Street, Siena ran. She zig-zagged across the tarmac a few metres in front of it. The car screeched to a stop in the middle of the road but she kept running. A voice called out: 'Are you okay?' Siena assumed that Axel wouldn't chase her with witnesses around.

Now, lying in her bed at home, she circled her hands protectively around her neck. Was Axel actually missing? If she told the police what had happened, would they blame her for his disappearance?

Siena typed out a quick email on her phone with the link to her video. She described the illegal entry to the park and the destruction of public property. The subject line read: *The desecration of the Killing Cave by Kinton Bay teenagers*. She addressed it to Detective Chief Inspector Poole, and added the email for the Channel Ten news desk.

The police would have to do something about the party gang now.

She ignored the tears on her cheeks, called the dog back to her bed and snuggled down hopefully for another hour's sleep. Without a nightmare.

19

Every news update repeats the same line over and over: 'We have to wait for forensics to make an identification.'

I haven't slept since the skull was found.

In the dead of night, I stare at the ceiling, wondering who it is . . . and if they'll find the rest of the bones.

Will they search the cave? Every nook and cranny?

The parties out there in the nineties. That was the start.

The parties are still going on now. I watch Siena's new video online. Last Saturday night. Teenagers drinking. Smoking dope. Axel Evans playing the guitar.

The comments under the video call Siena a crazy bitch.

Another vulnerable teenage girl.

Easy prey.

20

ROLLO

ROLLO HAD CANCELLED FOUR WHALE-WATCHING TRIPS LAST WEEK DUE to the storm but the calmer weather on Sunday meant the big one could go ahead. Another full boat. Business was finally picking up after two years. Preparing for the safety briefing, he hoped Owen wouldn't want to talk to him about the skull. But his old friend said nothing. No surprise there—they could both win gold medals if staying silent about stuff that mattered was an Olympic event.

As they motored through the heads, Rollo breathed in the salty air and felt all the crap disappear behind him. Last night, Meri had been shouting at Siena about the video and all the lies. Their daughter had sneaked out of Jasminda's last Saturday night, got a lift back into town with Kyle, and had gone to a drunken party at the Killing Cave. Rollo tried not to get involved. Taj retreated to his room and shut the door. His son spent too much time on the computer; Rollo should have brought him along today.

Kinton Bay's two watchmen rose high above the boat: to the north, Banks Head with its slopes of gum trees, and to the south, Oxley Head's rusty orange cliffs climbing upwards into the clear sky.

'Look, a pelican!' shouted a young girl.

The huge bird was skimming the water beside them, its black and white wings outstretched. Bizarre creatures. Rollo preferred the white-bellied sea eagles that swooped down to snatch fish with their powerful talons. They came back to the same nest each season to breed. And they chose one mate and stuck with them for life.

He'd chosen to stick with Meri, although she'd assumed he would run from the shock pregnancy. No-one in Kinton Bay had even known they were seeing each other. Their 'fling', as Meri called it, had been all about sex. Awesome sex. Meri had kissed him from his ankle upwards, licking the surfboard tattoo on his calf. Discovering the scar. 'A shark bite?' she'd teased. 'Almost,' he'd lied. 'Had a wipe-out at Wreck Beach and ended up on the rocks. Sharp as bloody shark's teeth!' He'd told everyone the same story, even the emergency doctor who'd sewn him up. 'It looks more like a knife wound,' the doctor had said, waiting for an explanation. But Rollo kept his mouth shut. Just as he'd been told.

With his sister trying and failing to get pregnant for the past three years, he'd felt embarrassed his own kids had arrived so easily. His parents adored the twins and thought the sun shone out of Meri's bum. 'We're lucky to have you, Meri,' Dad had said so many times. 'You put our lad back on track.' It was true: he never would've managed to own a business without her by his side, but he'd found his calling on the boat before they got together. When he was growing up, Dad drove bulldozers, and Mum served behind the counter at the petrol station. Long hours and backbreaking work with ball-breaking bosses. Rollo knew that wasn't for him. Even now, his parents didn't have enough money to retire; they were managing a caravan park up in Cooktown, on call twenty-four seven.

When he finished Year 12, he had decided surfing would be his priority; he surfed in the day and only did evening shifts at the pub. And it was through surfing that he fell into whale watching. One of the surfers asked Rollo to help on his dad's cruise while he was in Bali for six months. From the moment Gary took the boat out into the open sea, Rollo was hooked. When two young males lobtailed near the boat, he was mesmerised. *Showing off for the female.* Gary's commentary made the passengers laugh. But more than that, Rollo felt an affinity for those lads in the water. Sleek and fast, diving below and performing on top. Graceful. At one with the sea. Exactly how Rollo imagined himself in the surf. The shit of everyday life forgotten in the ever-changing ocean.

In all the years he'd been on the *Sirius*, first under Gary as captain and then later as the owner himself, his days had never resembled his parents' shitty work life. Even the admin—he did some of it, Meri ran the website and the marketing, and Chester from the marina helped with bookings.

'Okay, folks, time to keep your eyes wide open for the whales,' Rollo announced over the loudspeaker. 'We have two pods travelling north.'

The pods had been spotted earlier this morning, further south, a few miles offshore. Rollo had calculated a rough position for the boat to meet up with them, based on the whales swimming at four or five knots an hour. Pushing a flop of hair off his face, he admired the ocean: a perfect morning, eighteen degrees, the winter sun sparkling on a flat sea. That made spotting whales so much easier. In turbulent water, it was impossible to see their blow above the waterline or their trail after they submerged.

Owen stood on the starboard side, scanning the ocean with binoculars. He was the best spotter, with sharp eyes that didn't miss a thing. Standing there, he looked like a pirate with his thick scruffy beard and shoulder-length hair in a low ponytail. The beard covered his acne scars—the main reason he'd been bullied in high school. Or maybe it had been for his paintings. Detailed landscapes of Kinton Bay. The art teacher called them 'extraordinary' and said he had real talent. The boys called him a poofter. Blake stole his brush during class, Derek spilt dirty water across the wet picture. When the art teacher invited Owen for an extra lesson after school, the twins lurked in the corridor and threatened to break his middle finger. Despite the teacher's urging, Owen never chose art as an elective and stopped painting altogether. As far as Rollo knew, he'd never taken it up again.

'Dolphins at three o'clock,' Owen called.

Rollo relayed the message over the loudspeaker, reminding passengers how to find the right direction. There was no point using port or starboard, or even east or west—the clock approach was simplest for most people, with the bow of the boat as the number twelve. The sun reflected off sleek black fins as two smooth shapes broke the surface and leapt into the air.

'These are bottlenose dolphins,' Rollo explained. 'They belong to the toothed whale family, which is different from the humpback whales we'll see. Dolphins can travel at thirty-five kilometres an hour. An interesting fact is that they never actually sleep like we do. Dolphins have to stay awake to surface and breathe. So they only shut down half of their brain at a time.'

As he released the loudspeaker button, another call came from Owen. The main prize.

'Whales at one o'clock.'

Two weeks ago, Owen had lost his maintenance job with the council. That job had lasted longer than most—nearly eighteen months. He wasn't an easy employee, a whinger with a temper. But somehow he managed to keep it together for the three-hour cruises on weekends. Now Owen was asking for more hours on the boat, but Rollo couldn't promise anything—it all depended on bookings.

He scratched at the scar on his leg, then pressed the button on the loudspeaker. 'You're in for a treat today, folks.'

As Rollo began his usual patter of whale facts, he watched Owen moving among the passengers, helping them to spot the whales. Behind his friend, in the far distance, the treacherous rocks of Wreck Point jutted into the sea. The false headland that had, many years ago, smashed the *Lady Emmeline* into pieces. And above the point, a blue shape hovering. Presumably a police chopper bringing in equipment for the search. Teams of officers must be out there right now, looking for evidence related to the skull. What would they find from those parties and piss-ups back when he was a teenager, back when he made all his mistakes?

⌒

Rollo had farewelled the last passenger and was hosing down the deck when Owen came barrelling out of the cabin. He'd pulled a grey hoodie over his blue Seabreeze Cruises shirt; a vein pulsed in his forehead.

'What the fuck, Rollo?' Owen spat the words at him. 'I just got a call. Hayley's at the police station. What's your daughter's fucking problem?'

'I don't know what you're talking about.' Rollo took two steps back and put a hand on the railing to brace himself. Owen could do anything when he got into a rage.

'Siena sent a video to the police and said they should be fined for trespassing and some other shit. They're just kids having fun.'

What, like we were?

The skull had them both spooked. When he remembered that night from twenty-three years ago, it was a series of disconnected images. Derek punching Blake hard in the stomach. Owen drinking. Lance laughing. A girl unconscious by the campfire. Cigarettes and bongs and Bundy and Coke. The knife glinting in the firelight.

Now, Rollo stalled, preparing himself for Owen's anger. 'A video of . . . ?'

Of course, he'd seen the video. Meri had told Siena to take it off YouTube, but their daughter refused. That was the reason for last night's argument. *I'm just trying to keep you safe, Siena,* Meri had insisted.

'A video of a bunch of kids drinking at the cave.' Owen moved towards him. 'They're giving Hayley a fine. And me too. Fucking hell, mate. We don't have any cash. I can't afford that.'

'Don't worry. I'll sort it.'

'How the hell are you going to sort it?' Owen slammed his palms into Rollo's shoulders. 'It's your daughter who started this shit.'

'Calm down, mate.' He tightened his grip on the railing. Owen had pushed him overboard before. 'I'll figure something out.'

After every blow-up, Meri told him to cut his friend loose. 'He's not your responsibility,' she'd say. But Rollo felt differently. He and Owen had been surfing together since they were little, the youngest on the waves, and they always had each other's backs. But Rollo hadn't been able to stand up for his surfing buddy at school, that was social suicide. So, at sixteen, he'd convinced Owen to join the Wrecking Crew, figuring the twins would stop the bullying if Owen became part of the gang. He promised the others that Owen could get them a regular supply of Bundy rum. The plan had worked: the worst of the bullying stopped. Owen and Blake became friends, almost best mates, except Derek wouldn't allow that to happen. Jealous bastard.

Derek tricked and teased and cajoled and threatened. He had nicknames for all of them: the Blakester, Lucky Lance, Rollo the Stoned Loser, Crater Face for Owen, and Muscle Man for Scott Kinton. He called himself The Big D.

But after Blake disappeared, Owen shut down. Over the years, as the other blokes got jobs, made money, became their own bosses—or, in Derek's case, committed bigger crimes—Owen remained at a standstill. Angry, drunk, often unemployed. Whatever happened out there in the cave all those years ago had affected Owen for life.

'I can't afford these fucking fines, Rollo. So you'd better figure it out quickly.' Owen shoved him, not enough to send him backwards over the rail, but hard enough to deliver his message.

21

Student: *Taj Britton*
Year 9 Commerce, Mr Donovan
Assignment: Early industries, whale oil

Boiling the blubber

Whaling was one of Australia's first industries. After the Third Fleet brought convicts to Sydney in 1791, five of the empty ships went on to hunt whales. Numerous products were made from different parts of the whale—candles, soap and perfume from the blubber; corsets, whips and umbrellas from the baleen (the fringed bristles that humpbacks have instead of teeth). Whale meat had a dark red colour and tasted like beef.

But the most important product was the blubber.

In a procedure called flensing, long strips of blubber were cut from the carcass. These were boiled up in metal pots, known as 'try pots'. The Kinton Bay Historical Society has an old try pot which was used by the Byron Whaling Company. As the blubber boiled, it rendered into a clear, honey-coloured oil.

THE LIARS

This oil greased the wheels of industry for a few hundred years.
It was used in factories, machines, tractors, cars and explosives.
It powered the lamps in streets and buildings.

We even ate it in our margarine.

22

SIENA

ON THE FIRST DAY OF TERM, SIENA WAS TREATED LIKE A CELEBRITY: 'I saw you on three different channels!' Hayley and Jackson weren't at school and she managed to avoid the rest of their gang. When her history teacher praised her video, Siena bloomed with pride and hoped for more.

But on Tuesday, Hayley and Jackson stalked her at lunchtime. To lose them, she was heading for the library—those two wouldn't set foot in there—when a younger student approached her.

'Your friend Jasminda has been locked in the boys' toilets,' the kid said.

Siena ran towards the bathrooms near the quadrangle. This was her fault. Mum had warned her. They were targeting Jasminda because of the video. She barrelled into the boys' toilets, ready for war. *Please don't let them hurt her.*

The place was empty.

Not for long: Jackson followed her in. It was a set-up.

He shoved her into a kneeling position in front of the urinal. While everything in the boys' toilets was revolting, he'd blocked this bowl with toilet paper. A yellow pool of piss rippled centimetres from her face. Siena took short breaths through her nose, keeping her mouth shut, but still the smell stung her throat. Was Jackson really going to do this? She swallowed hard to stop herself from gagging.

'Take down the video, you stupid bitch.'

She should've listened to Mum—now, she'd be hurt for posting the video, for doing the right thing. From a distance, Jackson looked weedy with his glasses and gangly limbs, but close up, he was sinewy and strong. Why was Taj home sick today? She could've done with his help right now.

'Okay, okay, I'll take it down.' Not that it would make any difference—the police had a copy, and Channel Ten too. But he didn't need to know that.

'Right now!' Jackson instructed.

'I need my phone. It's in my bag.' The thought of the piss in her nose, her mouth, her eyes, made her gag again. 'Let me up and I'll do it.'

Instead of releasing his grip, Jackson squeezed her shoulders harder. 'You're gonna pay for this.' His fingers gouged into her muscles and she yelped. 'We'll take you back out to the Killing Cave. Give you what you deserve.'

'No!'

Her shout must have been loud enough to reach the quad. A female teacher called through the doorway: 'Is everything okay? Shall I send Mr Durham in there?'

Before Jackson could answer, Siena yelled as loudly as she could, 'Help me!'

In the deputy principal's office, Jackson wouldn't admit to anything. Nor would Siena. She decided her best option was to stay silent in front of him.

'I'm calling Chief Inspector Poole,' Mr Durham said. 'I'm sure this is related to Siena's videos in the forest. It's a police matter.'

Good. She could speak to the police privately, without Jackson around.

When the chief inspector finally arrived, he spent ten minutes in Mr Durham's office with Jackson, while she remained on the chair outside. As they finished up, the two adults moved closer to the door and she overheard a snippet of their conversation.

'Could the remains in the forest really be from an Aboriginal massacre?' The question came from Mr Durham.

'It's unlikely to be that old,' the chief inspector responded. 'But we haven't yet made an identification.'

Unlikely. Oh god, she had to tell Kyle and Aunty Bim.

'So the . . . person . . . it will be a more recent death?' Mr Durham's voice went soft and high. Nothing like his usual boom in assembly.

'I can't tell you anything else at this stage.' The chief inspector opened the door. 'Siena and Jackson, I want you both to come down to the station.'

～

This time Chief Inspector Poole refused to speak to Siena without a parent present; she was made to wait.

'What's going on?' Mum arrived and pulled her into a hug. 'Did Jackson hurt you?'

'I'm fine.' Blinking back tears, she nestled into the comfort of Mum's arms. The acrid scent of urine had lodged in the back of her nose. Tomorrow, she'd ask Jasminda, Taj and Kyle to be her protectors at school.

'Are you sure?' Mum brushed the hair off Siena's face and stared into her eyes. 'You look pretty upset.'

'He just said some stuff . . . But he's all talk, no action.' If she could convince herself then the fear would disappear. Thankfully, Mum didn't say *I told you so*. That would probably come later, when they got home.

When Mum went to the front desk to tell the officer they were ready, Jackson scuffed his way out from the inner doors. She could feel him glaring at her but kept her eyes focused on his trainers—bright red Air Max with a neon blue sole.

'I'm not finished with you,' he hissed.

In the interview room, Mum held her hand as the chief inspector asked Siena to describe what happened in the boys' toilets. They both made Siena feel like a child. She gently pulled her hand away and addressed the police chief.

'Didn't you get my email?' Siena leant across the table. 'Why haven't you arrested Jackson for trespassing and nudity and littering at the national park?'

'Thank you for sending through the video.' Chief Inspector Poole nodded. 'I've spoken with the park ranger, Hank Hoxton. Several individuals identified from the video have already been issued with fines under the *National Parks and Wildlife Act*.'

'Fines? Is that all?'

'The amounts aren't insubstantial. And Hank has changed the locks on the gate since you informed us that one of your fellow students had obtained a key from her father.'

Beside her, Mum groaned softly. Was that because Siena had snuck out to the party or because Owen would be furious with them all? So what. This issue was bigger than Owen and Hayley.

'Seriously—a fine?' She frowned at the chief inspector. 'That won't stop them, or the next lot. Kids have been partying in that cave since Mum was at school. They're desecrating a sacred place.'

Kyle wasn't going to believe this—or maybe he would. A fine: their parents would pay it and in a few months' time, when everything had calmed down, they'd start partying there again. Despite all her efforts, nothing would have changed.

'Siena, you need to be careful. You're stirring people up in town, and I've seen some of the comments under your video. Leave the policing to us, the proper authorities.'

'The proper authorities?' Siena scoffed. 'This country was stolen by so-called authorities. They sanctioned the decimation of the First Nations people. The authorities are not going to fix this.'

Mum laid a hand on her wrist. 'Come on, Siena, show some respect.'

'Where's the respect for the traditional owners?' she demanded. 'Where's the respect for their land?'

'Respect,' the chief inspector repeated the word slowly. 'It's one of my favourite subjects. I agree there's not enough respect in our community. But Siena, I need to ask you about something else. A few days ago, some of your friends reported a young man missing, Axel Evans. They believe you might know something about it.'

Perhaps it was shock at the abrupt change in topic, but the words came out before she could filter them. Bitter and angry. 'They're not my friends.'

'Do you know where Axel is?'

'Nope. You know he's, like, twenty-one or something? He's not at school with us. He's a man.' Freaking paedo scumbag. He shouldn't have been hanging around underage girls.

'Yes, we have his details. Hayley says you were the last person to see him on Saturday night.'

'Umm. I don't think so.' Maybe Axel had gone back to the rest of them after she'd run off.

'Look, we need to check on his welfare, make sure he hasn't come to any harm.'

Surely the blow with the rock couldn't have caused delayed concussion or bleeding in the brain or something.

'I . . . uh . . .' Siena took a ragged breath. 'He was with that whole group . . . Jackson and Hayley and Zoe and the others. I left. They were all still there, drinking, near the bowling club.'

'So you're saying that you weren't the last one to see him.'

Should she explain everything? And what about the car on Dolphin Street late that night—would the driver identify her and Axel? Whoever it was had seen them both.

'Chief Inspector,' Mum interrupted, 'this group clearly has it in for Siena. She's the victim here—Jackson just dragged her into the boys' toilets and threatened her. My daughter has given you a lot of information already. If she knew anything about this missing man, I'm sure she'd tell you.'

Go Mum! Sticking up for her. That made a change. Although maybe not the best time to do it. What if she *had* accidentally killed Axel with the rock? He could've collapsed walking home. His body might be hidden in a gully or washed out to sea in the storm.

⌒

Siena met Kyle outside the fish and chip shop. She wanted to cuddle and kiss him—recapture that incredible sensation they'd shared—to be close to him and banish Axel Evans from her thoughts. But other kids from school were hanging around and they settled for a brief hug. She couldn't tell him about Axel; he'd be horrified by that creep and want to get involved. Not a good idea—Jackson would eagerly start an attack on him. Of course, Kyle had heard about Jackson trapping her in the boys' toilets. After reassuring him that she was fine, she passed on the bad news: the bones were unlikely to be related to the massacre.

'You know what'll happen now?' said Kyle.

'What?'

'Nothing.' He touched the leather strap around his neck, flicking the silver turtle pendant with his thumb. 'Just like every other time Gran tried to talk about the massacre. All the attention will go to the dead guy.'

Siena understood his anger although she didn't like the dismissive way he referred to 'the dead guy'. She'd held that person's head in her hands.

'We should do something else, quickly,' she said. 'Before the police make an announcement.'

'Will that news channel interview Gran?'

'They want to wait until the skull is identified.' Siena's thoughts raced ahead. 'I'll interview her and put it up on YouTube. Get Mum to do something in the *Chronicle* too.'

'I don't know if Neville Kinton will print a story about the massacre. Gran has already spoken to him so many times. After all, he's descended from the murderer.'

As Dad had said, no-one wanted to 'dredge up the past'.

'I've got another idea.' Siena gave his hand a squeeze. 'Can you sneak out tonight?'

23

POOLE

POOLE SAW OFF SIENA BRITTON AND HER MOTHER, NONE THE WISER about the Axel Evans situation. Was the man actually missing or was it a distraction by Hayley Shuttlewood? She'd only started talking about Axel after being given a fine for trespassing in the national park.

It wasn't an offence to go missing, but Poole needed to ascertain that Axel was okay. Possibly he'd broken up with his girlfriend and was steering clear of her while his parents covered for him. Hmm, fifteen-year-old Hayley—under the age of consent.

Two officers had visited Axel's home and noted that his motorbike was still in the garage. But his mother had denied he was missing. 'Those girls are little troublemakers. One of them thinks she's his girlfriend, but Axel does his own thing,' she said. 'He picked up a job in the city. He'll be back in a couple of weeks.' The officers asked about the job and where he was staying in Sydney, but she couldn't say and wouldn't give them his mobile number. They requested she ask Axel to call the station as a welfare check. As they walked back to their car, the youngest child, all of eight years old, had oinked at them and yelled, 'Fuck off, pigs!' Knowing the Evans family, the 'job in the city' involved criminal activity. Axel wouldn't want his name on a police alert.

The informal chat with Jackson McCormack had also been unhelpful.

'Whatever Mr Durham said, I didn't do it.' Jackson's left sneaker bounced a rapid rhythm up and down on the floor. 'I was just talking to Siena about the party.'

'We could add a few more penalties to your fine for trespassing in the national park,' Poole warned him. Although Siena hadn't posted the full video online, she had described the actions of some of the group. 'Offensive behaviour, indecency and nudity.'

Red blotches appeared on Jackson's neck and face; he shifted in the chair and began a rhythmic tattoo with his right sneaker.

'Are you friends with Axel Evans?'

Constable Terry had labelled the twenty-one-year-old a toolie. But toolies hung out at Schoolies Week with Year 12 girls. Axel partied with fifteen-year-olds.

'He's my cousin.'

So, Jackson was his gateway to the schoolgirls. If Poole were a betting man, he'd put all his money on Jackson knowing exactly where his cousin had gone.

He should have known they'd be related. The Evanses and the McCormacks—two of the founding families. Proclamation Day must be coming up soon—a celebration of Geoffrey Kinton and a piss-up of the five founding families. Just what they needed after the storm damage and Siena's accusations. Privately, at home, Poole had dismissed the impact of Siena's videos. But Caroline disagreed. 'Stuff like this goes viral,' she warned him.

'You'd better make sure you act or you'll be hanged by the court of public opinion.'

⌒

Good news from the lab. The technicians had been able to extract DNA from the skull. It definitely wasn't historical as the teenagers had assumed. If a match existed on the database, the lab promised to have a preliminary report by the end of the day. Impressively fast.

Poole had sent them a list of possible IDs already in the database—familial DNA samples from relatives of Blake, Greyson and Stefan. Fabian Lavigne's family had handed over his toothbrush and hairbrush and those samples had gone into the system. But establishing the cause of death would be problematic unless the skull showed a bullet or blunt force trauma. Cold cases were notoriously difficult—evidence washed away, witnesses gone, memories lost.

'Ten bucks it's Fabian Lavigne.'

From his desk, Poole could hear officers placing bets on the skull's identity.

'Nah, my money's on Greyson Creighton.' Senior Sergeant Frawley's gravelly voice cut across the chatter. The older man should've known better.

Walking out of his office, Poole waited for them to catch sight of him and stop. They didn't.

'Didn't Greyson drown surfing?' asked Constable Terry.

'I'm doubling up.' Senior Constable Ernie Chan pulled out his wallet. 'Twenty bucks on Fabian.'

'That's enough.' Poole spoke softly but they all turned to him as one. 'Show some respect for the dead.'

'Sorry, boss,' Senior Sergeant Frawley boomed. 'It was inappropriate.'

Respect. As he'd told Siena, it was his buzzword at the moment. Respect for the dead. For women. For the elderly. For experience. Respect seemed to be sorely lacking everywhere. Poole had raised this at the last regional meeting. 'It's bloody Gen Z,' one of the superintendents had said. 'They should be called Generation Me—they think they're so important.' But Poole knew it wasn't that simple. The younger generations were inheriting a crumbling world; they didn't respect their elders, they blamed them.

⌒

Poole considered driving back to the high school to speak with the deputy principal. He'd met Anthony Durham before, of course, but the man seemed rattled today. Apparently Siena's second video had sent the students into a frenzy of gossip, and teachers were complaining that classes had been unsettled. When they were talking earlier, Durham had fidgeted with his reading glasses: taken them off thirteen times (Poole had started counting) and dropped them on the floor twice. They had bright red frames which made his actions even more noticeable. What was the man so nervous about? It was worth the short trip to chat with the deputy again, he decided.

But as Poole neared the high school, a phone call came through from the search team.

'We've found a backpack, sir. It was within a kilometre radius of the skull location, wedged between rocks.'

'Any identifying labels?' he asked. 'Anything inside?'

'It's a Rip Curl brand. Someone said they were producing that design in the nineteen-nineties. It's being bagged for forensics as we speak. There was broken glass inside—possibly a Bundaberg Rum bottle. Also, an old strip of tablets. Disintegrated.'

Had a Rip Curl backpack been listed in any of the missing persons reports? Blake had disappeared after school on a Friday; he might've been carrying a backpack. But so could have Greyson or Stefan.

Accelerating past the turn-off to the high school, Poole looped the car back around. He wanted to get to his desk and check those files. As he strode into the station, Frawley nodded at him without questioning his return.

He'd just opened the top file—Greyson Creighton's—when his phone rang again. More evidence from the search team before they packed up for the night?

'We have some results, sir.' It was the lab. 'We've found a likely match through a comparative mitochondrial-DNA-sequence analysis.'

'Mitochondrial . . . so it matches a sample from the mother.'

Whose mum would Poole be contacting with news about her dead child?

24

SIENA

OVER DINNER, MUM TOLD TAJ AND DAD ABOUT THE VISIT TO THE POLICE station. Of course, Taj already knew that Jackson had ambushed Siena in the toilets. Anything out of the ordinary raced through the school and across the socials like wildfire. When their parents were out of the room, she whispered to him, 'Please come to school tomorrow. I need you there.'

He nodded. 'Sure. I'll be good for tomorrow.'

What was wrong with him, anyway? Taj didn't seem sick. Her lucky brother didn't even have to put up with period pains.

'Was Hayley involved?' Dad asked, carrying in an apple pie, a special treat after her horrible day.

'Umm, not really.' Of course she was but Dad wouldn't want to know.

'Owen's pretty upset about your latest video . . .'

While Dad and Owen were old mates, the families had never been close. The Shuttlewoods used to invite them over for barbecues when Siena and Hayley were in the same Year 5 class. But Dad always drank too much, and Mum got cross; she didn't like Owen. Neither did Siena. His wild moods scared her.

And even though she hadn't understood his sexist jokes back then, they made her uncomfortable. Dad said he wasn't like that on the boat. If Owen could control his behaviour around the customers, why couldn't he control it all the time?

His wife, Aurora, was calmness and crystals in harem pants and jangly bangles. She gave Owen black velvet bags filled with green quartz and amethyst to 'soothe the negativity in his energy field'. She believed in body positivity and her tiny bikini barely contained her big boobs. They'd had what Aurora called a 'radiant blessing' four years ago—a cute baby girl. These days, Hayley seemed permanently embarrassed by her mother.

'You can tell Owen that I helped Hayley out that night,' Siena said. 'Twice. She was so smashed that she wouldn't remember.'

Owen had probably given her a case of Vodka Cruisers along with the key to the national park.

'I'll tell him,' Dad said. 'Have you taken down the video yet?'

'Yes.' Siena sighed. Mum had made her delete it before they left the police station. But if her secret plan went ahead, she would be posting a new one before morning.

⌒

After carefully arranging the pillows underneath her doona, Siena stepped back to check the final effect. Good. Her parents would assume it was her in the bed. The house was completely silent as she crept towards the back door. In the laundry, she tipped out some dog biscuits to stop Pirate from following her.

Kyle and Brooke were parked just around the corner, he in the passenger seat this time.

'I'm psyched that we're doing this.' Brooke grinned. 'I've got white and black paint—we'll see which stands out the best.'

'She's even dressed for the gig.' Kyle laughed at his sister. She was wearing overalls like a house painter.

As Brooke drove, they only passed two other cars. It was one am on a school night in winter. The pub would've shut at eleven, and the footpaths were completely empty. Along the seafront, streetlamps illuminated circular patches of green grass every ten metres or so. The half moon cast a sliver of light on the sea.

'Do they have security cameras down here?' Siena asked as they parked near Main Beach.

'I finished work early and came down to check,' Brooke said. 'My last customer didn't show up for her Brazilian.'

Genital waxing. Ugh. Did Brooke have to talk about that in front of them? Siena steered the conversation back to the cameras. 'And did you see any?'

'A few around the marina but none in the park. Unless they're really well hidden.'

Craning her neck, she studied the lamp poles and the toilet block. No visible cameras. The shops across the road would have their own CCTV, of course. Were any of them pointed this way?

'We should put on our caps now,' Kyle said, pulling one from his backpack.

He'd originally wanted to wear a balaclava, but Siena had suggested caps instead. 'We don't want to look like armed robbers,' she'd said. This was supposed to be a peaceful act. Siena had no intention of getting arrested. She didn't want to spend another afternoon facing Chief Inspector Poole.

Siena still couldn't quite believe she'd come up with this idea and was following through on it. Normally she'd do everything possible to avoid breaking the rules. But being trapped against the wall of the cave with Axel's hands around her neck had changed her. Finding the skull had shocked her. And Jackson holding her over the urinal had made her furious. Between those awful moments sparkled the kisses from Kyle. She felt like a different person, a century older and wiser than last month.

With their caps pulled low, paint cans and brushes in hand, they approached their target. It loomed above them.

'Wow, look!' Kyle pointed towards the beach.

Siena turned to see a swathe of tiny lights glowing in the waves. Phosphorescence, lapping against the shore.

'Magical.' She wished she could film it, but she'd changed her mind about videoing tonight's actions and had left her phone at home. If Mum checked, the location app would show that she'd been in her room all night.

'Like fairy lights dancing in the tide,' Brooke said. For a few minutes, the three of them stood transfixed, mesmerised by the shimmering sea.

Kyle finally called them out of their trance. 'Let's do this, yeah?'

Back on the damp grass, he hoisted her into a sitting position on his shoulders. While Brooke started on the base, Siena got to work at the top. It was tricky trying to keep her brushstrokes steady as she balanced on Kyle's shoulders. Spray paint would've been easier but the hardware store required ID for each purchase.

Five minutes later, Siena had finished and asked Kyle to lower her down. She'd been so focused on painting that she'd forgotten to worry if she was too heavy for him.

'Are you okay?' she asked. 'Have I broken your back?'

'All good.'

As her feet touched the ground, Kyle pulled her close to his chest. Kissed her softly on the lips.

'We're going to make them listen,' he said. 'For Gran. For the past. For our future.'

They were done and they hadn't been caught! During the Black Lives Matter rallies in England, Siena had seen protesters on TV pulling down statues of slave traders. Hopefully, this would be just as effective.

'Oh shit, headlights.' Brooke sounded the alert. 'Let's move!'

Siena and Kyle pulled apart. Lights were weaving along the road up on the hill near St Paul's. Had someone spotted them and called the police? They ran to the car and shoved the painting equipment onto the back seat. Brooke started the engine. To avoid the main road, she detoured two blocks down. The only sound inside the car was their panting breath. And then Kyle let out a 'Woohoo! We're an awesome team!'

Tomorrow morning, the town would wake to see their handiwork. A defiant reminder of what Geoffrey Kinton, their honoured founder, had done.

25

MERI

AN ELECTRONIC SOUND CUT THROUGH MERI'S SLEEP. NOT HER ALARM but Rollo's phone ringing. It didn't wake him, so she leaned over to his bedside table and glanced at the name on screen—Chester. The manager of the marina spoke before she could identify herself.

'Rollo, you gotta get down here, mate. Bloody hell, did your daughter do this?'

'What are you talking about, Chester? What time is it?'

'Shit, Meri. Sorry. It's just before six. Can you wake Rollo? Ask him to bring some turps and rags.'

They left the twins asleep and drove down to the marina. Meri wanted to find out what had happened before she spoke to Siena. The streetlights flickered off as they parked. Chester stood waiting for them, a navy Polartec zipped up to his chin, a beanie covering his grey shaggy hair.

'How did you even see it in the dark?' Meri asked, wishing she'd had the foresight to borrow Taj's beanie—her ears were freezing.

'Hard to miss. The white paint was shining.'

The sun filtered through the low clouds and a golden glow radiated across the park. The statue of Geoffrey Kinton loomed up from its pedestal as usual: one arm held high, his fist raised in victory; in his other hand a charter, in memory of the original Chartist movement, demanding voting rights for working-class men. The statue had been erected a hundred years after Kinton Bay was proclaimed a town. An inscription on the brass plaque read: *Vivit post funera virtus*. Virtue survives death.

It didn't this morning. The grand statue now boasted two words, repeated over and over in white paint along his back and legs, front and sides. Even on his upheld arm.

RAPIST. MURDERER. RAPIST. MURDERER. RAPIST. MURDERER.

'Is your daughter behind this?' Chester asked again. 'I've seen that video where she called Geoffrey Kinton a rapist.'

Everyone in town had seen *that* video.

'No, it can't have been Siena.' Meri shook her head, ignoring the quaver in her voice. 'She was asleep when I checked on her last night.'

Surely Siena wouldn't do something so reckless, especially after spending yesterday afternoon at the police station? But if not Siena, then who? Her friend Kyle? Either way, she'd be held responsible for inciting the defacement.

'We need to get it off.' Rollo rummaged in the bucket of supplies he'd grabbed from the garage. 'I reckon turps is a good start. I can try another paint stripper if that doesn't work.'

'What if it wrecks the bronze?' Chester asked.

Staring at the painted words, Meri remembered Bim Cooper coming into the office five years ago, a week before National Sorry Day. She'd overheard her pleading with Neville to write the 'true story' about the settlement of the town. Neville had fobbed her off, offered to print an article on a local Aboriginal artist instead.

'I could call Owen.' Rollo shook the turps bottle. 'He had that house-painting job for a few years up at Coffs Harbour. He'd know what to use.'

'God, no, don't ring him,' Meri said. Along with his paint-stripping skills, Owen would bring his resentment of Siena. 'Let me take a few photos while we figure out what to do.'

Snapping away on her iPhone, Meri considered their options. Clean it off and keep their daughter and her friends out of trouble? Or let the town see it, open up a debate about Kinton Bay's history and maybe create a stepping stone towards a different, more open future?

Other towns had done it. Taken down statues of violent colonial men who had waged war on Aboriginal people. Renamed their streets and landmarks. Commissioned public artworks recognising traditional stories.

'I don't understand why your daughter is so fired up about this,' Chester said. 'It's not like she's got Aboriginal blood.'

And in that moment, Meri knew what she had to do. Over the last four days, since her daughter had found the skull, the focus had been on Siena and her videos. Rollo's business buddies blamed Siena for showing Kinton Bay in a negative light; Jackson and his friends blamed her for their own illegal acts in the national park; even the chief inspector seemed to be implicating Siena with that missing guy. A familiar bitterness lodged in Meri's throat. Blame the girl with the message, avoid the real issue. She was guilty of it too—shouting at Siena for being at the party in the cave, and out in the forest with Kyle.

It was time to focus on the real issue. She turned to Chester. 'The history of this town affects us all. We're not going to clean it off. I'm calling the police to report that this statue has been vandalised.'

He frowned in confusion, looking to Rollo.

'Don't do that, Meri,' Rollo sputtered. 'We'll sort it out.'

But before either of them could stop her, she pressed the number on her mobile for Kinton Bay Police Station.

⌒

By lunchtime, Meri had finished her article. Neville wasn't happy, but they had to cover the story—by now, almost everyone had seen the defaced statue. The mayor had organised a cleaning crew 'to restore Geoffrey Kinton to his proper glory', but not quickly enough to stop the regional news station filming it for the evening bulletin.

When Meri had insisted on writing the story, Neville had ummed and ahhed before coming out with one of his lame puns: 'The good thing about statues is that you always know where they stand.' No doubt he'd change her headline before he published it online, but she still expected comments on the issue to come in thick and fast.

TOWN FOUNDER A MURDERER?

We've seen it happen in Sydney and cities overseas but no-one expected the sight that greeted locals at Kinton Bay this morning. The statue of town founder Geoffrey Kinton had been graffitied with the words 'rapist' and 'murderer'. It's a contested view of history that we must face: was our revered Geoffrey Kinton a sexual predator who killed men, women and children?

Local Aboriginal Elder Aunty Bim Cooper explains the story passed down from her grandmother. 'Our people saved Geoffrey Kinton from a shipwreck. In return, he raped one of our girls and murdered three families. But he's seen as a hero for his ideas of equality. Equal? Sure . . . as long as you're not black and you're not female.'

Two descendants of Geoffrey Kinton offer opposing views on the issue. Sixty-three-year-old potter Simon Kinton repeated the truism that 'History ain't black and white'. He said: 'It was different times and they were racist bastards back then. But we should find out the truth. I want to know if Geoffrey was a killer.'

Nineteen-year-old Alexandra Kinton, who works at the Sweet Cakes Bakehouse, has a different perspective on our founder. 'He was a good man who built this place from nothing,' she said. 'Everything you see here, Geoffrey Kinton started it. We should thank him for choosing such a beautiful spot to create our town.'

Kinton Bay Mayor Emmeline Redpath decried the vandalism. 'Young people today think they can take the law into their own hands. They don't understand we have processes in place to honour our Indigenous heritage. We have a Council Reconciliation Strategy and we work with local Elders. It's important for our residents to continue to live in peace and harmony like we always have.'

If Geoffrey Kinton murdered three Aboriginal families to establish this town, then we've never lived in peace and harmony.

Let us know your thoughts. Comment below or email us.

Would this latest stunt put Siena in more danger? Rollo said his business mates had started ringing and texting again, all with the same message: *Your daughter is destroying our town.*

⌒

Chief Inspector Poole was holding a media conference at three o'clock. Back to the station for the second time today. This morning, Meri and Siena had been interviewed by Constable Terry and Senior Sergeant Frawley. When the sergeant asked what she knew about the statue, Siena remained silent while Meri said 'No comment' for her. Was Constable Terry secretly pleased? He must know the history from his grandmother.

The police station had been built in the 1970s in an industrial block design, like something from the Soviet era. Chief Inspector Poole came down the front steps and positioned himself on the small patch of lawn. In his full dress uniform, he looked as grim as the institutional building behind him. The five reporters had their microphones and cameras ready.

'We have made a positive identification of the human remains found in Wreck Point National Park.'

Meri held her breath. If it were Blake, how would Glenda cope?

'Is it a local person, Chief Inspector?' the radio journalist asked, desperate to know.

'The technicians were able to match DNA from the remains with DNA from the deceased's mother.'

Oh god, it is Blake. I should've spoken to the police years ago. After Mum died, I could've done it then.

'We've notified the family. Due to the time zone difference, we had to wait until local authorities were available to contact the parents.'

Time difference. It couldn't be Blake. Meri let out the breath she'd been holding. Presumably it wasn't Fabian either. She'd phone both Glenda and Yuki with the 'good news' as soon as the media conference finished. Bad news, though, for the family of the dead man.

'The human remains have been identified as those of Stefan Schwarzenbeck, a Swiss backpacker who went missing from the area in 1999. Police are investigating the circumstances in which Stefan died. We encourage anyone who has any information related to his last movements to come forward and help us with our enquiries.'

Stefan had gone missing the year after Blake. Meri remembered the international media descending on Kinton Bay and Stefan's photo all over the news. But that photo hadn't done justice to his good looks and charm. Half the girls in Year 10 had taken up surfing for PE when they discovered Stefan was the new instructor. Later, they were sobbing over his disappearance.

The death of a backpacker. The tourism board and the development committee would be rushing into damage control.

'We'll also be asking the public if anyone recognises this bag. It's a Rip Curl brand.' Poole held up a printed image of the type of backpack everyone carried when she was at school.

'Excuse me, Chief Inspector,' she called out. 'Were any other personal items found? Is the death considered suspicious?'

'Stefan was last seen at the Time'n'Tide Hotel on the twentieth of November, with an anonymous sighting of him swimming off Grotto Rocks at midnight. Our investigation will look into all possibilities. Until we have evidence to prove otherwise, we will be treating Stefan's death as suspicious.'

A fit young man turning up dead in the forest, only twenty minutes from town. His poor parents had one answer now, but so many more questions.

26

Stefan Schwarzenbeck.

That was a fast ID. At least I know what I'm dealing with now but I still won't sleep tonight. The first time I saw Stefan, he was in the pub chatting to a bucks party from Dubbo.

'How can you be a surfer?' one of them said. 'Isn't Switzerland landlocked? Do you surf on the mountains or the lakes?'

Stefan answered in another language, his words sounded like a curse.

'What'd ya say, mate?' The buck took a step closer to him.

'The name of the mountain range where I live.' Stefan smiled, all teeth. He got the blokes back onside by buying a round; they joked that he must have a secret Swiss bank account.

A local girl, from Year 12 in KB High, pushed her way into the group and sidled up to Stefan. 'Your accent is sooooo sexy,' she cooed. 'How do you say "I love you" in German?'

Stefan knelt down, held out his arms like an opera singer and sang: 'Ich liebe dich.' The girl squealed and leaned in to kiss him.

'He loves to lick dick,' a Dubbo guy yelled. 'That's what he said. He's a poofter. Come over here, babe, and meet the real men.'

Putting his arm around the girl, Stefan ignored the blokes. 'Do you want to hear it in French and Italian too? I can speak four languages.'

Her answer was lost amid the shouting.

'Fucking faggot.'

⌐

The TV news shows the press conference outside the KB police station.

'We found a backpack but nothing else with the body. No clothing, shoes or jewellery. While clothing disintegrates, we would expect to find a watch or shoes. The storm has obviously swept through the area so we'll be widening the search.'

That night in the cave feels so long ago. But one moment sticks with me: when Stefan realised that his good looks and his four languages and his cheesy smile wouldn't get him out of this situation.

After he was reported missing, I called the hotline. Pretended to be another backpacker.

'Yep, I saw him swimming at Grotto Rocks at midnight.'

Nowhere near the Killing Cave.

The public appeals for information went on for months, then years. The first anniversary, the second, the fifth. On the tenth anniversary, his parents did a long TV interview with Sixty Minutes. On the twentieth, his parents stood near Grotto Rocks, and made another plea for answers.

Such ongoing, determined enquiries.

Unlike the others.

27

ROLLO

ROLLO KNEW THAT OWEN WOULD WANT TO HEAR AS SOON AS POSSIBLE. He typed out a short text message: *It's not Blake.*

The reply came within a minute: *Thank fuck.*

In the Killing Cave, they'd sat around the campfire, smoking and listening to Derek and Lance's grand plans.

'We're gonna grow dope in the forest. If the police find it, they can't connect it to us.'

'Rollo can be our tester!'

At the time, he would've done anything to keep up his dope supply—nicking cash from backpacker bags on the beach, sneaking money from Dad's wallet.

While Blake smoked with Rollo and chilled out, Derek got tanked on Bundaberg Rum. The Rip Curl backpack pictured in the newspaper—they'd used something like that to carry the beer and Bundy out to the cave. The rum riled Derek up, turned him into a nastier, louder version of himself. The version which, later, kept landing him in jail. Presumably Derek had heard about the skull near the cave.

The skull. Stefan Schwarzenbeck.

An arrogant shit in the surf. Kept dropping in when Rollo had the wave. Did it to everyone. They'd have a few words on the beach afterwards; a push and a shove helped Stefan get the message. But not for long. He was a wave hog, jockeying for the best position, snaking in below. Stefan always laughed it off, grinning with those large white teeth of his.

He pissed off everyone, especially Derek.

By then Blake had been gone a year, and Derek was meaner than ever. Thought he could get away with anything. So, although Stefan was older and better built, Derek and Lance started hassling him in the pub. He'd been in town about three months and had ingratiated himself by offering help for cash-in-hand jobs like gardening, cleaning boats and organising activities for kids. And he'd ingratiated himself with the girls.

'You think you're shit-hot around here, but you're not,' Derek told him in the pub. 'The chicks prefer us homegrown boys.'

They didn't though. And Derek and Lance weren't happy about it.

Since Blake had buggered off, Rollo tried to keep his distance from those two. So he copped the abuse as well: 'You're just like that backpacker wanker. Think you're shit-hot now you're working weekends at the pub. Send a few freebies over the bar and we'll leave you alone.'

The manager would sack him if he gave out free beers. Rollo poured them and paid from his own pocket.

It was a few days before anyone realised Stefan was missing. When he didn't turn up to his Wednesday job—helping out with the high school surfing classes—the sports teacher called the hostel, then the police. Rollo had been working on the night Stefan disappeared. In his interview with the police, he explained that he'd served the backpacker at the bar earlier but had finished work at eight and gone home. His statement was mostly true.

The bag found in the forest . . . was it his? After all these years, could it possibly have any identifying evidence inside? Surely he hadn't written his name on the tag.

⌒

It was bloody bad timing to have a development committee meeting. Rollo's phone had been ringing hot about the statue all day. *Does your daughter want to shut down business in town completely?* He checked Siena's YouTube channel and saw that she'd uploaded two new videos: an interview with Bim Cooper about the massacre, and a slideshow of Meri's photos of the graffitied statue. Meri wasn't helping the situation—she seemed on a mission to get maximum publicity.

Rollo had wanted a sausage roll for lunch, but he couldn't face walking down Dolphin Street to the bakery; he'd be accosted by everyone giving their opinions on the statue and the skull. But now he'd have to front the development committee. The monthly meeting was scheduled to discuss Proclamation Day celebrations—Rollo guessed they wouldn't be following the agenda.

He was about to leave for the meeting but Siena still hadn't arrived home. Taj said she'd gone to Jasminda's house after school. Meri was still at the office, setting up an interview with Stefan's parents in Switzerland.

'I put the meat pie on a tray for the oven,' Rollo told Taj. 'It'll take forty minutes.'

'Okay,' Taj grunted, as he walked off to his bedroom.

Rollo followed him down the hallway. 'How's your stomach? Will you be able to eat dinner?'

'Yep, I'm better now.'

Before the holidays, Meri had been talking about taking Taj to the doctor again and asking for an abdominal ultrasound. But then he'd seemed fine for the last few weeks, until yesterday. Was the cycle of sick days about to start again?

'Is everything okay at school?' Rollo asked. 'Any . . . issues with . . .'

'Jackson? No, he wasn't there. And Hayley kept away from us.'

Rollo's gut was cramping at the thought of tonight's meeting— an unusual feeling for him. Were Taj's stomach pains like that? Related to anxiety?

'Can you feed the dog, mate?'

Taj mumbled in agreement and moped towards the kitchen while Rollo pocketed his keys and headed for the front door. He heard the dog biscuits being shaken into the bowl. At the sound, Pirate would normally bolt down the hallway, skid on the tiles and come to a stop with his nose right in the food bowl.

'Have you seen Pirate?' Taj shouted from the kitchen.

Rollo went back and checked the bedrooms, but there was no sign of the black labrador. Shit, he didn't have time for this.

'He must've got out. Can you ask the neighbours? I have to go.'

His phone beeped in his pocket. Maybe someone had located the dog already? Whenever Pirate escaped, he always found his way to the house across the road, played with the border collie and ate from its bowl.

The text was from Meri: *TURN ON TV. Channel 10.*

Rollo's guts churned again. He went back into the lounge room, stabbed at the remote control. There on the screen was his daughter, standing in front of the statue.

'Our town was built on the massacre of Aboriginal people,' she was saying, her expression furious, defiant. 'Innocent families who were living in this area. We need to start telling the truth about our history.'

Rollo sank down onto the couch and dropped his head into his hands. He just hoped the other committee members were on their way to the meeting and had missed Siena's latest stunt.

⌒

From the corridor, Rollo could see Chester and Caroline already seated inside the conference room. Near the urn, making cups of tea, hovered Aunty Bim and Kath, the wife of Meri's editor. The other blokes—Lance, Alastair and Ned—stood in a huddle by the door. Despite being over seventy, Alastair still wore fluoro pink boardies with green thongs. He owned four buildings in the main drag, leased to the supermarket, the chemist and a few other stores. Not a bad bloke.

Unlike Ned, who was a know-it-all. And a walking advertisement for his surf shop, always wearing the trendiest brands. He'd run the shop for about fifteen years, expanding into rental boards and kayaks, along with scuba diving trips. In summer, he signed up customers for Rollo's cruises.

As usual, Lance thought he was at a different meeting from the rest of them. With his shaved head, designer stubble, white business shirt and blue jacket, he could've been mistaken for a Sydney real estate agent or the dude from *The Bachelor*.

'Rollo.' Lance stepped casually into the doorway, blocking his entry. 'I saw Siena on the telly again tonight.'

'Ah, yep.' Damn. 'I didn't know until . . .'

'You gotta stop her,' Lance hissed. 'It's affecting all of us.'

'And with that dead backpacker,' Ned muttered, 'no-one will want to holiday here.'

Caroline's voice cut across the conversations. 'Come and sit down, guys.'

At her instruction, Lance shepherded Rollo into the room as if he hadn't just been standing in his way. Caroline waited for them to take their chairs before speaking again.

'Let's begin with a minute's silence for Stefan Schwarzenbeck. The young man came to Australia to experience the world, but he never left our town. We hope his family will now be able to find some closure. May he rest in peace.'

Most of them had been living in Kinton Bay when Stefan went missing. Some of them would've known him. Lance and Derek used to harass him in the pub. That was long before Lance inherited his father's construction business, hooked up with some investment partners, and reinvented himself.

Lance was the first to break the silence. 'Look, I'm sorry the guy died, but we need to discuss how to handle the fallout. This will turn away tourists and investors for sure.' Shaking his head, he stared at each person around the table, then fixed his eyes on Rollo. 'And now your kid goes on television talking about a massacre. It's bad for business.'

'You do know, Lance, that there's more to development than money, don't you?' Aunty Bim never shied away from debating an issue, especially with Lance. It meant these meetings could get fiery. 'Think of how a child develops. Learns to walk, talk.

Grows up. Gets a bit smarter every day. That's development too. It's time for Kinton Bay to grow up. Get smarter and acknowledge its violent beginnings.'

Lance always underestimated Bim Cooper and regularly lost arguments with her. The old lady was quick-witted and direct with an air of wisdom. She had a way of making Rollo feel like a child. No doubt Lance felt it too, and hated it.

'We've got the Aboriginal mural near the shops,' Lance said. 'And totem poles at the school.'

'A mural,' Aunty Bim huffed. 'Is that enough to acknowledge the oldest living culture on Earth? Other places have started to recognise the wrongs that were done. But not here. Is that because half the town is related to Geoffrey Kinton?'

'I suspect so,' Caroline agreed. 'Apologies, Aunty Bim, if this sounds crass, but creating a memorial and showcasing our amazing local culture could attract the tourist dollar, as well as healing our town.'

'It can't be lip service.' Aunty Bim pushed her glasses up onto her white hair. 'We've been carrying this sorrow for too long.'

'Yes, of course.' Caroline nodded at her. 'What's our first step?'

'Getting the media to interview me. Not a pretty little white girl.' Aunty Bim glared at Rollo, adjusted her yellow scarf, then laughed. 'Yeah, I know she's better looking than me but it's time to listen to our voice, to the Elders.'

'Of course,' Rollo agreed. *Yes, let the Elders speak. I don't want Siena talking either.*

'You don't have any evidence of this massacre, though,' Lance jumped in. 'How do we know it happened?'

'We know. It's in our stories, it's in our hearts. If they got some archaeologists out there, they'd find something. I've been telling them for forty years but nobody's listening.'

'What about a memorial?' Caroline asked. 'Like the one at Myall Creek. Each year, descendants of both sides come together to remember.'

'Yeah, that would be a start,' said Aunty Bim. 'It'd have to go through council. And they'll probably want some kind of historical evidence, but we can get the ball rolling. What do you all reckon?'

No-one answered. Rollo glanced at the blokes. Lance shrugged his shoulders, while the others stared out the dark window.

'What about the backpacker, though?' Ned asked. 'That's a more immediate issue.'

'It's a terrible tragedy,' Caroline said. 'But I don't think it will really affect our youth tourism. Since the hostel shut down, we've hardly have any backpackers anyway.'

'Do the police have any idea what happened to him?' Rollo asked.

'I guess he didn't drown at Grotto Rocks after all,' Kath said.

Caroline picked up a glass and took a sip of water. He willed her to answer. What did she know? Her husband must have talked about the case with her.

'The police are investigating,' she murmured at last.

That was no answer, but Caroline returned his gaze—an intense look as if she could see inside his soul. A few times, Rollo had imagined her gaze upon him in bed. So physically different to his wife, Caroline was a woman to be noticed with her short blonde hair, bright clothes and oversized jewellery. Tonight, a huge black stone necklace dangled over her orange top.

'Back to our history, please,' Aunty Bim said. 'We can talk about the poor backpacker later. I'd like us to submit a motion for a memorial to the council.'

'Great idea. And maybe we can announce it on Proclamation Day. Who else agrees?' Caroline raised her hand and looked around the table.

Aunty Bim and Kath put up their hands. Three out of eight. Lance shook his head ever so slightly. After a moment, Alastair raised his arm. Half and half.

Caroline smiled encouragingly at Rollo. Bloody hell, he didn't like to be on the wrong side of Lance. His former mate usually got his own way with his charm and veiled threats and under-the-table bribes which no-one could prove. But Aunty Bim's theory of development had something to it; money couldn't be the only goal. His whale-watching and snorkelling business relied on clean seas. When Siena had been pursuing one of her environmental causes, she'd taught him a phrase—'symbiotic relationship'. The interdependence of two things, a mutually beneficial relationship. Rollo needed the whales and the spark-ling ocean to earn a crust.

And their town needed to deal with its past for their community and their business dollars.

Taj's words from this morning echoed in his mind: 'Nice work, sis.' He'd assumed that his sister had graffitied the statue and was proud of her for standing up for what she believed. And Meri had done the same by calling the police and writing an article about the monument.

Rollo took a deep breath. *Follow their lead. Stop coasting and stand up for what I believe.* He raised his hand.

Here we go. Time to lose all my mates.

He was home by nine o'clock, making Siena a hot chocolate and telling her the good news.

'We're going to recommend that council builds a memorial.'

'Really? That's amazing! And did you . . .'

'Mine was the deciding vote.' He couldn't help himself.

'You're the best, Dad.' Siena wrapped her arms around him and squeezed tight. His gut had stopped churning—he'd made the right choice. Hopefully Meri would be equally impressed when she got home.

'We might be able to announce it on Proclamation Day.' Rollo stacked the dishwasher with the dirty plates from dinner, setting aside scraps for the dog. 'Did Taj apologise to the neighbours for the breaking and entering?'

Siena's face was blank. 'What are you talking about?'

'Didn't Taj tell you that Pirate escaped?'

'I haven't seen Taj. He went into work because someone was sick. I thought Pirate must be with you or Mum.'

They ran through the house, calling the dog's name. Checked under beds, in the garage, around the bins, in the dark corners of the backyard. Knocked on neighbours' doors.

No-one had seen Pirate.

28

Student: Taj Britton
Year 9 Geography, Ms Adamou
Assignment: The cultural importance of whales to humans

From sacred to slaughtered

For coastal Aboriginal communities, the whale is a sacred spiritual totem featuring in creation stories. Ancient rock carvings of whales can be found all along the coast, including on a large flat shelf at the top of Grotto Rocks.

With colonisation came the whaling industry. In the town of Eden on the south coast, whalers employed the Yuin people because of their special relationship with the orcas, many of whom they knew and named. These orcas would herd whales into a bay and then alert the Yuin of their location. After the humpbacks were caught, the whalers would leave the bodies hanging from the boat overnight so the orcas could eat their tongues. It was called The Law of the Tongue. This is an example of mutualism—two different species working towards the same aim.

During the twentieth century, explosive harpoons made it even easier to kill. In 1963, with the whale population decimated, the International Whaling Commission banned the hunting of humpbacks in the Southern Hemisphere.

Three countries still allow whaling: Iceland, Norway and Japan. Some have old cultural practices. The Grindadrap is a cultural event which has been held on an island in the North Atlantic Ocean since the ninth century. Hundreds of pilot whales are corralled into a bay. The whales are dragged up the beach with a hook through their blowhole, then slaughtered by a lance that severs their main artery.

The sand and sea turn red with their blood.

29

MERI

MERI LEFT THE BACK DOOR AJAR OVERNIGHT, HOPING PIRATE WOULD find his way home, but morning came with no sign of the dog.

At seven-thirty, Rollo and Siena took the HiLux and searched the streets again, while Taj checked the nearby bushland and Meri jogged down the hill towards Main Beach. Pirate loved swimming in the sea. Spotting a dark shape ahead on the footpath, she sped up, her heart racing. What if he'd been hit by a car? As she drew closer, the shape became recognisable as a lost jumper.

She hadn't yet had a chance to chat with Siena about her latest media appearance. Her daughter had done it again—this time a TV interview without telling her. Siena didn't understand the sensitivities of Aboriginal issues in the media, and the negative bias of some reporters. In addition, she needed to be an ally, not a 'white saviour', and create space for Kyle and Aunty Bim to speak for themselves. How could a fifteen-year-old navigate all this without guidance? It was complex and, quite frankly, Meri was terrified about a shit-storm descending on her daughter. She'd seen stories blow up and abuse hurled from all quarters; by comparison, the comments on Siena's YouTube channel would look like friendly discussion.

Underneath her concern, Meri was still peeved. *Why the hell didn't Siena ring me first about the skull?* At least she'd landed the interview with the Swiss family; they were arriving tomorrow, no doubt with more media in tow.

After two blocks, Meri was puffing hard. Where had Pirate gone? Taj and Rollo had spoken to all the neighbours, Meri had posted messages on Facebook, and Siena on Instagram—nobody had seen him. At nine am, she'd ring the vet and the WIRES woman who helped injured wildlife. But Pirate had a microchip; if he'd been found, someone would've called.

As she came into the park, Meri slowed to a walk. The statue glowed, spotless after its big clean.

'What do you think about all this hoo-ha?'

Olive Kinton materialised from behind the statue in a turquoise tracksuit. As an active woman in her seventies, head of the historical society and church organist, Olive influenced the older people in the community.

'I think it's time to understand the truth about our history,' Meri answered. 'For our future.'

'Hmm.' Olive pointed to the paper that Kinton held in his hand. 'He stood for equal rights for men.'

'That doesn't stop him being a rapist and a racist.'

'I guess not.' Olive sighed.

'Do you have any documents from those early days?'

'Nothing about murder. I searched through everything years ago, when Bim first asked me. I know Geoffrey wrote letters home to his parents, but we've never found them.' Olive shook her head. 'But lately I've started a new project, mapping the extended Kinton family tree.'

Just what the town needed, more Kinton descendants.

'Well, please contact me if you find anything. I'm doing a series of articles.' As they talked, Meri had been scanning the park for any sign of Pirate. 'By the way, we've lost our dog. A black labrador. Have you seen him?'

'Not on my morning walk, love.' Olive frowned. 'But a barking dog kept me awake for hours last night. I had to do the crossword as a distraction.'

⌒

The four of them gathered around the kitchen table. Siena's eyes were red and puffy from crying, and Taj chewed his bottom lip. They'd driven and walked and jogged and door-knocked.

'I talked to Olive at the park.' Meri hadn't paid much attention to the old woman's comment earlier, but now it seemed like the only lead. 'She heard a dog barking last night. Let's drive past her place.'

'She lives near Hayley,' Siena said.

Taj nodded. 'And Jackson.'

'Do you think they . . .' Siena trailed off, her eyes filling with tears again.

Anger heated Meri's face. If Owen or Hayley had done something to their dog, she'd make sure Rollo sacked his old mate immediately. And now Siena should understand why she'd wanted her to take down the videos. The comments had been vicious enough, but sometimes people stepped out from behind their keyboards and followed up on their threats. Had poor Pirate paid the price for Siena's online exposé?

'We can't just knock on their door and ask if they've stolen our dog,' Taj said. 'Owen will go ballistic.'

Rollo cleared his throat. Was he trying to figure out whether Owen would stoop that low? Meri waited but still he didn't speak.

'I'll talk to Aurora,' she said, picking up her keys. 'Right then, let's move.'

As they headed to the car, Rollo's mobile rang. From his side of the conversation, Meri guessed it was a marine issue, nothing to do with Pirate. She jiggled the keys in her fingers—she had to check those houses, drop the twins at school, and get to work.

Finally, he hung up. 'Sorry, I have to meet the coastguard. There's a whale floating near Curlew Island. Injured or dead, he's not sure.'

Injured whales were difficult to treat; dead ones created logistical challenges. Either way, not what they needed right now.

Meri pulled up outside the Shuttlewoods' house and told the twins to stay in the car. She walked down the front path, preparing what to say, but Owen opened the door before she could knock.

'Hi. Rollo just rang. I'm going with him and the coastguard. He said your dog's missing.'

So much for the advantage of surprise. Meri had imagined Pirate rushing along the corridor to greet her.

'Yes, we can't find Pirate. Have you . . .'

'I don't know why you're asking me.' Owen glowered, tugging at his beard.

'Just looking everywhere. Can you and Aurora keep an eye out, please?'

There was a flash of movement behind him. Not the dog but Hayley running from the bathroom to her bedroom, wrapped in a towel. Wet hair dripping around her shoulders, fresh face scrubbed clean. She looked so young, nothing like the party animal in the video.

'Well, gotta go.' Owen nodded goodbye.

With his temper and the huge chip on his shoulder, Owen could definitely steal a dog. But if he or Hayley had anything to do with Pirate's disappearance, they'd have to hide it from sweet Aurora—she'd never approve.

In spite of Meri's instructions, neither of the twins had stayed in the car. She spotted them further up the street, peering over fences, calling, 'Pirate, come here, boy. Pirate, where are you?'

A few dogs barked in reply, but none sounded like Pirate.

They were standing near Jackson's place, a large two-storey brick house with brown columns flanking the front door. She sent the twins back to the car and pressed the fancy gold doorbell.

Jackson's parents ran the real estate agency, which was a major advertiser in the *Chronicle*. They were regularly invited to Neville and Kath's house for dinner. She guessed that the McCormacks would be furious with Siena, not only for getting their son into trouble but also for the effect her campaign may have on their holiday bookings. While Meri was desperate to find Pirate, she hoped that Shane McCormack wouldn't answer the door.

He did. With a surprise guest behind him—Neville. The flash of shock across his face rapidly changed to annoyance.

'We're having a breakfast business meeting,' Neville said. 'What are you doing here?'

Were they discussing advertising deals, along with some free good news stories on the McCormack agency? Full page spreads in the printed edition, extra ads and links online? A few years ago, Meri and the other journalists had sent an email to the editorial director of the media group which owned the *Chronicle*. They'd voiced their concerns about a number of Neville's decisions: articles in the summer holidays encouraging young people to 'spend up big' at the pub; biased coverage of the council elections in favour of Emmeline Redpath; and the promotion of new building developments in town, most of which were being sold by the McCormacks. The editorial director had rapped Neville over the knuckles and told him to separate out advertorial content but said nothing about encouraging drinking and gambling in the pub, nor the paper's influence in the council election. At the end of that year, the group leadership team congratulated Neville on his excellent advertising revenue and held him up as a role model for other small papers.

Meri wondered if it was time to raise the issue again, now that the paper had been bought by Regional Express Media. In the meantime, Neville was staring at her, waiting for an answer to his question.

'We lost . . .' she stumbled, her thoughts on his business meeting. 'I'm looking for my dog.'

Shane McCormack took a step forwards, towering over her. The beefy bloke still played prop for the KB rugby league team. 'I haven't seen any lost dog. Have you, Nev?'

'Nope.'

A look passed between the two men.

'But I keep seeing a teenage girl on the telly. A local girl. She looks pretty lost.' Shane ran a hand through his thick hair. 'I reckon she might need a bit of direction. Some supervision. Can you help her with that, Meri?'

How dare he threaten her? Just like his son had threatened Siena. She glanced at Neville for support, but she should've known better. Her editor gave a short nod of agreement.

'No, I think that—' Meri began but Neville cut her off.

'See you at the office.'

They stepped back inside the house and shut the door.

⌐

Meri was staring at the blinking cursor on her computer screen, her thoughts stuck on Shane McCormack, when her editor's voice gave her a jolt. She turned to face him. Neville was dressed in different clothes from earlier this morning—a red polo with a blue wave pattern, the McCormack real estate agency shirt.

'Kath told me what happened at the meeting last night,' he said. 'We won't report on it yet, not until the motion goes to council. Now, what about Proclamation Day? Have you spoken to Caroline?'

'Umm . . . not yet. I haven't had a chance.' So, he wasn't going to mention Shane. That shirt felt like a slap in the face. Meri closed her eyes against it, and tried to organise her thoughts.

'Ask her about the dead backpacker. She must have the inside goss.'

Was it ethical to interview the chief inspector's wife about a police investigation? Neville hadn't been interested before, but now that the skull had been identified, he wanted the 'inside goss'. Surprising.

After texting Caroline for a meeting, Meri decided to call the station about their missing dog and share her fear that it was retribution for Siena's videos.

'Has someone made a specific threat?' Constable Terry asked.

'Not directly. But we were at the station on Tuesday because of Jackson McCormack.'

'We'll keep a lookout, Mrs Britton, but it's not really a police matter.' The constable put his hand over the phone and she could hear him speaking with someone. Then he was back. 'The boss would like to talk with you. I'll put you through.'

Oh god, had they found CCTV footage of Siena defacing the statue? Meri knew it was cowardly, but she hadn't asked her daughter directly about it. Better that she didn't know.

The chief inspector's voice was croaky with exhaustion. 'Mrs Britton, I'd like to talk with you off the record. We cannot have anything compromising our investigation.'

'Absolutely, I understand.' She'd never do anything to jeopardise police procedure.

'The reason I'm speaking to you is because we need to ensure that no-one interferes with our evidence or spreads theories that could prejudice a jury in a trial.'

'Of course.' Was he worried that she might make a complaint about him interviewing Siena without an adult present?

'I'll be frank with you. I don't want your daughter filming any more videos in the national park. And I want all videos related to Wreck Point taken off her YouTube channel.'

Wow. Heavy-handed censorship of a fifteen-year-old girl. It felt like everyone in this town had it in for Siena.

'Okay, I'll speak to her.' Meri swallowed hard. 'Have you found something else?'

Please don't let it be the body of Axel Evans.

'We have located further skeletal remains.'

Skeletal, so not Axel. Thank god. 'More of Stefan's bones, then?'

'As I said, we're having an off-the-record chat. The bones have been submitted for forensic analysis. This is an active investigation, and I won't be speaking to the media until forensic results are confirmed.'

Poole ended the call and Meri wondered what the hell was happening.

Had they found more bodies in the forest?

PART THREE

FIGHTING
SEASON

The male humpbacks sing beautiful, sophisticated songs
as part of their mating rituals. They also violently attack
each other in the fight for the female. Up to ten bulls
battle for one cow. They smash each other with their
fins, splash their tails, headbutt and whack one another.
The competition is so brutal that, sometimes,
a bull kills its rival.

30

ROLLO

A BLACK BUMP FRACTURED THE SURFACE OF THE COBALT-BLUE SEA. IN the sunshine, it could have been mistaken for an overturned boat bobbing up and down. But as the coastguard motored towards it, Rollo spotted strips of flesh dangling around the edges, like a grass skirt flaring out in dance. The humpback must be dead.

The carcass moved with the swell, then jerked in a different direction.

'Don't get too close,' Rollo warned. 'I think there's a feeding frenzy below.'

Sure enough, two tiger sharks darted from underneath the whale, biting and ripping at its skin. The carcass would attract more and more predators. The tiger sharks, bull sharks and great whites would start the process—they were the only ones with teeth sharp enough to saw through the tough whale skin and thick blubber underneath.

'Can't see any fishing lines.' Owen peered over the bow. 'Do you think it was hit by a ship?'

'Probably,' the coastguard said. 'The current's going to bring it into the shallows and then we'll have putrefied whale flesh with sharks ripping at it.'

'Let's tow it further out,' Rollo suggested. 'Change its course. The sharks will demolish it in the open sea.'

Although he knew it'd take a long time for the sharks to finish this meal. They hadn't had a drift whale around here for years and years. When he had first started working on the boat, Gary told him about one that turned up further north: they'd inserted dynamite and the whale had erupted in a huge explosion of blubber, bone, oil and blood. That wasn't recommended anymore.

Whale carcasses that sank to the ocean floor created whole ecosystems, a feeding ground for sea creatures for decades. Scientists had even discovered new species of worms living off a carcass in the impenetrable darkness, kilometres underwater.

The sharks had become aware of the boat—they were knocking against the side, a warning to keep away from their dinner.

'Shit, they've really got the taste for it.' Owen shifted away from the edge.

Rollo watched the humpback's magnificent tail swaying intact below the water. So strong and graceful. As if it could somehow still propel the whale out of here, away from its attackers.

'We'd better ring the authorities before we arrange a tow,' Rollo thought aloud. 'They'll want to have their input.'

Hopefully the council, National Parks, and the Department of Fisheries would all agree. Rollo took a few pictures on his phone to send through to the various organisations. He knew this story would end up on the news. People were fascinated by fallen giants.

And thrilled by the ever-circling predators.

⌣

As they were finishing up at the marina, he asked Owen to come for a drink at the Time'n'Tide to calm him down after Siena's video, the bloody fines, and Meri turning up on his doorstep, asking for the dog.

The pub had been refurbished a few times since Rollo worked behind the bar, but it still had the same yeasty smell and sticky carpet. And the same vibe—screens showing horse racing and footy, a couple of pokie machines, deep-fried pub meals. Even though it was four o'clock, an hour when most other restaurants were closed between lunch and dinner, you could still order a meal at the Time'n'Tide.

A group of young surfers were doing just that, wolfing down steak and chips with their beers. Wearing boardies and wide grins, they'd obviously been out on the waves for the whole day. Rollo recognised Duke among them; he'd taken the boy under his wing ten years ago. In the surf, Duke had been impressive to watch, but he was a goddamn firecracker on land, getting into fights left, right and centre. His mum had moved them here from Brisbane, away from his aggro dad, trying to build a better life. But at fifteen, Duke didn't see it like that. Rollo had helped him settle down. Now he was too chilled—surfing and smoking, and not doing much else.

The young guy greeted him with a nod and a fist bump.

'How was it out there today?' Rollo asked.

'Started with some ankle slappers but then got decent.' Duke pushed his blond dreadlocks off his face. 'Pretty rad, all up.'

Rollo could almost taste the memories: no responsibilities, days that lasted forever, a permanent layer of salt on his tanned body.

'Sounds like it was pumping.' Maybe he could join Duke again in October, when this migration season had finished. 'I wouldn't surf at South Cove tomorrow, though. There's a dead whale near the heads and the sharks are flocking to it. Tell your buddies.'

The rest of the group caught his words and stopped speaking. They stared at him with respect and murmured between themselves. 'Shit, a fucken shark frenzy, hey?'

Rollo left them arguing about where to surf. He ordered two VBs, and carried them to the small bar table where Owen was perched.

'Look, mate, I can pay that fine for you,' he offered.

'Both fines? Hayley and I got one each.'

'Yep. Just give me the pieces of paper and I'll get it done.'

'Does Meri know you're paying them? Siena?' Owen slurped from his schooner, leaving froth around his moustache.

'Don't worry about them.'

Owen tapped his glass against Rollo's, a gesture of thanks. In the corner, two blokes started singing the Newcastle Knights song.

'The Knights are going to make it to the grand final this year,' predicted Owen.

'I dunno, mate.' Rollo stared at the top six ladder on the TV. Rugby league was the only game to follow around here. 'We've got to beat the Panthers and the Storm.'

Through the archway to the lounge area, Rollo spotted two men eating: Lance Nelson and Shane McCormack. The real estate agent. A big man, a few years older than them, successful; he was exactly the type of person Lance latched onto. In the last few years, they'd worked together promoting Lance's building developments to buyers. Shane would be even more pissed off than Lance about Siena's TV appearances. But that didn't excuse what his son had done to her in the boys' toilets. He'd love to confront the big man—but he just couldn't.

When the barmaid went to clear their plates, Lance sneakily patted her on the bum. The girl, Ebony, leaned into him briefly. Was she the one Lance had been seeing behind his wife's back? A few months ago, his third marriage had broken up. No kids involved, not like the first two. Rollo thought all the women in town would've heard of Lance's reputation by now.

Draining his beer, he bid farewell to Owen and ducked through the side door, avoiding Lance and Shane completely. He hurried back to the marina where he'd parked his ute, and reversed out.

It was only as he was turning into Dolphin Street that he noticed a folded piece of paper under his windscreen wiper. Pulling over, he grabbed the paper and opened it up. The words were written in big black capitals.

DEAD BACKPACKER + DEAD BLACKFELLAS +
DEAD WHALE = DEAD TOWN
STOP YOUR KID TALKING OR DEAD DOG NEXT ...

⌒

Meri had started cooking dinner. Rollo automatically stepped over the spot where Pirate curled up in the kitchen. The whole house felt off-kilter without him. Rollo had shoved the note into his glovebox—he didn't want it in the house, contaminating his family. If he told Siena, she'd blame herself for putting Pirate in danger. If he told Meri, she'd want to take it to the police. That would just inflame the situation. No, Rollo had to sort it himself.

Perhaps there was a clue in the note. Who knew about the dead whale? Owen, obviously. Chester at the marina. Rollo had just told Duke and his buddies at the pub. Meri would've mentioned it to Neville and the editorial team. Hmm, it could be all over town by now.

Meri suspected Owen of taking their dog, but his old mate wouldn't do that, would he? Jackson McCormack was definitely an option. His father maybe. Lance possibly.

'I just remembered I've got to pick up something from the council,' he told Meri, too jittery to sit still.

'Can you get some milk on the way back?'

Grey clouds obscured any hint of a sunset. Night was approaching. He parked a few houses from Lance's place and walked back. Softly whistled for Pirate. Called his name. No response.

Then he dropped by the McCormacks' mansion and accidentally set off the sensor light. No sign of Pirate anywhere.

Cruising along Kingfish Street, he took a squizz at Neville Kinton's place and caught the outline of two men in the front room. Was Neville's son home? Scott, aka Muscle Man, had been in the Wrecking Crew for six months or so. Derek had let him join because girls loved his chiselled abs and toned biceps. Whenever Scott was at a party with his shirt off, girls wanted to be there. But at the end of Year 11 after Blake had disappeared,

Scott suddenly left school and signed up to the Navy. Rollo had barely since him since.

As he pulled into his driveway, Rollo wondered who else might be upset about Siena's actions. The owners of the new wine bar? The company that had lodged the development application for the land opposite the church?

In the kitchen, Meri was draining a saucepan of pasta.

'Where's the milk?' she asked.

'Shit, I forgot. Too much on my mind.' Rollo grimaced. 'I can go after dinner.'

'Don't bother. I'll do it.'

Usually, Rollo would dash straight out again, appease his wife. But his energy—and optimism—had run dry.

'Any news on the backpacker?' he asked. 'Have they said how he died?'

Meri took her time to answer, combining the carbonara sauce with the pasta in the pan first.

'Not yet. His parents are arriving soon.'

From the expression on her face, he knew Meri was holding back.

'Do you know something else?' he snapped.

'Nope. What've you heard around town?'

'Not much.' That wasn't true, there was lots of gossip. Stefan had been injured bushwalking. Overdosed on drugs. Fought with another backpacker about money. Pissed off an angry local. Taken the wrong woman to bed and her husband had killed him for it.

'Rollo, what do you remember about the night Stefan disappeared? Were you working at the pub? Did the police interview you?'

God, what was this—twenty questions? He slumped into a chair. All he wanted to do was hug his kids and go to bed. He said the first thing that came into his head.

'I remember what Derek used to say to him: *You think you're so shit hot!* And he did. Stefan thought he was better than everyone else, that he could do whatever he wanted.'

If he kept talking about Stefan, he could avoid what was really on his mind.

The threat of a dead dog.

The image of a Rip Curl backpack in the forest.

31

POOLE

STEFAN SCHWARZENBECK'S PARENTS HAD BLOODSHOT EYES FROM THE jet lag and the emotional strain, but they insisted on going to the national park on Friday afternoon as soon as they arrived.

'We can't get into the exact location,' Poole explained. 'The forensic search is continuing.'

The lab had now confirmed that the other bones were from two separate individuals. A total of three bodies in the forest. The huge police team was meticulously digging through the mud and the leaf litter, amid rising concerns of another backpacker serial killer.

Poole tried to focus on the Swiss parents; both of them were nearing seventy but they looked younger, fitter. As if the search for their son had frozen them in time. 'This is Wreck Point National Park,' he told them as they entered the gates, guarded by two officers. 'The beach is popular with experienced surfers but it has some dangerous rips.'

The parents said nothing, so he kept talking. 'I believe Stefan enjoyed surfing. Is that the main reason he came to Australia?'

He'd met the parents once before, on their annual pilgrimage to Kinton Bay. They'd shown him a photo album in which their son grew from a cherubic baby to a gangly twelve-year-old to a sporty teenager. In later photos, Stefan skied icy slopes, played tennis, trekked along a ravine. The family had camped their way around Europe and posed atop the Empire State Building.

'He was a good swimmer and a good surfer,' the mother said. 'Do you think he came to the beach here?'

'We're trying to track his final movements. I have to be honest with you—so much time has passed that we may not find complete answers.'

'Was this area searched at the time?' the father asked.

'Yes, I had a look at the files. But where we found . . . Stefan . . . is very rugged and off the main trails.'

'*Das ist verrückt!*' the father growled. 'I do not understand why someone did not find him. Are you sure his body wasn't moved to the park recently?'

The parents thought of their son as having a body; all that remained of Stefan was a skull.

'We had a huge storm recently. We believe the erosion from the storm unearthed . . .'

. . . three sets of human remains.

His mind hadn't stopped spinning with possibilities. A triple homicide. A party gone wrong. Murder–suicide. A feast of deadly mushrooms. Some weird satanic pact. Another Ivan Milat picking up hitchhikers and taking them into the forest. Poole had cross-checked the names mentioned in Stefan's file— friends, drinking buddies, surfing mates, backpackers from the hostel. None of them was on the missing persons database; Stefan hadn't died with his mates.

The police media team was planning an announcement for Wednesday. A discovery like this meant sensational headlines, rampant speculation and panic. He'd prefer the remains were identified before the press conference; the lab was working overtime to get results.

This morning, Poole had called Rosalind Spencer, a detective on the case when Stefan had disappeared. She'd been stationed out in the far west until retirement a few years ago.

'If I said to you, hypothetically, that we'd discovered three sets of human remains in close proximity in the forest, dated to the late nineteen-nineties, what would you think?'

'Holy mackerel! I'd think those twins were involved. Blake and Derek O'Riordan.'

'They were teenagers back then. Could they have done this?'

Rosalind gave a bitter laugh. 'Oh yes. Especially if the victims are female. They were terrorising other kids, girls and boys. No-one would press charges, too scared. I should've done more, but Inspector Nelson told us the teenagers weren't a priority.'

'Why not?'

'Other stuff was going on. Scaffolding collapsed on the new wing of the hospital and killed one of the workers. There was a series of robberies at the shops and the bowling club. Our sergeant got injured in a brawl at the pub and went on sick leave. We had an American TV crew filming a documentary around the foreshore. We just didn't have enough officers.'

Poole ran a hand over his crew cut and tried to imagine the station back then.

'Not so sleepy Kinton Bay,' he grunted. 'Were people worried about three lads going missing in just over a year?'

'There was no link between them. Our investigations pointed to the likelihood that Stefan had drowned at Grotto Rocks after a night's drinking, and that Greyson had knocked himself out surfing, maybe encountered a shark at South Cove. Blake's disappearance barely registered with the locals—we were pretty sure he'd run away.'

'Was anything happening out in the national park?'

'Blake and Derek and their gang had parties out there.' Rosalind paused. 'One of the teachers, Miss Wilcox, talked to me about it, but as I said, the inspector insisted the high school kids weren't a priority. I kept my eye on those twins anyway. They were accused of all sorts of things, from killing the neighbour's dogs to stealing booze from the bowling club, but we never had enough on them.'

Wilcox: that name wasn't in Blake's file.

'Thanks, Rosalind, that's all helpful. Do you know where Inspector Nelson is now?'

'Greek Islands. Lucky bastard retired over there.' She whistled through her teeth, impressed. 'Is Derek still inside?'

'Yep. I'm arranging an interview with him. Any thoughts on what happened to Blake?'

'Probably killed those poor bastards in the forest and ran away so he'd never get caught.' Rosalind sighed thoughtfully. 'Wonder where he's hiding? Maybe he's been doing the same in other towns.'

⌣

Only three things helped Poole switch off from the job: sleep, which had been hard to come by; running, for which he'd had no time; and sex, ditto. On Sunday night, Caroline told him to lie down and relax. She dripped oil across his back and massaged the knots in his shoulders. Rubbed her thumbs along his spine. Rather than being aroused, he started to fall asleep. But then she asked him to turn over; that woke him up all right.

Afterwards, in the lounge room, he poured a golden-brown liquid into two brandy glasses.

'Shall we be Armagnac maniacs, madame?'

Their tenth wedding anniversary had been in Paris—he'd tagged along to one of Caroline's criminology conferences. Down an alleyway in the Marais, not far from their quaint hotel, they'd stumbled upon a tiny bar. The barman had introduced himself as 'an Armagnac maniac' and offered them tastings.

Caroline cradled her brandy balloon and asked how Stefan's parents were coping.

'They're obviously relieved he's been found after all these years.' He lifted the glass to his nose, sniffed it, took a sip and savoured the taste on his tongue. 'I haven't told them about the others yet. What do your statistics say?'

The possibility of a serial killer in Kinton Bay had shocked them both, even though they knew it could happen anywhere. Perhaps he could use some of Caroline's work to reassure the residents that this was still a safe place to live. A calm community would make his investigation easier.

'Three victims . . .' Caroline put her glass down on the coffee table and turned to face him. 'If the victims are male, statistically, the murder weapon will be a knife. If they're female, they're likely to have known the offender and cause of death will be strangulation.'

'There'll be no physical evidence for stabbing or strangulation.' Poole sighed. 'The bones are so decayed.'

He swirled the brandy around his mouth. Imagined himself a world away, in that candlelit bar with the Armagnac maniac pouring samples from different bottles. Shaking his head to clear it, Poole focused on another sort of maniac. 'And what are the statistics on serial killers? Didn't you do some research?'

'I'll print out a copy of my paper for you,' she said.

'Thanks.' He groaned at the thought of yet more late-night reading. 'I wish you could just download it all into my brain.'

'If only.' She laughed. 'Well, Australia doesn't have enough serial killers to be generalisable. But most of them are white males.'

'Clever loners?'

'The FBI's research debunked that hypothesis.' Caroline topped up the glasses. 'Not loners, not necessarily with a high IQ. Sometimes, seemingly ordinary people, with jobs and families. Look at the Golden State Killer in California—he'd been married and had three daughters.'

The Golden State Killer: a former police officer who committed at least thirteen murders and fifty rapes in the nineteen-seventies and eighties. The investigators had never linked the crimes and assumed there were multiple perpetrators until the introduction of DNA testing, which they used on evidence kept from the many crime scenes. And it was DNA that finally solved it. In a new technique, police collaborated with a public genealogy website and found a familial match. Through the relative's DNA, they identified the killer and caught him after forty years.

But Poole had no crime scene and no DNA evidence—only a few bones and a rotting backpack.

32

Student: Taj Britton
Year 9 Music, Ms Wright
Assignment: Music in nature

Songs of the humpback: music, fighting and mating

Humpback whales mature at about seven years of age, although they do not start mating until they are twelve.

The bulls form bachelor pods and swim and play together.

Like many animals in nature, some of them exhibit homosexual behaviour. But when the bulls are ready to mate, they'll violently fight each other to compete for the young female.

Only the males sing. They learn complicated songs to seduce the females. These songs are a series of moans and groans and clicks. Sometimes they sound like a creaking door, other times like a violin.

All the bulls memorise and sing the same song. The song can go on for up to an hour. It changes every few years.

33

MERI

FOR THE PAST FOUR DAYS, MERI HAD BEEN ITCHING TO FIND OUT ABOUT the skeletal remains. She'd heard nothing more from Chief Inspector Poole, but as instructed, she banned Siena from going to the national park, monitored her YouTube channel and checked the location app. Whenever Meri wasn't concentrating on work, her thoughts circled as she tried to guess what might have happened in the forest. Instead of shying away from that horrible year, as she usually did, Meri wanted to remember. She cursed herself for throwing out that box of Year 9 schoolbooks. And she couldn't ask her closest school friends—Kristie and Loretta had left town years ago, putting the past behind them. They hadn't stayed in touch, hadn't reconnected on Facebook.

Meri had found the old articles on Stefan, written by Neville in late 1999. Neville had been a senior journalist back then, in a team of ten, along with two photographers and two sub-editors. Over the years, the team had shrunk; these days journos were expected to be photographers and sub-editors as well.

Neville opened Tuesday's editorial meeting in his usual way. 'What's an astronaut's favourite part of a computer?' No-one answered so he went for the punchline: 'The space bar.'

Meri had heard that one about ten times. At least he hadn't tried to come up with a joke about the skull in the forest.

'We should run a public appeal for information about Stefan's death,' she said. 'Ask people to come forward and help the police work out his last movements. What do you think, Neville?'

While the other two journos nodded their agreement, Neville tilted his head back and stared up at the ceiling, cracking his neck from side to side.

'Mmm. Let's focus on the positives. Stefan has been found. After all this time. His parents must be relieved.'

Except that he's dead.

'Do the police think it's suspicious or just misadventure?' Josephine asked.

'They're calling it suspicious at this stage,' she replied.

'Okay, Meri, a small para towards the end of the story asking for info.' Neville raised his eyebrows, waiting for her to nod. 'Keep it low-key.'

'Neville, did *you* ever meet Stefan?' she asked.

Josephine and Hugh had been looking at their laptops but their heads snapped up to hear the response.

'I don't know.' Neville huffed. 'Maybe at the pub. There were so many backpackers passing through town in the nineties. I don't remember any individually. They were all the same.'

Apart from Stefan, who never went home.

⌢

Glenda called and asked Meri to drop in for lunch. There was an urgency in her voice. Was this about the new bones found in the forest?

Driving into 'Stinking Bay', Meri took in the full extent of the storm damage: roofs covered with tarpaulins, branches down, a thick stain of mud along the edge of the road. Rubbish snagged in the grass and the mangroves. The rotten-egg smell was stronger than usual. If Siena were here, she'd recite her assignment from last year: *Mangrove wetlands are an essential part of our coastal ecosystem. That smell is organic matter breaking down to release nutrients. It's nature in action!*

Glenda opened the front door and rushed her inside. The swelling had gone down, and her face was no longer lopsided, but she still had a band-aid on her scalp. It would take time for the scar to heal and her hair to grow back.

'How are you feeling?' Meri asked.

'I'm fine. Sit, sit.' Glenda pointed her towards the table, set with sandwiches. 'It's about Derek. Detectives interviewed him yesterday afternoon. He says they're accusing him and Blake of murder.'

'What?' Meri froze, her hand mid-air above the plate of food. 'The backpacker went missing a year after Blake. How could he possibly be involved?'

'Exactly!' Glenda held out her palms. 'Derek thinks they're trying to stop his parole in November.'

'They're probably just making enquiries,' Meri said. Trust Derek to over-react and kick up a fuss. 'What did the detectives ask him?'

'About the backpacker and that cave. But why aren't they finding out what happened to Blake?' Glenda pointed up at the photo on the wall: her twins on the first day of kindy, four years old, their short hair combed identically to one side, innocent smiles. Very cute. Nothing like the teenagers they became.

'How can they accuse my boys of murder?' Tears dripped down Glenda's cheeks. She pulled out a tissue from the crochet-covered box in the middle of the table. 'I know they weren't angels but they never hurt anyone.'

Blake and Derek had regularly hurt others. *They hurt me.* And Kristie and Loretta. They'd terrorised girls in and out of school. They'd bullied and beaten up boys.

With her blind mother love, Glenda had ignored the worst of her sons' faults. Meri went the opposite way with her own kids— quick to admonish them before anyone else could. If Glenda had disciplined her boys, would it have made a difference?

Taking a ham sandwich, Meri considered her reply: she couldn't upset Glenda right now, not with all she was going through—and what might be coming.

'I'm sure it's just normal police enquiries. If Derek is worried, he should talk to a lawyer.' Meri tied herself up in knots trying to ask the next question. 'And did Derek . . . does he know anything about . . . the backpacker?'

'He didn't say.' Glenda's hand shook as she lifted her mug. 'But what about my Blake? You promised to help find him, love. Have you talked to the police yet?'

Since the skull had been identified, Meri had focused on the backpacker. And all the issues raised by Siena.

'I spoke to Neville, but he didn't have space for a story,' she said. 'The police have been pretty busy.'

'I can't believe it was his fortieth birthday last month,' Glenda mused. 'Blake's favourite cake was chocolate, but Derek liked vanilla. One time, I did half and half. Derek was always jealous of his brother, though. And angrier. Blake was gentler. I never told anyone, but he used to paint my toenails.'

'Really?' Meri choked on a mouthful of bread. She couldn't picture Blake kneeling at his mother's feet, applying the nail polish.

'He had a soft side, my Blake,' Glenda continued. 'Kinton Bay was too rough for him.'

'But Blake was rough too.' She couldn't let Glenda re-write history completely. 'Especially with the girls.'

'What girls? Blake didn't like girls.'

Head spinning, Meri felt his weight on top of her in the cave, her inability to breathe. She could still see Loretta, hugging her knees as she sat on Meri's bed—the same bed where Siena now slept—crying because she'd come home with no underpants, blood on her thighs, her memory blank. And Kristie . . . poor Kristie.

Together, the three friends had gone to Miss Wilcox at the beginning of second term. Their kind English teacher promised to help, but nothing happened, and then she hadn't come back after the next school holidays. So Meri reassured her friends: *My dad will fix this.* But every time she'd tried to talk to him, he shut her down. Later, she realised he was avoiding her because all he cared about by then was Bonnie. And after he walked out, she couldn't tell Mum, couldn't give her more sorrow and pain.

Maybe Glenda was right about Blake not liking girls: he must've hated them to do what he did.

'I thought Blake . . .' She wondered how much she should say. Glenda had been her family's rock; Mum would turn in her grave if Meri inflicted unnecessary pain.

'Listen, love, I only ever said this to Cheryl. No-one else.' Glenda leaned across the table, tears still in her eyes. 'Blake was gay. That's why he ran away. I never told anyone 'cos of Derek. It would make him angry.'

Gay? Scruffy, greasy-haired Blake? It couldn't be true. He'd raped her.

'Did you tell the police?' Meri asked.

'No.' Glenda tugged out another tissue and blew her nose. 'When Blake told me, he was sobbing. He didn't want to be gay, but that's how he felt. And Derek . . .'

Derek would've been furious about a gay twin brother. If this was true, it certainly explained why Blake had decided to run away and never return. 'So, you think he went to Sydney?'

'Yeah. He could be who he wanted down there. Me and Cheryl went to Kings Cross a few times and showed his picture around. But no-one had seen him. He could've changed his appearance, though. Some of those boys had pink hair and earrings and tattoos.'

'You have to tell Chief Inspector Poole. It might be a clue to his whereabouts.'

Maybe this all explained Blake's denial—his last words. Maybe Meri should have believed him.

34

SIENA

SIENA DID ANOTHER CIRCUIT OF THE QUAD AT RECESS. ALTHOUGH IT didn't matter how many people she asked, the answer was always the same: 'No, I haven't seen a black labrador.'

Last night, in bed, she'd stretched out then curled up into a ball. Usually, Pirate slept beside her. She tried to fill the empty space by pushing a pillow between her spine and the wall.

It's my fault.

Over dinner, Taj had blurted out what they'd all been thinking. 'Whoever Siena upset with her video has taken Pirate.' Coming from her twin, the accusation was even more hurtful. 'He must be dead.'

Hayley, Zoe and their gang had commandeered the concrete steps leading from the quad up to the canteen. Some boys lounged behind them. Not Jackson. Siena hadn't seen him since last Tuesday at the police station. A whole week. Had he been suspended? Did he take Pirate in retaliation?

'What the fuck do you want?' Hayley demanded. 'I'm grounded 'cos of you.'

'Have you seen a black labrador running around town?' Siena scanned their faces, watching for any flicker of guilt.

'You asked yesterday. We already told you,' Zoe grunted without looking up, her eyes on her phone.

'I've got a question for you, though.' Hayley glared at her from the top step. 'Have you seen Axel?'

'And I already told you—no. He's a jerk. He tried to get with me.'

'You? As if! Watch your mouth,' Hayley snapped. 'He still hasn't turned up. If you know anything, you'd better say. His folks are scary people. They'll come after you.'

Geez, Hayley was jealous; she actually wanted to be with this guy who treated girls like dirt. But still, Siena was becoming more and more worried. Did that rock to the head have more impact than she realised?

Yesterday afternoon, while searching for Pirate, she'd detoured along the paths near Axel's house. At the end of his cul-de-sac, a track led into the bush towards Osprey Lookout. She'd trudged all the way to the top and back. Plenty of beer cans littered the sides of the path but nothing else. Where had Axel gone?

⁓

Mrs Genares clapped her hands enthusiastically. 'Thank you, Jasminda. Excellent work! A very insightful assignment on the treatment of homosexual prisoners in concentration camps. It's horrendous to think of the Nazis undertaking medical experiments to "cure" people's sexuality.'

Jasminda had finished her presentation with a love story between two men who'd met in a camp and survived. History was her favourite subject, and her gay uncle had told her how the Nazis wanted to eradicate homosexuality. Jas would get top marks for sure; Siena gave her a thumbs-up.

'These stories are now in the history books and that's important,' Mrs G continued. 'As Mark Twain said: *The very ink with which all history is written is merely fluid prejudice.* We need to keep that in mind as we interrogate the narratives of the past. That's a good lead-in to your assignment, Siena. You're next.'

Standing in front of the whiteboard, Siena began, 'My assignment is on the untold history of Kinton Bay.'

'Celebrity Siena,' a boy muttered. 'We've already seen it on the news.'

Mrs G had sat down in the front row for Siena's presentation, but she stood up again and faced the class. 'This is history in the making, Kaden,' she said. 'Or rather, the correcting of history. As I've told you before, history is written by the winners. They're the ones who record the battles and their own champions. The heroes on the losing side are forgotten.'

'Just like State of Origin.'

'Even though you're joking, you've got the right idea.' Mrs G hushed the titters. 'How many of you know the names of Aboriginal heroes?'

'Adam Goodes,' someone shouted.

'Ash Barty!'

'Yes, lots of great sports stars. What about the warriors who resisted the colonial occupation?'

Eddie Mabo came into Siena's thoughts, but he was more recent. The class stayed silent.

'The heroes protecting their families and their land were warriors like Pemulwuy around Port Jackson, Windradyne in the Bathurst War, and Yagan near Perth. You don't know their names because the winners—the colonials—considered them criminals.'

Aunty Bim didn't know the names of the people who'd been killed by Geoffrey Kinton; the winners didn't record their sins.

'Now, Siena. The massacre at Wreck Point.' Mrs G paused a moment. 'Do you think it's your story to tell? Remember, we talked about cultural appropriation. Should we be hearing it from the Aboriginal descendants themselves?'

'Umm, it's our combined history and we all need to tell it.' Siena hadn't prepared for this question. She spoke slowly. 'The early colonisers . . . our forefathers were responsible for some terrible atrocities. We need to acknowledge that this story is part of our town, part of us all.'

'But the skull she found wasn't Aboriginal,' Kaden called out.

His words reminded Siena of her latest nightmare: this time, the skull she held in her hands wasn't human. It had the shape of a dog. Pirate.

～

After school, with no-one else at home, Siena lay on her bed and wrote a list of suspects. Who could've taken Pirate? Jackson McCormack seemed the most likely culprit, followed by Hayley and Zoe. She couldn't bring herself to write the name Axel. The thought of him sent an involuntary shudder through her body.

She opened her laptop and checked the latest news on Kinton Bay. On the *Chronicle* site, the local headline read 'Strong growth in real estate'. Jackson's parents were pictured outside their agency. Ugh! The story of the defaced statue had already disappeared.

The police hadn't charged Siena and Kyle—much to her parents' relief. There was no evidence. But everyone knew that it could only be them. Mum said the mayor was on a warpath to 'make those kids pay for the desecration'.

Desecration. The same word Siena had used to describe the gang's actions in the cave.

She extracted Mum's diary from its hiding place under the bed and flipped it open to the first day of term three.

Monday, 20th July 1998
I wrote two stories over the holidays and couldn't wait to show them to Miss Wilcox. English was the first period after recess and I rushed into class early so I could talk to her. But she wasn't there. Eventually Mr Durham turned up and said he would be taking our class. I asked where Miss Wilcox was. 'She can't come back this term,' he said. 'The principal will talk to you all in assembly tomorrow.' He looked like he was about to cry. I think something really bad has happened.

Tuesday, 21st July 1998
SHE DIED. I can't believe it. We all cried in assembly when Mr Quinn announced that she had a sudden illness and died at home. I don't understand. She was so young. Mum said young people sometimes have a heart attack or asthma attack or tetanus from treading on a rusty nail. I just can't believe she's never coming back. After assembly, I saw Derek high-five Blake and I cried even harder. They're happy that she's gone. And now we have no-one to protect us. I can't stop crying. She was the best teacher.

Siena understood Mum's shock, even from the distance of two decades. If Mrs Genares died tomorrow, she'd be devastated.

But what did Mum mean by having no-one to protect them? From what? Or who?

35

ROLLO

NATIONAL PARKS AND WILDLIFE HAD ORGANISED A BOAT ON TUESDAY morning to tow the drift whale. Rollo, Owen and Hank motored out to the carcass, which was looking worse for wear. Hank Hoxton, the park ranger, had named the whale Nereus, after a Greek sea god. More strips had been torn from his belly. His magnificent tail sported bite marks. Occasionally, gulls landed atop his bulk and nibbled at the exposed flesh.

Rollo looped the second rope over itself and tied a knot. 'Hold on, nearly got it,' he called to the others. His fingers were slow in the cold wind, and the swell didn't help. For a moment, he saw himself slipping overboard, the circling sharks dragging him into the feast.

Finally, they had the ropes in place. As the boat towed the mighty carcass, the sharks followed. The white belly bobbing in the waves reminded Rollo of taking the kids tubing. They loved it when he revved the engine and they got air on the inflatable. When was the last time they'd done something like that as a family?

With the business, holidays were never easy. Rollo wanted to sail the family up to Cooktown to see his parents. Every so often, Meri's father sent messages through Nathan, inviting them over to Perth. Meri outright refused. 'I'm saving for when we can go to Europe,' she told him. As if Europe was the be-all and end-all.

When Meri was pregnant and wanted to name the twins after the city of Siena in Italy and the country of Tajikistan, he'd laughed. 'That's like calling them Brisbane and Vietnam.' Then he'd seen how much it meant to her, how much she felt she was missing compared to her university mates, and he'd agreed. These days, he didn't think about what the names signified—they were just his kids, Siena and Taj.

Their last holiday—if you could call it that—had been to Meri's brother's farm near Tamworth. Some holiday. Nathan had dragged him out of bed at six each morning to work in the paddocks. One day Nathan mentioned an upcoming trip to Perth. That night in bed, Rollo whispered to Meri, 'We could go to Perth too.'

'Nope. I can't bear to see my father playing happy families with his new wife and kids.'

'New?' Rollo coughed. 'They've been married more than twenty years. Their girls must've finished school by now. And our kids should be allowed to see their grandad.'

'He gave up any right to be a grandad when he walked out.'

After that, Rollo hadn't tried again. But the next time they'd seen Nathan and Sharon, the twins were fascinated by their Perth holiday snaps.

'Are they our aunties?' Siena asked about Meri's half-sisters. 'They look cool.'

'Stop showing those photos, Nathan,' Meri had said. 'I'm not forgiving him. He deserted me when I needed him. And Mum too. It was the worst time of my life.'

Sometimes it seemed like Meri's emotions were stuck at fifteen; and now with the twins at the same age, she was obsessed with tracking their movements.

'They're smart kids,' he reassured her. 'So much more aware than we were. And Siena would scream from the rooftops if a guy tried to do something to her.'

Although he knew that some teenage boys didn't take no for an answer.

Owen was at the stern of the boat, chatting with Hank. They weren't discussing the whale but the Swiss backpacker.

'He might've been rock climbing,' Hank said. 'Fell and hit his head. Do you remember him? Stefan was one of those dare-devil types.'

'Yeah, I remember.' Owen frowned. 'And you reckon he got stuck inside a secret cavern and that's why no-one found him?'

The backpacker and the backpack. Rollo should talk to Meri, tell her the backpack might be his. He should. But he wouldn't.

'Rollo, can you check the second rope?' Hank called. 'I think it's coming undone.'

Damn. The rope around Nereus's tail had loosened. Rollo was so distracted that he couldn't even tie a bloody knot properly.

⌒

The kids disappeared off to their rooms after dinner and Rollo sprawled in front of the television, utterly shattered. A rerun of *Border Force* played on the telly. Meri placed two mugs on the coffee table and sat next to him.

'Can I ask you something about Blake?'

'Sure.'

'Did you ever think . . . did he ever seem . . . gay to you?'

Rollo had picked up his cuppa; he put it straight back down. How the hell did Meri find out?

'Gay?' He gave a strangled laugh.

'If he was, Derek would have been furious, right?' Meri said. 'He'd have beaten him up and thrown him out of the gang?'

'Nah, 'course not.'

An image of Max Gupta flashed into his head. The night they'd seen him going home alone from the fish and chip shop, and cornered him in the small carpark behind the Chinese restaurant. 'I hate fags,' Derek had said, punching Max in the stomach and slapping him around the head. Lance pushed him to the ground and kicked him in the balls. 'Yeah, a good kick will get 'em working the right way,' Derek cheered. 'If you dob on us, you fucken poofter, we'll be waiting for you next Friday. And the next. And the one after.' On the concrete, Max had writhed in pain, begging for them to stop, promising not to tell.

Rollo had noticed Blake that night. While Derek and Lance were punching and kicking, Blake had danced around the edges. Like Rollo himself. And Owen. Pretending to brawl to keep Derek happy. At the time, he wondered if Derek had observed his twin's lack of involvement.

'Do you think that's why Blake ran away?' Meri asked. 'Because he was gay?'

'Nah. Who's spreading that rumour?' He picked up the remote and changed the channel.

Had Owen broken the pact after all these years?

36

MERI

THAT NIGHT, MERI'S BRAIN CHURNED OVER THE SECRETS OF KINTON BAY, trying to understand how it had all happened. While Rollo snored beside her, she started writing a new article on her laptop. One that Neville would never print.

A TOXIC, TROUBLED TOWN

Blame the girls—they shouldn't laugh so loud, they shouldn't wear short skirts. Blame the victims—they shouldn't go to parties, they shouldn't get drunk. Blame the parents—they should insist on earlier curfews, set stricter boundaries.

But whatever you do, don't blame those truly responsible.

The boys. The men. The culture.

Kinton Bay has always had a hard-drinking, macho culture. Men worked as timber cutters, builders and on fishing boats. It is alleged that our town was founded on an act of male violence—that Geoffrey Kinton kidnapped and raped an Aboriginal girl, killed her family and took advantage of her bush knowledge to settle here.

That violence was perpetrated at a cave near Wreck Point, the very same place where violence would later be perpetrated against teenage girls in the nineteen-nineties. When the victims spoke up, the men said 'not enough evidence' and 'boys will be boys'. Those boys were never charged.

The girls' lives were shattered; their belief in equality and justice destroyed.

From its very beginnings, this town has treated teenage girls as worthless. Has anything changed in the twenty-first century?

Meri closed the laptop and put it on the floor. She couldn't decide how to end the article; she'd have to talk to Siena about the current times.

Should Meri tell the truth about her own story—what she could remember of it, anyway? Shivering, she pulled the doona over her chest. It would take all her courage to name names. Next to her, Rollo shifted in his sleep and she recalled his reaction tonight. If Blake was gay, how did that tie into those parties and the culture of toxic masculinity?

~

On Wednesday morning, Detective Chief Inspector Poole stood behind a portable lectern outside the police station. His uniform was as neat as ever, but his usually ruddy face had a grey tinge and there were dark circles under his eyes. Meri counted the reporters—more than double than at the last media conference. A camera crew from the Newcastle regional channel, ABC TV from Coffs Harbour, and another two journalists she didn't recognise. Perhaps they were reporting back to Switzerland.

The Newcastle cameraman had prime position at the front. Meri edged to one side of him, held out her iPhone and pressed record.

'As you know, human remains found in Wreck Point National Park twelve days ago were identified as those of Swiss national Stefan Schwarzenbeck,' Poole began. 'Since then, teams searching the area have located some additional remains.'

He stopped for a moment and smoothed the paper on the lectern.

'Initially, we assumed these remains would be identified similarly. However, DNA results show this not to be the case. Sadly, we have identified two more people.'

Muttering spread through the assembled news crews.

'We have notified their families,' Poole continued. 'They have been identified as two males who both went missing in 1998. Greyson Creighton, a nurse from Brisbane, and Blake O'Riordan, a local high school student.'

Oh god. Blake.

He'd been in the forest all this time.

Swaying slightly, Meri put a hand on the cameraman's arm to steady herself.

'Are you all right?' he whispered.

She nodded but didn't let go. The police would reopen the investigation. Into Blake's death this time, not his disappearance. They'd want to question her again. And Rollo too. Find out who was the last person to see Blake alive.

'We're asking the public to help us. Rewards are being offered as an incentive for people to come forward. Half a million dollars for Stefan, two hundred thousand for Greyson, and fifty thousand for Blake. Their families deserve answers after all this time.'

The chief inspector continued speaking but Meri couldn't concentrate on his words.

On the drive from the police station to Glenda's place, Meri considered pulling over to phone Rollo. But Glenda was her first priority. And she wanted to tell her husband face to face, gauge his reaction. When she'd asked him about the possibility of Blake being gay, he'd denied it, turning away from her, the edge of his mouth twitching slightly. Why had he lied?

She tried to remember the details of Greyson Creighton's disappearance: he was a Brisbane nurse doing a placement at the community hospital and there was some tragic element. What was it? His parents had been distraught, obviously, and so was—Meri suddenly seized on the fact—his fiancée. He'd proposed to her only three months before, in the Botanic Gardens in the city.

Three young men left in the forest. What could possibly link a local teenager, a surfing Swiss backpacker and a Brisbane nurse?

Knocking on Glenda's door, Meri wondered how to help. The desperate mother had been so sure her son was alive, somewhere. And Meri had promised her that she would find some answers. She'd let Glenda down.

Twice.

The guilt flooded through her, made her stomach churn.

She'd have to talk to the chief inspector. Tell him. How would Glenda react to her withholding information for so many years?

Paul, the brother-in-law, answered the door. Good, that meant Glenda's sister, Cheryl, must be here supporting her.

'You've heard the terrible news, then. We can't believe Blake never left Kinton Bay.' Paul sniffed back tears. 'Come into the kitchen and have a cuppa, love. I've got some more bad news.'

'What is it?' Meri heard the tremor in her voice. As she walked down the corridor, there was no sign of Glenda. In the kitchen, the chairs and table had been pushed against the walls.

'The coppers called us all here first thing this morning and told us. Glenda was shocked and upset, but she got it together after a bit.' Paul moved a chair for Meri to sit down. 'And then, half an hour ago, some visitors were here and she tripped over the mat and collapsed. We think she hit her head again. The ambos took her straight to hospital. Cheryl went with them.'

'Was she conscious?'

'In and out. She didn't look good. They said it's real bad to hit your head a second time.'

Glenda's strange comment from the last hospital visit came back to her: *I want purples and pinks at my funeral. Same colour as my hair.* Poor, poor Glenda. She'd been certain her son was still alive; the hope had kept her going.

'I'll pop into the hospital later.'

Paul had put out two mugs on the counter. Clearly, he wanted some company after this morning's events. He opened a cupboard, stared into it blankly and closed it again.

'I have to get going, Paul.' She put a hand on his shoulder. 'I'm so sorry about . . . everything.'

And she was. Sorry for Glenda, for Cheryl and Paul, for all the family and friends. Sorry for her own dishonesty. But deep down, a tiny sense of karmic satisfaction gleamed, a miniscule flame to start thawing the cold teenage fear. The bastard who'd assaulted her was dead.

She stared at a photograph on the wall—not the one of the twins at four years old which Glenda had pointed out last time—but them as teenagers, a school portrait from Year 10. She couldn't tell the two apart.

That tiny flame of karmic satisfaction fizzled out. Maybe her attacker wasn't dead after all.

37

That first death was accidental: I meant to humiliate him for his disgusting behaviour.

When he was unconscious, I stripped him and left him in the cave. Took all his clothes away. I expected him to stumble out of the forest by late afternoon, starkers. Or be found in the cave that night when everyone turned up to the next party. Either way, humiliation.

Two days later, I went back. He lay spreadeagled, face down on the rock, like a sacrifice to the cave itself. I thought he was playing a trick. Waiting for me to get close so he could jump up and attack me.

Then I saw flies buzzing around his bum. A very white bum. Blood had pooled downwards, into his chest and stomach, all the parts nearest the ground. They'd turned reddish-purple.

I puked on the rock platform. It splattered onto my jeans. Fuck, fuck, fuck. This wasn't the plan. The trick was now on me. Sprinting down the path, I planned to get help but when I banged my shin on a rock, the pain made me stop and think: Inspector Nelson would be the one investigating this . . .

I could make an anonymous call but my vomit was up there. I'd have to go back and clean it up.

Using gum leaves to brush it off the edge of the rock platform, I nearly puked again. This situation, it wasn't what I'd planned. I felt bad, of course I did—sick to my stomach.

But self-preservation was starting to kick in.

Dragging the body into the depths of the cave was harder than I expected. His skin snagged on rocks, sticks caught in his hair. This is his punishment, I told myself. It's his fault. He chose to act the way he did.

In the darkest corner of the cave, a black hole gaped like a narrow tunnel into hell. After I'd shoved his body into it, I stacked piles of rocks over the top.

I got lucky. It rained for a month. No parties, no bushwalkers.

I dumped his belongings in a charity clothing bin. They disappeared completely, just like him.

38

ROLLO

BLAKE'S BONES FOUND IN THE NATIONAL PARK. AND GREYSON'S . . . Sitting in his HiLux in the marina carpark, Rollo let out a strangled sob.

Thank god he wasn't with Owen when he heard. His mate was waiting on the boat, expecting him to come back with pies from Sweet Cakes Bakehouse. They were supposed to be cleaning the deck after lunch. But he couldn't face Owen. Couldn't face going home. Couldn't face the Time'n'Tide. Couldn't face talking to Meri.

On the passenger seat, his mobile rang and Meri's number flashed up. He ignored it.

With shaking hands, Rollo started the engine and drove without thinking. He took the highway out of town, relieved to see Kinton Bay disappear in his rear-vision mirror. But then he realised that in ten kilometres he'd have to pass the gate to the national park. Would it be manned by coppers? A road appeared on his right and he turned down it. A rural enclave with a few small farms, an orchard, horse paddocks. Nothing to remind him of Blake along here.

As he slowed for a bend, Rollo recognised the next pro-perty—Duke's place. A long dirt driveway leading up to a blue weatherboard cottage. The young surfer wouldn't mind if he crashed on his couch for an hour, took a moment to process this shit.

A station wagon was parked out front, a surfboard leaned against the verandah wall. At the sound of the ute pulling up, Duke opened the screen door.

'Rollo, my man, good to see you.' Duke hugged him hard.

'Can I come in?' he asked. 'Hang for a bit?'

'Sure, man.' Duke's eyes were glassy; he must've had a smoke already today.

Duke looped an arm around his shoulders and walked him into the lounge room where a collection of bongs stood proudly on a side table. Stuck on the walls were surfing posters of the greats.

'Got a new one.' Duke pointed it out. 'Duke Kahanamoku when he came over here in 1915. That's Freshwater Beach behind him.'

'Cool. The birth of Aussie surfing.' Rollo nodded at the retro poster. Flopping onto the couch, he closed his eyes while Duke rolled a joint.

'Good batch,' Duke said. 'It's from a new guy.'

The rich scent filled the room. Oh god, twenty-three years. After Blake disappeared, Rollo had spent the next four months completely out of it, doped up to the eyeballs, blaming himself. Then Greyson went too. And all the time, Derek and Lance were strutting around town, bolder than ever. After Greyson's disappearance, he made a vow to stop smoking. He didn't want to be the next missing man.

He hadn't realised he was staring at the joint until Duke spoke again.

'Sorry, mate. Do you want me to put it out?' All of the young surfers had heard Rollo's inspiring tale of his doped-out teenage years, quitting drugs and, eventually, buying a business.

'Nah, that's okay.' He gestured for Duke to hand it over. 'It's been a fucken rough morning.'

Rollo put the joint between his lips and sucked slowly. His mobile rang. Meri again. As if she knew what he was doing. He switched it off and put it in his pocket. Took another long, slow drag.

'I heard about the bodies in the forest,' Duke said. 'One of them was your friend, wasn't he? That's heavy.'

'Yeah, heavy,' he echoed.

Unlike his body, which was starting to feel very light. Maybe he could float away and no-one would notice. He looked up to the ceiling and saw Blake sitting on top of the cupboard, laughing. Naked apart from his white jocks. Lance must've stolen his clothes again. Or Derek. Those shitheads loved that prank.

Weird that he was hallucinating, dope never used to do that. Must be his grief and guilt.

Hey, Blake, how're you doing? he asked.

Yeah, good. Blake put his hands over his eyes, then his mouth, then his ears. *See no evil, speak no evil, hear no evil. Hey, man, how do you know I'm Blake? Not Derek?*

It was a game the twins played. Tricking teachers, kids around school, girls. Rollo had thought he could always tell them apart. But one time, he bumped into Blake at the fish and chip shop and talked to him for twenty minutes before realising it was Derek. For months afterwards, the smug prick had boasted about fooling a mate.

He had another drag and focused on the teenager on top of the cupboard.

Do you hate me, Blake?

Blake kicked his feet like a kid, banging them against the wood. *Why did you do it? You knew Derek was a mean bastard.*

Getting wasted at the cave had been Rollo's favourite pastime in high school. No parents, no teachers, no judgement. A joint permanently in his hand, he sat by the campfire with his mates, enjoying the buzz, laughing his head off, chilling, then falling asleep. Sometimes girls joined them but Rollo was normally out of it by the time they all hooked up.

Until that last party with Blake. That night at the cave, he saw Derek and Lance crushing tablets into an orange juice bottle, and topping it up with vodka.

'What are those?' he'd asked.

'Roofies.' Lance grinned. 'Greyson was busted again last week so we got a new supply. Party time!'

'Who's Greyson?' Rollo didn't understand, didn't know that they'd been using roofies. Maybe this explained the strange vibe of the past few months—the feeling that made him want to leave the Wrecking Crew.

'He's a nurse at the hospital,' Derek had answered. 'What a poofter job. But he's been getting some gear and selling it.'

'Didn't you just say he got busted?'

'Yeah, but my uncle doesn't arrest him. Just confiscates it. And these little beauties find their way to us and into the girls' drinks.'

Even in his half-cut state, Rollo could see that was pretty fucked. 'I don't think we should—'

'Jesus, Rollo, you big baby.' Lance scowled at him. 'You're getting paranoid from smoking so much of that shit. Which, you know, is coming via my uncle too.'

'I thought you were buying from Trev at Harbours End?'

'Nah. He left town when the bikies started selling.' Lance screwed the lid on the juice bottle and shook it. 'Mate, you haven't paid me for this week.'

'Yeah, I'll get it to you.' For a few moments, he'd tried to understand the drug chain—but did it really matter as long as it kept coming? The roofies, though, that wasn't right. When Derek and Lance went to collect the girls from the party down at the beach, they took the juice bottle with them.

But he'd seen Lance put the rest of the Rohypnol tablets inside his backpack. When the others weren't watching, he tossed the bag off the rock platform into the dense bush below.

That last night had ended in one humungous mess.

I'm sorry, Blake.

But the top of the cupboard was empty. His friend had gone. Disappeared again. Blake was one big fucking disappearing act. He felt the laughter erupting from deep inside himself.

'Are you right, man?' Duke held out a bottle of Coke for him. 'Too strong? It's been a while.'

'I'm okay. It's just . . .' He burst out laughing again. 'You got any chips?'

As Duke went to the kitchen for snacks, Rollo pushed himself off the couch to get some air. About to open the sliding door, he stopped and stared through the glass. His mind was playing more tricks on him. Not Blake this time, but a dog who looked just like Pirate.

'I've got Cheezels and chips and a family pack of bickies.' Duke put the packets down on the coffee table. 'Don't take the Monte Carlo, it's my fave.'

The phantom dog barked.

'Ah shit, that dog must be lonely.' Duke nibbled on his biscuit. 'I'm not really into dogs. I'm being paid to look after it.'

Pirate.

Rollo opened the sliding door and the dog came running. Licked his fingers, rubbed against his legs, sniffed his crotch. Squatting down, he buried his face in the black fur and whispered Pirate's name. Marvelled at his dog. Alive! He couldn't wait to tell the kids.

'Who asked you to look after him?'

Duke shrugged, then winced. 'I'm not s'posed to tell anyone. It's a birthday surprise.'

'I'm really good at keeping secrets.' Which bastard had taken their dog? Terrified his kids, upset his wife. Left a threatening note on his windscreen.

'You gotta keep this secret too,' Duke insisted.

Surely Duke was mellow enough to spit it out. 'Listen, man, I've been keeping secrets my whole life.'

'It's for your mate, Owen.'

What the fuck? While Meri had believed the worst of him, Rollo never really entertained the idea. Not Owen. He knew how much Rollo and the family loved Pirate. Their friendship had survived so much but this was the lowest of the low.

'You mean Owen asked you to look after the dog?'

'Not exactly.' Duke scratched at his groin. 'Okay, so you know the barmaid at the Time'n'Tide . . .'

'Yeah, Ebony.'

'She asked me to look after it because I live out of town. She said it was for your friend, Owen.' Duke patted the dog awkwardly. 'Ebony paid me cash, but I reckon the money came from that guy. The one who thinks he's so shit hot.'

'Shane McCormack?'

'No, you know, that guy on the bike, man on the moon.' Duke screwed up his eyes. 'What's his name? It's coming to me . . .'

Duke must be smoking too much. Was he thinking of the film *E.T.*, with the bike flying across the moon? Rollo couldn't remember the names of anyone in that movie. Only the director.

'Steven Spielberg?'

'What the hell are you talking about? Steven Spielberg doesn't live in Kinton Bay. Sorry, I got confused about the man on the moon—he's got the same surname as the guy on the bike.'

'Jesus, Duke. Spit it out. Who?'

'The bald guy with the construction company. Snappy dresser. Shares a first name with that famous bike rider. The one who got done for drugs.'

Lance.

39

MERI

AS SOON AS MERI ENTERED THE OFFICE, SHE WAS ACCOSTED BY her editor.

'Where have you been? It's midday. The media conference was hours ago.' Neville's cheeks puffed out in anger. 'The biggest story in the town's history and you're missing in action.'

'I went to interview Glenda.' It wasn't really why she'd gone there but her editor didn't need to know that.

'Good idea.' Neville shifted gear. 'The grieving mother. Yes, much better than the serial killer angle other media will be pushing. Great thinking. I assume she talked to you.'

He spoke as if he cared. All these years of refusing to listen to Glenda and suddenly he was her number one supporter.

'No. She's in hospital. They won't let me see her for another hour or so.' Meri brushed at the tear that threatened to fall and switched to work mode. 'What sort of lead do you want?'

It would be hard for Neville to put a positive spin on this one. Three dead men—terrible for tourism, business, investment.

'Let's start with a few quotes of disbelief. From Mayor Redpath, maybe? This sort of thing doesn't happen in our town, et cetera, et cetera. Kinton Bay is a safe place. Then focus on the victims and their families. The shock and sadness of our community. But no mention of murder or serial killers. None of that.'

She could certainly do sadness. And try to bury the regret.

Sitting at her computer, Meri wrangled her chaotic thoughts into sentences. She had a quick look back at her first story on the skull and saw Aunty Bim's quotes about the massacre. What had Neville just said? *The biggest story in the town's history.* But according to Aunty Bim, worse things had happened here before. That perpetrator was long dead and buried.

Unlike now, when the killer could still be living in town. Walking down Dolphin Street. Shopping at the supermarket. Ordering fish and chips from her son. Drinking at the Time'n'Tide.

For the sixth time, Meri rang Rollo. She wanted to tell him about Glenda. His phone went straight to voicemail. Damn him for refusing to download the location app. Chester said the *Sirius* was moored at the marina, but Rollo wasn't onboard.

The other journalists and the editorial assistant all dropped by her desk on their way to the kitchen and the bathroom.

'Do they think it's a serial killer?' Josephine asked.

Hugh wondered if the forensics results could be wrong. 'Are they sure the bodies aren't from the massacre?'

'I've heard ghost stories about that cave.' The young editorial assistant fluttered her hands dramatically. 'Spooky!'

The trouble with a small newsroom—and a small town—was that gossip and conjecture travelled fast. And, as with Blake's actual disappearance, gossip sometimes became a form of fact.

Meri had almost finished her story when Neville leaned against her desk.

'Nearly done,' she told him. 'Is it okay if I leave after this? I need to visit Glenda and pick up the kids from school.'

And find my bloody husband.

'Sure. Do the police have any theories?' he asked, lowering his voice. 'Were they killed by the same person?'

'They're keeping all lines of enquiry open.' She repeated Poole's phrase. 'What do you think happened, Neville? You were living here when they went missing. Any ideas about Stefan? Or Greyson? Did you interview his fiancée? Was there some creepy bastard hanging around town who could've murdered three young men?'

Neville, who had been so keen to discuss the police's theories, suddenly pushed away from her desk.

'Check the old files.' He threw the words over his shoulder. 'I noted down everything I knew.'

He would've written bald facts, nothing about his impressions or his interactions with the missing men. Greyson had lived in KB for a year. Had they drunk together in the pub?

～

A strong sense of déjà vu flooded through Meri as she entered the hospital. Except this time, Glenda was in the emergency ward, her face even more bruised and swollen, eyes closed.

'Has she been awake?' Meri asked the doctor.

'In and out of consciousness,' the doctor said. 'It's serious. We're transferring her to Newcastle. You can sit with her for a few minutes. Her sister just went to make some phone calls.'

Sweet Glenda, always caring for others. But the police hadn't cared for her; they'd never taken her concerns seriously, never properly looked for Blake. Meri perched on the chair and took her hand.

'I'm so sorry,' she whispered. 'I didn't do enough to help you. I knew something and . . .'

A nurse leaned in to check one of the machines, and Meri changed the subject.

'It must've been hard bringing up twins on your own, Glenda. You're a good woman.' Kind-hearted. Generous. Jovial. Her sons hadn't inherited any of those qualities.

Glenda's eyelids flickered open and her mouth moved. 'Warn Derek for me.'

'About what?' She wriggled closer.

'Lance,' Glenda groaned. 'Wants Derek . . . to stay away.'

'Why?' Did Lance want to hide their old friendship when Derek came out of prison? Or was this about something more recent?

'Derek knows too much . . . I'm scared.' Glenda was breathing heavily, her words harder to understand.

'You'll be fine.' She hoped it was the truth. 'They'll fix you up in Newcastle and you'll be feeling better in no time.'

'He caused this . . .' Glenda waved her left arm towards her head, dropped it back by her side and closed her eyes again. 'Lance did.'

Dear god. Had Lance tripped her down the steps of her own home two weeks ago? Surely that was too much, even for him.

'What did he do exactly?' Meri pressed.

She remembered the elaborate bunch of flowers Lance had brought to the hospital last time. Had he visited her to make sure she kept her mouth shut? Intimidation was Lance's speciality. He and Derek and Blake used to do it together at school. Whatever Derek knew must be dangerous to Lance, dangerous enough to start threatening his old mate's mum.

'Glenda, can you hear me?'

She whimpered and closed her eyes.

⌒

Meri had texted the twins to say she was picking them up after school; neither asked why, which meant they understood her concern.

'I can't believe it's Blake,' Siena said as she clambered into the front seat. 'Glenda must be so upset.'

After hugging her daughter and waiting for Taj to get into the back, Meri told them about Glenda's head injury.

'Is she going to die?' Taj asked.

'No, no,' Meri said, and then burst into tears. God, she hadn't meant to break down in front of the twins. Siena reached over for a quick squeeze and Taj patted her shoulder from the back seat. Oh, her beautiful, caring children.

On the way home, Taj asked about the dog.

'We still haven't heard anything,' Meri said.

Siena was focused on the forest. 'Everyone thinks it's a serial killer. Is it, Mum?'

Fear would be bubbling around town, at the school, in the pub, the shops, homes. Like the base of a volcano, simmering and simmering until it erupted. The fear was already etching grooves into her children's foreheads.

'The police haven't determined that yet. But there are lots of very experienced detectives here working on the cases. They'll figure it out.'

Pulling into the driveway, Meri let out a sigh of relief to see the HiLux parked by the garage.

'Dad's home,' she announced brightly.

'Does he know about Blake and Glenda?' Taj asked.

Siena jumped out, ran up the path and disappeared inside the house while Taj was still gathering his school bag off the floor.

'Let's go and find out,' Meri said.

They heard Siena scream. Piercing and high-pitched. Had Jackson broken into their house? Running towards the door, Meri realised, too late, that she should've told Taj to stay back and call the police. But he was right on her heels.

And then she heard another sound.

Not a scream but a laugh. Bizarre in the midst of everything.

She rushed into the hallway to see Siena kneeling on the floor. A blur of black spun in circles around her.

'Pirate, where have you been?' Meri bent down to stroke his neck.

Rollo appeared from the lounge room, holding a mug of tea.

'Surprise!' He grinned. 'Pirate's home and he's fine.'

The dog's tail thumped a beat on the floor. Then he threaded around them, accepting cuddles and licking their faces.

'Where did you find him?' she asked.

'I didn't.' Rollo shrugged and took another sip of his tea. 'When I got home Pirate was lying on the back deck like he'd never left.'

40

POOLE

TASK FORCE OWL. WHILE THE NAME HAD BEEN RANDOMLY SELECTED, it seemed ironic to Poole. If only they knew what the owls had seen in the forest two decades ago.

Three men, three investigations, three sets of reports. At the time, each disappearance had a different set of circumstances and none appeared to be linked. Now their final resting places had converged.

As always, Poole would keep an open mind. However, the fact that the bones were found close together in the forest pointed to deliberate killings, and possibly one killer.

The forensic reports showed no knife injuries, no bullet wounds, and no projectile trauma. The bodies had decomposed over time and were likely to have been dislodged from their original location during the recent storm. The search team hadn't located any clothes or shoes, only the backpack. Were the victims naked when they died? Those lads would've worn sneakers or hiking boots in the forest. Although if they'd been at the beach first, they could've worn thongs and board shorts. But were their belongings deliberately taken away?

The police commissioner asked Poole if he expected more bodies to turn up. All the chatter around the station focused on the backpacker murders down south in the early nineties: seven bodies discovered over fourteen months in the Belanglo State Forest. A phenomenal investigation, with data from so many sources, including a public hotline. They'd had two hundred and thirty suspects—the massive amount of information required a whole new database program to be designed.

Aren't three bodies enough? Poole wanted to say to the commissioner. *Three young men with their lives cut short.*

'The teams are still searching,' he said instead. 'It's difficult terrain.'

A team from the Homicide Squad in Sydney was combing through the old files and investigations database looking for any links—common threads, common timeframes or associates known to all three men. They were trying to identify any convicted offenders in the area at the time. With Poole, they'd started a list of persons of interest. Not suspects yet.

Some detectives believed that, in big cases like this, the offender's name popped up early in discussions. But detailed analysis was needed to rule out other suspects before they narrowed their sights.

Who'd had the *opportunity, motive and capability* to commit all three murders?

One name kept coming up.

Derek O'Riordan.

They'd interviewed him in the correctional centre in Cessnock last Monday, before the discovery of the other bones. Derek had loped into the room, intrigued by their visit, and draped his tall frame over the chair. His muscular arms and legs hung off the sides, his chest puffed out. With his black buzz cut, he resembled the spider tattooed on his neck—a redback crawling upwards. He listened to their questions about Stefan Schwarzenbeck and answered in short sentences, never elaborating. He wouldn't be drawn out.

'Yeah, I saw him in the pub sometimes. Cocky bastard.'

'Nah. I never got in a fight with him.'

'I dunno who he was hanging round with.'

'Nup, don't remember where I was that night.'

Studying him in the interview, Poole had observed that anger was Derek's emotional default. And jealousy.

The discovery of the two other men had changed everything. They'd have to interview Derek again. Was it possible that this man, in jail for robbery and assault, could also have committed murder?

In the team briefing yesterday, Poole explained that of the three men, Greyson Creighton's last movements might be easiest to determine. 'Greyson was working at the community hospital and renting a house with another nurse. He had regular shifts and regular contacts.' Poole addressed two female detectives who'd come up from Sydney. 'Singh and Coleman, can you re-interview all the contacts from his original missing person's report? Ask about any links with Blake or Derek O'Riordan. And find out if he used to visit Wreck Point for surfing or bushwalking.'

'His parents engaged a private investigation firm from Brisbane,' said Detective Sergeant Sarah Singh. 'I'll ask his family for a copy of the PI report too. It might contain some additional detail.'

'Good. I'll be across them all, but my focus is Blake. I know his old school friends and his mother. She's in hospital so

I'm waiting to hear when I can talk to her.' Glenda had been transferred to Newcastle—that didn't sound good. 'It's a small community here. We're looking for any links between the three. Knowing this town, there'll be many connections.'

On Monday, Poole had ten spare minutes while waiting for the regional chief superintendent—enough time to wolf down a chicken sandwich and read Caroline's research paper on serial killers. Caroline had been in Sydney last week lecturing but they'd discussed the serial killer angle together over the weekend. He turned to the section entitled 'Childhood and Background'.

Childhood trauma is a common feature in the histories of convicted serial killers. Trauma can disrupt child brain development and lead to emotional dysregulation. Many offenders have committed minor criminal acts from a young age, including theft and property damage. They may torture or kill animals.

As a result of childhood trauma, the individual may develop a fear of abandonment, making it difficult to form intimate relationships. In some cases, the first killing may stem from a desperate desire to be close with another person and the terror of being rejected or humiliated by them. Killing the object of their desire (whether a parent, sibling or potential lover) is preferable to experiencing what they believe will be a short period of affection followed by inevitable betrayal.

'Nature or nurture?' is the constant question in any analysis of offenders. Many offenders come from violent families who undertake criminal activities.

Nature or nurture. As a baby, had Derek suffered child-hood trauma? Poole flipped through Blake's file, searching for any mention of the twins' dad. Nothing in the original inves-tigation. But he remembered asking Glenda last year: could Blake have gone to stay with his father? 'The boys don't know him,' Glenda had said. 'Their dad was in a bikie gang. A bad influence. I kicked him out when they were four.' She'd refused to give his name.

Raising twins must have doubled the stress on Glenda and her partner. He glanced down at the report again. *Minor criminal acts from a young age. Torturing or killing animals.* Both of those applied to Derek. Had he murdered his own brother to avoid the 'inevitable betrayal' of affection as Caroline's paper theorised?

'Excuse me, boss.' Senior Sergeant Frawley approached his desk. 'We've got an anonymous phone call saying we have the wrong timeline for Blake. This person also claims to have infor-mation about why Greyson was killed. They want to discuss the reward money and they'll only speak to you.'

Poole sat in the interview room, adjusting his headphones, waiting for the call to be put through. A public appeal for infor-mation always drew a range of responses: genuine tips, confused half-memories, snippets of a sighting. Those were the helpful calls. But it also attracted people with other motivations—a desire to insert themselves into the investigation, or get their hands on a reward when they had no real information. A guilty conscience might prompt a person to dob in a friend after years and years. Or it could be the killer himself, phoning in to provide false information and set them on the wrong path.

Which kind of call would this be?

'Connecting you now, sir.'

Poole grasped a pen between his fingers, ready to note down any thoughts that leapt out at him. The conversation would be recorded so he could go over it again later.

'Thank you for calling,' Poole began. 'I understand you wish to remain anonymous at this point. That's perfectly fine. We appreciate any information that will lead to—'

The caller interrupted him. 'How much money are you going to give me?'

A male voice. Deep. Slightly rough. Belligerent attitude. Had he been drinking?

'We really need your information first. Until you start talking, we won't know if it can help with the investigation.'

'Oh, it'll help,' the man said.

'Great,' said Poole. 'If you have genuine information leading to an arrest, then you'll be eligible to receive part of the reward.'

'Part of it?'

'A reward is sometimes divided up between a few informants.' It was becoming evident that this caller was only interested in the money. Perhaps he knew nothing useful. But if he did, he'd have to reveal his identity to receive the reward. Poole wouldn't mention that yet, no need to spook him. 'We're acting in good faith, sir. We want to pay for information to resolve these cases. You can trust the police process.'

'Trust the police? Ha! You weren't around in the nineties.'

'No, I wasn't. That's why I'd really like to hear what you have to say.'

'Greyson was killed 'cos of drugs.' The man grunted. 'He was stealing drugs from the hospital pharmacy and selling them at the pub. He got caught by Inspector Nelson but never charged.'

'Do you know why not?'

'Nelson had his own scam running. He'd confiscate drugs and money, then give the drugs to his lackeys to sell. All with a kickback to him. He had the bikies in his pocket too.'

A corrupt cop. Bloody hell, he'd heard no rumours about Nelson. Or did this caller hold a grudge against the former inspector? Poole would have to start digging.

'Can you tell me the names of these lackeys?'

'Yep, if you give me the fifty-thousand-dollar reward.'

The money again—it was all this guy could think about. He wasn't unburdening himself because of a guilty conscience.

'This is very helpful information,' Poole said. 'The reward is certainly a good incentive for you to keep talking. Was Blake's death also related to drugs?'

'Nah, I don't think so.'

Two murderers???? Poole scribbled on his pad. 'You told my officer that we had our timeline wrong. What did you mean by that?'

'They're saying the last sighting of Blake was leaving school on Friday arvo. That's bullshit. We . . . they had a party that night. Out at the Killing Cave. Afterwards they made a pact not to talk about it.'

'Who did?' asked Poole.

'The Wrecking Crew. Derek, Blake, Owen, Scott and Rollo. That backpack you found—it belongs to one of them, Rollo Britton.'

PART FOUR

HUNTING SEASON

Humpbacks and orcas are social animals. Orcas are
known as 'the wolves of the sea' due to their pack
mentality. They'll surround and attack the youngest,
weakest or most vulnerable whale. Humpbacks can use
their pack mentality for good—they have been known to
rescue other species, like grey whales and seals,
from an orca attack.

41

ROLLO

A CALL CAME THROUGH FROM THE PARK RANGER AT TUESDAY LUNCHTIME. The whale carcass had drifted back in and snagged on Grotto Rocks at the end of the little beach. By the time Rollo and Owen arrived, a small group of onlookers had already gathered. Each time a wave thrust the whale against the jagged rocks, the crowd gasped.

Ten metres from shore, tiger sharks circled, snapping at the whale whenever it drifted deep enough. They were smart: the sharks wouldn't beach themselves for a feed, but they'd steal a mouthful at any opportunity.

Rollo walked towards the rocks with Owen trailing behind. His mate had been quiet all morning. Neither of them had mentioned Blake's name. Rollo wondered if he knew that Glenda had been taken to Newcastle Hospital. But the way Owen wouldn't meet his eyes stopped him from asking. Everything was so fucking shit. And it had all begun with Siena's discovery.

He watched a couple with a German shepherd; the dog barked each time the whale's body crashed into the rocks.

At least he'd found Pirate. Meri had accepted his explanation that the dog turned up by himself. Fucking Lance. Threatening him and his family with that note. Rollo should've guessed straight away. Lance had made a habit of saying, *Keep your mouth shut.* He'd copied it from Derek, but he would hate for anyone to have known how he'd idolised him at school. Followed each of Derek's commands. And now he was a slyer version of Derek, a charming manipulator disguised as an entrepreneur, with a few development deals that shouldn't have been approved. Aunty Bim said Lance had offered money to the local Aboriginal Land Council to change their classification of a heritage site. They refused but Lance did it so carefully that there was no trail. Rollo didn't know how to approach him without stoking a fire.

The barking German shepherd dashed forwards on the sand. It growled at the head of the whale, sniffing and nipping, as the gigantic creature moved in the waves.

'Get that bloody dog out of here,' Owen shouted.

The whale stank to high heaven. With the warmth of the sun, the open wounds, and the sludge of the sea, his body had turned into one stinking mess of potent gases. The vast belly could explode at any moment.

Hank Hoxton stood near the rocks speaking with the guy from Fisheries. Both wore disposable face masks.

'Don't go near it unless you're wearing protective gear,' Hank warned them.

Together, the men outlined a plan to drag the whale onto the sand, cut open the carcass to release the gases, then divide it into pieces, crane them onto trucks and take them to the tip.

'Jesus, that's gonna be fun,' Rollo said.

Nereus, old man of the sea, *Megaptera novaeangliae*, killed by a freighter, dismembered by sharks, sawn up by humans and discarded in the local dump. What an end for this majestic creature. The whale lay on his side, one pectoral fin waving in the air as a final farewell. Most of the dorsal fin had been ripped off. Close up, the tubercles on Nereus's head were bigger than Rollo expected, bumps larger than his fists; no-one understood the purpose of these oversized hair follicles.

'Any marine biologists want to come and look at him?' he asked. 'Could be of scientific interest?'

Hank shook his head. 'I sent them photos. They said it's too decomposed.'

'What about the lice?'

Pale pink star-like creatures clustered around the blowhole and barnacles. Researchers were studying these tiny crustaceans to find out more about whale movements and their interactions with other species.

'We haven't had any requests for the lice.'

The white throat grooves—the ventral pleats which expanded to feed—had chunks torn out of them. They were now stained a rusty red colour, blood. Rollo had never seen a whale in this state before. If his old boss Gary were here, he'd be praying over the carcass and contacting an Elder to hold some kind of ceremony. Rollo hadn't paid much attention to Gary's practices back then, but maybe it was the right thing to do. Should he ring Caroline Poole and ask her to speak to Aunty Bim? Or should he simply stand up for what he believed in himself? Like his brave daughter. His brave, truth-telling, troublemaking daughter.

Staring at the whale, Rollo felt the heaviness of death around him. Just fifteen kilometres from here, the bones of three men had been found. So far, there had been no ceremonies for any of the dead.

Rollo cleared his throat. 'Hank, we should ring the Aboriginal Land Council. They've got that new sea country custodians' program.'

'Shit, I completely forgot about that. Yep, you're right. I'll call them.'

It wasn't the response he'd expected; Rollo lifted his shoulders, stood taller and nodded briefly at the carcass. *You'll get a good farewell, Nereus my friend.* The whale was a totem to some groups around the bay, so the Elders would conduct a proper cultural ceremony over the animal.

He'd promised the twins a photo. He pulled out his phone and took a close-up of the pink lice; that seemed the least distressing part.

An elbow in his side made him look up. Owen was frowning at him. 'We need to talk.'

Rollo followed his mate as he leapt across the jagged rocks, sure-footed in his rubber thongs. Owen crouched down suddenly by a deep rockpool. A small octopus floated along the bottom. Brown with blue markings on its body and legs. A deadly blue-ring.

Rollo spoke first. 'Lance took my dog. He tried to pin the blame on you.'

'That prick! He's still doing it—bullying us however he can.' Owen shook his head. 'I owe him money.'

'Aw, Jesus. Why'd you borrow from him?'

'I was desperate, mate.'

It put Owen right back into his high school role as Lance's dogsbody. Lance would've delivered his loan with enough humiliation to make Owen feel like a no-good, worthless piece of shit. And now he was causing trouble with the dog. Just another reminder for the Wrecking Crew to keep the pact.

'I guess you heard about Glenda,' Rollo mumbled.

'Yeah, the news nearly killed her. And it's killing me too.' Owen balled his fists. 'I really thought Blake had run away to the Cross. Thought he'd come back one day.'

'Me too.' Although Rollo wasn't so sure.

'Now he never will.'

Owen seemed to have tears in his eyes, something Rollo had never seen before.

'And it's all your fault,' he said, blinking furiously.

Rollo went completely still. 'Why?'

'You know what you did.'

Slumping down to avoid Owen's glare, he traced the ridges of the scar on his leg. A memory came to him. Droplets of blood, the same rusty colour as the grooves on the whale's throat, oozing down the blade of a knife.

'What about Lance and Derek? You should be blaming them.'

With that parting shot, he stood up and left Owen at the rockpool. After all these years, after all he'd done for his mate, Owen still blamed him. Deep down, Rollo knew the score: it was a mistake he could never fix.

Striding through the trees back to the small clearing, he spotted a police four-wheel drive parked behind his HiLux, blocking him in. An officer climbed out of the driver's side. Wes Terry, the young constable.

'The chief inspector was wondering if you could come in for a chat,' Terry said.

'Sure.' His mouth was suddenly dry and he swallowed before speaking again. 'About what?'

'Your old school friend, Blake O'Riordan.'

Oh fuck. Who had started talking?

When Poole showed him a photo of the backpack, Rollo put his hands over his mouth. Realising that might make him look suspicious, he moved them to the top of the table. Then he saw his fingers were shaking and put his hands in his lap, out of Poole's sight.

'Is this your backpack?' the chief inspector asked.

'Dunno. Might be. We all had the same type.'

'If it is yours, why would it be in the forest, near the cave?'

'We used to have parties out there.' Rollo shrugged, attempting nonchalance. 'We carried booze in our backpacks.'

'And do you recall the last night you partied out there with Blake?'

For years, Rollo had tried so hard. To be a good husband, good father, mate, employer. And now here he was in this fucking interview room. Which bastard had dobbed him in? Was it Owen or Lance or Derek? All three would love to get their hands on the reward money.

It was definitely Rollo's fault how the party blew up. The Saturday night before, they'd been on Main Beach, Blake chugging back the beers, and they'd almost finished all their grog. Derek and Lance went off to lift a few bottles of vodka and rum from the bowling club; they took Owen as bag carrier and lookout.

On the beach without the others, Rollo imagined curling up there with Joanne Keane. She was on his mind constantly.

'I really like this girl,' he'd told Blake.

'Who?'

He was drunk enough to share his secret but not so drunk he'd name her. The crew would start hassling Joanne Keane at school. He couldn't even say that she surfed because they'd guess straight away. Joanne—stylish surfer, very cool and super smart. She'd be dux next year. Too nice a girl to look twice at Rollo, especially when he was hanging around with the deviant twins.

'I can't stop thinking about her, but she'd never go out with someone like me.' He gulped a mouthful of beer, suddenly melancholic. 'Forbidden love, that's what it is.'

'Nah, mate, that's not forbidden love.' Blake dropped his voice to a whisper. 'I'm gonna tell you a secret. But you gotta keep your mouth shut.'

That's not forbidden love . . . Keep your mouth shut. Rollo was so sick of the twins and Lance telling him what to do. All he wanted was to smoke and surf and ask Joanne Keane out on a surfing date.

'Who's your forbidden love, then?'

'It's not about one person . . .' Blake started. 'More about . . .'

God, Blake was so drunk that he couldn't even string a sentence together.

'Spit it out, mate.'

'I don't like girls. I reckon I prefer . . .'

Rollo choked, and the beer spurted up into his nose. He had to cough and blow and spit to get his breath back. That was one pretty big secret. Bigger than Rollo liking Joanne Keane.

Fuck . . . Derek wouldn't want a gay man in his crew, a gay brother in his house. Look what he'd done to Max Gupta.

'Don't tell no-one.' Blake's words came in a big rush. 'I don't wanna be gay. I'm just telling you 'cos I know you'll understand.'

But he hadn't understood. Why had Blake shared the secret with him, not Owen? They were closer. Did Blake think he was the most sensitive one in the gang? That the others would've reacted by teasing him and beating him up?

And then Rollo made his mistake. A few nights later, puffing on a joint, he got the giggles, thought it hilarious that one of the hardass twins could be gay. Especially after what they'd done to Mr Durham: spreading rumours about him having sex with a male student; writing graffiti about it in the toilets; spray-painting words on his car. Rollo couldn't keep his mouth shut. Laughing so much that he could barely get the words out, he told Derek. *It's so funny that your twin brother is gay.*

Owen was right: it was his fault that Blake had died.

He tuned in to hear Poole rephrasing his last question: 'Were you at a party in the cave on Friday the fourteenth of August? Was that the last time you saw Blake alive?'

He stared at the grey wall behind the inspector's head as if he might find the answer there. Which one of the old Wrecking Crew had broken the pact?

42

Student: Taj Britton
Year 9 English, Mr Durham
Assignment: Speech on a non-fiction topic

Predators of the humpback whale
As one of the largest animals on earth, the humpback has few predators. Humans, of course, are the deadliest. We almost hunted these whales to extinction. It's estimated that by 1966, humans had killed 90 per cent of the population.

Natural predators include killer whales, also known as orcas, and tiger sharks. With their razor-sharp teeth, these animals are fast and vicious. They attack in packs, ganging up on the youngest or weakest whales.

Sharks and orcas are strategic—they sink their teeth into the whale's dorsal fin and roll it over. Their aim is to keep the blowhole underwater, to stop the whale from breathing and drown it. Other strategies include severing the arteries to the tail so the whale cannot swim.

Humpbacks retaliate against their attackers. They use their huge knobbly flippers to dislodge predators; the flippers are covered in barnacles that can rip into the shark's flesh. Another evasive tactic is to go deep. Unlike sharks and orcas, humpbacks can dive down two hundred metres and hold their breath for half an hour.

They can hide silently, in the depths, waiting.

43

MERI

EVERY NIGHT FOR THE PAST WEEK, MERI HAD GONE TO SLEEP WITH the same thought running through her mind: *I'll speak to the chief inspector tomorrow.* And every day, she'd found some excuse to avoid entering the station. As she stared at the ceiling yet again, with another day past, she struggled to understand her inaction—was it about hurting Glenda? Or implicating her father? Or the shame of having to admit it? The secret had been buried so deep, for so long, that she couldn't let it out.

On Tuesday morning as she sat down at her desk, Meri made herself a promise: *I will do it today.* One excuse had been her workload. Not only was she busy writing stories on the dead men, she was also battling with Neville to run them. The current situation did not fit well with his good news philosophy. Sighing, she opened her inbox and read the top email.

I hope you don't mind me writing to you after all this time. I saw the news about Blake and I couldn't believe it.

Scanning to the bottom of the page, she found a name. Kristie. After so many years, her old school friend had got back in touch. Holding a hand over her heart, Meri kept reading.

Did you know that I moved to the other side of the country to get away from those memories? And then there was Blake's photo, on the television. When I started crying, my husband asked what was wrong. I've never told him anything. Please can you give me a call and tell me what's happening?

I'm so, so sorry I didn't come to your mum's funeral. I couldn't face returning to that place. I'm sorry I dropped out of contact. Let's talk soon.

I've missed you. Love Kristie xx

Kristie had written two phone numbers—her mobile and her home number. The area code was Perth. She'd gone as far away from Kinton Bay as she could, without leaving Australia.

Sidestepping the locals who wanted to gossip and ask her questions, Meri raced down Dolphin Street to Sandy Cafe, where Caroline sat at a table by the window, already drinking a coffee. Shit, Meri was the one who had arranged this meeting.

'Sorry I'm late,' she panted.

'Don't apologise. I'm early.' Caroline smiled, looking up from a report she'd been reading.

Meri never arrived anywhere early. Too busy juggling work and family. She ordered a coffee and sat down.

On the table was a report titled *Why Killers Kill*. Some light reading there. Was Caroline helping her husband? Officially, this interview related to Proclamation Day, but everyone was talking about the forest.

'How's your husband doing?' she asked. 'He must be hectic.'

'I've barely seen him for two weeks.' Caroline sighed. 'He's not getting much sleep.'

'And do you know how the investigation is going?'

'They're checking the old file notes. Re-interviewing key witnesses. It's so hard, though. No-one remembers much after all this time.'

The waitress placed the coffee down and Meri waited for her to leave. She wasn't sure how to approach this conversation—she always felt slightly intimidated by the criminology professor.

Caroline leaned forwards and said, 'So, what exactly do you want to ask me?'

Stalling, Meri took a big sip from her cup and scalded her tongue. 'Sorry, I'm usually more organised. Can we talk about the case first, then Proclamation Day?'

'You keep apologising for no reason.' Caroline smiled. 'We women are constantly apologising for things that aren't our fault. You don't hear men doing that. It's like we have to apologise for just being ourselves. Well, I'm on a mission to stop it.'

Meri had never thought about how many times she said 'sorry' during a day. To appease and calm other people. To avoid an argument with Rollo. To justify a decision to the kids. To get through a crowded supermarket aisle. To convince Neville to run a story. To encourage the waitress to hurry up. Caroline was right—most of the time, it *wasn't* her fault.

'Sounds like a good mission,' she said. 'I'm on board.'

'Great. So let's get down to business. This is all background information and off the record, of course.' Caroline rested her elbows on the table and stared intently at her. 'Obviously, I can't speak about the investigation, but I can talk to you about my specialty, criminal profiling. It's likely that one person was responsible for all three deaths. The probability of unrelated remains being found in the same location is very small.'

'And this is what the police think?' As soon as she'd asked the question, she regretted it. Caroline's lips turned down, as if Meri were a student in a lecture hall who'd given a disappointing answer.

'I'm not speaking for the police. I'm talking to you as an associate professor of forensic criminology.' Caroline sat up even straighter. 'I've created a profile of the possible killer.'

Would Meri recognise the person she described?

'Three male victims is unusual,' Caroline continued. 'In most cases, we see multiple female victims. Usually the result of a sex crime. Obviously here the police only have bones, so they can't determine if there is a sexual element, but I think there must be.'

'Uh-huh.' She wrote *sexual element* in her notebook, fingers shaking as she gripped the pen.

'My theory is that the killer feels threatened or disgusted by gay men and that these murders are actually gay hate crimes.'

'Right . . .' She tried to keep her expression neutral, but her mind was racing. This theory reinforced Glenda's claim that Blake was gay.

'I think the men all had homosexual relationships or they were flirtatious with other guys. This set the killer off.'

'How do you know they were gay?'

'Some of the old interviews refer to it in an oblique way. But I feel their friends didn't want to tell the police. You know Greyson Creighton was engaged?'

Meri nodded.

'I've studied gay hate crimes in Sydney in the eighties and early nineties. A number of those murders were by gangs of young men. None of them happened quite as late as 1998, but sometimes things trickle through more slowly to the regional areas.' Caroline spoke as if she were discussing the latest trends in clothing . . . not murder.

'People are certainly more homophobic here than in the city.' At uni, no-one had even blinked at Adam strutting into class in a cut-off t-shirt, ripped denim shorts, eyeliner, necklace and diamond studs; Meri couldn't imagine that in Kinton Bay.

'I'm working on a full profile to give to the police. I expect they'll share it with the media.'

Meri took a sip of her coffee, not so hot now. 'How old do you think the killer or killers would've been?'

'Early twenties. Maybe even younger. They'd need to be fit and strong to hide the bodies.'

Did the Wrecking Crew kill Blake because he was gay? And then Greyson, a male nurse, and Stefan, a traveller who enjoyed language and culture—outsiders, much more sensitive than the men who'd grown up in Kinton Bay? The local gang may have felt threatened by these different types of men.

Meri's phone beeped with a text message. Apologising for the interruption—oops, she'd said she wasn't going to do that anymore—she checked the message. It was from Rollo.

I'm at the station. They're questioning me about Blake. Sorry I can't get bread for lunch. Can you?

Were they questioning him as a witness? Or as a suspect? Rollo still hadn't satisfactorily explained where he'd been that Wednesday when Blake's death was announced. He claimed he was checking the hulls using scuba gear, but his eyes were bloodshot and he smelt like dope. After all this time, had he started using again? With him in that state, she hadn't mentioned Glenda's warnings about Lance. And this morning Taj had refused to go to school again—no stomach ache but sore joints and a sore head. Meri had been wondering about anxiety, but now she had another thought. What if her son was following in his father's footsteps? Catching up on sleep after a big night sneaking out and smoking pot? Or staying home from school to smoke by himself? Rollo had admitted it was what he used to do. Had he done other things with the gang in those teenage years? Meri didn't want to know.

She could feel Caroline watching her. What would this intimidating woman do if she suspected her husband of lying, smoking pot and god knows what else? Ridiculous question. Douglas Poole was a fine, upstanding policeman. Caroline would never have married a man like Rollo. She had much better instincts.

'Everything all right?' Caroline's brow creased in concern.

'Yes, thanks.' She took a deep breath and asked her next question. 'Do you think the murderer is a local?'

'Definitely local at the time of the killings.' Caroline lifted her coffee cup. 'He might have moved away afterwards. We need to ask why there were only three murders. Did the person take a job elsewhere and continue offending in another town? Did they go to prison for a different crime? Did they die? Get married?'

Meri stared at the words she'd just written on her notepad: *job out of town—prison—married*. A few years after Stefan's disappearance, Lance was working in Newcastle, and Owen on a farm in Grafton. Derek had been sent to jail for the first time. And Meri and Rollo were walking down the aisle at St Paul's. The criminal profile could be describing every member of the Wrecking Crew.

44

I google Kinton Bay and pages of results come up. Even the papers in England are reporting it. I've made our town famous all over the world. The development committee won't be happy with this publicity, though. Definitely bad for business.

SUSPECTED SERIAL KILLER IN SEASIDE VILLAGE
Police believe the discovery of three sets of human remains in a sleepy seaside village in Australia points to the work of a serial killer. Statistically, the killer is likely to be male and he would have been in his early twenties at the time of the suspected murders in 1998.

Serial killer, yes, but unlike those famous American ones, I didn't kill for my own desire. The opposite. I was doing a good deed for others—ridding the world of degenerates.

Stefan must have tried it on in every town and city he visited across Australia. And then he was employed as a surfing instructor for high school sport. I saw how he helped the teenagers—a quick touch here, a smile and a smirk there, leaning close to whisper in their ears. His broad grin concealing his true motives. I saw how he spotted a target and zeroed in.

In the days after he went missing, a caller rang the police to say the Swiss backpacker had been swimming at midnight near Grotto Rocks. That witness was me. Just like the witness in Blake's disappearance. 'He's in Kings Cross. He wants his mum to know that he's okay.' Me, ringing the police from a public phone booth.

Three scumbags in a forest, dead as a result of their immoral behaviour. If it wasn't for the storm and Siena's 'research' out there, this could have stayed buried forever.

But the police don't know much.

I just have to stay smarter than them.

45

SIENA

AT LUNCHTIME, SIENA OPENED THE PHOTO THAT DAD HAD SENT HER: a close-up of the pink lice on the side of the dead whale. Hopefully she would be able to get there later, after the interview. The ABC app had a video about the murders; it included aerial shots of the national park with tiny white dots moving around, the search team near the cave. Mum had told her to stay away from the forest, by order of Detective Chief Inspector Poole.

On the other side of the quad, Kyle slammed a ball into the basket. When the game finished, she showed him the video. He rested his chin on top of her head to watch it, wrapping his arms around her waist. They'd given up trying to be discreet.

'Look at all the police resources they're putting into it,' Kyle snorted. 'Teams of police from Sydney, a task force, a public hotline. And here we are with three dead families and they don't want to know.'

'Maybe they'll find some of the bones when they're searching.' Siena turned around to hug him.

'They'll probably bury them again, like the property developers back in the nineteen-seventies. Gran said that's what they did all over Australia. Old gravesites complicate everything and no-one wants to deal with the implications.'

'But they'd have to investigate if they found something,' Siena insisted.

'Haven't you learned by now?' Kyle rolled his eyes. 'There's one rule for whitefellas, another rule for us.'

'I've got that interview lined up after school with *The Top Story*. Everyone watches that show. Let's make them listen.'

He shook his head and stepped backwards, releasing her. 'Mum and Dad don't want me on TV. They don't like that show and they've had some threats. Dad's worried he'll lose his job.'

Standing in front of the statue near Main Beach, Siena squinted into the camera lens. Before the other interviews, she'd felt confident with Kyle by her side. Alone, she had butterflies in her tummy. And Mum would be furious. Again. Should she call it off?

'Siena, are you ready?' the interviewer asked. Fleur Lloyd was dressed in a black wind jacket, even though it wasn't windy and no rain was forecast. Siena had noticed that reporters always wore wind jackets when broadcasting bad news from regional areas, not just during storms and cyclones.

She glanced at the bronze statue—Geoffrey Kinton shone in the sunshine. Bastard. No-one would guess he'd been daubed in paint two weeks ago. A cover-up by the mayor this time. Siena rubbed her tummy and took a deep breath. Even though it was melodramatic reporting, *The Top Story* was one of the most popular news shows across Australia. Right. She had to do this—tell the story, get the true history out there, and make Kyle and Aunty Bim proud.

The interviewer began with the same questions as the other reporters. 'How did you feel about finding the skull? Was it a shock? Could you imagine it would lead to the discovery of two more bodies and the search for a serial killer?'

'A terrible shock. I've been having nightmares. I feel so bad for their families.' Siena knew from doing media studies that it was a good idea to give them what they wanted before moving on to your own agenda. 'Some people say the Killing Cave is haunted. That's not true, but our town *was* born in bad blood. Blood spilled by the town founder, Geoffrey Kinton.'

'Born in bad blood.' Fleur repeated the phrase breathlessly. This TV show relied on scandal and crime for its ratings.

'It's a very sad story.' Fleur arranged her face in an expression of concern. 'But it happened almost two hundred years ago. What does it have to do with the dead men in the forest today?'

Siena delivered the speech she'd prepared. 'Maybe our town isn't haunted but cursed. Cursed until we change its name from Kinton. Until this town is honest and acknowledges Geoffrey Kinton's crimes.' She pointed to the statue behind them. 'We know the identity of the murderer. We honour him every day. But there's no police task force for the families he killed. No justice for them.'

Fleur was trying to interrupt her. Would they just cut what she'd said about the massacre? No-one wanted to listen: it made them feel bad. Dad and the development committee wouldn't be happy either.

'And what about justice for the men whose bodies were found in the national park?' Fleur got her question in. 'A serial killer has been operating in Kinton Bay. Do you feel safe living here now, Siena?'

Oh shit, she hadn't role-played that question with Kyle. Of course she didn't feel safe—not with guys like Axel and Jackson around. And Kyle's answer would've been the same but for a different reason: *How can I ever feel safe? Blackfellas are fifteen times more likely to be jailed than other Aussies.* But if she implied that Kinton Bay wasn't safe, Dad would blame her for destroying the town single-handedly.

'I've . . . um . . . lived here all my life. My parents grew up here.' She bit her lip. Quick, quick, what to say? 'I love Kinton Bay. It's a beautiful place. But we need to understand that our town has been founded on violence. Like so many other towns across Australia.'

Fleur nodded but raised her eyebrows slightly. She was about to change the subject back to the more recent case, so Siena rushed on, repeating something Aunty Bim had said.

'There's a Great Silence. Australia has amnesia about its past.'

⌒

Pirate was standing by the back door, wagging his tail, welcoming her home after the interview. Siena dropped to her knees and hugged him. He reached a paw up to her shoulder and his claws caught in her hair. She could probably start wearing it in plaits again now; the bruises had healed. Hayley's Insta posts were still all about Axel. *Where was he?* Siena hadn't told anyone about the rock, not even Taj. Her brother never seemed to be around lately, and when he was home, he stayed in his bedroom.

'Taj, are you here?' She walked down to his room with Pirate shadowing her, expecting him to be under the doona, just like this morning when he'd been too sick to go to school. But he wasn't in bed, nor anywhere in the house. She clicked on the location app—it occasionally came in useful when she wanted to track her brother—but Taj had switched it off again.

Where are you? she texted.

Taking advantage of the empty house, she pulled out Mum's diary from its hiding spot. Did Mum have any insights about Blake's disappearance at the time? Flicking through the pages dated September 1998, Siena spotted his name in the middle of a paragraph.

Inspector Nelson was at assembly today, talking about Blake. He said Blake has run away. 'Blake isn't in trouble but his mum's worried and wants to check that he's okay. If anyone knows anything, come and talk to the police.'

Blake's mum was on stage too, but Derek sat in the back row with his gang. When I looked at him, Derek was punching Lance in the arm. With Blake gone, Derek has been strutting around like he's king of the school. My knees start shaking whenever I see him. Yesterday at lunch, I ran in the other direction. I'll never tell anyone what Blake said. Especially not Inspector Nelson. Dad is the only person I'd speak to but he's not here. I wish he was. I need him.

Siena went back several pages, searching for the day Blake went missing. What would Mum never tell the police?

Friday, 14th August 1998
We got our short stories back today. Mr Durham gave mine 17/20 and said 'It conjures up a fascinating, imaginative

world.' Loretta had to take her story to Mr Quinn because it mentioned rape but she wouldn't tell the principal anything. No point now that Miss Wilcox isn't here to help anymore.

Nathan is finally on his P plates so he drove us into town for dinner at the Chinese. Mum put on a happy face but she was cross because Dad had to work at the club and couldn't come. I had fried spring rolls, Mongolian lamb and deep-fried ice-cream. I bet I get pimples from the fried stuff.

While Blake was being killed, Mum was eating Chinese and worrying about acne. Siena read all of the previous week's entries to see if there'd been a conversation with Blake. Nope, nothing about him. She went back another week. Nothing there either.

Pirate yawned and flopped his head onto her leg. Siena yawned too. Mum's diary was mostly full of boring stuff about homework, friends and what she ate for dinner. Mum was so naïve. Not a word about the big issues of the day—the first National Sorry Day, the rise of Pauline Hanson and her One Nation party, uranium mining approved at Jabiluka. That was why the world had got into such a mess: Mum's generation had allowed racism and capitalism to rise while they worried about their outfits and their pimples. Did her grandfather protest the big issues in the seventies? Mum wouldn't talk about him. A great silence in her own family.

Maybe Siena could get her own answers. On her phone, she googled 'Peter Carmody, Perth' and a match appeared—it must be the right one, he was Facebook friends with Uncle Nathan. Before she could overthink it, Siena typed a message and pressed send.

Hi Peter, this is your granddaughter, Siena from Kinton Bay.
I follow a few environmental causes and I wondered if you
were in any protests when you were young? I'm doing a school
assignment about how protest can change the world. By the
way, you might have seen Kinton Bay in the news. Mum sends
her love.

She shouldn't have written that last sentence. From the
photos in the album, Siena knew that her grandfather hadn't
been at Mum's wedding. One time at the farm, she'd overheard
Uncle Nathan arguing with Mum. He'd said, 'You should've
let our father come to the funeral.'

Harsh. Mum had banned him from her wedding and Granny's
funeral, and refused to see him in two decades.

Siena planned to find out why.

46

POOLE

ROLLO BRITTON PUT HIS HANDS OVER HIS MOUTH, TUGGED AT AN EAR, scratched his calf, raked his fingers through his shoulder-length hair. Definitely uncomfortable in the interview room. Absolutely not telling the truth. *Opportunity, capability, motive* . . . He'd had the opportunity and the capability—did he have a motive for murder?

Poole eyeballed him. 'Do you know how Blake died?'

'No.' Rollo's tanned face had lost a few shades of colour. 'The last time I saw him, Blake was fine.'

'That was on Friday night at the cave, correct? When the police spoke to you back then, you said you'd last seen him at school earlier that day. Why?'

Scratching at his lower leg again, Rollo seemed to weigh up his options. 'Derek. He made us swear an oath.'

'And did you always do what Derek said?'

'He had a knife.' Rollo sucked in a breath. 'He'd cut you if you didn't.'

'There's no point protecting your old mates.' Poole smiled encouragingly. 'Especially not Derek. In fact, one of your old gang has already spoken to us.'

Rollo shut his eyes briefly. 'Which of those bastards is trying to set me up?'

The anonymous call had been made from the town's public phone box near the pub. That only ruled out Derek. But as the caller clearly wanted the reward, he'd need to identify himself at some stage.

'Why would someone want to frame you?'

'To protect their own arses. Let's start with Lance. He stole my dog. Threatened me, threatened my daughter. I'd reckon he has something to hide, wouldn't you?'

'And Owen?'

'He's got a temper, but Blake was his best friend. If Owen wanted to kill anyone, it'd be me. Thinks I betrayed my mate.'

'By killing Blake?'

'No, I didn't kill him.' Rollo clenched his jaw. 'I told them Blake was gay.'

'And that was a problem?'

'A big problem for Derek. Not his idea of a real man.'

Poole looked down at his notes, considering this new information. Caroline had floated the theory of a homophobic killer, and the detectives were looking into it. And now, one piece of the puzzle had slotted into place. But perhaps the men were murdered for different reasons—the anonymous caller had claimed that Greyson was killed over drugs. Did that indicate more than one perpetrator and more than one motive? Rollo *and* Derek?

A knock interrupted his train of thought. Frawley was at the door to deliver some information.

With all the media in town, this news would travel fast, so Poole decided to inform Rollo. After all, they were family friends.

'We'll finish up now, but I'd like to continue our discussion on Thursday. Please don't leave town without letting me know.' And then he broke the sad news. 'I'm sorry to tell you that Glenda O'Riordan had a bleed on the brain. They tried to save her but there was nothing they could do. She died a few hours ago.'

⌒

For years, Glenda had been coming into the station and asking for Blake's case to be 'properly investigated'. Poole's predecessors assumed the teenager had run away. When he'd first read Blake's file, Poole had felt that Nelson was lazy or incompetent or both. However, the anonymous caller implied that the inspector had been running a drug racket. Did Nelson half-heartedly investigate the disappearances of the missing men, worried it would draw attention to his own misconduct?

Officers using police powers for their own ends were the lowest of the low. Poole wanted to know if Nelson was living in the Greek Islands courtesy of protection money, backhanders and bribes. He'd ask his team to look into Nelson and speak with the Professional Standards Command. In his last role, he'd sent an officer to jail—he wasn't afraid of stirring up trouble again.

And that meant Poole had to ensure his own behaviour was exemplary and followed the CYA procedure: Cover Your Arse. *Write down everything, explain all your decisions, dot every i, cross every t.*

Yuki Lavigne had been into the station again yesterday, asking if Fabian's remains could possibly be in the forest as well. Poole reassured her that the search team had found nothing. His team had worked hard on Fabian's case, covered off numerous angles and followed up the threatening letters. They'd checked CCTV, bank accounts, his personal and business contacts. Despite not discovering any leads, they'd been thorough.

But what about Axel Evans—had the team done as much as they could there? None of Axel's friends had come forward with new information, and Jackson McCormack was refusing to speak to the police. Yesterday afternoon, though, Poole had chatted with Hayley Shuttlewood again and she'd finally provided Axel's number. 'I'm scared that his body is going to turn up in the forest,' she'd said, echoing Poole's own worry. When he called the mobile, it went to voicemail: *Send me a text. Don't leave a message. See ya.* Frawley was now requesting a data dump from the telco for the past three weeks. Hopefully it would reveal the young man's movements, and if he really was in Sydney. Poole suspected that Axel was involved in illegal activity and keeping a low profile.

He radioed Senior Constable Chan, who was on foot patrol with Wes Terry.

'Can you two drive out to Axel Evans's house?' he asked. 'Check in with his parents. And go back to the mechanics where he used to work.'

'Yes, sir. We can be there in about fifteen minutes.'

Missing young men. Too many of them. He opened up Blake O'Riordan's file and read Derek's 1998 statement again.

*My brother said he wants to get away from Kinton Bay.
School's shit. Mum's making us do the HSC but he just wants
to get a job and start living. I reckon he's gone to Kings Cross
in Sydney. That's what he used to talk about. A bag and some
clothes are missing from his cupboard.*

Derek had started the Kings Cross rumour.

*Last time I saw him was Friday arvo at school. I think he had
dates with girls on Friday and Saturday nights. I dunno if he
met up with them or not. He had lots of girls.*

Kings Cross. Lots of girls. Derek had been covering his tracks.
The next statement was from Anthony Durham. Back then,
he must've been just out of teaching college, not much older
than the senior students. At the time, he was regarded as one
of the last people to see Blake.

*I took Friday afternoon detention with eight students, including
Blake O'Riordan. He was on detention for being disrespectful
to the geography teacher. He's always rude to the young
teachers. Blake, Derek and Lance basically harassed the English
teacher, Frances Wilcox, to death. I blame those twins for her
suicide. They haven't stopped; now they're harassing me.*

The former detective, Rosalind Spencer, had mentioned
that teacher's name—Wilcox. She'd said Frances Wilcox had
known about the parties in the cave, and here was a claim that
the twins had bullied the woman to death. Time to speak with
Durham again.

~

As Poole sat down in the small lounge chair in the deputy principal's office, he sized him up. Shorter than him, younger, fifty-ish perhaps. Durham had a thick crop of grey hair, carefully styled and swept to one side. The red glasses gave him an inner-city look; he would've fitted perfectly into Surry Hills or Paddington.

'Thanks for seeing me so quickly.' Poole opened his notebook on his lap. 'As I said on the phone, I hoped we could chat about Blake and Derek O'Riordan. You taught them?'

'Yes, I taught English and I was their careers adviser. They weren't interested in either area.' Durham took off his glasses and began fiddling with them. 'Derek said he planned to be a career criminal. I guess he achieved that particular goal.'

Durham wasn't making a joke; bitterness emanated from him. He said the twins were always being accused of one thing or another. Most of it didn't stick.

'They were slippery,' he explained. 'They'd confuse people with the twin thing and say it was a case of mistaken identity. But then if the other twin was accused, he always had an alibi from one of their mates. Their little gang would do whatever Derek told them.'

This aligned with what Rollo had said earlier today—do what Derek commanded or face the threat of his knife.

'In your statement to the police in 1998, you mentioned a teacher called Frances Wilcox. Can you tell me about her?'

The last time they'd spoken, Durham had seemed nervous, fiddling with his glasses constantly. This time, he took them off and laid them on his desk; then he removed his jacket and hung it on the back of his chair. All very deliberate movements, done with a cold fury in his eyes.

'Frances Wilcox was a new graduate, first year out. An English teacher like me, she was enthusiastic and excited to be starting her career. We became good friends very quickly.' Durham stopped for a few moments, lost in a memory perhaps. 'At the end of term one, some girls came to her. They thought they'd been sexually assaulted at a party in the cave, but they couldn't recall much. It sounded like they'd been drugged.'

'And what happened? Did the police get involved?'

'Frances talked to our principal, Mr Quinn. He felt it was a case of *he said/she said* and it was difficult to understand what had actually occurred.' Durham shook his head. 'Then Frances talked to Inspector Nelson. He wouldn't listen either. I suspect that's because he was just as bad—blackmailing backpackers to have sex with him by taking their passports.'

'That's a serious allegation.' Poole frowned. 'Did you have evidence of this?'

'I heard him upstairs in the pub one night.' Durham snarled his disgust. 'I had to stay there for a week because they were putting new floorboards in my place. Two different girls came and went. The Brazilian asked for her passport back as she was leaving.'

It seemed more and more likely that Inspector Nelson had been running the town as his personal fiefdom. A drug racket, blackmail, kickbacks, and a sextortion scam too. Bloody hell. What a piece of work.

'Did anyone else know?' he asked.

'No. It wasn't common knowledge. The only person I told was Frances. She mentioned it to her best friend but no-one else. I couldn't report it.' Durham stared at him without blinking. 'I was the only openly gay guy in town. Inspector Nelson made it perfectly clear that he hated *pooftas*, as he called them. I couldn't risk being harassed by the cops as well. You see, the twins were harassing me. Then they started harassing Frances because she'd spoken up about the parties. Nelson let it happen.'

Poole swallowed his anger. No-one in town had been safe. 'What did the twins do to her?'

'All sorts of things. They spread a rumour that she was having an affair with the maths teacher. Ripped the side mirror off her car. Left a dead rat on her doorstep. Poured tomato sauce into her handbag. It went on and on.' Durham slapped the desk with his palm in time to these last words. 'When Frances complained to our principal, Quinn told her to toughen up. Implied she wasn't cut out to be a teacher.'

'And you think this harassment drove her to suicide?'

'Yes. On top of everything else. She cared for those girls and she couldn't help them—that really affected her. Her boyfriend dumped her on the night of her sister's wedding. And then the principal and the police dismissed her concerns. Frances felt she'd become invisible.'

'What happened afterwards?'

'Everyone called it a terrible tragedy and that was that.' Durham paused. 'The twins were never held to account. They kept harassing me; told everyone I was sleeping with a male student. Wrote homophobic slurs in the toilets. I think the parties continued and they just cycled through different groups of girls. Quinn left a few years later. He's dead now.'

It seemed that the twins had taken the authorities' silence as a chance to act with impunity.

'How did you feel when Blake went missing?'

'I'm not going to lie.' He sat straighter in his chair. 'I was relieved.'

Interesting that Durham would still admit this after the boy's bones had been found in the forest.

'Did you ever meet Stefan?'

'He worked for the surf school that took the kids for sport in summer.' Durham ran his fingers over his jaw for a moment. 'I talked to him each Wednesday about student numbers and safety.'

'And Greyson Creighton?'

'We were in a pub trivia team together for a few months, along with some other teachers and nurses.'

So Durham had known them all. 'Were either Greyson or Stefan interested in men?' Poole asked.

'I never got that vibe.' He patted his styled hair and put his red glasses back on.

'And did you ever see Inspector Nelson in the pub with Stefan or Greyson?'

'Nelson was in the pub all the time. He spoke to everyone. I think he had a finger in every pie.'

⌒

Settling behind his own desk, Poole considered Durham's comments about the man who'd previously sat in this chair. Inspector Nelson. He dialled the former detective, Rosalind Spencer.

'We've had an allegation that Nelson wasn't above board,' he started.

'Really?' She sounded shocked. 'He was always on at us about standards. I didn't see anything dodgy.'

'What about girls? Backpackers, in particular?' Poole explained the allegation.

Rosalind made a clicking noise and it was a short while before she spoke. 'He made sexist comments and ogled girls in bikinis on the beach. I guess that part is possible . . . I did find a woman's passport on his desk one day.'

She gave him the names of three other officers who had worked with Nelson. He'd ask the team to call them; either the inspector was above board or he'd covered his tracks well, apart from an errant passport.

Poole didn't know what to think. Durham and the anonymous caller had both labelled Nelson as corrupt. If he was a bad egg, had that contributed to the men's death and the investigation at the time? With Caroline's theory about a gay hate crime, Durham was lucky not to have been the fourth victim.

Unless Durham was the one covering his tracks—making up allegations about Nelson to deflect from his own crimes. He'd had the opportunity and capability for all three murders, but as yet, a motive only for Blake's. Had he killed Blake in a burst of rage, seeking revenge for the twins' bullying and teasing?

And where did Rollo and Derek fit in all of this? Poole would interview Derek again, armed with the new information. Opening Caroline's report, he reread the section on motivation.

The FBI Serial Murder Symposium found that the motives of a serial killer may be difficult to identify and may change over time. They suggested investigators consider the following broad categories: anger; criminal enterprise (drugs, gangs, organised crime); financial gain; ideology; power/thrill; psychosis; and sexually-based motivation.

Poole's thoughts kept ticking over, one theory and then another. With so little evidence, it was all guesswork at the moment. Another possibility flashed up: the gang had been planning a gay hate crime for Durham . . . and he'd turned the tables on them.

47

I see Greyson's parents on the news, crying.

Greyson Creighton. Engaged to a young woman and still picking up every weekend in Kinton Bay. With his sharp nose and round glasses, he wasn't good-looking but he had a charm and arrogance that made people listen to his stories. And Greyson bought round after round of drinks. Spirits. Dropped a roofie in one for an unsuspecting victim. By the end of each evening, his target was unable to resist.

After Blake's accidental death, I hadn't planned on another one. But then Greyson started boasting about Frances Wilcox.

'I'm going out with a bang,' Greyson said one night to a group after pub trivia. 'This time next year, I'll be married. I've got a week until I leave Kinton Bay and I'm partying every night. Who's joining me?'

A few people responded, but not enough for his liking.

'I can get whatever pills you want.' Greyson spread his arms wide. 'Ketamine. Valium. Rohypnol. Just name it and it's yours.'

'Bullshit!' someone called him out.

'You'd better believe it. I've been supplying everyone in town, from the kids to the teachers. Just ask Frances Wilcox. Well, you can't actually. The drugs did the job for her.'

Greyson Creighton, a nurse dedicated to saving lives, had sold the tablets that ended hers. And now he was bragging about it. That was the moment I decided to give him a taste of his own medicine. In preparation, I bought some roofies from him.

⌒

Two days later, I knew he was coming off night shift and made sure I bumped into him in the hospital carpark. Early Sunday morning—the rest of Kinton Bay wasn't yet awake.

'Do you want to come for a swim?' I asked.

'Yep. And let's party after. I'll get some beer and a few tabs.'

'Don't worry, I've got it sorted.' I smiled. 'And I know the best place. Bet you've never been there.'

We went for a swim at Wreck Beach and then I showed him the cave. He drank a vodka and orange in one quick gulp, never guessing it contained a lethal dose.

I led him to the back of the cave, ready for his collapse. Not so far to drag him; I'd learned something from Blake's death.

48

MERI

ALONG WITH HER THEORY ABOUT THE GAY HATE CRIMES, OVER COFFEE Caroline had given Meri a copy of the development application for the Blue Waters Panorama Residences. It named a big national company and Lance's Construction & Development as the main applicants for a new building opposite St Paul's. The supporting documents listed Neville and Kath Kinton as investors.

Bloody Neville. Telling Josephine to write those articles about the 'innovative design of an exciting new luxury holiday precinct that will bring visitors to our town'. All with no disclosure of his own financial interest. Nothing like positive press to help council vote in favour of *his* development application. While she'd grown accustomed to Neville's good news mantra, Meri couldn't accept his flagrant breach of journalistic ethics.

After checking that he wasn't in the office, she printed out all the articles they'd run on the Blue Waters Residences over the past nine months. She placed them in a manila folder with a copy of the development application and supporting documents. Should she challenge him or go straight to senior management?

As she was weighing up each option, Neville struggled through the front door of the office with a takeaway coffee in one hand and a cake box in the other. After slipping the manila folder into her laptop satchel, she went to help him.

'I've got chocolate cake for afternoon tea,' he said. 'You've all been working so hard, I thought you might need a sugar fix.'

Normally, Meri or Josephine supplied the spontaneous cake. It had been months since Neville provided a treat.

'Thanks.' She took the box and followed him to the meeting room. 'I searched the database for your articles on the disappearance of Greyson Creighton. I only found one.'

'You should know better than to speak with me before I've had my afternoon coffee fix.' He grimaced and Meri realised that he hadn't yet done his usual cake pun.

'Sorry,' she said, then remembered her mission to stop apologising. 'Can you tell me where I can find the other articles and your notes?'

'We've changed systems three or four times since then. They've probably been lost.'

'Do you remember if there was any indication that Greyson might be gay?'

'Gay?' Neville sounded surprised. 'He was engaged to a woman.'

'Bisexual, then?'

'I don't know but he was a sleaze. He cracked on to Kath's little sister at the pub and she was only seventeen. Kath's dad wanted to punch his lights out.'

'Did you tell the police?' she asked. 'It might've been related.'

'Honestly, I can't believe you'd say that. Kath's father had nothing to do with Greyson's death.'

'Every little piece adds to the puzzle.' She flushed slightly. 'Can you think of anyone who had a link to all three men?'

'I'll get plates.' Neville strode towards the kitchen. 'I know you all like to have your cake and eat it too.'

Ah, there was the pun. As he was walking away, Meri noticed his shirt. The same one he'd worn a few weeks ago—the yellow polo with Lance's logo.

Neville never gave a straight answer about anything. There was no point trying to discuss his breach of ethics. She'd phone the editorial director in Sydney and send him the documents. Hopefully he would take more notice than the last time staff had made a complaint.

And she couldn't sit here and eat cake with him. Grabbing her satchel, Meri announced that she had to dash to the post office. She'd ring the editorial director, Bernard Emery, then send the documents by overnight express. On the street, away from the office, Meri pulled out her phone. But before she could dial, a text came through from Rollo. *I'm done at the police station. I need to talk to you urgently. I'll pick you up.*

⌒

After she'd climbed into the ute, Rollo drove them around the corner to the bowling club. Three o'clock in the afternoon and the carpark was empty. When he switched off the engine and told her about Glenda, she rested her head against the dashboard and wept. Her old friend had been a link to both of her parents, working first with Dad at the club and then in their house when Mum was sick. And she'd been the twins' surrogate grandmother.

I'm an orphan. The strange thought came to her. Both of her parents were only children—there were no uncles, aunts or cousins. *Your father is still alive,* Rollo would say if he could read her mind. But Glenda had been the one who'd helped them through Mum's sickness and death. She'd been more of a family member than her absent father.

Rollo rubbed her back and she scrabbled in her bag to find a tissue.

'I can't believe it,' he said. 'Just when they'd found Blake. And Derek's getting out in a few months. It's cruel timing.'

She blew her nose. 'At the hospital Glenda said: *Lance caused this.* He wanted Derek to stay away from Kinton Bay.'

'Why?'

'I think he's worried about what Derek knows.' She'd been trying to make sense of Glenda's disjointed words.

'About Blake?'

'No.' She blotted her tears with a fresh tissue. 'Glenda's first head injury occurred before Siena found the skull.'

'Fucking Lance.' Rollo thumped his hands against the steering wheel. 'I've gotta tell you a few more things. Just hear me out. Lance stole Pirate, hid him at Duke's house.'

'That jerk . . . Why didn't you say? I knew you were lying.'

'Sorry.' He shook his head. 'I didn't want to worry you. I got Pirate back—that was the most important thing. I thought Lance was angry about Siena's videos. But if he's threatened Glenda . . .'

Lance's dirty fingerprints were all over town. Meri knew one thing: she'd speak to Bernard Emery as a priority. Lance had just made it personal. She couldn't stand the thought of her paper helping that bastard make more money through shady deals.

Why the hell had Rollo kept that secret? She stared at her husband—he was picking at the skin around his thumbnail.

'What else haven't you told me?'

'Oh god, Meri. I'm in trouble.' He heaved a huge breath. 'I think Lance is trying to make it look as though I had something to do with the dead men. That's why Poole interviewed me. It's my backpack they found.'

Rollo's fear filled the cabin. She could feel it snaking inside her, multiplying and splitting off into new worries. Pushing down the guilt of doubting her own husband, she made herself turn to look him in the eye and ask the question: 'Rollo, *did* you have anything to do with it?'

He stared back at her, scared. 'I think I caused Blake's death.'

She wanted to get out of the ute and run. Hide under the manager's desk in the bowling club, like she had as a child. The small space beneath the dark heavy wood had been Meri's cocoon from the world. Sometimes, her father's hand would appear from above, offering a glass of lemonade. But that wasn't an option now.

'And I might be . . .' Rollo inhaled shakily in the silent car. 'I might be implicated in Greyson's death.'

Meri wrapped her arms tightly across her front as if she could deflect his words. He'd been acting so strangely since the identification of the remains, and this was why. She stared at his hands on the wheel—were they the hands of a murderer?

'The trouble is that I can't remember it all.' He touched her leg and she flinched. 'Maybe if we went back to the cave, it would help?'

She didn't want to go back there. Not with him. Not with anyone.

'Please,' he begged.

The father of her children. The man she'd slept beside for the past sixteen years. What had he done before that?

He took her silence as agreement, started the car and set off on the road towards Wreck Point.

⌣

The gate at the entrance to the national park was open. Blue and white police tape flapped along the sides of the trail.

The track had been flattened by the search team and their diggers, making it easy to follow. As they began walking, Meri shivered; she hadn't been back here since she was fifteen.

Those first parties on Wreck Beach had been fun. Meri and her friends were the youngest girls there; they stuck together by the campfire, watched and learned. Older couples would vanish into the dark, return later flushed and dishevelled. Kristie kissed her Year 12 crush; Meri shared a drink with a cute Year 10 boy; and Loretta eyed up Lance Nelson. 'He's so sexy,' she sighed.

By their third party, the girls were feeling comfortable. With the bravery of two Bacardi Breezers, Meri asked Lance if they really did have a list of virgins.

'Yep! And you three should be stoked that your names are on it.' Lance squeezed Loretta's thigh. 'It means you're sexy babes. Not ugly slags.'

Thankful for the darkness, Meri took another swig of her drink and hoped it would cool the heat in her cheeks. She'd never been called a 'sexy babe' before.

'Next time, come up to the cave. That's where we have the best parties. Secret parties. You girls will love it.' He grinned at them, then turned and winked at Derek.

Heady with the attention from these cool older guys, the following weekend the three girls had followed the Wrecking Crew from the safety of the beach party up to the cave.

Back then, Meri barely noticed Rollo—he'd been on the edge of the gang, always smoking, laughing, chilled, sometimes asleep. He didn't chat up girls, not in the same way as Lance and Derek. Could he really have been involved in Blake's death?

Now, Rollo held out a hand and pulled her up the last steps to the rock platform. The sandstone roof of the cave arched above her, the bright sunshine outside illuminating orange and golden walls. It felt like a horrible trick: the place of her worst nightmares revealed as a serene glowing haven. Running her fingers over the cool rock, Meri wandered further into the cave and found the evidence that matched her memories. Graffiti from all those years ago: *Kristie gives great head.*

She sank onto the floor, her back against the wall, her knees curled up. The earthy damp smell filled her nostrils and took her back to that night.

Wafting smoke, cigarettes and marijuana. The taste of vodka and orange—no bitterness to indicate another ingredient. The guys had been laughing and whispering to each other. Meri watched Lance pull Loretta into his lap and start kissing her. The light in the cave was strange. Meri's head felt heavy, dull. She'd been talking to Blake about the movie, *Titanic*. He wanted to see it.

'I must've drunk too much,' she slurred. 'This cave is tipping like the *Titanic*.' She leaned against his shoulder, closed her eyes to stop the spinning, must have fallen asleep. Then she woke with rough hands on her breasts, her boob tube around her neck, her skirt pushed up. The rocks scratching her back. She tried to focus, felt Blake on top of her. Couldn't think, couldn't move, couldn't act. And then it was all foggy again.

The next day, Loretta had freaked out about the blood on her underpants, the scratches on her thighs and her blank memory. Kristie recalled moments here and there—her head being pushed towards Derek's penis, stumbling over rocks in the dark, throwing up in someone's car. Their bodies were exhausted, their heads ached. This was no normal hangover.

The sick feeling in Meri's stomach wouldn't go away. This was all her fault. She'd asked about the virgin list, she'd laughed with Lance, she'd practically invited them to do it.

The girls had cried and hugged each other. When Monday came, they claimed they'd all caught gastro and stayed home. They decided to face school together on Wednesday. The Wrecking Crew were all smiles and winks. *It's the good-time girls*, they shouted across the quad. *When are you coming back to the cave for some more fun? You girls were ace!*

Rumours went around about the 'easy girls' who loved to party. Kristie, Loretta and Meri hid from the boys as much as they could, spending lunchtimes in the library or the toilets. They didn't plan to tell—it felt impossible when they couldn't even remember—but then Kristie's period was late.

Their parents would be furious that the girls had sneaked out to parties. Miss Wilcox had given the safe sex talk—she was young, she'd understand. They confided in her and she helped Kristie organise a trip to a clinic in Newcastle, even paid for some of it. And then she spoke to the principal and the police, without mentioning their names.

A week later, vile words were scrawled across her desk in the English room: *Wilcox, will our cocks fit in your mouth?* Telling the principal and the police had made everything worse.

And then, when Miss Wilcox died in the July school holidays, the girls were heartbroken. They decided the only way to survive in this school without her kindness was to block out that night. Pretend it never happened. The authorities obviously didn't believe their story; there was no point fighting it. Kristie started drinking more and eating less. Loretta kept her head in a book. And Meri began retreating to her room. She'd tried to tell Dad after Miss Wilcox died but he was never home, too busy, always changing the subject.

While Rollo had been part of the Wrecking Crew, Meri hadn't seen him that terrible night. In all their time together, she'd avoided this topic.

'Did you know about the rapes that happened here? The girls being drugged?'

'I was stoned and half asleep most of the time, but Derek always boasted about girls the next day.' Rollo rested both hands against the curved wall and pressed his forehead against them. 'For ages, I didn't realise Lance was slipping roofies in the girls' drinks. One night, they put the roofies in my backpack, so I threw it over the ledge. That's what the police found. But I should've done more.'

It was time to acknowledge it—to him, to herself. She'd never said the words aloud, they tasted like mud in her mouth.

'Blake raped me here when I was fifteen.'

Horror blanched his face. 'Oh god, no. Meri, I'm so sorry.' He crouched down, wrapped his arms around her. Rocked her to and fro. She could hear him sniffling.

'I never knew you came to a party up here.'

She stared at the grooves in the ceiling of the cave; felt the solidity of the rock underneath her, thousands and thousands of years old, and the strength of her husband's arms around her. Loyal Rollo, who'd stood by her when she wanted to go ahead with the pregnancy, and when her mum was dying.

'I'm going to write about it,' she said. 'If Neville won't publish it, I'll go above his head. Now that Glenda has gone, I can tell the truth about those boys—about Blake—without hurting her.'

'I'll do everything I can to help. I should've done more when I was younger.' Rollo gulped. 'Ask me anything, quote me in the paper, I'll talk to the police. Whatever's needed, I'll do it.'

'Thank you.' She had to believe in him. But first she needed the truth. 'Let's start now. Tell me about the last party with Blake. Why do you think you caused his death?'

49

ROLLO

ROLLO WANTED TO PUKE OFF THE EDGE OF THE ROCK PLATFORM. IT ALL made sense now: Meri's refusal to discuss the cave; using the location app to track the kids; her constant anxiety about Siena; her discussions with Taj on sexual consent. He'd assumed it was her father's desertion that had caused all of this.

But it was one of his mates. Fucking hell. And probably not the one she thought.

That party must've been when Rollo was in Townsville for a few weeks. Grandpa had broken his hip and wasn't getting better. The hospital had called to say he was dying, and Rollo's family set out on a three-day road trip. On his return, he didn't recall the gang boasting about young Meri Carmody and her friends. Later, they were harassing her, along with Miss Wilcox, but he never knew why.

If Blake hadn't disappeared, what might Rollo's life look like now? Would the gang have stayed together, with Derek and Lance manipulating them? Leading them into a life of crime. Those two thought they were untouchable with Lance's uncle in charge of the police station.

Thank god for Meri. His parents were right: without her, he never would have bought the boat or been able to run the business.

His wonderful, brave wife was waiting for him to tell the story of the last party.

'You know you asked me about Blake being gay,' he started slowly. 'He was. And I think that's what got him killed.'

'What do you mean?'

'Derek came up with a plan to stop his brother being gay.'

'Well, that's ridiculous and impossible,' Meri said.

If Rollo hadn't spilled his secret, would Blake still be alive?

⌒

A winter party, not cold but darker than usual. Thick cloud obscured the moon and the stars. Derek had taken his mum's car again without asking. Driven them out to the forest, with cases of beer, a bottle of Bundy and some roofies. There was a big party on Wreck Beach, a farewell for a guy in Year 12, but someone convinced a group of girls to come up to the cave. Tourists—Rollo didn't recognise any of them.

He'd already been smoking and was freaking out on the walk to the cave, jumping at shadows and strange rustling sounds in the bush. When they came to the rock platform, Derek, the shit, started to make ghost noises. Eerie cries that echoed around the cavern. The girls screeched in fear. Rollo felt a spiderweb on his face, batted at it with both hands, lost his balance, fell onto the ground and curled up in a ball.

'Look at the Stoned Loser,' Derek mocked. 'What a baby.'

As usual, Owen was carrying the beers and rum. 'Hurry up, Crater Face, we're dying of thirst.' Derek snatched the drinks from him and passed them around the girls. 'Crater Face is a virgin,' he told them. 'No-one wants to kiss a face like that.'

Later, when the roofies had taken effect, Derek made Blake observe as he did it with a girl from Sydney.

'Watch and learn. It's your turn next.'

'I know what to do, mate,' Blake said. 'But I reckon you're hurting her. Get off her, Derek.'

Rollo realised something—he'd seen Blake kiss a girl but nothing more.

Derek was on a mission, though. He finished with the girl, then got Muscle Man Scott to hold Blake while he stripped him. He and Scott forced him to walk around the cave naked, like a bull for sale.

'Look at this fine specimen.' They pushed him towards the girls. 'Who wouldn't want to have sex with this top root?'

'Leave me alone,' Blake complained.

'Nah, brother, this is your lucky night. Which girl do you want? Your choice.'

Blake hissed at Rollo, 'You fucker. You told him, didn't you?'

Ignoring his attempts to break free, Derek, Lance and Scott manhandled him into position on top of a girl with blonde hair. She was semi-conscious, her eyes closing and opening. One of her friends seemed to understand what was going on. As Derek made everyone slow-clap Blake, she said, 'I think Vicki is too out of it.'

Her comment emboldened Rollo. He'd fucked up by telling Derek, he had to stop this now.

'Derek, mate,' he drawled. 'Don't do this to him.'

'Keep your mouth shut, Stoned Loser.'

His head spun. The bodies in front of him—Blake furiously gritting his teeth, the blonde girl hardly moving—the gunshot sound of each clap, the screeches of owls in the trees, the rustle of possums, and Derek laughing, urging his brother on. All Rollo's fault, because he hadn't kept Blake's secret.

He stumbled forwards, trying to pull Blake free. But before he could get a grip on Blake's shoulder, Derek grabbed him by the back of his t-shirt and slammed him away, against the wall of rock.

'You're ruining the plan, Stoned Loser.'

When he saw the rip in his jeans, his first thought was that he'd landed on a jagged rock. He put his hand over the cut, but blood seeped through his fingers and dripped down onto his sandshoes. And then the pain kicked in.

'You stabbed me.'

Everything stopped. The others all turned to look at him.

'Shit. That's a lot of blood.' Owen spoke up for once. 'We need to take him to hospital. I can drive.'

As he limped to the mouth of the cave, Derek followed him, muttering, 'Keep your fucking mouth shut. Say you cut it on a rock.'

Derek, Lance and Scott all stayed behind at the Killing Cave with Blake and the girls. By Monday afternoon, with no sign of his brother, Derek had enforced a pact: the party never happened. None of them were to speak about the night again. If they did, they'd be knifed, same as Rollo. When the police questioned them about Blake's disappearance, they stuck to the story: the last time they'd seen Blake was on Friday afternoon. The tourist girls had left town by then. In any case, Inspector Nelson kept his enquiry low-key. Presumably he didn't want to draw attention to his own drug dealings with Lance and the twins.

Friggin' Derek. He'd always carried a blade. What had happened after Rollo went to hospital that night? If Derek could stab a mate, what might he have done to his gay brother?

As he told the story, Meri listened closely, frowning and asking questions.

'So that scar on your leg isn't from surfing? Derek stabbed you.'

'Yes.' He paused. 'At the time, I thought Blake got away. Escaped from his brother. But now I realise that they killed him that night.'

She nodded, gazing around the walls of the cave as if picturing the scene.

'Umm . . . I have my own confession.' Meri chose her words carefully. 'I should've spoken to the police . . . I was scared. '

He glanced at her in surprise.

Meri was struggling to speak. 'Blake didn't die on Friday night.'

50

MERI

THE TWO SECRETS SHE'D BEEN KEEPING FOR SO LONG WERE FINALLY out—and they both related to Blake.

'I saw him on Saturday morning. He was hiding inside the shed at the hockey field.' Meri let out a sob. 'I thought he was going to attack me again.'

'Fuuuck. Why didn't you ever tell me?' Rollo stared at her in disbelief. 'Or the police? They've been eyeing me as a suspect.'

She'd always prayed that her sighting wouldn't have made a difference; that Blake had run away and the exact timing didn't matter.

But, of course, if he never left Kinton Bay, if his death was suspicious, then timing was crucial.

'He asked for money and said he was running away.' Her breath came in short sharp bursts. 'When I went to scream for help, he put a hand over my mouth. He said that Derek would stab us both. And then he threatened . . .'

Meri could still see his furious expression; could still feel his cigarette fumes on her own face. All of it a flashback to that night in the cave. The fear was buried deep inside.

Rollo rubbed her back, encouraging her to finish.

'. . . Blake threatened to destroy my dad. If I didn't do what he said, they were going to steal some cash from the bowling club and set it up to make it look like Dad had taken it. According to Blake, Inspector Nelson would go along with it, accept a bribe and charge him. Nelson had done nothing to stop the twins before, so I believed him.'

'You were protecting your father.'

Protecting a father who didn't protect me.

'I thought that, even when Blake was gone, Derek would follow through on the threat.' She tried to explain her thinking from back then. 'I know it was crazy, but I was frightened and ashamed. Blake had drugged me and raped me and got away with it. And now he was threatening Dad. I couldn't tell anyone.'

She'd been bullied into keeping a secret for two decades. But where had Blake gone after the hockey sheds? Did he run into Derek and his knife?

Derek. The one who had taunted and threatened the whole town, including his brother. Forced him into committing sexual assault. Everything that Rollo had told her was reinforcing her suspicion.

'I've realised something after talking to Glenda and hearing your story about that last party.' She crossed her arms over her chest, as if protecting herself. 'It probably wasn't Blake who . . . I had a moment of relief over his death, but now . . . I think that my abuser is still alive.'

51

SIENA

GLENDA WAS GONE. CHEERY, CUDDLY, COLOURFUL GLENDA—HOW COULD she be dead? Yesterday, Siena had been writing her a get-well card when Mum arrived home to break the news. *Dead.* She kept saying the word in her head to make sense of it. Mum thought the funeral would be at St Paul's.

And today, they were attending a different kind of funeral. She and Taj had the morning off school for the ceremony. They'd been told to wear masks. Dad had warned them about the stench, but Siena had never smelt anything like it. She kept trying not to gag. The sight of the dead whale was just as distressing, up on the beach out of the cool water where he should have been. Buzzing with flies. Parts of him missing, ripped off by sharks.

Uncle Travis, an Elder from Harbours End, had come to do the ceremony; his saltwater people had a totemic connection to whales. Gathered on the small beach, not too close to the carcass, they listened to Uncle Travis singing. Kyle put his arm around her shoulders, and she nestled into him. He gave her a flower in memory of Glenda. 'It's a hellebore,' he whispered.

'A winter rose.' Touching the soft white petals, she thought of death—Glenda and the whale, the bones in the forest. Rose's family all those years ago.

Siena would just stay for the first part of the ceremony; the rest was private, for the saltwater people only. When Uncle Travis finished singing, she placed a palm frond on the sand and left the beach. She trailed behind Dad, Owen and Caroline Poole.

As they walked back to the car, Siena pulled off her mask, relieved to be away from the smell. She hadn't had time to talk to Kyle about yesterday's TV interview; she hoped that he'd be impressed with her when it aired tonight.

'Are you okay?' Caroline slowed to walk beside her. 'That stench is horrendous. Something to do with all the blubber. Out of the water, it's still insulating so the insides are being cooked like they're in an oven.'

'Ugh. That makes me feel even sicker.'

'Well, let's try for a better topic.' Caroline smiled. 'Did your dad tell you we've got council support for a memorial?'

'No—that's amazing!' Dad had been too distracted lately to tell her anything.

'There's still some negotiating to do, though. They don't want to use the word "massacre". But they've agreed to move Kinton's statue away from the middle of town.'

'Fantastic. Do you think they'll agree to change the name of Kinton Bay?'

'We'll try our hardest. It's tricky when half the town shares his surname.' Caroline put a hand on her shoulder. 'You helped set this in motion, Siena. You should be proud of yourself.'

A warm glow fizzed inside her. She hoped that she was just like Caroline when she grew up.

～

After school, Siena lay on her bed and opened her laptop. The TV channel had broadcast a trailer for tonight's show. The camera panned across Kinton Bay township, the forest and a random cave—not the actual cave. Photos flashed up one-by-one of Blake, Greyson and Stefan. The voiceover was deep and dramatic.

'Is this the village of the damned? One local girl believes an Aboriginal curse has been placed on the town in retribution for past atrocities. She says this curse has led to the murders of three young men.'

Oh no. That wasn't what she'd said.

No, no, no, no, no.

She'd been trying to point out the injustice and whitewashing of history. Shit, shit, shit. Now the other half of the town—the ones who had supported her—would turn against her too. And Aunty Bim and Kyle . . . they'd never speak to her again.

Siena sent Mum the link and then rang her at work.

'Everyone's going to hate me,' she sobbed. 'Watch the trailer.'

'No-one will hate you.' Mum went silent as she played the video; she remained silent after it had finished.

'See!' Her sobs came again. 'They will hate me.'

'Hmm. Some reporters selectively edit their interviews to sensationalise—'

'I know how it works,' Siena interrupted. 'I just didn't think I was saying stuff that could be edited and twisted.'

'They shouldn't have interviewed you without me there.'

'Please, Mum, not that again.' When would she stop treating her like a child?

'Siena, I've been working as a journalist for nearly twenty years.' She could hear the anger in Mum's voice. 'If you'd bothered to tell me that you were talking to this trashy program, I could've given you some tips.'

'You're still angry I didn't ring you when we found the skull,' Siena lashed out. 'Your dumb newspaper wouldn't have printed the story anyway—they wouldn't be able to spin it into a positive, upbeat article to keep the advertisers happy.'

'You're upset, but there's no need to be rude.' Mum sighed. 'I think we need to make a complaint to the station. But, please, Siena, you shouldn't be talking about these issues without Aunty Bim.'

'Oh god. I didn't mean to say the wrong thing.' She felt numb. So much for getting the point across and impressing Kyle and Aunty Bim. She'd just destroyed everything.

'Let me give Prisha a call and ask her opinion. I'll see if she agrees that the story is racist and breaches industry standards.' She could hear Mum tapping on her keyboard. 'Then I'll contact the producer, the station and ACMA.'

That sounded bad. Really, really bad.

⌇

Normally, the smell of salt and vinegar in Mick's fish and chip shop made Siena's mouth water. Not today. After talking to her mum, she'd called Kyle. He'd agreed to meet but he was barely speaking—apart from ordering two calamari rings.

'Is your brother coming in this Saturday?' Mick pushed the hot packet of chips across the counter.

'I guess so. Doesn't he normally work Saturdays?'

'Yeah, but he's been sick the last few weekends.'

'Uh-huh.' She instinctively covered for Taj. He'd left the house at the same time as usual each Saturday. If he hadn't come to work, where had he gone instead?

In silence, they crossed the road to Main Beach and sat down on the sand, opening the old-fashioned fish and chip packet between them. A cool breeze through the heads made the paper flap onto the chips.

'I'm so sorry, Kyle.' She put a tentative hand on his leg. 'I didn't know the journalist would do that. They turned what I said into something else altogether.'

'Yeah.' His voice was deep, sullen. 'That the ancestors put a curse on the town. Fucking fake news.'

Siena couldn't tell if he was angry with her or with *The Top Story*. He'd always said he hated those programs.

'It'll be okay.' She tried to reassure him, and herself. 'No-one watches *Top Story* anyway.'

They both knew that wasn't true. Only yesterday she'd been raving about it being the most popular current affairs program in Australia. Everyone in Kinton Bay—and across the country— would flick on their TV sets tonight.

'Gran says it's typical. Whitefellas trying to make us look primitive. If they can portray us as uncivilised and super-stitious, they can ignore us as irrelevant.' He held a calamari ring between his finger and thumb but didn't eat it. 'We can't trust any TV reporter.'

'We're contacting the producer and the network, and submit-ting a complaint of racism to the Australian Communications and Media Authority.'

Kyle didn't respond.

Fiddling with the end of her plait, she braced herself. 'Is Aunty Bim really mad at me?'

'A bit. She says you shouldn't be talking for us. But she's more angry at the media who won't listen to her. She's annoyed they want to focus on the cute little white girl.'

Flushed with shame, she stared down at the chips and tried not to cry.

'Her words, not mine,' Kyle added. 'I think you're cute but . . . I'm not sure this all . . . This isn't really working.'

'We can make it work.' Siena kept her eyes on the chips. If she looked at him, the tears would come again. 'I'll stay far, far away from any journalists and TV crews. We can post a clip from Aunty Bim on my YouTube channel. And I'll ask Mum to interview her again too. We'll get the story out properly.'

'I know you think you're doing the right thing but . . . you're upsetting people. And you've got to stop calling it by that name, the Killing Cave. Gran says it's offensive and disrespectful.' He finally ate the calamari ring in two quick bites, unfolded his long legs and stood up. Brushed the sand from his jeans. 'Sorry, Siena. Let's just leave it.'

Watching him walk away from her, past the statue of Geoffrey Kinton, she cursed herself for setting all of this in motion. For insisting on finding the cave. For speaking to the reporters, saying stupid things that they could twist for their purposes.

She was the one who'd put a curse on this town.

Once Kyle had crossed the road, she got up, dumped the chips in the rubbish bin and hurried home through the side streets, her face blotchy from crying.

The house was empty. Where was Taj now? She closed the door and curled up on her bed. Pirate snuggled against her, licking her wet face, salty from the tears. Should she text Kyle? Beg for a second chance? Her fingers hovered over the phone.

She messaged Jasminda instead: *Kyle dumped me because of that shitty TV show.*

Her friend fired straight back: *Oh no, babe! I'll be at your place in an hour with chocolate. It's just a blip. He loves you. Hugs xxxx*

Grabbing a tissue from her bedside table, Siena blew her nose. Wiped the tears and Pirate's saliva from her cheeks. Leaning down under the bed, she brought out Mum's diary. Anything to stop her thinking about Kyle and *Top Story*. She flicked back to the entry that had puzzled her: *I'll never tell anyone what Blake said, and I'm never speaking to Inspector Nelson.*

Surely the diary would explain that somewhere? Siena began scanning the pages for any mention of Blake. Paragraphs and paragraphs of teenage ramblings. After forty-five minutes, Siena wondered if 'never telling' might also mean 'never writing it down'. Was Mum keeping the secret locked in her head?

On a page from May 1998, Siena's eyes snagged on the word 'DIE'.

They should be arrested and charged, that's what Miss Wilcox says. It's called date rape and it's a real thing that happens. I love Miss Wilcox but every time we speak to her, I have to stare at my shoes. She tells us it's not our fault and that we shouldn't be ashamed but I can't help feeling that way. If the boys did get arrested, then the whole town would find out.

I would DIE.

And what evidence can we give? We hardly remember anything. The boys all know what happened. They have all the knowledge and all the power.

Whenever I spot the Wrecking Crew at school or on the street, I think about how they've seen me naked. Blake has touched every part of me. Invaded my body. He's taken away my dreams. Destroyed any ideas of love. I've told Miss Wilcox that all the romantic classics are ruined for me now. I'll never watch Romeo and Juliet *again.*

Siena dropped the diary, her hands shaking. Axel's stupid story was true—a gang had been raping teenage girls in the cave. Her own mother.

52

POOLE

MYTHS ABOUT SERIAL KILLERS
Although Hollywood suggests otherwise, serial killings are rare. The public, and even many law enforcement officers, have skewed perceptions based on movies, television shows and books that perpetuate a number of myths such as the dysfunctional loner, the evil genius, and the psychotic attacker. Another myth is that serial killers cannot stop killing. In fact, some stop before they are caught.

Poole nodded as he read Caroline's research report again. It didn't mention journalists, though. They perpetuated the myths too. All the tabloid headlines screamed SERIAL KILLER, and the current affairs program on Wednesday night had sensationalised not only the case but also the historical massacre. Just what the investigation needed—a muddying of the waters by a racist, melodramatic TV show.

Since Glenda's death five days ago, the team had been pulling together detailed information for their next interview with Derek. They'd searched the O'Riordan house but found nothing of note.

Not surprising after all this time. The interview was scheduled for Thursday at the correctional centre; however, they would be seeing Derek today—at his mother's funeral.

Derek had forced his mates into a pact of silence about Blake's final hours at a party on Friday night. Poole had assumed that was the last sighting. And then last Wednesday, Meri Britton had delivered some unexpected information.

'I saw Blake on the Saturday morning.'

Apologising for not speaking up before, her face red with shame, Meri had described finding Blake in the sports shed when she was putting away the goalie kit after her hockey game.

'Blake threatened me, and threatened to get my dad in trouble with the police. I was already scared of him because he'd'—it took her a full minute to say the word—'raped me at a party. Well, I thought it was him but now I realise it must've been Derek. I was one of the teenage girls who the gang invited to parties and drugged.'

He asked her theory on what had happened next.

'I think Derek killed him. And Lance was probably involved too. I'm not sure about Scott.'

The chat with Owen Shuttlewood at the end of last week had been interesting. While listening to his voice, Poole became certain that Owen was their anonymous caller; he'd sent the recordings off to the techs to confirm it. However, Owen in person, had very little to say. When Poole had pressed him, he turned angry. 'I've got nuthin' to do with this', he'd insisted, 'Blake was my friend'.

Poole recalled anger as one of the general motivations in Caroline's report.

The Wrecking Crew—he was ticking off interviews with each member, one by one. He'd called Neville Kinton and asked about his son: Scott was in the Navy and on a five-month deployment in the Middle East. Poole would organise a call to the ship. He'd hoped that Neville, with his newspaper knowledge, could shed some light on the town at the time but he offered no insights.

Poole had left a message for another member of the gang, Lance Nelson. Was he related to Inspector Nelson? In Kinton Bay, highly likely. Lance had been out of town on business, but he'd be back for Glenda's funeral today.

⌣

The old sandstone church on the hill brimmed with mourners. Most wore an element of dark pink, as requested. Crimson scarves, ruby shirts and cherry dresses. One group of older women had even dyed their hair burgundy, just like Glenda's. While some were dressed to the nines, others looked as if they'd come straight from the beach. Glenda O'Riordan had certainly known a broad cross-section of Kinton Bay.

Pink, purple and mauve flowers adorned the lid of the glossy white coffin, so shiny it almost glowed at the front of the church. Poole sat at the back with Caroline and two officers, Frawley and Chan. When the organ began playing and everyone stood, he scanned the pews. No sign of Derek yet, although he should've been here by now with his prison guard escort. The congregation finished singing and the organ moaned an extra note; it echoed off the sandstone bricks and faded out, the soft bellow of a dying animal. St Paul's really needed to train someone younger to play—Olive must be seventy-five in the shade.

Meri Britton and her family perched in the third row from the front. Owen was behind them with his wife. Further along the wooden bench sat Neville and Kath Kinton.

At the front, next to Mayor Redpath, their shoulders almost touching, was Lance Nelson. One of the richest, most powerful men in town. A success story, transforming from teenage gang member to slick businessman. With a little help from his uncle, perhaps? Poole had discovered the connection just before coming here. Was Lance one of the reasons Inspector Nelson had let the gang run wild? They'd tracked down a phone number for the retired inspector in the Greek Islands; so far he hadn't returned their calls.

Glenda's sister, Cheryl, made her way to the pulpit. She unfolded a piece of paper, shifted from foot to foot, and cleared her throat into the microphone. As she moved, sequins sparkled on the neckline of her bright pink and gold dress. It was the same style that Glenda used to wear.

'My sister was the life of the party. She'd be pissed off not to be here for the party after church today.' Cheryl waited for the hoots of laughter to stop. 'Glennie knew how to make the most of things, even though life gave her a shit sandwich. She tried not to be angry at the world. Only at the coppers who did stuff-all to help.'

Poole clenched his teeth—that corrupt bastard in charge, Nelson, had barely looked for her son. Cheryl's criticism was entirely fair.

'Glennie loved her boys. My Terror Twins, she called them, when they raced around on their bikes. Or kicked a ball and broke someone's window. She was so proud of them when they got into the top footy team at school. They had talent—they coulda played for the Newcastle Knights.'

Poole had heard this story from Glenda herself. He'd asked Durham about it last week, wondering if it was why the school had seemed to allow them a free rein. Were they rugby league superstars? *They lasted about three games*, Durham said. *They couldn't turn up to training on time, didn't want to run and argued with the coach. Then one of them punched out a player on the field. Their own team-mate, no less.* A very different account.

'Now Blake has finally been found.' Cheryl's anger danced on the edge of every word. 'I wish Glennie could've had the chance to say goodbye to him. Here's hoping they'll be together in the big place upstairs. Blake was so tender-hearted. He put on a tough front, but he was a softie underneath.'

Poole stifled a cough of disagreement. Tender-hearted Blake and his brother had killed the neighbour's dogs. Drugged and raped girls. Bullied kids and teachers.

'And where the hell is Derek?' Cheryl suddenly asked, staring out across the congregation. 'He's s'posed to be here. That bloody prison mustn't have let him out after all. As if he hasn't suffered enough this week. We all need to be there for Derek.'

Derek was due for parole in November. But if he was responsible for the deaths of three men, he'd be inside for the rest of his life.

During the final hymn, four funeral directors wheeled out the white coffin on a trolley. No sons to carry their mother aloft on their shoulders at the end.

Poole put a call through to the correctional centre as soon as he got into his car.

'We were expecting an inmate, Derek O'Riordan, to attend a funeral service this morning, but he hasn't turned up,' he said. 'Can you check the location of the van?'

'Just give me a moment.' The officer put him on hold, then returned. 'I can confirm the van is approaching Kinton Bay now. There was a delay in leaving. A problem with his cell-mate.'

Caroline climbed into the passenger seat to accompany him to the wake. Poole guessed she wanted a word with the mayor about the memorial. She'd been lecturing in Sydney last week and missed a follow-up meeting with Bim Cooper.

'I won't stay long at the wake—just do a quick walk-through,' he said. 'I meant to ask you, did you ever meet Blake or Derek when you were up here on holidays?'

'I saw them around. They stood out because they were identical but also very loud and drunk, down at Main Beach in the evenings. Of course, they were a few years younger than me. I was in third-year uni by then.'

'Did you meet any of the teachers?' he asked. 'There was a young graduate who would've been around your age. Frances Wilcox. It's alleged she was bullied by the twins and that it contributed to her suicide.'

'Good god, how awful. What happened?'

On the short drive to the bowling club, Poole told her what he'd learned about the twins' harassment of the young teacher.

Inside the bowlo, Cheryl had organised sandwiches and cake, as well as beer and wine. She was making an announcement as they entered the room. 'I've paid for some bottles and jugs, but don't chug them down too fast or the tab'll run out.'

The number of mourners had multiplied since the church. Laughter and chatter filled the room. But it stopped suddenly as they were walking towards Cheryl. Everyone turned to look at the door.

'Is that him?' Caroline murmured. 'He looks hard.'

Derek wore black jeans and a black shirt dotted with pink palm trees, both clearly brand new for today. His short black hair was freshly cropped. Two guards followed him, monitoring his every move.

One of the cousins chanted as if he were at a footy match. 'Derek! Derek! Derek!'

Pushing past other family members, Derek made a beeline for his Aunty Cheryl. He bent down to wrap his heavily inked arms around her small frame.

People started chatting again and Poole watched Derek take in the room, wave to family and friends, hold up both hands and beam like a rock star at a concert. His gaze fell on Poole and his expression changed into a sneer.

'What the fuck are you doing here?'

'Showing my respect for your mother.' He kept his face neutral.

'Is that your wife?' Derek asked.

Looking around, he saw Caroline walking away from them, towards the mayor. Good. He didn't like suspects knowing about his private life. Instead of answering Derek's question, he gave his condolences. 'I'm very sorry about your mother.'

'Yeah, and my brother. Are you gonna find out what happened to him?' Derek demanded. 'We were so close, like one.'

'We have a team of detectives investigating.' Poole nodded. 'No stone will be left unturned.'

'No stone unturned. That's a good one for a murder in a forest.'

Derek was standing so close that he could smell his breath—hot chips. Had he somehow convinced the guards to stop at

Maccas? Was he even later to his mother's funeral because of a burger and fries? It seemed consistent with what Poole understood of his personality: callous, uncaring, incapable of empathy or remorse. The same psychopathic tendencies identified in Caroline's report on serial killers.

'As I said before, I'm sorry for the loss of your mother and your brother.' He stared into the prisoner's eyes. 'We're interviewing his old friends and establishing his last movements. And we'll be speaking to you again soon.'

Derek's eyes widened slightly. If he *had* killed his brother and the other two men, Poole wanted him to understand that the police were coming for him.

'Good. Then you'll talk to that poofter teacher, Durham. He got me expelled. He's the reason I never finished school. Durham always had it in for me and Blake.'

53

ROLLO

WHEN DEREK SCANNED THE ROOM, ROLLO SHRANK AGAINST THE BAR, wishing he were invisible. Resisting the urge to grab his family and slink out the back door of the bowlo, he hunched over and rubbed his scar instead.

'You all right?' Meri whispered, touching his shoulder.

'Yep.' How would his wife be feeling with the predator from her teenage years now in the same room? 'What about you?'

'Uh-huh.' Meri handed her car keys to their daughter, who stood motionless, fascinated by Derek, the star attraction. 'You and Taj wait in the car. We won't be long. I'll just go to the loo.'

The twins left and Owen sidled up to him at the bar, as if his mate could protect him. Seeing Derek here in person today triggered a memory—he'd had an ulterior motive for spilling Blake's secret.

'I'm sorry for telling Derek that Blake was gay,' he said.

'Fuck me, an apology at last.' Owen threw up his hand, and beer slopped over the side of the glass.

'I was young and stoned and confused . . . But the truth is, I did it on purpose.'

'Why would you do that?'

'To break up the Wrecking Crew. Derek and Lance were getting worse and worse. They expected us to do whatever they said. I was trying to set us all free.'

'Well, it didn't work for Blake.' Owen scowled. 'And we're still not free. Lance thinks he controls this town, and us.'

Where was Lance? He'd been at the church earlier, but Rollo hadn't seen him here. Time for their escape too. Rollo glanced over to see Meri coming back from the toilet. And behind her was Derek.

'Ah, my main man, where the fuck have you been?' Derek held out his arms for a brotherly hug with Rollo. This was what Lance would've wanted to avoid: a public embrace with the convicted criminal. Derek slapped him hard on the back, then turned his attention to Owen. 'Great to see you, Crater Face. Come and visit me sometime with the Stoned Loser.'

Crater Face. Stoned Loser. The old nicknames. *I've changed. I'm not a stoned loser anymore.* Rollo wanted to throw him onto the floor, kneel on his chest, shout in his face: *You raped my wife, you're the fuckwit loser. Get back to prison where you belong.*

Derek must've been lifting weights in jail; his forearms and chest were thick and strong. But other than that, he hadn't changed—he was the same fuckwit he'd always been. Meri had said that there was no time limit on reporting historical sexual assault in New South Wales. Could he be locked up as a serial killer *and* a serial rapist?

'Meri, sweet Meri, how are you?' Derek tried to kiss her on the cheek; she stepped backwards, leaving him hanging in midair.

She didn't speak so Rollo answered for her. 'We're sorry about Glenda. We'll really miss her.'

'You'll miss her doing your cleaning,' Derek sniggered.

'Glenda was a friend to my whole family.' Meri tightened her jaw and stared over the top of Derek's head. 'She helped out when Mum was sick, and she loved the twins.'

Rollo wished she hadn't mentioned their children. But he was amazed that Meri could manage a conversation at all with this man—his own hands were balled into fists behind his back.

'How are those twins?' Derek asked. 'Mum said they're teenagers now. Cute girl, I heard.'

They both moved at the same time; he landed a quick jab to Derek's kidneys while Meri slapped his arm. In a flash, the prison guards were upon them, pushing them back.

'You're disgusting,' Meri hissed. 'Your mother would be ashamed of you.'

Derek fired back, 'Yeah? Well, Mum said you were gonna find out what happened to Blake. You haven't found out shit.'

'Don't worry, Derek.' The look on her face was one of pure hatred. 'I'm going to expose exactly what happened in this town.'

54

SIENA

'HE DEFINITELY LOOKED LIKE A MURDERER,' TAJ TOLD HIS FRIENDS. 'AND he had a redback spider tattooed on his neck.'

Siena was eating her lunch with them on the oval. Jasminda hadn't come to school today, and she couldn't risk bumping into Kyle near the basketball courts.

'Sick.' Dominic sounded impressed.

'He's sick in the head.' She didn't want them to picture Derek as some kind of hero. Yesterday, when Mum and Dad had walked out of the bowling club, they'd looked shell-shocked. And then they'd been quiet all night at home.

A blue campervan zipped past the school fence, two surfboards on its roof.

'That's the sort of van I want.' Taj pointed. 'They go for about ten thousand bucks.'

'What are you talking about?' Siena asked.

'End of year twelve, I'm doing a road trip up the coast. Just me, my board and the van.'

She'd never heard this plan before—assumed they'd do something together to celebrate the end of school.

'Cool. How much have you saved?' Dominic asked.

'Six grand.'

Dominic and the other boys let out a soft whistle. Six grand—that was huge! Siena only did occasional babysitting and had no savings. But she'd found the right moment to ask him about the fish and chip shop.

'Mick said you haven't even been at work this month.'

'I'm doing some other stuff online. Pays more.'

'What?'

Taj inclined his head towards his mates and gave her the look that meant *Not now*. What was he up to? And whoever he was working for, could she get a job with them too?

As soon as she finished her sandwich, Siena escaped to the library. It was usually empty at lunchtime. She opened her laptop to a long message. Yay! He'd written back! It was the first communication she'd ever received from her grandad.

Hello Siena. Such a great surprise to hear from you! Thank you so much for getting in touch! I'd love to call you for a chat if your mother allows it.

In answer to your question, yes, I did go to some protests in the 1980s. I was involved in a huge march against uranium mining in 1985. And I went to a women's march too. Do you need to interview me for your school assignment? I'm happy to do that for you. My father was in the printers' union in London and involved in a strike in 1955 when the papers weren't published for nearly a month. They missed reporting on Winston Churchill's resignation! No internet back then, so they couldn't just publish on the web.

No internet . . . impossible to imagine.

I've read your mum's articles online about the Kinton Bay deaths. It's very strange and tragic. I gave the O'Riordan twins a job at the bowling club but they didn't last long. I was helping out Glenda. I'm sorry to hear she died. She certainly had her hands full with those two boys. But I'd actually met all three young men. Greyson used to bring his parents to the club for dinner when they visited, and I once gave Stefan a lift when he was hitchhiking into KB. Such sad news.

Grandad was keeping up with Mum's articles from over there. Did Mum know? And he'd met all the dead men. Maybe she could interview him for her channel?

It would be wonderful if you could visit us in Perth. I can organise plane tickets for you and Taj. Have you flown to Siena and Tajikistan yet? That was your mum's dream. My phone number is at the bottom of this message—please call if you can. Or I'll call you. I'm so happy to hear from you. We have so much to catch up on. I subscribed to your YouTube channel.

No way! He'd subscribed to her channel!

I'm so impressed that you're taking after your mum and my father in the news business! You're an incredibly passionate young woman. You're just like your mum. She was always interested in current affairs and injustices too.

Siena stuck out her tongue at the laptop screen. How could her grandfather make that comparison? Mum had taken no risks; she'd stayed in her home town and worked in a dead-end job. She wasn't passionate about anything.

Except for how it was everyone else's fault that she'd ended up there. Shit, Mum was going to kill her for writing to Grandad.

310

'Are you sticking out your tongue at me?'

Kyle was standing behind the desk partition.

'Definitely not.' She twirled the end of her plait as a distraction and hoped her cheeks weren't going red. 'I've just heard from my grandad for the first time in my life.'

'That's big news! So why the face?'

'He said I reminded him of Mum. That she was passionate about injustice too. But it doesn't sound like her.'

Kyle leaned against the edge of the desk. He was staying long enough to get comfortable and chat. A good sign. Although she didn't want to talk about that horrible TV show.

'People change,' he said. 'I reckon your mum was passionate. Probably still is, under all the bullshit. She's interviewing Gran for a long article about the massacre. Your mum says it'll be hard to get her editor to publish the story but she's going for it.'

'I guess that's passionate,' Siena conceded.

'Maybe you should work with your mum on it,' he suggested. 'You two would be an unstoppable team.'

The conversation had been making her hopeful, but his last comment undid everything. Kyle used to call the two of them an 'awesome team'. Basically, he was handing Siena back to her mum.

'If you team up with your mum, we might get to see more of each other.' He raised his eyebrows. 'She's interviewing me next.'

⌒

As Siena was walking home past the bowling club, her phone beeped with a text from Mum. *Where are you? Why aren't you home?* Oops, it looked like she'd turned off the location app. Had she done that accidentally in the library? Her fingers flew over the buttons: *Nearly there. Home in ten.*

She hurried past the steps to the bowlo. The funeral yesterday had been weird; she'd assumed it would focus on Glenda, but Cheryl's speech was more about the twins.

She hadn't told Kyle but she'd already teamed up with her mother: at the funeral, Mum had known she'd be too upset to take notes on the eulogy so Siena offered to do it for her. Now Mum was fighting with her editor to run the obituary. He was dismissive because Glenda was a cleaner.

Coming into the kitchen, she stopped dead at the sight of Mum, Dad, Owen and Hayley sitting around the table.

'Hayley wants to ask you about Axel,' Mum explained. 'She said someone saw you arguing near the surf shop on the night he was last seen.'

Oh shit. They couldn't accuse her of anything, could they?

'I got a message on Insta.' Hayley crossed her arms and jutted out her chin. She looked like she'd been crying. 'You saw him last.'

'Do you know where he went?' Dad asked.

'Hayley's very upset,' Mum added. 'Do you have any ideas?'

Seriously! Her parents were taking Hayley's side? After everything that had happened to her: the trolling, the harassment, Jackson bullying her at school, Pirate going missing, and the horrible TV show? Stuff Dad and the way he tried to appease everyone. That never worked—they'd studied World War II last term and look at how Chamberlain's attempt at appeasing Hitler had turned out. Stuff them all. Time to go on the attack.

She put her hands on her hips. 'I'll tell you what happened. Axel trapped me against the wall of the cave and put his hands around my neck. He tried to choke me because I wouldn't kiss him.'

'Good god.' The colour drained from Mum's cheeks. She jumped up and hugged Siena to her chest.

'It's okay, Mum, I stopped him.'

'How?' Owen asked.

'I clocked him in the head with a rock. I didn't hit him hard.' It might be a mistake to admit it but, at least, everyone would know of his awfulness.

Now Dad looked like he was going to cry.

Owen focused on his daughter. 'Were you okay, Hales?'

Hayley slouched in the chair, her arms still crossed. 'Fine. No-one saw Siena with Axel. She's lying. He wouldn't do that.'

After the amount she'd drunk, could Hayley even remember that night?

'I'm so sorry, darling.' Mum kept patting Siena's back softly, but her voice turned hard. 'These men . . . they can't just keep doing whatever they want out in the cave. This has been going on too long.'

Was Mum talking about Axel or further back—the events in her diary? Her mother turned and glared at Dad and Owen.

'We're going to the police,' Mum said, grabbing her hand. 'We're telling them everything.'

55

They're closing in, I can feel it. A noose around my neck being drawn tighter and tighter.

The strongest temptation is to run. But another part of me wants to explain why I had to act. No-one would listen, no-one would help. Not the parents, not the principal, not the police. Frances tried and then when she was bullied to death, I thought the school or the coroner would investigate, and blow the whole thing wide open. But nothing changed.

I had no other option. I was the only one seeking justice.

The first killing was accidental, the second and third intentional—all of them, though, done for other people. For the public good. And it worked: that behaviour stopped. But who knew that altruism could hollow out your insides? Along with the fear eating me up: when would the bodies be found?

I didn't plan on coming out of retirement but the rage about Axel Evans started to consume me. I heard stories. People told me things. Teenagers especially; they sought my advice. I started watching him around town. Why didn't the victims say something? Why didn't they go to the police? It's not like it was in the nineteen-nineties, the police would do something now.

That Saturday night, when Siena ran into the empty street, I slammed on my brakes to avoid hitting her. In the headlights, I saw the terror on her face, the bruises on her neck. And there, chasing her along the road, was Axel Evans.

I couldn't let him get away with it.

I just never imagined they'd find the bones the week he disappeared.

PART FIVE

HEALING
SEASON

These beautiful, altruistic, intelligent animals are helping

to heal our oceans, our climate, our planet.

We must let them live in peace.

56

MERI

INSIDE THE POLICE STATION, WAITING FOR A FEMALE OFFICER TO BE available, Meri couldn't stop cuddling her daughter. *My poor baby. How could I have let this happen after all my worry and precautions?* In the interview room, though, Siena shrugged her off. Her daughter spoke clearly, articulately, just as she did on her YouTube videos. Impressive. If only Meri and her friends had been able to do the same in 1998, perhaps everything would have turned out differently. Or perhaps not, with Inspector Nelson in charge.

As she listened to Siena describe what had happened at the Killing Cave that night, it sounded like nothing had changed in two decades. Except, of course, some of today's teenagers behaved differently. Her own daughter was here at the station— so aware and assured. Siena's friends, the lovely Jasminda and caring Kyle. And Taj. Kind, hardworking, polite Taj. She'd brought him up to be nothing like the boys of her youth.

Afterwards, Meri drove them up the winding hill to Osprey Lookout. Standing high above the town, with the bay spread out beneath them, she pulled Siena against her.

319

'I wish I could've protected you from Axel.' She stared at the sea, tinged orange by the setting sun. 'That's all I've ever wanted. To keep you safe.'

'It was good to report him to the police. Hayley can't see what those guys are really like—Axel and Jackson and the rest. They were so disgusting at that party. They treat girls like dirt.'

'Toxic masculinity.' Meri used a term that she'd never heard in her teenage years, but it applied to the Wrecking Crew back then and Axel now.

'Mum, did something like this happen out at the cave when you were my age?' Siena asked the question tentatively.

Meri wondered what she'd overheard. 'Yes, something similar.'

It would all come out eventually, but Siena didn't need to deal with it today, right after speaking with the police about her own ordeal.

'It's okay.' Siena's arm crept around her shoulders. 'I know about it . . . I found your old diary in the recycling bin. From when you were my age. I'm sorry . . .'

'Oh god, no! Please tell me you didn't read my diary.' Meri moved out of her daughter's embrace. Even though she couldn't recall what she'd written, she knew it would have been raw and honest.

'Sorry,' Siena repeated.

'It's an invasion of privacy.' She shook her head. 'You can't read other people's diaries. Especially not your mother's.'

Two kookaburras landed on a branch nearby and began a raucous conversation. Meri headed towards the carpark; she couldn't hear herself think with that racket. As she reached the car, Siena rushed around in front of her.

'Listen, Mum, I told you about the diary because I thought it meant we understood each other. We've been through the same . . . stuff. I'm really, really sorry.'

'Okay.' Tears welled in her eyes—she'd so wanted to protect her daughter from it all. 'But give my diary back. I'm cringing about what you must have read.'

Had she written about that heady teenage feeling of sexual power, the ability to attract older boys? It had been an illusion.

Her diary would have also outlined her dream of becoming an investigative journalist in London.

At Glenda's funeral, she'd remembered walking down the aisle on her mother's arm, five months pregnant. She hadn't invited her father to the wedding. Even as she'd said her vows, she expected Rollo to disappear and disappoint her as well. But he hadn't. He'd kept proving himself over and over.

For too long, Meri had been so preoccupied by not making it to the BBC in London that she'd missed the achievement right in front of her: a relatively happy family. No more blaming the people around her for how life had turned out. With Mum's cancer diagnosis, she'd chosen to accept her accidental pregnancy, create a family, stay in Kinton Bay, work here, and focus on community news. It didn't mean she was a failure. Maybe she never would've made it to the BBC even if she'd tried: she wasn't as brave as Kimberley. Although her friend had once said that Meri was brave to go ahead and have the twins.

And it was her own daughter inspiring her now. Even though Siena had made plenty of mistakes in her approach, her passion couldn't be faulted—she stood up for what she believed. Meri used to do the same; it was time to get back to her old self.

First thing tomorrow, she'd visit Lance. He must have been involved in Blake's death. Why else would he have stolen their dog? Her pretext for the visit would be the Blue Waters Panorama Residences—she wanted to know if Neville's articles had made any difference to the progress of the development application through council.

After that, she'd meet with the development committee for an update, and Caroline for any inside information about the police case.

And then she'd follow up with the editorial director of Regional Express Media. Last Friday, Bernard had listened to Meri's concerns for an hour. He'd already received the documents and clicked his tongue as she'd explained each issue. But Meri had another concern; she'd only recognised it when Rollo had been remembering that Friday night in the cave.

Tomorrow afternoon, she'd speak to Kristie and discuss telling their story.

Meri was on a mission.

For justice. For healing.

⌒

Meri arrived at Lance's office at eight am, hoping to catch him. The place was empty apart from his mum. She was dressed in the yellow polo shirt worn by all the staff, except Lance himself.

'Morning, Ninetta,' Meri greeted her. 'Is Lance here or out on site already?'

'Sorry, love, he's back in Sydney for a few days. To see suppliers and the divorce lawyer.' Ninetta shuffled papers on her desk. 'His ex reckons she can take half the business. Well, she can't. If she does that, we'll go bust.'

Lance's third marriage had broken up earlier in the year; his wife must've had enough of the many affairs. But Ninetta would defend Lance to the death, and vilify his ex, as she'd done twice before.

'Do you know when he'll be back?' Meri asked.

'After the weekend. I'll tell him you dropped in.'

That was in five days. Was Lance hiding from his ex-wife? Or the police?

Her next meeting was more successful—a chat with Aunty Bim, Caroline and Alastair from the development committee. They were pushing ahead with a motion to council to change the name of Kinton Bay. It would be a battle. Meri had seen these debates divide opinion in other towns. Up north, a vote to change the name of a village which honoured an alleged colonial murderer had been supported by just six residents, the rest—three hundred and fifty-five—voted against it. But in Western Australia, Fremantle Council was considering renaming Kings Square to pay tribute to Midgegooroo, a local resistance leader who'd been executed without trial by order of the Governor in 1833. The Northern Territory had re-named so many places. And quite frankly, if major cities like Mumbai, St Petersburg and Ho Chi Minh City could change their names, then surely it was possible for tiny Kinton Bay.

Siena had asked if she could come to the meeting too, but it was a school day—and privately, Meri wasn't sure if Bim would want to see Siena after the disastrous television interview. At least Bim approved of Siena's suggestion: a competition for people to submit names to create a shortlist.

After the meeting, Meri and Caroline walked half a block to the Sandy Cafe. Along with the coffees, Meri bought a small lemon tart to share. She needed the sustenance today.

They began talking about the police investigation almost immediately. Meri explained how the Wrecking Crew had been lacing girls' drinks in the cave, without naming herself as a victim.

'Derek O'Riordan was the leader,' she finished. 'He terrorised everyone—the girls and his own gang of boys.'

'And Blake terrorised them as well?'

'Mostly Derek. Sometimes he pretended to be Blake.'

'But didn't Blake sexually assault girls when they were drugged?' Caroline asked.

'I don't think so. Your theory about a gay hate crime might be right. Blake had recently told Rollo he was gay. At that last party, Derek was forcing his brother to have sex with a girl as some kind of fix for his homosexuality. Stupid and wrong in every way.' Meri snorted. 'We think Derek stabbed his own brother because he was gay.'

A small mercy that Glenda wouldn't have to face this possibility: that one of her sons had killed the other.

'After all these years, it'll be difficult to find the evidence to convict him.' Caroline took a sip of her coffee. 'Does Rollo remember much about that night?'

'I'm not sure his evidence will help. Blake didn't die on Friday night.' Meri realised she hadn't explained everything. 'I saw him the next day.'

'Well, I hadn't heard that.'

'Lance must know something. He's the one with the key to all this.' She couldn't quite work it out, but it tied in with the warnings to Glenda. 'That's why he left town.'

⌒

On her way back to the *Chronicle* office, Meri thought about Kristie. When she'd spoken to her a few days ago, Kristie had sounded happy, with a lovely husband, three young kids, and a job as a primary school teacher. It had taken her a long time to trust men, though. 'I didn't have a boyfriend until I was twenty-two. And even then I had to take everything super slow.' Kristie had finally told her husband everything she could remember about those events in the Killing Cave, including the termination in Newcastle.

Meri's phone buzzed: the editorial director. She'd been watching Neville this week—he'd given no hint that head office was investigating him.

'We've assessed the documents you sent through,' Bernard said. 'And done an analysis of the editor's bias over a cross-section of stories. We've come to a decision.'

'Right.' She swallowed. Surely it was a clear breach of ethics. But would they just rap him over the knuckles like last time? 'Before you tell me your decision, I need to bring up one more issue.'

'Okay, go ahead,' he said.

She only had one piece of evidence. Would it be enough to make a case? Muscle Man, aka Scott Kinton, had left the bay so many years ago that she'd almost forgotten about him. But Scott had been there that Friday night, he'd been involved in the date rapes, maybe even Blake's death. The Muscle Man *must* have helped move the unconscious girls; Meri had no memory of how she'd returned from the cave.

'I believe that Neville has been avoiding reporting on a missing teenager, now confirmed dead.' Meri rubbed at her temples. 'Over the past two years, I've written three articles about the case, which Neville has refused to run. From when the boy disappeared in 1998, I suspect that he has downplayed the story.'

'If this is true, why would he do it?'

'His son was good friends with the missing teen. I think he was . . .' She couldn't say 'covering up', that was too serious an accusation. 'I think he was protecting his son.'

'Do you have evidence?'

Meri's mouth had gone dry; she licked her lips to speak. 'I only have my three articles which he didn't publish. We've changed computer systems numerous times over the past twenty years—I'm not sure if I can find you anything more concrete.'

It wasn't just the stories which Neville didn't run, it was the stories he stopped from being written.

'This is a very vague complaint but a major allegation.' Bernard sounded irritated. 'Although I understand it's difficult to prove. Has Neville's son been charged with any crime?'

'No.'

'Well, I feel this adds to the picture we already have of Neville's editorial approach. I'll be coming up to Kinton Bay on Monday to speak with him. But I'd like to know your availability.'

'My availability?'

'If we were to require an acting editor for a period of six months?'

Meri stopped walking and stared at the *Chronicle* sign above the door of the newspaper office. Shit. They were actually going to do it—fire Neville. *Be brave*, she told herself as she took the last few steps towards the office.

'I'm available,' she said. 'I'd be honoured to be considered for the role.'

She had no idea what the editorial director would say to Neville. But she refused to feel guilty.

Like Derek, like his own son, Neville had made his choices and would now face the consequences.

57

POOLE

INFORMATION WAS PILING UP IN TASK FORCE OWL, WITH HUNDREDS of phone calls coming in from the public. Some cranks, several psychics, and a handful of families who wondered if the remains of their missing sons were out in the forest as well. But for the most part, people recounted useful snippets that were helping to build a picture of the men's movements before they disappeared. Poole had re-interviewed the former hostel manager and received an updated list of people staying there at the same time as Stefan. One of those English backpackers was now residing in Belmarsh Prison in the UK, convicted of manslaughter; more details were being sent through on him. A detective was looking into locals who fitted the profile that Caroline had provided.

As yet, Lance Nelson hadn't come into the station for a chat. The property developer was back in Sydney. They'd set a time with him on Monday and if he didn't show, Poole would be tracking him down.

Apart from Rollo's backpack, no other material evidence had been located. The search team had found rubbish from more recent parties: cigarette butts, broken glass, chip packets and used condoms. A Solo can and Malibu bottle from the nineteen-nineties. But no clothes or shoes or watches or bags. Forensics had been unable to determine the cause of death from the bones. Most likely the deaths were linked, but it was still possible that one or more of the men had died by accident or suicide.

Another call had come through late yesterday from Fabian Lavigne's wife. She'd been ringing regularly since the discovery of the bones.

'Have you looked into whether this person could have taken Fabian as well?' Yuki asked.

'Yes,' he assured her. 'Our detectives are working on it.'

A gap of twenty years between murders. A much older victim. Unlikely to be the same offender but not impossible.

Back in the nineties, they hadn't investigated any links between the three disappearances. Poole wouldn't make the same mistake now. He'd asked a team to cross-reference all of the information in Fabian's case with the others. Days and days of meticulous analysis.

Caroline had come into the station to discuss the criminal profile and her gay hate crime hypothesis.

'The homophobic aspect is interesting in relation to twins,' Caroline explained to the team. 'Imagine you're aggressively masculine, that's your driving force. Your sense of worth comes from dominance over girls, including through rape, and violence and threats against boys. And then you find out that your twin—essentially a mirror of yourself—is gay. Obviously I'm talking about Derek O'Riordan. He would've been asking himself: *Am I gay too?* He may have perceived Blake's revelation as a direct attack on his identity. It would have shaken him at the deepest level.'

He could see her point. 'But if it was Derek, why would he kill the others?' he asked. 'Neither of them were openly gay.'

'Derek's fear of his own sexuality, of being gay like his brother, could have been focused on other men as well. They didn't need to be gay necessarily, just different, to pose a threat. Greyson and Stefan were both different. At that time, guys in this town conformed to certain behaviours—macho, hard-drinking, sexually aggressive to women.'

Poole nodded; she'd just described the Wrecking Crew.

⌒

At the correctional centre, with a solicitor by his side, Derek was more talkative than at his mother's wake. Not necessarily cooperative, but talkative.

'I'm up for parole on the tenth of November. That's a hundred and four days away. You're not keeping me in here. I've done nuthin' wrong.'

Poole identified everyone present for the tape—himself, Detective Sergeant Sarah Singh, the prisoner and his solicitor. The inclusion of Singh had been deliberate: to see how Derek responded to a younger female. Poole hoped he might under-estimate her, show off and give away more than he intended.

'Can you tell us about your brother?' Poole began.

'You should get one thing straight—I didn't kill him. He was my best mate.' Derek sniffed and rubbed the back of his hand across his nostrils. 'How could I kill him? It'd be like killing meself. I thought he'd run away and left me.'

'You said at the time that he went to Kings Cross. Why?'

'Just a guess. I thought that's where they all went.'

Poole glanced at Singh, indicating for her to take the lead.

'Who do you mean by "they"? Gay men?' When Derek nodded, she asked, 'Did you have a problem with Blake being gay?'

'Fucking Rollo—he's been talking to you, hasn't he. Okay, I mighta said some stuff, but I didn't really care. That last night, it was just a game.'

'A game?' Singh raised her eyebrows. 'A game where you forced your brother to rape a semi-conscious girl and you stabbed Rollo in the leg? Your brother must have felt threatened.'

'Maybe . . . Yeah, I guess. He didn't come home with me. Stormed off into the forest. Told me to get fucked.' Derek put his hands over his face. 'Those were his last words to me. *Get fucked.*'

'I'm sorry about that,' Singh said. 'It must be a distressing memory.'

Derek looked slightly taken aback at this display of empathy. 'Uh, yeah,' he mumbled.

'So where do you think he went that night?' Singh asked.

'I dunno.' Derek scratched at his neck. 'I never saw him again.'

Poole decided to move on; they could return to Blake at the end.

'Did you see Greyson Creighton on the tenth of December that year?' he asked.

The prisoner shrank in his chair. Tugged on his solicitor's arm. They leaned away from the detectives for a whispered conversation. When they'd finished, Derek sat up straight again.

'I saw Greyson at the pub. Dunno what day. But like I said, I'm not going down for this shit.' He hesitated, made eye contact with his solicitor, then spoke. 'Lance was getting drugs off Greyson.'

'Did you threaten Greyson?'

'Nah, not really. He was going back home and Lance wanted him to send tablets down from Brisbane. A regular shipment, like. But they were arguing about price.' Derek had been staring at the floor—suddenly, he looked up at Poole. 'You need to talk to Lance. Aunty Cheryl said he'd been hanging around Mum's place. He was always a jealous bastard. Hated me having a twin. If he killed my brother . . .' Derek thumped his fists on the table.

'Easy,' the solicitor warned him.

'I'm not staying in this place for life because of Lance fucking Nelson.' Derek hit the table again. 'He was threatening my mum. I reckon he caused her death.'

'Why?' Poole asked.

'Can't say . . . but he did a lot of work for that new resort out of town. You might want to look into that.'

Poole hid his smile—the former mates were turning on each other. They'd get some answers now.

⌒

At last, they had a connection between two of the dead men: drugs were being sold from Greyson to Blake's gang, via Lance Nelson. On the drive back to Kinton Bay, Poole asked his team to examine Lance's involvement in 'the new resort out of town', Fabian's place. By the time they walked into the police station two and a half hours later, Detective Senior Sergeant Coleman had found something.

'Lance's company did a lot of work for the resort. Fabian complained it was substandard and sent numerous emails requesting it be rectified. When those first COVID cases hit the resort, Fabian was in the process of engaging lawyers.'

'And what happened?'

'Nothing. Fabian went into damage control over the virus,' Coleman said. 'He never engaged the lawyers.'

'Why didn't we know about this?' Poole asked. 'His wife never mentioned Lance.'

'The emails were from a private account, not Fabian's business one. Perhaps Yuki didn't know. Do you want me to talk to her?'

'Thanks, that would be good.' He considered Fabian's last known movements. 'Can you get someone to pull up the CCTV footage from the night Fabian went missing?'

Poole had studied the footage before, of course, and his officers had spoken to everyone in the pub that night. Yuki had watched it too, looking for any of the people who'd made threats to her husband over the COVID outbreak and its impact on the town.

Murder to protect one's reputation and business. Financial gain. Criminal enterprise. Those motivations had been listed in Caroline's report on serial killers. Could Lance Nelson be responsible for the murders in the nineties, protected by his uncle, and Fabian's disappearance now? It seemed highly unlikely but Poole knew that sometimes truth was stranger than fiction.

⌒

The data dump on Axel Evans's phone came back mid-afternoon. His mobile hadn't been operated for a month—its last use just a few hours after the alleged assault on Siena Britton in the cave. The final phone call was to Jackson McCormack at five thirty-six am from somewhere around Main Beach.

Poole rang Jackson and asked about his last conversation with his cousin. 'Do you know where he was when he called you?'

'Yeah, on the marina.'

They could check the CCTV. Hopefully Chester kept his tapes and at least one of the angles had caught Axel's movements.

'Any idea what he was doing there?' Poole considered the options. 'Was he getting on a boat?'

'I dunno. He said something about the *Sirius*.'

With two officers, Poole went down to the marina.

'See if you can find the *Sirius*,' he instructed. 'If it's not here, ask Chester for the logs.'

The search didn't take long. The *Sirius* was the biggest catamaran on the marina, its hulls painted with whales and dolphins. Rollo's cruiser. *What the hell?*

Poole and his officers were squatting down, trying to get a closer look at the boat, when Rollo himself appeared, sprinting along the wharf towards them.

'What're you doing?' He held his sides, breathless from running.

'Has Axel Evans been on your boat?' Poole asked.

'Have you found him?' Pushing his hair off his forehead, Rollo glanced towards his boat. 'I only heard about the assault on Tuesday. Siena didn't tell us before.'

'Would you mind if we took a look?'

Rollo opened his mouth, closed it again. 'All right. I've got nothing to hide.'

But it turned out that he did.

Constable Terry called softly from the cockpit. 'Boss, in here.'

When Poole joined him, Terry pointed to a mobile shoved into a compartment below the controls—its distinctive phone case featured an electric guitar and matched the description from Hayley.

He bagged it and disembarked to show the evidence to Rollo. 'Do you know who owns this phone, and why it's on your boat?'

'Nope.' Sweat beaded on Rollo's forehead. He wiped it off with his thumb. 'I've never seen it before. I think someone's trying to set me up. Like I told you, Lance threatened me and stole our dog.'

Lance's name again.

'I'll need your logbooks,' he said. 'Were you out on the first weekend of July?'

'Yeah, I think so.' Rollo squatted on his haunches and put his head in his hands. He muttered something under his breath and Poole strained to hear it. 'I didn't do anything. As if I could push a man overboard in front of forty passengers.'

'I'd like you to come back to the station with me.' He heard Rollo groan in response.

Why was the phone on his boat? It would've been so easy to throw it into the ocean, miles out.

Unless, as Rollo claimed, he was being framed.

Or unless he'd forgotten about it.

58

ROLLO

WHAT THE FUCK WAS AXEL'S PHONE DOING ON HIS BOAT? LANCE, OWEN, Jackson, Hayley—which one of them had put it there? He'd had enough. Rollo wasn't keeping his mouth shut any longer. Even if it meant incriminating himself.

Another bloody interview at the police station. Chief Inspector Poole asked about Axel again, but Rollo had nothing to tell him.

'I don't know anything about the phone,' he repeated. 'But can I talk to you about something else?'

Shit, he should've googled aiding and abetting. Could he be arrested for what he'd done?

Poole prompted him. 'About what?'

'Greyson Creighton.' Rollo saw the surprise on the policeman's face. 'He was stealing drugs from the hospital pharmacy store and selling them . . . Lance was using his Rohypnol tablets to spike the girls' drinks at the parties.'

'Right.'

'And then Greyson was going back home and Lance wanted his regular supply to continue. But Greyson said the hospital in

Brisbane had tighter security. Lance was super pissed off and threatened to expose him to the matron at the hospital if he didn't figure out a solution.' Rollo could hear himself blathering. *Jesus, just get it over and done with.* He blew out a long breath through his nose.

'And then what happened?'

'I should have told you lot years ago . . . I'm sorry . . .' He shifted in his chair, steeled himself to get the words out. He understood why Meri had never mentioned seeing Blake at the hockey fields. Utter fear. 'Lance stole Greyson's surfboard. He told me to take it to South Cove, break it up and put it into the waves. Let it get washed up again.'

'Which day was this?'

'The day before he went missing. I didn't even know it was Greyson's board until I saw the picture in the paper the following week.' He'd nearly shat himself, reading about it. 'I never told anyone because Derek would've knifed me. I was lucky the first time. The doctors said if it had hit the artery, I would've bled out. But I still had damage to my muscle. That leg has always been weaker.'

'I understand you were afraid.' Poole nodded at him sympathetically. 'Did Lance ever discuss Greyson with you after that?'

'No, I stayed away from them.'

'But what did you think had happened?'

'I thought Derek had stabbed him and Lance had thrown his body out at sea.'

For all these years, he'd kept the worry to himself, afraid that one day they'd do the same to him. It was a relief to say it aloud.

⌒

Rollo waited outside the Time'n'Tide, his anger growing. This town, this shitty town where he'd spent his whole life. These people were supposed to be his friends, but someone had placed Axel's phone on his boat. Siena and Meri had this idea that they could 'move everyone forward, together, to a place of healing'. Ha! How could that be possible with guys like Lance around?

When Lance came out the side door, he followed him for a few paces until they were away from the pub windows, then grabbed him from behind. Spun him around by the collar of his fancy business shirt and pushed him against the wall of the pub.

Lance reacted instinctively, ramming a fist into Rollo's stomach. Then he saw his attacker's face.

'Rollo. What the hell?'

'You took my bloody dog, you're humiliating Owen again, you hurt Glenda and now you're trying to set me up.' Spittle flew with his words.

'Get your hands off me.' Lance wrenched out of Rollo's grasp and pulled at his shirt to straighten it. 'How did you even know I was here? Mum's telling everyone I'm in Sydney.'

'I know you're seeing the barmaid. Figured you might be camping out in her room at the pub to avoid the coppers.'

'If you're so smart, Rollo, then you should get everyone to shut up.' Lance mimicked a zipping motion across his mouth. 'Your daughter, your wife. And keep your own mouth shut.'

There it was again. *Keep your mouth shut.* He'd hated being told that at seventeen by Lance and Derek. He hated it even more now.

'Too late, Lance. It's all coming out.' Rollo lowered his voice slightly. 'Was it a hate crime, like Caroline says? You killed Blake because he was gay? Or were you just jealous that he was

Derek's twin? And what about the other two—how did they piss you off? Drugs? Girls?'

'You're still a stoned loser. Is Meri making up this shit to protect you?'

Turning, Lance went to walk away, but Rollo snatched his arm. He'd known Lance all his life. Their parents had been friends; hell, their grandparents had been friends, but even when they'd hung out at school together, Rollo had never liked him. Lance used people to get what he wanted. Underneath the expensive clothes, Lance was the loser, not him.

'Why is Axel's phone on my boat, huh?' He stood taller to make the most of his height advantage.

'Axel?' Lance seemed genuinely confused. 'Shane's nephew?'

'Yeah, the toolie who assaulted my daughter.'

'I don't know what you're talking about.' Lance frowned.

'Police are searching my boat. They're questioning *me*. I don't even know the guy.'

'It's those crazy bitches in your family. They probably attacked him.'

Crazy bitches. His wife, who'd been raped when she was just fifteen—thanks to Lance's roofies. His daughter, who'd been assaulted by Axel and threatened for trying to discuss the town's history. Rollo shoved him. Hard. Lance stumbled back, lost his balance and fell onto the footpath. This was it—Lance would come for him now; he was never one to walk away from a fight. His eyes dark with rage, Lance was pushing himself up, preparing for attack, just as Aunty Bim came around the corner.

'Are you okay?' Bim put out a hand to help him up.

'He's fine,' Rollo cut in. Having finally worked up the courage to face Lance after all these years, he itched to punch the bastard, even though he would lose the fight. Flexing his fingers, he glanced at Aunty Bim. Why did she have to come along right now?

'I'm good, thanks, Bim.' Lance flashed a smile at her. 'Rollo tripped me. We were just mucking around.'

Mucking around? Fuck me, this man still thinks he's untouchable. Rollo had to do something. He focused on Aunty Bim; she knew what this prick was like—she'd want to see him punished too. 'We're just on our way to the police station. Will you walk with us? You can tell us how council is going with the memorial plans.'

'Actually, I have to get back to work,' Lance said. 'I've got a meeting at four. I'll see you later.'

'Come on, mate, it's only a block away. Aunty Bim has lots to tell us.'

Lance needed Aunty Bim's support on the development committee; he wouldn't kick up a fuss.

Rollo hooked his arm into Lance's and winked at Aunty Bim. She understood, casually stepping forwards and taking Lance's other arm. With his spare hand, Rollo texted Meri: *Come outside*. Hopefully she'd read it before they passed her office.

'It's going to be quite a process to get agreement,' Aunty Bim started. 'We're trying to find some written record of the massacre.'

Rollo wanted to hug her—he could already tell that this long yarn would take them all the way to the police station.

'Olive is looking into it, and some historians in Sydney too. You whitefellas won't believe anything till it's written in your own history books. History books written by white men. Anyways, Olive is trying to track down a letter Geoffrey Kinton sent back home. She has a theory that he mentioned Rose, the teenager he took.'

They continued up Dolphin Street with Aunty Bim barely drawing breath.

'We'll need your help, Lance. You know all about development applications and getting council onboard.' She sent a sly look across to Rollo. 'You can guide us through the process. We want the memorial built in the park, near where Kinton's statue is now, but under the trees.'

They reached the newspaper office with no sign of Meri. Only half a block to the police station. If Lance was going to make a run for it, he'd do it now.

'What do you think the memorial will look like, Aunty Bim?' Rollo asked, tightening his grip on Lance's arm.

'That's a discussion for way, way down the track. We'll probably talk to some local artists. Lance, have you worked with any sculptors in your buildings?'

Quick footsteps sounded behind them. Rollo glanced over his shoulder to see his wife marching up the street, forming a rearguard to stop Lance from bolting. And up ahead, ten metres away, was the police station. The door opened and Chief Inspector Poole stepped out to greet them.

'Good to see you, Lance,' Poole called out. 'You missed our three o'clock appointment. I was just coming to find you.'

Stoned loser. Lance had used Rollo's old teenage nickname outside the pub, just like Derek had at the funeral. Back in 1998, Rollo would never have guessed that one day he—the bored, drunk, no-good-at-school stoned loser—would own a business, marry the smart girl and father two amazing kids. If Blake had lived, what would he be doing now? Might he have moved away from Derek, found his feet and done something with his life?

Rollo pictured his own twins. Such strong independent teenagers at fifteen. But they were still incomplete, only part of the individuals they would become. Who knew where Siena's campaigning would take her? And with his work ethic, Taj would find his purpose one day.

Aunty Bim accompanied Lance all the way up the steps to the front door of the station.

When Meri leaned against him for a hug, he had to balance his wobbly legs, as if he were on the boat in rough seas. *Please let Poole see through Lance's bullshit and find out the truth. Don't let him pin anything on me.*

Everything Rollo loved was right here, in this town. He didn't want to lose it.

59

SIENA

ON THE BUS, SIENA HID UP THE BACK WITH HER HEAD DOWN, EYES ON her phone. She'd begged Taj to come to school today, but he'd said his stomach hurt again. Axel's disappearance was on all the news sites—the police must have put out a missing person's alert last night after they'd found his phone. On Dad's boat. WTF? How did it get there? Kyle sat up the front of the bus with his mates; Hayley and her friends were in the middle. None of them had seen her get on.

When the bus pulled up at school, she waited, letting them all off first. But as she came down the steps, one person remained: Kyle, leaning against the Norfolk pine. He *had* spotted her.

'Are you okay?' he asked. 'I saw all that stuff on the news about that guy, Axel. He was at the cave, wasn't he?'

'Yeah. I went to the police and lodged a report about him assaulting me.'

'Shit, Siena. Why didn't you tell me?' His arms went around her, and she snuggled her face into his jumper.

'I'm sorry.' Pressed against his chest, she could smell his deodorant, hear the thump of his heart. 'It was better you didn't know, so no-one would think you were involved. I wasn't trying to keep a secret. I was protecting you.'

She felt his lips on her forehead.

'I understand,' he said eventually. 'But you should've told me.'

She glanced up to check his expression and his lips moved to meet hers. *Please, please, please, let this be the start of us making up.*

⌒

By recess, the gossip had spread around the school. Some people even said things to her face.

'Hayley reckons you hit that missing guy in the head with a rock. Did you kill him?'

'I thought you were just a nerd but you're doing some really weird shit now.'

'Is Axel out in the Killing Cave with the other dead bodies?'

At lunchtime, Siena was sitting on the concrete stairs watching Kyle play basketball. Hayley stomped up the steps and stood in front of her, blocking her view.

'You'd better be ready to start answering questions.'

'I haven't done anything,' she declared, trying to sound stronger than she felt. 'I told you that.'

'Axel is alive. He's on his way home. Someone spotted him in Brisbane. He got amnesia from where you hit him in the head. You're the one who's gonna be arrested for assault, not him.' After delivering the news, Hayley turned on her heel and strutted off.

For one moment, Siena felt her shoulders loosening, her back relaxing—she wanted to collapse on the ground in relief. *The sleazebag is alive! I didn't accidentally kill him.*

But now they were blaming her.

She called Mum from behind the gym, holding the phone close to her mouth so no-one would hear. Axel's re-appearance was news to her; it hadn't yet hit the media.

'Mum, can you ring the police? Find out more?'

'Of course. But why are you worried? He's been found alive. That's great! It means no-one can accuse you or Dad of anything.'

Siena squeezed her eyes shut for a moment. 'Hayley says I'm going to be arrested for assaulting him. For giving him amnesia.'

'Fuck that for a joke!'

'Mum! Did you just swear?' Siena didn't know whether to laugh or be shocked.

'I will not allow that man to play the victim. He's the one at fault here. Not you.'

'I didn't even hit him that hard.' The rock had been small, not particularly heavy—she could still feel the weight of it in her hand.

'Don't worry about it,' Mum said. 'Amnesia is a convenient cover story to avoid any assault charges.'

The bell rang for next period.

'I've got to go,' Siena said. 'Promise me you'll call Chief Inspector Poole?'

'I'll do it right now. That creep is not going to start victim-blaming. No way.'

Walking back to class, Siena realised she hadn't heard her mother talk like that before. A sign of the younger Meri, the passionate young woman her grandfather remembered.

60

POOLE

THE MISSING PERSON'S ALERT AND THE MEDIA BLITZ HAD WORKED. MIDDAY on Friday, Axel's mother phoned the police station to report that he was safely home, and demanded they 'stop hounding the family'. Poole drove to the house and Mrs Evans reluctantly admitted him to the living room, but didn't offer him a seat.

He was relieved to see Axel Evans in the flesh; this young man had not met with the same fate as those others in the forest. Dressed in faded jeans and a black t-shirt, Axel had a nervousness about him, twisting his fingers through the messy man-bun on top of his head. A week's worth of stubble covered his chin and dark circles ringed his eyes but apart from the tiredness, he appeared healthy.

Axel stood behind a lounge chair, as if he needed a barricade between him and the police. 'I can't remember what happened. I think I caught a train to Brisbane.'

'And what made you come home?'

His hands moved from his hair to the back of the lounge chair, where he began kneading the leather. 'I saw my face all over the news.'

'Why can't you remember?'

'I got amnesia. That crazy chick, Siena, hit me in the head with a rock.' He pointed to a spot behind his ear. 'It knocked out my memory for two weeks.'

'Did you go to hospital in Brisbane?'

'Nup.'

'Well, we'd better take you to the community hospital now.' Poole inclined his head towards the door. 'We need to get you assessed.'

'Nup. I'm all good.' Axel shrank further away from him.

'Can I ask you about your phone? Do you know where it is?'

'Dunno. I had amnesia.'

Late last night, when the alert about Axel Evans had been blasting out of every TV and radio station, an anonymous message had come through the CrimeStoppers hotline.

'Axel Evans is safe,' the caller had said. 'Someone told him to leave town for a few weeks. It was about the girls. He's fine.'

Now, in Axel's living room, Poole came straight out with it. 'Who told you to go away?'

The lad shoved his hands into his jeans' pockets and mumbled: 'I . . . um . . . dunno what you mean.'

'I heard that someone told you to leave town. Can you tell me what's going on?'

'Nothing.' The word came out in a rush. He looked to his mother for back-up.

'Okay, that's enough.' Mrs Evans stepped close to her son. 'Axel's tired. He's got to recover from that amnesia.'

'We'll be in touch.' Poole smiled.

Axel's next interview would be with a specialist detective from the Sex Crimes Investigation Team.

When Poole returned to the station, Meri Britton was waiting for him in the reception area. She leapt to her feet and rushed across the small room towards him.

'I've heard Axel's back,' she said. 'I'm concerned he'll come after Siena when he learns of the charges against him.'

'Mrs Britton. The safety of victims is our top priority in these situations.'

But she refused to accept his reassurance. 'Axel has to be stopped. You know what happened to me and my friends. No-one listened to us.'

'I promise we're listening now,' he said.

The front glass doors opened and Caroline walked through with three large books in her arms.

'Just thought I'd drop these in.' She smiled at him, then nodded at Meri. 'I mentioned this book about serial cases to the team. It's by a leading English criminologist. And I've got two on the psychology of serial killers.'

After placing them on the counter, she gave him a quick peck on the cheek.

Meri interrupted them. 'Caroline, I'm so worried about Axel. He assaulted Siena in the cave. Now he's back and blaming her.'

'Siena too? I'm sorry.' Caroline took Meri's hands in her own. 'One of the parents of the other girls contacted me. I'm going to help them through the process. Unofficially. Just as a support.'

Poole frowned. The police hadn't even charged Axel yet. He and Meri spoke at the same time.

'They'll have legal aid,' he said.

'What other girls?' Meri asked.

'Three girls. Alleged sexual assault at the cave,' Caroline said. 'I can take Siena under my wing too. A trial is a horrible, complicated system for anyone, let alone teenagers.'

He wished she'd spoken to him first. Not that he could prevent her from getting involved. Caroline always stepped in to help others; that was her nature. But they certainly couldn't talk about the case at home if she was supporting the victims.

'When Axel is arrested, the magistrate is likely to consider him a flight risk, so bail won't be granted,' Caroline explained to Meri. 'Your daughter will be safe.'

'Thank god.' Meri turned to face Poole. 'And what about Lance? When will my family be safe from him?'

'As you know, we interviewed him yesterday. Lance is continuing to help with our enquiries today.'

'You should speak to Neville Kinton,' she said. 'He's involved in Lance's development near the church. Everything Lance touches is tainted.'

⌒

In yesterday's interview, Lance had denied buying drugs from Greyson, denied slipping them into girls' drinks, denied asking Rollo to break up the surfboard, denied everything. He'd acted like they were all mates and he was doing them a favour by explaining their mistakes and setting them on the right track.

'I'm so against drugs.' Lance pulled on the cuffs of his striped business shirt, like a magician showing there was nothing up his sleeves. 'Always have been. Not good for the body or the mind. Rollo, though, he was smoking dope from a young age.'

'But you and Derek ran this gang,' Poole said. 'You were using date-rape drugs at the parties.'

'No, no, you've got the wrong end of the stick,' he said patiently. 'It wasn't a gang, just a group of mates playing silly buggers. And Rollo was the head of the Wrecking Crew. Not me.'

Accusations and counter-accusations. Lance's lies were as smooth as his shaved scalp, but with the statements from Owen, Rollo, Meri and other witnesses, the detectives were building a case against him. And Derek. The two friends had the opportunity, the capability and the motive to commit at least two of the murders.

Not surprisingly, nothing in the old files linked either of them to the disappearances. Lance's uncle, Inspector Nelson, had kept very sparse records. Had he looked the other way or was he actually complicit in the deaths? Poole's team hadn't worked it out yet.

And then there was Fabian Lavigne.

Yuki had been unaware of Lance's substandard work on the resort and her husband's demands for him to fix it. 'Fabian never told me. He knew I would insist on delaying the launch until it was repaired. And we couldn't afford that.'

Poole and his team watched the CCTV footage of the night Fabian disappeared, the thirtieth of October last year. They'd studied it before, but this time they were focusing not on Fabian's movements, but Lance's. At six fifty-seven, Lance entered the frame. He joined Fabian in conversation at the bar. There was no audio, but the body language told the story: Fabian spoke pleadingly, his hands out; Lance stepped closer, menacing the older man. His back to the camera, Fabian suddenly jerked as though he'd received a quick jab to the abdomen. Lance walked away wearing a toothy grin.

An hour later, Fabian approached the mayor, who had just finished dinner at one of the long tables. But before Fabian could reach her, Lance intervened. He escorted Emmeline to the bar, where a champagne bucket was placed in front of them, and Lance gestured for others to join them. At ten-thirty, Lance left with the mayor, while Fabian remained for another hour. He was unsteady on his feet and unable to open the door to exit. A staff member came and turned the handle for him, patted him on the shoulder and sent him out into the night.

Poole squinted at the TV screen, trying to figure out if Fabian was drunk or whether Lance had slipped him a sedative, the old trick from his teenage years. The images couldn't give him an answer.

Fabian staggered down Dolphin Street towards the marina, then simply vanished into the darkness of the park.

While Lance had been in the interview room yesterday, Detective Senior Sergeant Lena Coleman visited his office and met with the office manager, his mother. Initially, Ninetta had been wary, assuming the detective wanted to talk about Blake and the teenage gang. But when Coleman began asking about Fabian Lavigne, she'd been happy to assist: 'Anything to help his poor wife. Fabian was such a dish with his French accent. A nice change from the other old blokes around here. He always wore lovely shoes. Not very practical, but very stylish.' Ninetta had handed over some paper documents and a thumb drive relating to their work at Fabian's resort. 'It was a big project for us,' she'd boasted. 'We hired extra subbies and extra equipment, so there are numerous job sheets.'

Late yesterday, Coleman had looked over the paperwork and discovered the compliance certificates had been falsified. The certifier who'd approved Lance's work at the resort did not exist. She found the same fake name on multiple projects.

Now Meri Britton had mentioned the Blue Waters Panorama Residences, an expensive investment with a lot at stake. Poole walked over to the desk where Coleman was working.

'Did Ninetta give you anything on the Blue Waters development yesterday?' he asked.

'I don't think so. But we had a whole bunch of electronic documents.' Coleman opened up a new window on her computer. 'What are you looking for precisely?'

'Not sure. Anything from the week Fabian went missing— late October, early November last year?'

A needle in a haystack. He didn't understand enough about corrupt building practices to know where to search. Coleman tapped on the keyboard and brought up job sheets and invoices. Flicking between documents, she read quickly.

'There's a job sheet related to Blue Waters,' she said. 'They hired a digger on the twenty-fifth of October and kept it onsite until the third of November.'

'Good work.'

'Also, forensics re-examined the abusive letters sent to Fabian,' she said. 'It just came through. They believe that two of the letters match the formatting and style of Lance's correspondence.'

'I'm getting a warrant.'

He was infuriated that they hadn't found this in their investigation last year. They'd spoken to Lance and many others, but nothing had indicated his strong connection to Fabian.

Poole would be going in hard now.

'I'll need a search team, shovels and a backhoe on standby. And see if we can organise a cadaver dog from the Dog Unit.'

61

Student: Taj Britton
Year 9 Technology, Mrs McKellar
Assignment: Unusual ideas to combat climate change

Saving whales can save our planet!
Whales are ancient creatures that evolved into their current form around 30 million years ago. Humans nearly hunted them into extinction. When humpback whaling was banned in 1963, as few as 100 whales remained off the east coast of Australia.

The protection laws, along with marine research, have led to an amazing success story. Surveys estimate around 40,000 whales on Australia's east coast today, with a growth rate of 10 per cent a year. The humpback whale has been taken off the list of threatened species. However, whales face new threats—the effects of pollution and climate change.

But scientists have discovered that whales actually help to fight climate change. Their waste products encourage the growth of phytoplankton, which contributes to more than 50 per cent of the planet's oxygen levels. Whales also capture tonnes of carbon in their bodies—equivalent to planting thousands of trees. When a whale dies and sinks to the bottom of the ocean, it locks the carbon away for hundreds of years.

The International Monetary Fund has put a figure on the value of an individual whale to the economy—$2 million. It noted that nature had created this whale-based carbon-sink technology, and humans needed to revitalise whale populations to let it work properly again for our planet.

62

POOLE

OUTSIDE THE FENCE TO THE BLUE WATERS PANORAMA RESIDENCES, Poole presented the search warrant to Lance's solicitor—the developer had insisted on having him here, while simultaneously claiming he had nothing to hide. Lance undid the padlocks on the wire fence around the building site with a smile. But when he spotted the yellow backhoe rumbling up the street, his smile twisted into a snarl.

The search team consisted of twelve officers plus the cadaver dog and its handler. Despite Poole's concerns about timing, they'd managed to get the search warrant issued by the magistrate and the equipment in place by Saturday mid-morning.

The Blue Waters Panorama Residences currently consisted of grass and dirt. The storm had created furrows where water cascaded down the incline. Black plastic, sticks and bits of metal clumped together like a dam wall against the fence at the lower end of the block. As promised, the location offered panoramic views over Kinton Bay, to the heads in the distance. It was yet another stunning winter day, the water sparkling in the sunshine. A yacht set sail from the marina, its red spinnaker a defiant blot against the green-blue sea and the bright blue sky.

Poole's officers started methodically searching the block while the dog got to work. A black and white English springer spaniel, it followed the handler's orders and began sniffing the area closest to the fence.

At one end of the vacant block sat a small, prefabricated site office.

'Can you unlock the shed for us?'

'There's nothing inside,' Lance said. 'We don't have approval to start work yet.'

Poole waved him towards the door and Lance drew a key from his pocket. When Poole walked inside, the air smelt damp. A fine layer of mud coated the floor. The roof must've leaked in the storms.

'What's underneath here?' he asked.

'Just some footings. We levelled the earth.'

'Concrete?'

'I don't really remember. It was last year. I think I was in Sydney when the portable arrived.'

Walking out of the shed again, Poole noticed the cadaver dog. It had stopped moving and was focused on the dirt right next to the shed.

'Sir, we might have something,' the female handler said.

'Right.' He sized up the shed. 'We'll need a crane to get this moved.'

'I've got a business to run,' Lance whined. 'I don't have time to wait for a crane. It'll take hours to get here.'

And how much would Lance be squirming during those hours?

⌒

Poole left the team, asking them to call him once the crane was in place, and returned to the station. The detectives working on Stefan's case had contacted the hospital to check on his medical history and any links with Greyson. There was no overlap: Greyson had already disappeared by the time Stefan arrived in Kinton Bay. However, they'd found something else.

'A few weeks before he went missing, Stefan presented to the hospital with a laceration to his hip,' Detective Sergeant Singh explained. 'I've tracked down the doctor who sewed him up. She was a resident at the time and it was one of her first knife wounds.'

'Good work. What did she say?'

'Stefan lied about the injury.' Singh read from her notes. 'He insisted that he'd cut himself on rocks, although she could see the injury was made by a knife. She suggested going to the police, but Stefan wouldn't hear of it. I suspect he told no-one—his parents didn't know about it.'

A knife. Derek's trademark.

'I don't suppose there are any reports of a brawl that night?' he asked. Even if something had happened, it was highly unlikely that Inspector Nelson would have kept a record.

'No, but I spoke to the former bar manager. He'd seen Derek and Lance harassing the backpacker a few times. The arguments seemed to be about high school girls. Derek said the girls were off limits, they were "theirs". It was around the time of his eighteenth birthday. Derek was finally allowed into the pub legally.'

A turf war about girls. A milestone birthday without his twin. Had that triggered Derek to commit another killing?

All the evidence they had so far was circumstantial, but the pieces were adding up. Soon, there would be enough to charge him for the murders. Although it wasn't ideal, a jury could convict on strong circumstantial evidence.

'The bar manager gave some other information, sir,' Singh continued. 'He said the pub owner and Inspector Nelson had special negotiations about extended trading hours. The bar staff was also encouraged to report any drug deals which weren't by *approved* dealers. Nelson was taking a cut of all the profits from the pub and the dealers. And he kept a regular room for sex with female backpackers.'

'Is the bar manager willing to make a formal statement?'

'Yep.' Singh nodded.

Excellent. It looked like they'd have enough evidence to bring in Nelson. The inspector shared part of the blame for the sexual assaults and murders in Kinton Bay. Perhaps he'd end up in the same facility as his nephew, whom he'd allowed a free rein.

In the meantime, Meri Britton had made a formal statement relating to historical sexual assault by Derek O'Riordan. She believed that others would be coming forward. Two women had made similar allegations about Lance. The statements also mentioned the involvement of Scott Kinton, the editor's son. The naval police coxswain on the ship had set up an online conference for them to interview Scott tomorrow.

Two detectives were investigating whether Lance had threatened or caused injury to Glenda O'Riordan. Her sister confirmed that Glenda had been scared of Lance in the last few weeks of her life, ever since they'd got Derek's parole date. From what Poole could extrapolate, Lance had been using Derek for intimidation a few years ago—to Fabian and to others. Yuki recalled some strange events when they were in the building process: a deliberate flat tyre on Fabian's car, broken windows, a dead possum on their doorstep, noises at night. Not enough to call the police but enough to cause worry.

Perhaps Derek knew something about Fabian's whereabouts and that was why Lance wanted him to stay away? The detectives had set up an interview with Ninetta, Lance's mother, who'd found Glenda after her first fall. She might also have an address for Inspector Nelson, her brother-in-law.

God, this small town was so inter-related.

⌒

Poole arrived back at the vacant block to see a huge red crane positioning its chains over the top of the shed. Amid steel ropes and hooks, shouted directions and workers in hard hats, the portable office rose into the air. It was manoeuvred it into a flat area in the middle of the site.

Where the shed had been, a rectangular cement slab shone in the sunlight. The backhoe began its work, breaking up the concrete. Next came officers with spades, digging by hand, the soil dark and soft. Four feet down, an officer called out for everyone to stop. He'd spotted a patch of colour in the black earth.

A tan leather shoe.

He always wore lovely shoes. Not very practical, but very stylish.
They'd found Fabian.

63

MERI

THE EDITORIAL DIRECTOR, BERNARD EMERY, ARRIVED FROM SYDNEY ON Monday morning and had a long closed-door meeting with Neville. Then Meri was invited in. When Bernard explained the changes, she avoided eye contact with her editor. They spent two more hours together as other staff were called in, one-by-one, to provide updates on their work.

As she sat in Neville's office, Meri hoped that Hugh had finished the follow-up to her breaking story about Fabian. Poor Yuki—her husband buried under a building site. For the past ten months, she'd been driving past him every time she went to the supermarket. The fact that his body was found on the Blue Waters site had shaken Neville. Meri suspected the development wouldn't go ahead now. And at last, Lance would be behind bars, where he belonged.

Neville called a full staff meeting for five o'clock, but first, he wanted to speak to Meri alone.

With butterflies in her stomach, she silently recited Caroline's approach—do not apologise, do not pander to the men, their emotions are not your responsibility. The shelving unit behind

Neville's desk was almost empty. He'd packed all his books and photos into boxes. After Meri came in, he slammed the door behind her and motioned for her to sit.

'I've been here for over thirty years. My whole working life.' He stood on the other side of his desk, leaning forward, arms rigid, the veins in his neck bulging. 'I've kept this paper going when all the other regionals around here have closed. And *this* is my thanks.'

'Neville, I'm sorry.' Damn, the apology had slipped out. No matter, she still planned to speak her mind. 'But you kept this paper going by doing dodgy, unethical advertorial deals.'

'Unethical. Bah!' He waved a hand through the air, sweeping away the word. 'We live in a small town, Meri. Everything's connected.'

'But we have standards. Rules we have to follow.' She couldn't believe his excuses. 'We, of all people, have to be above board or how can our readers trust us?'

'It was you, wasn't it.' He stood up again. 'I took you on even though you had no training, no experience, because your mother was sick. And this—this is how you repay me?'

He'd been kind and understanding when Mum was dying and the twins were young. Part of her felt like a traitor; the other part was angry and righteous.

'I'm grateful for the opportunities you gave me. I've also worked bloody hard and followed your stupid "good news" guidelines.' She rose to her feet as well. 'I will not, however, support your unethical behaviour, nor allow you to make your reporters complicit in these practices. You've repeatedly breached the media code of ethics. Honesty. Fairness. Independence.'

'Get off your high horse, Meri. We need to work with businesses to survive. This is the real world.'

'And does that involve downplaying murder?' She handed him the ethics page printed from the Media, Entertainment and Arts Alliance website. 'You did not report Blake's disappearance with fairness. All the time, you were protecting your son.'

The piece of paper shook in Neville's hands. He stumbled back into his chair and the page fell to the floor. 'Scott didn't break any laws. He was just in the wrong place at the wrong time.'

Typical Neville—trying to spin a positive slant right to the very end.

⌒

Meri arrived home to dinner preparations: Rollo was cutting up potatoes while Siena peeled carrots. They cheered when she told them about her new role as acting editor.

'I'll be shaking up the place,' she said. 'You'll be seeing much more than good news stories and business-friendly articles.'

'Go, Mum!' Siena gave her a hug.

Was her daughter actually proud of her?

The feeling was mutual.

Meri was so impressed with her daughter for standing up to Axel. And so very, very scared. She wanted to swaddle Siena in her old orange baby wraps and tuck her safely into her cot. Protect her from this ordeal. But the time for swaddling and coddling had passed. Meri kept picturing the trial: the effect it would have on Siena, on all of them. She knew communities could operate in one of two ways—gather around and protect a victim, or pile on in a personal attack. And she'd do everything in her power to stop Axel Evans, or his supporters, from hurting Siena. But they had extra support on their side. Associate Professor Caroline Poole, criminologist, knowledgeable about the system, and with a husband who was head of the local police: she'd make sure justice was dealt.

But right now, Meri wanted to enjoy this moment; she decided they needed to get out of the kitchen and celebrate.

'Put the veggies back in the fridge for tomorrow,' she said. 'Let's go and have fish and chips with Taj.'

Mick greeted them at the shop and took their order himself. Only two other customers were waiting but he seemed harried, his face red and his glasses steamy.

'Is Taj on a break?' Meri asked. 'We were hoping to eat dinner with him.'

Mick stopped writing on his order pad and looked up at her. 'He's not working tonight. I haven't seen Taj for months.'

'What do you mean? He said you called him in.'

The happiness she'd been feeling about her new job popped like a balloon. Months? He hadn't been working for months.

She turned to Siena. 'Where's your brother?'

64

Axel will be charged soon. An unexpected bonus was those girls coming forward during his absence.

That Saturday night when Siena ran in front of my car, I'd seen the group near the bowling club and decided to do a lap of the town, checking on the girls. The sight of Siena, bruised and terrified, made me furious. After all these years, after all my efforts, she shouldn't be going through the same as her mother.

Of course, it was Axel chasing her. The toolie, they called him, hanging around teenage girls, supplying booze and dope to make them even more vulnerable. Blake and Derek all over again. Except he was smarter than them. Years ago, Frances had warned the twins, told them to stop. They'd taken no notice. Not Axel. He'd followed my directions on the anonymous instructions perfectly; apart from the mobile phone—I don't know how that ended up on the boat.

I'd been watching him for months, hatching a few different plans. But when I saw Siena, I just wanted the girls to be safe immediately. Even if it was only for a short time while I sorted out the next step. I left a bottle of rum outside his front door that very night. Attached to it was an envelope with his name and an anonymous note inside.

You know what you've done, Axel. Sexual assault of girls under sixteen. Legally, they're children. The maximum penalty is ten years in jail. Is that what you want? If not, get out of town immediately. Go to the blue bench near the marina. Take the envelope taped underneath the seat. It has cash for a train ticket to Brisbane. Leave your phone there. Don't contact anyone. Don't tell anyone. Stay away from girls.

I'll be watching to make sure you go. The only other option is the police. And JAIL.

Times have changed. The police and the law are catching up. If only it hadn't taken so long, Blake and the others would still be alive.

65

POOLE

AFTER A BUSY WEEKEND PULLING TOGETHER ALL OF THE EVIDENCE FOR the murder charge against Lance, the team finally celebrated with drinks at Poole's house on Monday night. They could hardly have a beer at the Time'n'Tide, where the victim had spent his last hours alive. And Poole was mindful of the family's grief. While Yuki's concerns had been substantiated, she was obviously devastated by the discovery.

Ten officers lounged on the back deck around a table laden with chips and dips. Caroline had put out plates ready for Chinese takeaway. Later tonight, when they were alone, he'd tell her his plan. Before the pandemic, Caroline had attended two international conferences a year. She missed the travel and the collegiate learning. But next November, one had been scheduled in Istanbul. His proposal was to go to the conference together, then fly to Jordan afterwards and visit Petra. It was on their bucket list: an ancient city carved into pink sandstone cliffs in the midst of a desert two thousand years ago. Such incredible history. The names of the structures could have come from a mythical book—the Temple of Winged Lions, the Street of Facades, and the High Place of Sacrifice. She'd love it.

'Do you think we'll get Derek for the murders?' Frawley's booming voice cut into his thoughts.

'Yep, we will,' he said. 'The evidence is building up.'

'But why would he kill his own brother?' Constable Terry asked.

'Twin killings are rare but they do happen.' Caroline put down her wineglass to explain. 'Sometimes the sibling rivalry is so intense that a twin decides the other has to die, so he can live freely. There have been a few interesting cases in America. Some premeditated, others committed in an impulsive rage.'

Poole fetched his wife's report from the dining table inside and brandished it to the team. 'Have you all read Caroline's research? It's got some good background on serial killers. Really useful stuff.'

Detective Sergeant Sarah Singh took the report from him. It fell open at a page and she began reading aloud. '*Female serial killers are uncommon, comprising around one in ten offenders or even fewer. This makes research into the phenomenon more difficult; however, it has been determined that their motivations and methods are very different from those of male killers. Generally, females are less violent and less sadistic. Known as the quiet killers, they are more likely to use poisons and drugs than guns and knives. They plan meticulously and often kill people close to them. Some female serial killers are motivated by rage—they kill as a result of perceived injustice. They are less likely to be arrested.*'

'Motivated by rage, hey?' Frawley guffawed. 'I'd better watch out for my wife then. She's going through menopause and getting angrier every day.'

'Just keep doing your job properly, at home and at work.' Caroline patted Frawley's shoulder. 'Then women won't have to rage at all the injustices.'

Poole smiled across the table at her—Caroline would fight injustice wherever she encountered it. Returning his smile, she opened another bottle of wine and refilled the glasses.

66

On 15 August 1998, I turned up to Kinton Bay police station. Senior Constable Rosalind Spencer stood at the front desk. She was the only one who'd vaguely listened to Frances; I hoped she'd listen to me. I was determined to get justice for my best friend.

'Today is Frances Wilcox's twenty-second birthday but she isn't here to celebrate it,' I announced. 'Miss Wilcox tried to help those girls and instead she was bullied to death by Blake and Derek O'Riordan. They should be investigated and arrested.'

The policewoman held up her hand, signalling me to stop. 'What's your name and occupation, please?'

'Callie Maguire. I'm doing a teaching degree. Frances and I lived in the same college at uni in Sydney and she was my best friend.'

Two years older than me, Frances sometimes acted like my big sister. She looked out for me. I hadn't done the same—I'd failed her.

'My condolences on your friend's death,' Senior Constable Spencer said. 'Frances was well liked in Kinton Bay. But the coroner has already prepared a report.'

We were interrupted by a middle-aged woman and two teenage girls shuffling through the front door. The mother approached the desk, stepping around me. When she whispered to the senior constable, I could just make out her words.

'My daughter and niece think they've been raped.'

The policewoman called Inspector Nelson and I studied the girls. Faces blotchy from crying, eyes glazed. They seemed so young in their pink and blue shorts, with their plastic jelly shoes. Had Frances's death made no difference to the safety of girls in this town?

'They don't remember anything,' the mother was saying. 'What am I going to tell my sister? We're up from Sydney and we brought Janey on holiday with us for a week. I'm responsible. It's my fault. But Vicki can't remember anything either. What am I supposed to do?'

The mother kept gabbling and I stepped closer to the girls.

'I'm so sorry.' I kept my voice low, hoping the older women wouldn't hear. 'Where did this happen?'

'There was a party at the cave last night.' The teenager in the blue shorts answered me. 'Out in that national park.'

'And who was there?'

'A group of boys. There were twins.'

Frances had told me the stories of the cave. Nothing had changed.

A tall man in uniform came through the internal doors. Inspector Nelson. The one who hadn't helped Frances and the girls; the one who blackmailed female backpackers for sex. Nelson smiled down at the mother and placed a hand on her shoulder. Patted her gently.

'I'm sorry you're going through this, madam. How confusing for you all.' He nodded at the girls. 'Come on through and I'm sure we'll work out this misunderstanding quickly. Kinton Bay is a safe place, but some teenagers are using drugs. I expect your girls got caught up in a party atmosphere.'

The mother nodded. The girls glanced at each other.

'It's the beach culture.' Inspector Nelson guided them towards the door leading to the interview room. 'I know it's exciting for young girls and they want to try out new things. Don't worry, I'm sure we can figure this out in a jiffy and we won't need to even talk about charges of illegal drug use and possession.'

Before the door closed, one of the teenagers stared back at me. Her dazed look had given way to wide-eyed fear. Now I could see how the Inspector must have fobbed off Frances. Blame the girls for making trouble, not the boys who were causing it.

Storming back to Rosalind Spencer, I caught her frown before she rearranged her features into a neutral mask.

'Did you hear that?' I asked. 'Those girls have been raped by Blake and Derek O'Riordan and your Inspector just threatened them with drug charges. This is exactly what Frances was trying to stop. Why aren't you doing something?'

I could taste salty tears on my lips. Tears for Frances. Tears for these girls. Furious tears at the hopelessness of the situation.

I'm sorry, Frances. I was just trying to give you justice for your birthday. But we can't trust the police to do anything. I'll have to deal with it myself.

When the policewoman refused to listen, I set off to find the O'Riordan twins. As I drove around town searching for the unmistakable boys, I decided that teaching was no longer a career option for me. I had to work out how to change the warped police system.

I spotted one of them outside the back of the supermarket near the big garbage bins.

'My little sister was at the cave with you guys last night,' I said. 'She left her watch there. Dad gave it to her and he'll kill her if she's lost it. Can you help me find it? I can drive but I need you to show me the path to the cave.'

I didn't know if he'd buy my story. He seemed sceptical, cautious. Or perhaps calculating at which point he could drug me so I'd be his next easy victim.

'Do you a deal.' He finally spoke. 'I'll come to the cave with you. And then after, can you give me twenty bucks and drive me to the bus stop at Harbours End?'

'Okay. Deal.'

Scumbag. He'd raped those girls and now he was asking me to give him money and drive him around. The pills were in my wallet—ironically, they'd come from Lance. Months and months ago, Frances had confiscated them during an English lesson. He'd been showing off to the other boys in class. I had beers in my backpack, ready for the tablet.

He was silent in the car and on the walking track. Inside the cave, we searched for the watch. After five minutes, I pretended to find it, on a rock ledge. 'Yay! My dad will never know, and my sister will live to see another day.'

'Great . . . well, I gotta catch that bus now.'

'Yep, I'll drive you there.' But instead of walking, I sat down on the rock, cracked open a beer and took a sip. 'It's nice getting away from my crazy family for a few hours. This place is so calm. Have a quick beer with me?'

He took the can from me, and then his hand hovered near my neck. Oh god, he was going to attack me right now. Ducking, I reached for my backpack, preparing to run.

'You okay?' He frowned. 'You've got a leaf in your hair.'

Without taking my eyes off him, I ran my fingers through my hair. Felt the crunch of dry leaves. He hadn't been lying.

'Yep, all good.' But how was I going to spike his drink without him noticing?

Suddenly he put the beer can down on a rock. Oh no.

'Just gotta take a piss,' he said, wandering off to the side of the cave.

While he was peeing, I crushed the tablet into his beer can. I could hear the stream of his urine. What a disgusting jerk. Acting so nonchalant when he'd bullied Frances to death and raped all of those girls. A nasty piece of work. Quickly, I added another tablet to the beer. A double dose should work faster.

Later, after he collapsed, I stripped him. Put his clothes in my backpack. Left him naked, drugged, humiliated.

Like he and his mates had done to the girls.

~

So many times, I almost admitted my crime to Mum. She must've guessed something was going on—the sudden change from my teaching degree to criminology; the new feminist friends I brought home; my constant lectures about bad men; the Reclaim the Night marches.

The image of Blake's body in the crevasse had imprinted itself in my brain.

Had I killed him with the double dose? Or had he banged his head when he fell? I didn't know. Would I be charged with manslaughter? Murder?

Over and over, I argued each side in my head: How could I have done that? I must confess. No, he deserved it. It was justice. He's evil. They're not looking for him.

At the time, I didn't understand the impact Blake's disappearance would have on others—his mother, his friends, his classmates, his teachers, even his revolting brother.

And on me.

⌒

After Blake and Greyson, I should've stayed away from Kinton Bay. But I kept coming back. No-one else was looking out for the girls. The school had failed them, the police didn't care. They needed me. I appointed myself their unofficial protector, an old-fashioned chaperone, spying on beach parties from the shadows. The Avenging Angel.

One Saturday afternoon, I saw the Swiss backpacker on the beach, helping teenage girls with their surfing, flirting and touching them. I watched him. After dark, he bought alcohol, sat on the sand and gave them drinks until they could barely walk. And then he took the underage girls into the dunes.

Those three men thought they could have whoever they wanted, without consent. The victims couldn't remember what had happened. Too confused, too scared to go to the police. To an inspector who wouldn't do anything anyway.

So I dispensed justice for the girls.

Stefan was the easiest. 'Meet me in the carpark by Main Beach when the pub closes,' I purred in his ear. 'I know a special place we can go.' He was so sure of himself, so sure he could have sex with any girl, that he got into my car. I passed him the spiked vodka on the way to the cave. He tried to kiss me but I made him wait. 'It'll be worth it,' I promised him. In that last moment, he finally realised—the hunter had become the prey.

Of course, I know now that vigilante justice has its flaws.

Until I saw the small article in the newspaper about a missing teenager, I thought that I'd killed Derek.

And now Meri is saying Blake wasn't involved with the sexual assaults at the earlier parties; that the only time was when his brother forced him that Friday night.

I made a terrible mistake.

67

MERI

ROLLO MOTIONED FOR THEM TO STEP ONTO THE FOOTPATH FOR A FAMILY discussion away from Mick and the other customers at the fish and chip shop.

'I'll phone Taj,' he said. 'I'm sure there's a simple explanation.'

Meri's mind was racing. Mick said he hadn't seen her son *for months*. What was Taj doing on Friday nights and all day Saturday? And all the other nights? *I've been called in because Mick's daughter can't work*, he'd told Rollo. Months of lies. She'd trusted him without question. Easygoing Taj. Never a problem. It was her daughter she'd worried about—vulnerable Siena up against violent boys, alcohol and drugs.

Had she been worrying about the wrong twin? The days off school, the headaches and stomach pains.

'No answer,' said Rollo.

Meri tried calling on her phone—no answer again—then she checked the location app. His face didn't come up. He'd switched it off yet again. She made Siena ring from her number as well. Still no answer.

'Where is he?' she asked Siena. 'What's he been doing?'

'I'm sure he's fine, Mum. He's got another job online. He said it pays better. I don't know anything else.'

But Siena's forehead crinkled with worry, mirroring her own.

An online job. How on earth did a fifteen-year-old boy make money online? Gambling? Pornography? Cryptocurrency? Sports betting? Buying vapes or synthetic pills and selling them at school? None of that sounded like her smart, sensitive son.

'But if it's online, why isn't he at home?'

'He'll be okay.' Rollo echoed their daughter's reassurance. 'Why don't you text his mates, Siena? And look him up on that Snap Maps thingy.'

A gentle sea breeze lifted some food wrappers in the gutter and made them dance briefly. Meri peered down the street: the pub windows shone with light while, further away, the marina was enveloped in darkness. She heard the familiar *tink-tink-tink* of ropes knocking against masts. In the park, a small group of people sat at a picnic table. Geoffrey Kinton's statue loomed darkly above them. Was Taj at a beach party? A mate's place?

She shouldn't be this worried; it was only seven o'clock. He'd come home as soon as his fake shift ended, walking in the door, pretending he needed a shower to wash off the smell of fried fish. But why would Taj lie to them?

As Siena received messages from each friend, it became clear that no-one had seen him tonight.

Mick called out from the shop that their fish and chips were ready. Meri asked him to put the packets in the warmer, saying they just had to pop to the supermarket for something.

They could scour the streets of Kinton Bay, the cafes, the pub, the bowling club. Drive to the hockey fields and the high school. Check the marina, walk along Main Beach and over to Grotto Rocks. But what if he'd gone to the Killing Cave?

If Taj wasn't with his friends, then where could he be? Did he have a secret girlfriend? Or boyfriend? He hadn't shown any interest in relationships, unlike some of his mates. Meri had assumed that he was still developing, a step behind his sister as he had been since birth.

'Let's walk to the bowlo,' Rollo suggested. 'Someone might have seen him.'

They started up the main street with Meri checking her phone every minute. She'd rung him five times now—Rollo said to stop. Outside the Chinese restaurant, Caroline Poole was waiting for takeaway. She said she hadn't seen Taj. The one set of traffic lights in town changed on their approach and the red man flashed up. Meri looked at her phone again. No response from Taj.

She clicked on the useless location app—what was the point of it? Siena had left her phone at Jasminda's the night she went to the Killing Cave; Taj just turned his off or let the battery run down. These teenagers she was trying to safeguard were too clever for their own good. And they believed they were immortal.

On the app screen, two faces—hers and Siena's—clustered together at the corner of Dolphin and Redpath streets. The app froze for a moment, and then another circle flicked on—Taj's face. Down to their left, two blocks away on Dianella Street.

'Look.' She showed the others.

Siena reached over to her phone and enlarged the map. 'I think he's at the historical society building.'

'I can smell . . .' Rollo was sniffing the air.

They'd just passed the Chinese restaurant with its aroma of garlic and ginger. How could he be thinking about food now?

'Smoke.'

They could see the fire as soon as they turned into Dianella Street. Flames racing up the wall and verandah at the southern end, licking across the roof. The Kinton Bay Historical Society was based in an old weatherboard house filled with wooden artefacts and old papers. All highly flammable. They sprinted up the street, their shoes slamming on the concrete: Rollo the fastest, followed by Siena, and Meri in the rear. As she came closer, Meri recognised Hayley on the footpath, yelling into her mobile for the fire brigade to hurry up. Then she saw two more figures bolting in the opposite direction—teenage boys, one chasing the other and screaming, 'Bring back the key, you fuckwit!' Neither of them resembled Taj.

A car pulled up next to Hayley, and the occupant rushed out to help.

Orange glowed where there should have been dark windows, smoke billowed from the roof. Staring at the building, Meri willed herself to keep running, to move, to act. But her legs were frozen; the world had suddenly fallen into slow motion. *Please, God, no. Don't let him be inside there.*

A strangled sound came from her throat.

'Taj! No, no, no.'

68

Meri asks if I've seen Taj as she passes the Chinese restaurant. I wonder if I should mention the Kinton Bay Historical Society. A few evenings I've spotted Taj going in there. But he never took anyone or anything inside with him—no girls, no alcohol, no drugs. He wasn't coaxing his prey into a hidden location like Axel or Derek.

Meri has been so busy protecting her daughter that she forgot about her son. That's part of the reason I never had kids. Impossible to keep them safe in this world. Instead, I became the protector of the girls here for a few years. And then, when the position came up for Doug, it was his turn. I debated whether it would be a mistake to move up here with Doug's job. Having to face the memories.

But no-one has ever recognised me. I discarded my nickname long ago. And with my dyed hair, my married name, my academic job, I'm a million miles from the young woman who spied on beach parties. And no-one knew that I was Frances's roommate at college. Our friendship blossomed in my first year at uni, an isolated bubble of independence, away from our families and childhood friends. When she got the job in Kinton Bay, I came up to visit her almost every weekend. We went swimming and had picnics; we didn't go to the pub or the cafes. She wanted to stay away from all the school kids, their parents and the other teachers. While I knew all about Inspector Nelson, Durham and the Wrecking Crew from Frances, none of them knew me.

Every decision I've made since then has been to build a foundation for an impeccable character. Who would ever suspect a twenty-one-year-old woman as a serial killer? A high-achieving uni student with a double degree in criminology and psychology. An associate professor. A volunteer for women's shelters. The wife of a police chief.

If I'm ever considered a person of interest, I have my defence ready. I've been creating it for years. Diaries to show I was with friends on the significant days. Trinkets to support my alibis. A photo album labelled with the wrong dates.

And as if the killer would come back to live here after so many years. That's counterintuitive.

Who could ever suspect me over someone like Lance or Derek?

But my conscience has been troubling me in the small hours. Blake did not deserve my 'justice'. I got the wrong twin. In my nightmares, I apologise to him and his mum. But to admit to his accidental death would expose my involvement in the others. I've dedicated my life to protecting girls. Made sacrifices. I will not be sent to trial by Doug and his detectives.

Those detectives who are now waiting for me to bring back the Chinese takeaway. My conscience is also niggling me about the ways I've misdirected their investigation. I could not believe it when Sarah Singh read out the section from my report about female serial killers. They're smart, Doug and those detectives—super smart. And I know how dedicated they are to seeking justice for the victims. That's exactly what I was doing too.

The containers of Chinese food sit on the passenger seat releasing spicy aromas. As I turn the corner, I see flames lighting up the dark sky.

'The fire engine's coming,' Hayley shrieks as I hurry out of the car. 'Taj is in there.'

When I first joined the development committee, Olive Kinton and Aunty Bim gave me a tour of this small building. The main room held glass cases of old coins, colonial knick-knacks and historical drawings of the town. A boiling pot from the whaling industry. In another room, Aunty Bim had created a display of spears, nulla nullas and boomerangs. Photos of the stolen generations. A list of words in the local language. They'd showed me the files in the back room—boxes and boxes of historical documents, a bookshelf lined with three different sets of encyclopaedias.

Old paper, brittle and dry. Is that where the fire had started?

Flames leap across the verandah posts towards the front door. I see Rollo darting down one side of the house. Meri and Siena are hovering around the windows.

'Axel locked all the doors,' Hayley tells me, tears dripping down her face. 'We told him not to but he just laughed at us.'

'There's a back door,' I say. 'I'll see if I can get in.'

I'm already running, unlatching the side gate, flying along the narrow garden path. I'll have to smash a window. Will that create a surge of oxygen and accelerate the fire? Too panicked to think clearly, I pick up a rock from the border of the flowerbed and keep sprinting. Three steps up to the back verandah.

The back door is locked, as Hayley said. I kick at the handle for a few moments but it doesn't budge. Along the verandah, I spy a window, waist high. Inside is the little office where Olive works. After smashing the rock into one of the panes, I twist my hand into an awkward hook and undo the latch. As I lift up the window, a whooshing sound pulsates through the house. Oh god, I've made the fire explode. Scrambling inside, I slam the window down again, praying it will shut out some of the oxygen source.

'Taj!' I scream. Inhale smoke, and cough. Pull my shirt up to cover my mouth. 'Taj, where are you?'

Get down, I remember that advice. I drop and crawl along the floor towards the flames. Fear constricts my throat.

'Taj,' I call again. Where can he be? Through the thick grey haze, it's difficult to determine the layout of the building. I crawl forwards and see the door frame burning, a gateway to hell. Go, go, go! I urge myself, trying to overcome the terror. The smoke stings my eyes, I'm blinking and crying. Taj must be suffering so much more.

Amid the creaking and crackling of the fire, I hear a voice. 'In here!'

He's lying beside a heavy, old-fashioned cabinet in the main room. I can't understand why he hasn't escaped to the back office. And then I see his ankle. It's encircled by an old colonial chain, with the other end wrapped around the cabinet leg. It's fastened tightly with a gold padlock.

As an avenging angel, I helped countless girls but I took three lives. That's the other reason I didn't have kids—a self-imposed punishment. Perhaps in saving Taj, I can begin to redeem myself. Atone for the pain I inflicted on those men's families when I delivered my justice.

The flames are in the ceiling, leaping and dancing in our direction.

'You have to lift the cabinet,' Taj gasps.

Splinters of wood are scattered on his jeans and the floor. He must have tried to kick over the heavy piece of furniture with his free leg, risked tipping it on top of himself. Still kneeling, I grasp the underside of the cabinet, but it doesn't budge. I'll have to stand to use my full strength. The hot air and smoke burn my throat. Sweat drips from my hair, down my back. Bracing myself, I grip the edge and heave with all my strength. The cabinet jolts up an inch. Taj rolls to one side, releasing his leg.

'Back room,' I tell him, pointing.

He's crawling, the chain still attached, dragging behind him. The wall where we'd just been is ablaze, the cabinet on fire. He's not going fast enough—I can feel the heat on my bum, my legs, my feet. The crash of a beam from the ceiling makes him speed up.

'The office.' I choke out the words. 'The window . . . open.'

Through the flaming doorway we go, the return from hell. The office is still intact, although the grey haze has filled this room too. Taj opens the window, pulls himself through. He's safe. I can hear voices outside. A siren shrieks through my chaotic thoughts. The fire brigade has arrived.

As the breeze comes in the open window, I hear a soft whoosh. It's fine, I'm nearly there. But then there's a huge cracking noise from the front of the building. The fireys must have smashed open the front door. Air rushes down the corridor and flames roar into the office. I'm still on my hands and knees. My feet are hot, my sneakers feel like they're melting.

The house seems to shudder. Contracting in pain. The crackling of the fire is so loud, but beneath it, I can hear the house rupturing. The roof is caving in.

69

ROLLO

TAJ STAYED IN HOSPITAL FOR THE NIGHT. NO BURNS, THANK GOD, BUT the doctors wanted to monitor his lungs for the effects of smoke inhalation. They gave him oxygen and dressed the wound on his ankle where he'd jerked at the chain. A tetanus shot for the old rusty metal. Painkillers for his body, which ached from his efforts to escape.

The police interviewed Taj briefly. He said Axel, Jackson and Hayley must have seen him go in the back door of the building that evening. He claimed he wasn't breaking in. Olive had given him a key because he was helping set up an electronic catalogue. Why he had to do that at night, Rollo still didn't understand. He and Meri were waiting to ask their own questions when Taj was feeling better.

On Monday evening, when Taj unlocked the door to the historical society, Axel and Jackson had followed him inside and shoved him to the ground. They told Taj to make his sister retract her statement about the assault. When Taj refused, they found the old chain, grabbed a padlock from the office and attached him to the cabinet. Axel turned off his phone, kicked it out of reach, and took the key to the building.

'I'm going to set this place on fire,' he threatened.

Taj didn't believe him until Axel ran into the other room, pulled out his cigarette lighter and ignited the brittle, dry pages of the encyclopaedias. Then he'd dragged a shocked Jackson out of the building. In between trying to free his leg, Taj had managed to hook his phone with a spear and bring it closer. He'd switched it on and rung the fire brigade at the same time as Hayley. The location app had come on automatically.

Axel was being charged with starting a fire, and destroying property with the intention of causing bodily injury. Serious offences. Jackson said he'd tried to get the key back, but Axel had thrown it in a bush. Apparently, Axel kept telling the police he was drunk and not thinking straight—they hadn't been impressed with his excuse.

Rollo had been trying to kick in the back door when Taj climbed out of the window. Weeping with relief, he'd dragged his son away from the fire, into the garden. Between ragged breaths of fresh air, Taj had pointed back at the house and wheezed, 'Caroline.'

Jumping through the window himself, he'd found her on the floor and pulled her from the flames. She'd been wheezing, conscious but disorientated. When he tried to get her to stand, she'd screamed and fallen back to the floor. Rollo had managed to lift her halfway across the window ledge when Owen appeared on the verandah. Together, they bundled her out and onto the grass. Behind them, the windows flared and the inferno had engulfed the back of the house.

Caroline had been taken to hospital with Taj. They were in the waiting room with Poole when the doctor delivered the news about his wife's feet.

'No marathons for a while, then,' Poole said grimly, a soft sob escaping his lips.

'She's brave and strong and tough.' Meri had stepped forwards and grasped his hands. 'She'll get through this with your help.'

From the community hospital, Caroline was airlifted to Newcastle; the specialist burns unit there would do everything they could to heal her feet.

⌒

Last night, as water from the hoses splashed and hissed over the flames, Owen had turned to Rollo, his face stricken in the smoky glow.

'I'm sorry, mate . . . I didn't have a clue that Axel was . . . so dangerous.'

'Like Derek. Like Lance.' Rollo shook his head. 'Just the same.'

'Yep. You're right.' Owen slung an arm around his shoulder. 'I have to confess . . .'

'About what?'

'I called the police station anonymously. That's why you were dragged in for questioning.' Owen made a strange gulping sound. 'I needed the reward, the cash—and I wanted them to know what Derek did to his brother.'

Owen, not Lance, had broken the pact. Broken the gang's power over him.

'Don't worry, mate.' While Owen was feeling apologetic, perhaps he'd take this news better. Rollo sucked in a breath.

'Listen, Meri is writing a series of articles about the parties at the cave in the nineties. I'm going on record.'

'Shit!' He whistled through his teeth. 'Derek will go ballistic.'

'Will you talk to Meri too?' Rollo asked. 'Tell your side of the story? How the gang treated you?'

Waiting for his answer, Rollo scanned the building. The fire was almost extinguished. One end of the old house had been razed but near them, the blackened verandah posts still rose to the charred roof. Four walls stood. Could any of it be saved?

Owen finally answered. 'Yeah. Maybe.'

⌒

On Friday, Rollo knew what they needed. Sea air. A cleansing of their lungs. A break from the curious townspeople—their questions and their casseroles.

As Rollo started the boat's engine, he glanced at the compartment where Axel's phone had been found. Axel had admitted to police that he'd hidden it there himself, with the aim of causing trouble for Siena.

They motored out of the heads on a calm sea, the drone of the engine and the swish of the water against the hulls the only sounds. Meri sat with her arm around Taj, no space between their bodies. Siena shared the wheel with Rollo, steering the boat towards Curlew Island.

The tiny island had two sandy beaches and lots of rock platforms. In summer, he brought tourists here. A safe location for snorkelling—clear, shallow water with all kinds of fish. And it was picture perfect for Instagram: white sand against a turquoise sea, rounded russet rocks and emerald-green bushes.

Today, fluffy clouds dotted the sky, on a bright blue backdrop of winter sunshine.

As they approached the island, Siena broke the silence. 'Dad, did you know this is a culturally significant place? Kyle said the local women used to fish in the cove.'

'I didn't know that.'

'You should employ Kyle as a guide for your summer trips out here.' Siena grinned. 'He'd be great!'

Did that mean she and Kyle were friends again? Boyfriend and girlfriend?

'Good idea. I'll have a chat.'

Dropping the anchor, he ran his eyes over Curlew Island. Although named for a seabird, it was shaped like a humpback—a bulge in the middle and flatter towards the southern end, which flared out like a tail. He wondered if the traditional custodians had called it by a whale name. He'd ask Aunty Bim at the next meeting. And he'd float Siena's latest idea with her too; he wanted to learn more about this island and its past.

They picnicked where the beach met the grass, perching on rocks. Waves lapped gently against the shore; this side was so sheltered that they could see a stingray gliding along the sandy bottom.

Meri handed out chicken and mayo sandwiches, and opened a packet of barbecue chips. As usual, the twins each took a handful and shoved them into their sandwiches for extra salt and crunch.

'Did you know Taj got top marks for his whale assignment on climate change?' Siena was clearly trying to give him a boost.

'Fifty-eight out of sixty. Mrs McKellar was so impressed that she read out the last section in class.'

'Well done, mate.' Rollo patted him gently on the shoulder.

Meri, however, was not so congratulatory. 'That has to be the last one on whales, Taj. I can't believe the teachers haven't figured it out yet. You can't keep doing the same topic for different subjects. Next time, you'll get zero.'

'It's not my fault that teachers don't communicate.' Taj stuck out his bottom lip, just as he had when he was a toddler.

'You're right, communication is very important. Communication and trust,' Meri said sternly. Rollo caught her eye, and she softened. 'Why didn't you tell us about the historical society? Why did you lie to us about going to work?'

'I'm sorry.' Taj wouldn't look at them, stared at the horizon instead. 'Olive didn't know I was going there at night.'

'But she can't have been paying you,' Meri said. 'The historical society doesn't have any money.'

'No, she wasn't paying me anything.' He picked up a stick and drew circles in the sand. 'I was using the encyclopaedias to do online . . .'

'Online what?'

'Assignments.' Taj snapped the stick in two and slumped forwards with his elbows on his knees. 'Students have been paying me to do their assignments. And some online exams. That's why I was staying home sick from school. I had to do their exams in real-time. It was easy with all the online schooling.'

'Students from Kinton Bay High?' Rollo asked, confused.

'No, all over Australia. Private schools. Lots of rich kids who wanted to keep up their grades. Everyone liked my assignments so they asked me for more. They paid me heaps.'

In the past two months, he and Meri had discussed their son's illness and all the time Taj spent in his room, on his computer. They'd wondered about gastro, appendicitis, irritable bowel syndrome, food allergies, chronic fatigue, anxiety, bullying, video game addiction, buying vapes online. Nothing like this.

'You've been cheating?' Siena jabbed him in the shoulder. 'Seriously, Taj? I can't believe you'd do that.'

'It was really good money.' He shrugged. 'I wanted to start saving for a new surfboard and a van.'

'And that's why you did the whale project over and over.' Meri spoke at last. 'You were too busy working on assignments for other kids.'

'Yeah, but I've learned heaps about lots of different topics.'

Rollo didn't know how to feel. At Taj's age, he'd been smoking dope and shoplifting cigarettes and bottles of Coke for Derek. His entrepreneurial son was using his brain to rake in the dollars. Smart—but wrong.

There was still one thing Rollo didn't understand. 'Couldn't you research everything online? Why did you need the encyclopaedias?'

'I had so many assignments that I couldn't finish them on time. And then I discovered the plagiarism software most schools use doesn't check against old texts. So I was copying slabs of information from them.'

'We'll need to talk to all the schools,' Meri said. 'Tell them which students have been cheating.'

'No, Mum, please.'

When Meri said nothing, Taj looked to him for support.

'Thanks for telling us the truth,' he said. 'Let's talk about this later and enjoy the picnic now.'

He just wanted his son to relax; they were all so lucky that Taj was still with them.

After lunch, despite their objections that the water was too cold, Rollo insisted everyone had a swim. It'd be good for them all—immersion in the cool sea, the opposite of fire.

'But I'll have to go in my undies and bra,' Meri complained. 'And it'll be freezing.'

'Doesn't matter. Just ten seconds,' he bargained. 'Duck your head under. You'll feel amazing.'

Taj didn't require any coaxing; he pulled off his t-shirt and plunged into the waves.

'Beautiful,' he shouted when he came up for air.

Siena followed, splashing water at her brother. Taking Meri's hand, Rollo walked in with her, the water knee high, then thigh high, then waist high. Too slow for his liking. A fast entry was his preference. She gasped as the cold enveloped her body.

'Swim with me,' he suggested. 'It'll warm us up.'

They did three laps across the small bay, their bodies adjusting to the temperature. He felt his head clearing, the chaos of the last few weeks settling. While the twins raced each other, Meri whispered to him, 'I just got my boss sacked for unethical conduct, and look at my son! How can I . . .'

'It's hardly the same, hon. Neville is sixty-something and running a newspaper. Taj is fifteen. He made one bad decision.'

The twins surfaced near them and Rollo stopped talking. His family would be okay, he was sure of it.

'Look, Dad!' Taj pointed south-east. 'I think there's three of them.'

Rollo glimpsed a sleek shape curving through the swell, not far from the island. They stood and watched in silence until the whales disappeared under the sea again. And then a fourth whale emerged.

'That was—' Meri started.

'Mum, Dad, look! Wow!'

After so many years spent spotting black backs and tails, Rollo had to blink to process the sight. White back, white fin, white tail, almost luminescent in the water. The white whale. Migaloo. Sacred. One of a kind.

Migaloo blew out a column of air, the noise close and loud. He vanished for a moment and then his tail came up. A shock of white again. Slapping and splashing, the whale began lobtailing. Migaloo was putting on a cheeky performance just for them.

'Shall we get the boat?' Meri asked. 'Go closer?'

He shook his head. Right now, they were together, sharing the same sea, the same experience, as Migaloo. The most famous, elusive whale in Australia. The only whale with additional laws to protect him. Rollo's cheeks were wet, not from the saltwater, but his own tears. He wished Owen was here to see this too.

Migaloo rolled again onto his side. This time, he lifted up his flipper, almost waving to them.

In the cold water, hugging his family against him, Rollo felt that his beating, bursting heart must surely be as large as the whale's.

70

SIENA

Four weeks later

PROCLAMATION DAY. THIS YEAR, IT WASN'T GOING TO BE THE SAME OLD Kinton family piss-up at the bowlo.

The celebrations were held in two parts. The first, a small gathering at the cave which began with a smoking ceremony to release the spirits of those who had died there. Siena hadn't been to the cave since the police search—they'd created a wide track. Never again would it be a predator's hidden lair with a difficult escape route.

Inside the cave, Aboriginal Elder Uncle Travis invited them to take off their shoes. Siena felt the cool sandstone under her feet, a physical connection to the years past, the people past, the earth mother. The cave, stained by a dark history, was a keeper of secrets, although Siena and Kyle's discovery had exposed some of them. But the mysteries of this cave—they stretched further back, thousands and thousands of years, long before the murderous Geoffrey Kinton had arrived.

As Uncle Travis placed a handful of green leaves on the small fire, the smoke wafted towards Siena. She inhaled the scent of the land. But the smell reminded her of Axel and his fire. He'd accused her of blackmailing him into leaving town with a note and money for a train ticket. Another of his lies, blaming the victim. She didn't want to think about him, not here, not now. Instead, she focused on Kyle's profile next to her. They were coming out again on Sunday, a field trip for her koala club; he was giving them a talk about the natural habitat.

'This smoking ceremony is for healing the cave, restoring balance and harmony here.' Uncle Travis tipped another clutch of leaves onto the fire. 'We're thinking of our past, our ancestors. And our present, where we come from and where we're going.'

When Uncle Travis began singing in language, low and deep, Siena had to blink back tears. In the firelight, the ceiling had a soft pink glow. A dusty rose colour. Rose, the symbol of eternal love. Rose, a survivor. According to Olive's latest research, Kinton had fathered five children with Rose. Now Olive was working out the lineage to see if any of Rose's descendants still lived in town.

Aunty Bim spoke next. 'We call this place Ngarrgan Cave. Ngarrgan means morning or daylight.' She held her arms out wide. 'This cave connects the sea and the land. It's about beginnings, a new morning, a new day.'

Siena stepped into the smoke and scooped it over her body. Cleansing the past. Bringing harmony to the present. A new dawn for the future. Exactly what the town needed.

The second part of the celebration had been moved from its usual location, in front of Geoffrey Kinton's statue, to the paved courtyard outside the council building. The mayor welcomed everyone and then Aunty Bim spoke about the plans for a new memorial. Some of the crowd jeered, others cheered.

'Change the name!' The shout came from somewhere behind Siena. She'd been reading all the letters to the *Chronicle* and the comments on the website; the townspeople were evenly split, half for and half against. On her YouTube channel and at school, Siena and Kyle had been campaigning for the name change.

After Mayor Redpath presented the Living Legends awards to Uncle Travis and Olive, Kyle was called to the podium. He bounded up the steps with a big grin on his face.

'I'm proud to be descended from the First People who walked on this land,' Kyle began. 'We've looked after our Country for more than sixty thousand years. But some of you have got it the wrong way around. Stop treating the land as if it belongs to you. *We belong to it*. We're all part of it, all connected. It's our obligation to care for it.'

Siena raised a fist and yelled 'Yes!' Shit, he was amazing. Kyle would be prime minister one day.

Next up, Taj described the magical moment of meeting Migaloo the whale. Her brother seemed to have recovered from his ordeals, both of them. Mum had made him talk to all his 'clients' and then she'd rung their schools. It had been messy and uncomfortable, but they'd got through it. She'd made him donate his income to a literacy fund for kids. *At least your dishonesty can contribute in a meaningful way to someone's education*, she'd said. But one good thing had come from it all: a science teacher in Melbourne had invited Taj to write articles for a children's nature magazine. Of course, his first story would be about whales and Migaloo.

And now it was Siena's turn on stage. Letting out a deep breath, she positioned her notes on the lectern and tried to put the disastrous TV interview out of her mind. That was the last time she'd spoken up. The program had been instructed to run an apology following her complaint, but Siena still felt sick about it.

Mum and Dad were standing right at the front of the crowd, along with Caroline in a wheelchair and the chief inspector— they beamed up at her. Siena focused on them and her group of friends nearby, rather than the four hundred faces behind.

'Our history is written by the white men in power. We need to listen to the stories that have been suppressed. The truths from local Aboriginal people, the truths from women and teenage girls, from individuals who haven't traditionally held power. By respecting all of those stories, and respecting every single person in this community, together we will build a stronger, more harmonious town.'

Her friends clapped loudly, some of the men sneered, and others appeared bored. Owen, of all people, was nodding his head in agreement. Dad said he'd had fewer angry outbursts since Lance's arrest and was painting landscapes. Owen painting— who knew? After the fire, he'd come over with Hayley, who had sat in the kitchen crying. *I'm so sorry he did that to you, Taj. I honestly thought you were going to die.* While Axel would be on remand until the trial, Jackson was out on bail but Siena rarely saw him. His parents had offered their services to help out with re-building the historical society.

As Siena left the podium, Mayor Redpath took her place. 'Aren't these young people simply wonderful!' she gushed. 'I think our future is in good hands.' A turnaround from two months ago when she'd been cursing the young people for desecrating Geoffrey Kinton's statue. But Mum said the mayor was frantically trying to distance herself from Lance Nelson and align herself with the 'right' people. That was why the teenagers had been invited to speak.

'A few more things before you crack open the bubbly and celebrate our day,' the mayor continued. 'We've applied for a grant to re-build our historical society. And we're getting financial support for a separate Aboriginal cultural centre. Aunty Bim is in charge of that. Now, with the photo this year, we want everyone in it, not just the founding families. As you're all getting organised, we're going to hear from some local singers.'

Siena had only learned the news about the cultural centre yesterday—Aunty Bim and Uncle Travis had been quietly working towards setting up their own keeping place, along with the plans for the memorial.

Kyle's mum and three other countrywomen began singing, slow and melodic. The haunting chorus made Siena think of the day they'd found the skull. If she could go back to that moment, she'd do it all so differently—include her mother; talk less and listen more to Kyle and Aunty Bim; tell the truth about Axel earlier. But they were here now. They'd exposed some of the lies and change was coming. Slipping her hand into Kyle's, she looked up at him and smiled.

71

I can't get to the ceremony in the cave—too difficult in the wheelchair. But I make it to the celebrations at the council building and listen to the teenagers with happiness in my heart. Siena, the girl who demands to be heard; Kyle, the boy who cares about the past and the future; and Taj. Dear Taj who looks cheerful and healthy and has his whole life ahead of him.

When the photos are finished, the mayor approaches me.

'We'd like to honour you for your brave actions,' she says, grasping at my hand.

'No, no. Absolutely not.' I almost shout the words and Emmeline takes a step back.

I don't deserve to be honoured for what I've done.

An image of that burning doorway is seared in my brain. Not when I was going through it, forcing myself onwards despite the fear, but when I came out, when I thought we were safe. I had rescued Taj and we'd almost escaped. And then came the roar of flames. That noise is on a loop inside my head. I'm haunted by other sounds, too. In my dreams, I hear the voices of the dead men calling for my blood and the howling of their families' grief.

While I am remorseful, it will benefit no-one if I confess to the murders in the forest. The police say Derek and Lance will be charged on circumstantial evidence, any day now. Perhaps their defence lawyers will get them off. Whatever happens, Lance faces at least twenty years in prison for Fabian's murder and Derek will go down for sexual assault.

Justice doesn't always work the way we expect. They'll pay for their crimes. And mine.

Although I face my own sentence. The doctors tell me that within a few months, my feet will be able to bear my weight again. In a year, maybe I'll jog a little, but not the fun runs and half marathons of old. Never again will I run next to the man I love.

Siena and the other three girls visit me regularly to discuss their cases against Axel. I have a feeling he will plead guilty to the assaults and focus on defending himself on the charges related to the fire. That would be a relief for the girls—not having to testify nor hear his lawyer twist the situation. It would suit me too; I don't want any further investigation of the note which sent him off to Brisbane. Despite the topic of these chats, it's a joy to listen to the teenagers asserting themselves, discussing the law, taking back control.

And the earlier victims from the nineteen-nineties—no longer the girls I remember seeing at beach parties but grown women with children of their own—have returned to Kinton Bay. To record their statements against Derek and Lance, to renew friendships, to make peace with this town.

Meri invites them to lunch at the bowling club and asks me to speak. How can I refuse? When I come into the function room, she introduces me to her friends and classmates. One woman tells me about her old English teacher, Miss Wilcox, who was such a support at the time. I feel a lightness in this space: their secret horror has been acknowledged and shared, their abusers identified and charged.

Tears stream down my cheeks. Meri assumes it's from the pain in my feet or the trauma of the fire. It's neither.

Unlike Frances, these women have made it through.

My tears are of happiness and relief.

72

MERI

CONFRONTING BUT CATHARTIC. CAROLINE DELIVERED HER SPEECH WITH the right blend of legal jargon, real stories, empathy and hope. She talked about the culture of toxic masculinity in Kinton Bay, the importance of listening to victims, and the support available. Then finished her speech with a toast.

'I'd like you to raise your glasses to female friendship and support,' she said. 'We're all here today because Meri Britton has broken the silence and uncovered the truth with her news articles. I also want to pay tribute to one of your old teachers, Frances Wilcox, who sadly died in 1998. Many of you mentioned how she tried to help the girls. Women supporting women can make a real difference. Here's to female solidarity and friendship.'

'To female friendship,' Meri echoed, clinking her wineglass with Kristie, then Loretta. But that wasn't enough. Jumping out of her chair, she scooted around and pulled her old friends into a hug. 'I still can't believe you're both here. It's so good to see you.'

Even though they'd spoken by phone over the past month, Meri had worried that their face-to-face reunion would be polite, superficial chit-chat. Instead, they'd gone deep after twenty minutes: Kristie explaining how hard it had been to tell her husband about the abortion; and Loretta admitting to a prescription drug addiction for the first two years of university. She was now a medical researcher into rare childhood diseases.

'I just wish I'd got back in touch sooner,' Loretta said.

Apart from a few wrinkles, Loretta looked exactly the same as she had in high school with her black hair in the same high ponytail. She'd been married and divorced twice, and had an adorable five-year-old boy whom she promised to bring next time. Next time. Their friendship would continue.

It was interesting that Loretta and Kristie had both chosen jobs which related to children: the age group before they'd experienced trauma themselves.

Meri had been watching her twins walk that tightrope between childhood and adulthood. Completely naïve one minute, wise beyond their years the next. Perhaps that was why her fifteen-year-old self had got stuck—Meri hadn't been able to properly process everything. Her innocence had been destroyed in one gigantic swoop. As an adult, she could finally see the situation from a different perspective: the all-encompassing teenage shame and the failings of the grown-ups to stop the Wrecking Crew.

When Siena had admitted that she'd contacted her grandfather, she'd opened with: 'I know you're going to be mad at me, Mum.' But after everything they'd just gone through, Meri found she wasn't angry at all.

She still pictured Dad as he had been in 1998—handsome, dressed for work at the bowling club in a collared blue shirt and black pants. So it was a shock when Siena brought him up on FaceTime, this older man with hair greying at the temples, loose skin on his neck and jowls, but wearing a Mambo t-shirt.

'I read all your articles online,' her father said. 'You're an excellent journalist. And congratulations on the promotion to editor! I'm so proud of you.' He'd been following her career all these years when she'd been feeling abandoned by him.

Her teenage self had internalised the guilt for Dad's abandonment—*He's leaving because I'm disgusting, because of what happened in the forest*. She'd tried to make him proud again by keeping him safe from Blake's threat but, of course, it was all a fabrication in her head. Her father never knew any of it. And now he was beside himself with his own guilt, for being unaware, for her burden in trying to protect him, and for not supporting her when she'd needed it most. So many complicated feelings on both sides.

In the next school holidays, they'd be seeing him in real life. Keen to make up for lost time, Dad had paid for their plane tickets to Perth. The twins had already started researching places to see, including some Aboriginal sites. Siena and Taj, named for her dream of experiencing the culture and history of Europe and Asia; yet so many places around Australia, including Ngarrgan Cave, were older than the castles of Europe. She'd never realised there was so much right here.

Today's luncheon, a smoking ceremony in the cave, healings and blessings, new beginnings with old friends. A trip to Perth to see Dad and meet Kristie's family in September. By then, the humpbacks would be swimming south. Home again. New mothers returning to Antarctica with their calves, creating new family pods. Meri remembered a family dinner for her twelfth birthday in this room in the bowling club. They'd taken a family photo, Nathan giving her bunny ears, Mum and Dad both smiling, both happy. Wherever Mum was now, she'd be smiling about this trip to Perth—long overdue, she'd say. It was Meri's moment to create a new family pod.

⌒

Under Meri's editorial eye, the *Coastal Chronicle* was reporting real news, interviewing a range of voices, discussing the issues— good and bad. Josephine had covered Fabian's murder and exposed Lance's corrupt business dealings, without fear or favour, just as Kimberley would have done for the BBC. As Meri mentored the younger journalists, she felt she was making a difference, right here in her community. No-one else could write about Kinton Bay like Meri.

Her writing focused on exposing the town's true history. She'd combined Aunty Bim's oral stories and Olive's records, with some extra research from Siena and Kyle, to write the story of Kinton's arrival and the massacre. Another article had been on Rose and tracking her descendants.

Of course, she also wrote about Derek and Lance most days, in relation to one or other of the many charges they were facing. Detective Chief Inspector Poole said they'd be arresting them for the murders of Blake, Stefan and Greyson next week. While he'd taken leave to care for Caroline, he dropped into work regularly. The biggest shock for Meri was Inspector Nelson— they were extraditing him from Greece to face multiple charges related to drugs, extortion and perverting the course of justice. Corruption, crossing the line, twisting the facts—she hated it as much as Poole did.

When Meri heard about Nelson, everything suddenly made more sense. She was writing it into her series of articles about the rapes at the Killing Cave in the nineteen-nineties. To tie all the pieces together, she contacted Frances Wilcox's parents. They were delighted to hear from a former student inspired by their daughter to choose writing for a career.

'That's super,' they enthused. 'Frances would've been thrilled.'

'I'm writing about that year,' Meri explained. 'Do you still have any photos or letters or a diary from then?'

Meri's own diary contained evidence which they could use; she was so relieved that Siena had plucked it from the recycling bin. The embarrassment of hearing her entries read aloud in court would be outweighed by the possibility of sending Derek and Lance to jail.

'You phoned at the right time,' Mrs Wilcox said. 'We're moving into a retirement village and trying to sort out Frances's things. She and her best friend wrote lots of letters back and forth. I'll pop them in a package for you, along with a photo of the two of them in Kinton Bay.'

Female friendship. Meri ended the phone call by telling the parents how they'd toasted female friends and Miss Wilcox at a luncheon last weekend. Their joy at people remembering their daughter made Meri tear up.

Her own memories of Miss Wilcox were interrupted by a ping on her mobile. A message from the location app: *Taj has 0% battery.* Despite everything, their son still hadn't learned the lesson of re-charging his phone. But Meri knew he was safe, in school today with Siena. Her daughter's face came up on the app, at Kinton Bay High.

A quick gratitude list ran through Meri's head:

1. *I'm back in touch with my school friends.*
2. *We're seeing Dad and his family soon.*
3. *Bookings for whale-watching are still strong.*
4. *I've told the truth about Blake and Derek.*
5. *Siena and Taj are happy and safe.*

Taj. Her heart thudded whenever she thought about the fire. They could be standing in the same shoes as Miss Wilcox's parents. Every night, she kissed and hugged her son good night and said a silent prayer. Her gratitude was eternal: *thank you, Caroline. Thank you, thank you, thank you.*

Meri could never thank her enough.

ACKNOWLEDGEMENTS

TO MY WONDERFUL READERS, THANK YOU FOR TAKING THE TIME TO read or listen to my books. I've had such lovely messages, conversations and book club meetings, which continued to inspire my writing over the pandemic years. The best thing is when a reader talks about a character like they're a real person—I love that!

Thank you to my fantastic publisher, Allen & Unwin: everyone in editorial, the teams in sales, marketing and publicity, and of course, all those behind the scenes. Extra special thanks to Annette Barlow and Christa Munns; I really appreciate your incredible expertise and support.

The book community is the best—it certainly kept me going in lockdown! Many thanks to our booksellers, reviewers, authors, readers, podcasters, bloggers, festival organisers and attendees—online and in real life. I appreciate the additional effort everyone has made over these strange few years.

When my daughter turned fifteen and started going to teenage parties, I was relieved that so much had changed for women since my own teenage years. My original story idea was about these differences between the experiences of a mother and daughter. But then, as a number of issues related to violence against women came out in the media and the Women's March 4 Justice protests swept the country in 2021, I realised it hadn't changed as much as I'd hoped.

It made me think about my teenage years, the parties and the strong friendships which kept the secrets of those times and shaped who we became. We cared for each other and stood by each other. I've dedicated this book to the power of all female friendships, and in particular, to my high school friends. All these years later, we remain connected, despite being in different states.

I grew up on Wiradjuri Country in Bathurst and, at school, we learned nothing about the Traditional Owners and the Frontier Wars, even though our town was the first inland settlement and the site of terrible conflict and martial law. At university, I first heard a snippet of a different history and I still remember my shock—both at the colonists' horrendous treatment of Aboriginal people and that there could be an alternative, untold story. For this book, I was interested in how a community learns about, and faces up to, its own violent history. From all the research I did, I'll mention just two informative sources: the University of Newcastle's mapping project, *Colonial Frontier Massacres in Australia, 1788–1930* (accessible online); and Tim Elliott's article on the Elliston massacre (*Sydney Morning Herald*, 25 January 2020), which highlights the different responses in a community. As I've written a fictional story which could have happened anywhere in Australia, it is not set it in any specific Aboriginal Country.

I'd like to thank Gamilaroi writer Judi Morison for her generous advice. There are incredible First Nations' writers telling their stories and, over the years, I've read books by Melissa Lucashenko, Nardi Simpson, Tara June Winch, Anita Heiss, Bruce Pascoe, Tony Birch and Marcia Langton, among others. I am grateful to Terri Janke for the guidance in her works, *Indigenous Cultural Protocols and the Arts* and *More Than Words: Writing, Aboriginal and Torres Strait Islander Culture and Copyright in Australia*.

Many thanks to the people I interviewed across a wide range of topics: Fiona B, Suzanne S, Hal E, Roger M, Beth M, Dave K and Dawse. Your explanations and experiences were extremely helpful in creating the world of Kinton Bay and its characters.

Part of this book was written in my last semester of a Masters in Creative Writing at the University of Technology, Sydney. Special thanks to my very insightful lecturer, Claire Corbett, and my excellent fellow writers, India Hopper, Zoe Downing, Theresa Miller and Louise Sinclair.

Heartfelt thanks to my former agent, Brian Cook—enjoy your travels in retirement!

I appreciate the comments from those who read the manuscript at some point in the process. You're all awesome: Jo Barges, Caz Hardie, Nicole Davis, Krishaa Tulsiani, Maddie Watson and Angus Chaffey. Many thanks to Liane Moriarty and Marisa Colonna for their friendship and support. Cheers to my writing group: Cath Hanrahan, Katy Pike, Frances Chapman and Margaret Morgan. Special thanks to my super supportive online writing crew: Rob McDonald, Ashley Kalagian Blunt, Anna Downes and Josh Pomare. And thanks to the Not So Solitary Scribes for the laughs in our Friday Zoom meet-ups.

Two very special friends read the manuscript twice— Christina Chipman and Ber Carroll. I really appreciate your discussions, questions and encouragement which helped shape this into a more layered story.

For giving me some quiet time to write away from home, thank you to Jo and Dave for your luxury shed, and to Varuna, The National Writer's House in Katoomba for a week-long residency.

To all of my extended family, thanks for being my cheer squad! To Jamie, Jeremy and Tia, I love you to the moon and back. Thank you for all your help (including cups of tea, food, reassurance and manuscript reading), especially during the busy times.

I inherited my love of reading and writing from my mum. I dedicated *Six Minutes* to her and she came along on my 'launch' road trip from Sydney to Bathurst to Canberra. While Mum read the first draft of this book, sadly she died during lockdown last year. Ingrid McGovern was a doctor, volunteer, writer and book lover, who enriched the lives of others. Mum believed in the power of books to comfort, entertain, educate, enlighten and change lives. We miss you, Mum. xx

NEW FROM PETRONELLA McGOVERN

THE LAST TRACE
PETRONELLA McGOVERN

*'Part family drama, part high concept thriller =
100% compelling.'*
SARAH BAILEY, author of The Housemate **and** Body of Lies

Family. It means everything to Sheridan. She has missed having her brother around. At last, Lachy is back in Australia, and Sheridan can't wait to spend the Easter holidays all together in the mountains with their kids.

But, on Good Friday, something devastating happens that rips their two families apart, and now she can't imagine ever forgiving him.

Lachy knows he's not coping, but his sister doesn't have the full story. And, terrifyingly, nor does he. There are some critical gaps in his memory. How is he connected to a missing woman, a hit-and-run, and a request for DNA?

To untangle the truth, Lachy must decide who he can trust. His sister? His friends? Even himself?

The Last Trace is a gripping thriller about siblings and secrets, and the traces we can never erase.

ISBN 978 1 76087 925 9

1

LACHY

MEMORY'S A SLIPPERY BASTARD, LACHY THOUGHT. HIS FACE HOT WITH shame, he blinked and tried to focus on the teenager sitting opposite him. Kai was devouring a hamburger, elbows propped on the table, a soft groan of delight accompanying each mouthful.

Lachy took in the long bar, a sprinkling of diners at wooden tables and the historic photos on the walls. They were at the Dalgety pub. Bloody hell, he must have had a blackout. That had never happened before with his son around. Oh God, had he driven here from the cabin?

Kai licked a blob of barbecue sauce from his lips and continued their conversation. 'So, if the ski fields open in June, when can we go snowboarding?'

On Lachy's placemat sat a half-eaten bowl of vegetarian nachos and a schooner of sparkling water. He lifted his glass, desperate for something cool to douse the burning shame. But when the liquid fizzed on his tongue, he was surprised by the sugary taste of lemonade.

'We can drive up any time,' Lachy said, relieved his voice sounded normal. 'Apart from opening weekend. It's always too crowded then.'

How the hell had they ended up at the pub for dinner? His last memory was from hours ago, just after lunch. He'd opened the package with the DNA results, alone in the cabin while Kai was at school. A short report had already been sent to him online but this package contained extra detail and a few brochures, including one on counselling. His mouth had been as dry as four months ago, when he'd been trying to work up enough saliva to fill the tube. Even though the report told him little more, the physical sight of it had him reaching for the whisky bottle. With the alcohol burning in his throat, he typed out an email, double-checking each word, hoping Juliet would answer this time. She must have received her report by now—it would indicate if his DNA was a match. Pressing send, he noticed a new message from head office pop up. He slammed the laptop shut, but it was too late: the sounds from the Kenya project flooded his brain. He'd slugged another whisky, blocking out work. And another.

Those moments, and the forgotten ones in between, had led to here, now.

'What about the July school holidays?' Kai was asking. 'Is that a good time to—'

'Yeah, great. Sorry, just have to use the loo.'

In the men's, he locked the cubicle door and slumped on the toilet lid. How was it that the things he wanted to forget wouldn't leave him alone while other stuff vanished into the ether? Jesus, he was a mess. A shit parent, shit employee, all-round failure. He must have driven along the twisty road, lined by gum trees, in the windstorm. They were lucky a mob of roos hadn't leapt across their path. Idiot. At least he'd only driven as far as Dalgety, fifteen minutes from home, and not all the way into Warabina.

A knock on the door startled him. Had his son spotted something wrong?

'Just finishing,' he shouted and flushed the toilet.

Waiting outside the cubicle stood an old bushie, sporting an impressive beard and a huge bruise on his forehead.

'It's you!' The bushie clapped him on the shoulder. 'I owe you one, remember. What's your poison?'

Normally Lachy wouldn't forget a face like that but he'd spent the last five hours in a blackout state. Had he been chatting to this man at the bar and bought him a drink?

'Don't worry about it,' Lachy said. 'I'm here with my son.'

'Yeah, good lad, Kai. I'll get him one too. He's not on the beers yet, though, is he? Reckon I was drinking at his age.' The bushie winked. 'What does he like? Coke?'

Head spinning, Lachy stared at him for a beat too long, then rushed out an answer.

'Yep. Coke.' He cleared his throat. 'I mean, you really don't have to . . .'

'I owe you heaps, but I'll start with two drinks. I'll bring 'em over after.' The bushie nodded towards the toilet and Lachy hurried to step out of his way. As he did, he felt a hand on his wrist. Gentle, surprisingly intimate.

'Hope you don't need stitches. You've had a big night, mate.'

Lachy pulled up the sleeve of his jacket and stared in shock at the bloodstain on his shirt. After the bushie had gone into the cubicle, he took off his jacket and rolled his shirt cuff back.

An angry, red graze covered his forearm with two deeper gashes. Shit, he had to clean this up. What had he done to himself?

Was Kai injured too?

Surely, he'd remember that.

No, he wouldn't.

He splashed water over the cuts, grimacing at the sudden pain, watching droplets of blood swirl down the plughole. When he turned the tap off, it kept dripping: clean water going straight into the drain. Tomorrow morning, he'd drive back and replace the O-ring and the jumper valve. He should be doing more; he should be in Kenya right now setting up a water system. Instead, he was hiding out here in the mountains, being absolutely useless. He rubbed the tattoo around his left bicep, a circle of interconnecting lines, tiny waves of never-ending water. A symbol of everything he believed, and yet he didn't recall getting it.

These goddamn blackouts, he'd had them when he was younger then got them under control. For the past decade, his memory would only slip once a year, when he finished an aid project and flew back to head office in Washington DC. He drank fast to ease the transition from the drought-stricken communities in Africa to the wasteful West. The blackouts were never intentional but he couldn't seem to avoid them on those particular nights. The rest of the time, he prided himself on his excellent memory, responsibility and moral code.

Years ago, he'd read up on the science: he was drinking too fast for the alcohol to be absorbed and his brain couldn't form new memories; they'd last three minutes then whoosh, disappear into nothingness. Some people, like him, were predisposed to blackouts and didn't always appear intoxicated. A surgeon had done a successful operation in a blackout state: his brain accessed his skills and experience but he had no memory of the procedure. His nurses didn't even realise because he presented as sober.

God, Lachy hoped that he'd presented as sober tonight, that he'd made good decisions. Although if he'd driven the ute, that was unforgivable. Had he endangered his son when he'd wounded himself? Fucking hell, this wasn't supposed to happen back home in Australia.

Checking his watch, he reorientated himself. Seven-thirty, Tuesday, the fourth of April.

Sheridan, Nick and the girls were arriving on Friday for the Easter family gathering at Mimosa Hideout. His big sister would be checking that he was properly looking after Kai and the farm. Sheridan already thought he was a crap dad. If she found out about tonight, she'd be ropeable. But they'd been doing okay—he'd settled Kai into the local high school and taken him hiking in the mountains. Sure, he wasn't strict, but Kai didn't need another adult telling him what to do; he already had an enthusiastic mum and a follow-the-rules stepfather. Lachy had always been the good-time dad, cramming all the fun into one adventurous week when he came home between projects. Until this year.

A phlegmy cough from the cubicle snapped Lachy from his thoughts. He stared at his bloodstained sleeve. If only he could just ask about the missing hours but then everyone would learn the truth: he wasn't the man he made himself out to be.

When Lachy returned from the bathroom, Kai raised his eyebrows at the extended absence.

'I just ran into'—was he supposed to know the man's name?—'the old bushie. He's buying us drinks. And he asked about my arm.'

'Is he all right?'

'Yeah, I'll put some antiseptic on it when I get home.'

Lachy realised he'd misheard the question. Could it possibly be *his* fault that the bushie had a bruised head?

He was totally against drink driving; never, ever did it. Except one other time. During his very first blackout, nineteen years old and working at a summer camp in Pennsylvania. They'd partied hard on a night off without any kids. Apparently he'd borrowed a car and driven Tiffany, another camp counsellor, to meet a friend in the middle of the night. He never saw her again.

His first blackout had been in America and so had his last, six months ago. The reason for his DNA test.

No, his last blackout was today. Here in Australia. *You've had a big night*, the bushie said. What had Lachy done? And what had his son witnessed? A familiar shame washed over him. He wanted to curl up in bed and hide from the world. Hide from his son. Hide from himself.

Because Lachy never knew how he behaved when he was a stranger in his own life.